AFTER ROME

By Morgan Llywelyn
from Tom Doherty Associates

Bard

Brendán

Brian Boru

The Elementals

Etruscans (with Michael Scott)

Finn Mac Cool

Grania

The Horse Goddess

The Last Prince of Ireland

Lion of Ireland

Pride of Lions

Strongbow

THE NOVELS OF THE IRISH CENTURY

1916: A Novel of the Irish Rebellion

1921: A Novel of the Irish Civil War

1949: A Novel of the Irish Free State

1972: A Novel of Ireland's Unfinished Revolution

1999: A Novel of the Celtic Tiger and the Search for Peace

AFTER ROME

A Novel of Celtic Britain

MORGAN LLYWELYN

FORGE®

A TOM DOHERTY ASSOCIATES BOOK
NEW YORK

AFTER ROME

Copyright © 2013 by Morgan Llywelyn

All rights reserved.

Map by Jon Lansberg

Design by Mary Wirth

A Forge Book
Published by Tom Doherty Associates, LLC
175 Fifth Avenue
New York, NY 10010

www.tor-forge.com

Forge® is a registered trademark of Tom Doherty Associates, LLC.

Library of Congress Cataloging-in-Publication Data

Llywelyn, Morgan.
 After Rome / Morgan Llywelyn.—1st ed.
  p. cm.
 ISBN 978-0-7653-3123-6 (hardcover)
 ISBN 978-1-4299-8740-0 (e-book)
 1. Wroxeter (England)—History—Fiction. 2. Great Britain—History—To 1066—Fiction. I. Title.
 PS3562.L94A69 2013
 813'.54—dc23

2012027562

First Edition: February 2013

Printed in the United States of America

0 9 8 7 6 5 4 3 2 1

For Sonia Schorman

And always, always, for Charlie

History and myth are both suspect—
and for the same reason.

AFTER ROME

PROLOGUE

In the beginning Albion was a shaggy wilderness belonging only to itself. When the glaciers melted and the seas rose Albion and the neighboring land of Eire became two large islands on the western edge of Europe. Stranded together in a cold ocean, they awaited an uncertain future.

Their earliest human inhabitants were nomadic hunters whose existence depended on circumstance alone. In this respect they were little different from the wild animals they hunted. Life was lived at subsistence level and always a struggle. They were born and mated and died within a brief span of years, during which nothing much changed except the islands. Gradually these grew warmer. And greener.

As a result the hunters became gatherers as well, collecting the random edibles produced by the improving environment. The long slow centuries rolled on and on. Eventually a few resourceful men and women began to plant seeds to raise their own grain, and domesticate wild animals for a reliable supply of meat and milk. A more settled way of life became possible. Stone was the all-purpose tool. The chipping and shaping of flint axes was almost an industry.

When prehistoric farmers found the tough sward of Albion difficult to plow with Stone-Age implements, they turned to the forest that covered most of the island. The earth beneath the trees, deep and rich with leaf mold, was easier to cultivate. Where trees were cut down and light let in, crops thrived. The limitless abundance of timber provided both shelter and fuel. Worship, responding to an impulse buried deep in the human spirit, developed around the sacral trees. They were revered both for their practical and their spiritual value, little distinction being made between the two.

After uncounted generations in solitude the islands were visited by a seagoing race. These voyagers, who navigated by the stars, roamed the western seaways. Wherever they went new art forms appeared and new rituals began. On Eire, west of Albion, the natives created stone- and earthwork monuments of astonishing complexity for observing the cosmos and employing the energies of the sky to improve their pastoral culture.

On Albion the reaction was much the same. The first temples the natives erected were made of timber, but over time the wood rotted and had to be replaced. They began using stone instead. Under the guidance of their astronomer-priests they searched out massive boulders, which contained sky magic, and transported them long distances. Giant megaliths soared upward from the plain. Elaborate ceremonies demonstrated that earth and sky were one and man was joined to both.

Albion celebrated the heavens.

Centuries became millennia. A new wave of strangers from the vast land mass to the east reached the islands in the sunset. They stayed to found colonies and utilize such natural resources as copper and tin, the necessary components for making bronze. Bronze was more malleable than stone and could be used for everything from axe heads to personal ornaments. The extreme southwestern peninsula of Albion was particularly rich in tin; there as elsewhere, metal became a valuable commodity.

The Bronze Age had arrived.

The natives of Albion and Eire, who believed the earth was alive and sacred and anything taken from it constituted a debt that must be repaid, began burying metal artifacts with their dead.

After generations of intermarrying the colonists considered themselves natives. Tribes were formed along the lines of ancestral heritage. Fertile fields were plotted and pieced together; claimed and named and fought over. On the hilltops tribal chieftains built earthwork fortresses and called themselves kings. In the valleys their followers fought with bronze weapons and called themselves armies.

For more than five hundred years the two islands retained their small, scattered populations. Their seclusion ended with a fresh influx of settlers led by fair-haired warriors with sweeping mustaches. Ardent, impetuous and fearless, the Celts burst on the scene and quickly made themselves at home. The newcomers absorbed and were absorbed by the indigenous people. Celtic language and Celtic culture triumphed.

In their original homeland on the continent the Celts had learned to work with iron. Albion had iron ore in abundance. The almost impenetrable primeval forest began to shrink as trees were felled and burned to make charcoal for smelting the new metal. The Bronze Age surrendered to the Age of Iron. As if by magic, smiths produced nearly indestructible iron cauldrons, spearheads, helmets—and chains to bind captives taken in war.

Ruts made by iron plow scarred the land like sword slashes. The amount of available land for agriculture dwindled, but foreign trade increased along the coasts. Seaports were developed in the shelter of convenient headlands. Red Samian tableware and black glass jewelry from Gaul began to appear in chieftainly households. Such imported luxuries were purchased with quantities of native tin, as well as silver, lead, wheat and slaves.

The name of Albion began to be known abroad.

Yet the spirit of Albion did not change. Her gods remained nature gods. From Stone Age farmers to Iron Age kings, the inhabitants of the island were pantheistic. Life was lived according to the seasons. Man with all his accomplishments was recognized as a part of nature and not its superior.

Fifty-five years before the birth of Christ a small military force landed on the southeast coast of the island. Having crushed Gaul, Gaius Julius Caesar was turning his attention to Albion. After fierce fighting Caesar had advanced only a little distance into the country when he learned that many of his ships and supplies had been lost in a storm. He called off his troops and left. A year later he tried again. His second incursion was terminated when a revolt broke out in Gaul and Caesar was needed. Yet within a matter of years those early expeditionary forces were followed by a full-scale Roman invasion.

The invaders were not interested in agriculture, but in empire building. In Albion the Romans saw what they perceived as ignorant savages infesting a land ripe for the taking. As far as they were concerned the island's resources had but one purpose: to serve Rome. The struggle was long and bloody. In the end, Albion was renamed Britannia and Roman rule was the law of the land.

Britannia Prima—the Western Empire—was not an easy posting. The damp cold was a palpable presence, like a brother; known and familiar, to be endured or ignored. Born to it, the British tribes were indifferent to the weather until the Romans came. The legionnaires in the tavernae, drinking imported wine late into the night, talked continually of the palm-fringed coasts of the Mediterranean until native Britons began to dream of sunnier climes.

In place of hundreds of elected tribal kings ruling over a patchwork of territories, the Roman administrators installed a highly organized system of central government. To provide the large number of civil servants this required, the authorities set out to educate selected natives. These were mainly chosen from chieftainly families. Many of the noble Britons, already besotted with imported luxuries, were eager to embrace a more materialistic lifestyle. Thus was created a Romano-British aristocracy, which maintained control over the lower classes for their Roman masters. They were rewarded with tutors for their children and rare holidays under the Iberian sun.

Latin became the language of the privileged few. The upper and middle classes aspired to Roman fashion, Roman food, Roman architecture. Some gave their children Roman names. Abandoning the life of field and forest, they settled into new towns and cities built after the Roman pattern. "Urbanus" became a compliment; "rusticus" an insult. Urban men exchanged the hooded cloak for the toga;

urban wives and daughters copied the hairstyles said to be fashionable in far-distant Rome.

Urban homes were warmed by hypocausts: tubes molded of kiln-dried clay carried smoke out of the house from an underground furnace while transmitting heat to the interior walls. Urban centers were proud of their public privies, which could seat as many as eight or ten at a time. A statue of the Roman goddess Fortuna was kept in public bathhouses to protect men when they were naked and at their most vulnerable. For almost three centuries these bathhouses served as a focus of city life, a sophisticated meeting place where the social elite could gather to sneer at the "peasantry."

Then the Romans left.

Their armies were recalled to defend the Roman Empire from the hordes of barbarians that were sweeping across the continent. The last legion departed Britannia in AD 410. Unwilling to remain without an armed force to protect them, the Roman-born administrators and their families fled with the soldiers.

They did not take with them the educated native members of the civil service. Beneath a veneer of Latin sophistication many of the Romano-British still possessed the passionate, impetuous temperament of the Celt. They would not be welcome in Rome. Only a few generations removed from paganism, they practiced a Celtic version of Christianity at variance with the official version. They remembered and sometimes even used the language of their ancestors. Worst of all, they retained a stubborn belief in the rights of the individual over those of a monolithic state.

They were left behind to try to make the best of things in a land that was no longer Albion.

And could never be Rome.

CHAPTER ONE

Dark.

The moon is dark; the stars are smothered by clouds. Autumn is upon us now. This morning the rain rushed down the hills like silver snakes, yet nothing is moving tonight. Even the mice and moles cower in their burrows. The earth holds her breath as if waiting for disaster, but the disaster has already happened.

Civilization has collapsed.

Lucius Plautius, who studied with the Athenians, would say I am suffering from depression. He could be right.

Dinas, who laughs at everything, would say there is no such thing as depression. He could be right.

Cadogan leaned his shoulder against the door, braced his feet and shoved again. Nothing happened. The oak planks did not even creak.

The door was like the woman on the other side. Obdurate. The woman who had slid the bolt across the door. There was no other way in. The walls were constructed of solid logs. The few windows provided ventilation and a modicum of light, but they were too narrow to admit an intruder. In cold weather they were shuttered with two planks.

Cadogan stepped away from the door and rubbed his shoulder. He was weary to the bone. He had been riding for most of the night. Alternately trotting and cantering through the haunted darkness, up and down hills, splashing through streams, dodging trees at the last moment only to be slashed by low hanging branches. Trusting his horse to take him home.

To sanctuary.

In years gone by a traveler might have found a comfortable inn along the way. In such an establishment Cadogan would have enjoyed an ample meal and a flagon of the local brew while the hosteler rubbed down the bay mare and gave her a heaping measure of oats. A few coins more would have purchased a dry bed for himself— with a minimum of fleas—so he could resume his journey in the morning feeling refreshed.

There were no comfortable inns anymore. No lantern's gleam to welcome weary travelers. Windows were shuttered if any shutters remained. Doors sagged from rusting hinges; arrogant weeds thrust through floorboards. Business was very bad indeed.

The bay mare would have no oats tonight. Cadogan had removed her saddle and bridle and turned her loose to graze, knowing she would not wander far. She was too old and too wise to stray. This was the only home she had known for two years and she was content.

He could hear her tearing up mouthfuls of dry grass.

Cadogan stopped rubbing his shoulder and stood deep in thought. Then he walked around to the rear of the building, where he had stacked a quantity of firewood along the north wall. Heavy branches had been chopped into neat lengths, ready for burning. Kindling was wedged between the logs and the wall to create an added layer of insulation. Cadogan reached in and pulled out a handful of sturdy twigs. Ignoring the protestations of his aching body, he crouched and set them on the ground. Quietly.

His night-adapted eyes could make out general shapes but no specifics. Still crouching, he ran his hands over the nearby earth until he found several thick clumps of grass. Dying grass left from summer. He ripped them up, roots and all, and carried them with the kindling to the west side of the building. The side nearest the forest. A single narrow window was set in the wall.

Cadogan turned his back on the window and took two measured paces forward. He rolled the clumps of grass together until they formed a loose ball, which he placed on the ground before him. Loosening his linen underpants, he dribbled a few drops of urine onto the grass, just enough to dampen the center while leaving some dry tips. He used the twigs to fashion inward-leaning walls around the grass to hold it in place. Next he took a set of flints from the leather pouch on his belt and began striking sparks over his construction. After several tries, the dry grass tips ignited in a sizzle of red and gold.

Cadogan crouched and blew gently on the blades to keep them burning, then sat back on his heels and waited.

Although light was visible through the window, he did not call out to the woman inside. Not again. After taking care of his horse he had hammered his fist on the door. Called out his name. Expected her to welcome him. Instead she had bolted the door before he could push it open and enter.

Obviously another method of communication was required.

The smoke began to seep out of its enclosure like a timid creature poking its nose out of a burrow. Cadogan waited until it formed a pale cloud, dimly lit from beneath. The small ball of grass was too damp to fuel a substantial fire, but perfect for making smoke. He leaned forward and blew again. Sat back with eyes narrowed, calculating the exact moment when a final, well-placed breath would send the cloud upward.

When the column of smoke had thickened sufficiently he stood up and unfastened his hooded cloak. Waving it in front of him, he began wafting the smoke toward the window.

Some distance away, the mare raised her head and snorted.

A nightingale called among the trees, immediately answered by another. Even in the dark territories must be defined and boundaries respected. Nature's laws were strict.

Cadogan moved back and forth, almost dancing on the balls of his feet as he directed and redirected the smoke. Even something as diaphanous as smoke could be controlled with persistence.

The woman inside called out, "Are you still there?" Her voice was unpleasantly sharp, with an edge like a knife. It was almost the only thing he remembered about her.

He continued shepherding smoke.

"Is that you, Cadogan? What are you doing?"

Weave and twist, draw patterns in the air. Try to ignore the sudden stitch in his side.

"Cadogan! You said I could stay here. You said!" Her voice shrilled upward. She could smell the smoke now. In summer the lightning, the random finger of God, set trees ablaze to renew them. And the trees were very near.

"I'm in here, Cadogan!" she cried. "Answer me!"

He flung his cloak over his shoulder like a toga and walked around to the front of the building. Flattening himself against the wall beside the door, he waited.

He heard her groan as she lifted the heavy bolt and set it aside. The iron hinges, which he never greased, protested loudly when she pulled the door open. She thrust her head into the night. It was too dark to see anything. Holding her breath, she listened for the crackling of fire. Was it coming nearer? What should she do?

She ducked back inside. Looked wildly about the room.

The smell of smoke was growing stronger.

When she ran through the open doorway Cadogan lunged forward and caught her. He could feel how thin she was beneath her gown. All angles, with no comfort in her body to offer a man. Strong, though; she fought like one of the savage wildcats from Caledonia. Screeching, squalling, writhing in his grip and trying to scratch his eyes out.

A plague on the wretched woman! thought Cadogan. He immediately repented, reminding himself that he was a Christian. But even Christ had lost his temper with the money changers.

By the time Cadogan managed to pinion her wrists they were both panting.

"You said I could stay, you said I could stay!"

"Only until my cousin came back for you," Cadogan replied. He had been told his deep voice was "reassuring," but his next words were anything but reassuring. "If Dinas hasn't come for you by now he's not going to."

"You don't know that!" she shrilled.

"I know him. You're not the first woman he's abandoned."

"He hasn't abandoned me, he never would! Dinas adores me. Many men have said they loved me, but none are as passionate as Dinas. He swore he'd throw himself on his sword if he ever lost me!"

Cadogan began to feel sorry for her. And sorry for himself, for his aching body and leaden weariness. Sorry that his life—which only a month ago had been filled with a hermit's simple pleasures— was being torn asunder through no fault of his own.

"You should go inside now," he said, releasing her wrists.

"But there's a fire coming!"

"Don't worry, you'll be safe. There's no real fire, only damp grass smoking."

She caught her breath. "Do you mean . . . did you trick me?"

"I had to make you open the door."

She furiously pummeled his chest with her fists. "You're a terrible man and I hate you! Hate you, hate you, hate you!"

"That's too bad." He captured her wrists again and started to force her into the house. Thought better of it. Pulling her after him, he went around to the back of the building.

She made no effort to free herself. Instead she kept up a running commentary on his failures as a human being while he stamped on the fire. "You're worthless compared to your cousin, do you know that? Dinas is a twelve-pronged stag and you're a pile of goat dung. Goat dung with flies on it!"

Cadogan noticed that she had begun drawling her vowels. "Dinas is twice the man you are, he has balls like melons and a prick like a stallion. What do you have under your tunic, a dead eel? The first time I saw you I knew you were nothing. If Dinas was here you couldn't treat me like this, because he would knock your teeth out."

"Dinas likes to fight," Cadogan said. "I don't."

"So you're a coward as well."

He ignored the insult and continued extinguishing the fire. It took a while to hunt down and crush the last tiny spark. When he was satisfied there no danger of the blaze flaring up again, he took her back inside. Still yammering at him. Her voice was seriously beginning to grate on his nerves.

A bronze oil lamp on a three-legged table supplied the only light. The draft from the closing door caused the flame to gutter, flickering as if it might go out. Cadogan released the woman so he could slide the heavy bolt across the door, then he took a large tin ewer from beneath the table. When he lifted it his heart sank. He thumbed back the lid and peered inside anyway. The ewer was empty. She had burned all the herring oil.

"There isn't any more," she confirmed. "I already looked."

He turned to find her sitting on the bed. The only bed.

"Why did you have to burn all of it?"

"What did you expect me to do, sit in the dark? You're not much of a host, Cadogan. In fact I don't like anything about you. Not your splotchy face, not your flabby body, not even your feet. You're the ugliest creature I've ever seen."

The man to whom she spoke was above average height, with a sturdy body sculpted by hard work. He had a clean shaven, affable face that still retained a smattering of boyish freckles, and wore his thick brown hair cropped in the Roman style.

Puzzled, Cadogan asked, "What's wrong with my feet?"

She did not answer.

He rubbed his shoulder again. "I'm tired; I'm very tired. I've had several bad days and I need some sleep, so I'm afraid you'll have to sit somewhere else."

She raised a pair of overplucked eyebrows. "Why should I perch on a stool when there's a comfortable bed? Dinas never told me you were brutal, Cadogan. He said you were kind. He said I could rely on your kindness."

"Dinas says too thundering much and none of it true," Cadogan
growled. Taking her by the elbows, he moved her off the bed. She
hung like dead weight in his hands. When he released her she flounced
over to a stool and sat down. "I hate you," she said flatly. "I always
have and I always will."

"You don't even know me."

"That makes it easier."

Cadogan stretched out on the bed and folded his arms behind his
head. It was easier to ignore her than have a conversation with her.
His eyes wandered around the room. As always, his handiwork gave
him a sense of satisfaction in spite of his somber mood.

Seen from outside, his home was unimpressive. A rectangular
timber building with a steeply pitched roof, it melted into its forest
setting. To the casual observer it might have been a woodcutter's
cabin, though it was too large for one. It more nearly resembled a
small fort.

A fortlet.

That had not been his original intention. During construction
the house had seemed to choose its own shape. By the time it was
finished he realized what he had wanted all along was a fort. A building sufficient to protect its occupant from the intrusions and abra-
sions of the outside world.

His first choice for the exterior walls was stone and mortar, his
second choice was brick. Stone was impossible for one man to quarry
and transport, and the nearest brickyard was many miles away. That
left only the raw materials at hand. Cadogan had felled the trees and
sawn the wood himself, learning the necessary skills as he went
along. Trial and error. Axe and adze and plane. Use the mare to drag
the heavy logs into place. Laboriously raise them one by one, chink
the gaps with mud. For two years he had pushed his body to its limits, promising himself he would correct his mistakes later. When
there was time.

The interior of the building showed a certain refinement. It consisted of one large room whose unpeeled log walls were covered by

smooth planks. The roof was supported by tree trunks shaped into columns. The clay floor had been pounded until it gleamed, then incised with patterns imitating mosaic tiles. In the center of the room was a raised stone hearth surmounted by andirons decorated with boars' heads. Above this was a smoke hole, cleverly concealed within the angle of the roof.

One end of the room was given over to storage. Crates and bags and boxes of various sizes were neatly stacked beside an assortment of tools, some of them handmade, all of them well maintained. Cadogan's clothing was hung on pegs. Hunting spears leaned against the wall with their feet ensnared in fishing nets. A large iron cauldron complete with flesh hooks was stored beneath a row of shelves. The bottom shelf was crammed with tin cooking utensils and everyday plates and cups cast in pewter. The shelf above this boasted a complete set of glazed red tableware, plus a single, exquisite glass bottle the color of emeralds. The top shelf was fitted with cubbyholes designed to hold Cadogan's cherished collection of manuscripts. Scrolls of Athenian poetry, Alexandrian maps, books of Latin history and theology. The books had been written on thin sheets formed by pounding together crisscross slices of the pith of a sedge called papyrus.

At the opposite end of the room was a wooden bedstead, held high off the floor by oak stumps. The bed was equipped with a horsehair mattress, a rather grimy sleeping pad stuffed with goose down, an equally grimy linen sheet and three woolen blankets. Near the bed a naturally formed stone basin was set atop another broad stump. Cadogan had found the object in the river the preceding autumn, when the water was low enough to allow for easy fording. Over many centuries the river had shaped and polished the stones in its bed as it slowly changed its course. Following the way of least resistance.

The remainder of Cadogan's furniture consisted of a brass-bound chest inlaid with silver and copper, two brightly painted wooden stools, a battered campaign table with folding legs, and a larger oak table. The lamp on that table had been one of his mother's treasures. When he was a child she had guided his chubby fingers around the swirling acanthus leaves engraved on the bronze surface. "See how beautiful, Cadogan?" He had loved beauty ever since.

The woman followed the direction of his eyes. Where he saw achievement she saw failure. Crude construction and a dirt floor covered with chicken scratches. Most of the furniture looked as if it had been hacked out with an axe. Sacks of grain and dried meat were hanging from ropes slung over the rafters to protect the food from rats. Although she could not see them in the dim light, she knew there were spiderwebs in the corners. Worst of all, the place had a damp, musty smell, as if moisture were seeping up from the earth below. She had wasted the last of her tiny vial of perfume trying to sweeten the air.

"It's cold in here," she complained.

"There's no fire on the hearth," he pointed out.

"You're out of firewood."

"There's plenty stacked behind the house, didn't you look back there?"

She said indignantly, "I'm not accustomed to bringing in firewood. Why are you hiding in this miserable hovel anyway?"

"This isn't a miserable hovel, it's my home. And I'm not hiding." Cadogan wanted to close his eyes but he couldn't, not with her staring at him. "I live alone out here because a solitary life appeals to me."

"You want to make this pitiful hut a *hermitage*?"

"That's not what I said. I said the life appeals to me, I didn't say I wanted to *be* a hermit. There's a difference." He was too weary to explain the difference to her, even if he could. His need for isolation had come on him gradually and would, he suspected, fade in time. Of one thing he was certain: he had not wanted it interrupted by a crazy woman. "Put out the lamp," he said. "It will be dawn soon anyway."

"I'm not going to sit here in the dark. You might abuse me."

He almost laughed. "Abuse you? No fear of that . . . What's your name? I don't even know your name."

"Don't know my *name*!" She sounded as if it were the ultimate insult.

He tried to be patient. "You may recall that I left here shortly after you and Dinas appeared at my door. The brief conversation I had with my cousin was not about you, but something much more urgent. He never even mentioned your . . ."

"His horse is dangerous, you know," she interrupted. "It's killed people. I myself am a splendid rider, but Dinas wouldn't let me ride behind him because he was afraid I might get hurt. He insisted I walk; it proves how much he loves me."

Cadogan responded with a noncommittal grunt. Felt the pressure of her eyes on him. He must make more effort; hospitality was a virtue. "Dinas didn't tell me your name," he explained. "He said only that you needed shelter for a couple of days. Perhaps I should have questioned him further but . . ."

"My name," she interrupted again, "is Quartilla."

"Quartilla?"

"It's a perfectly good Roman name! My father was a centurion."

Cadogan was by nature a kindly man, but the woman's attitude was becoming intolerable. Before he could stop himself he said, "Any number of people make that claim these days. And even if your father was a centurion, I doubt if he stayed around long enough to name you. Tell me what your mother called you."

She lowered her eyes and gnawed at her thumbnail. "I don't know," she said sulkily. "She died when I was born."

He was instantly remorseful. "I'm sorry."

"Why? You didn't know her any more than I did."

Cadogan's head felt hollow and his eyes were full of sand. The conversation was going nowhere. With an effort, he propped himself on one elbow and tried to smile at her. "Let me rest for a while, Quartilla, and I promise we'll sort this out in the . . ."

"Did you bring anything to eat? I'm hungry."

"There were adequate supplies here, what about them?"

She shrugged. "I guess I ate them."

"You what?"

"I ate everything that was fit to eat, but not those dreadful dried things. I would have eaten those wretched chickens but I couldn't catch any. And then that wretched rooster bit me. On my leg! He took a whole piece out of it!"

"Kikero was only protecting his family."

"His *family*?" Quartilla sounded scandalized.

"I don't eat the hens, I eat their eggs," Cadogan tried to explain. "If I ate the hens they'd be gone and I wouldn't have any eggs. Did you at least throw some corn to them?"

"I don't tend livestock," she said icily.

"They're not just . . . I mean . . . in the morning, Quartilla." Cadogan gave a deep sigh. "In the morning." He fell back on the bed and put one arm across his eyes.

She moved her stool close to the lamp so she could examine her fingernails. They were bitten and broken but still stained with henna. She began picking at the ragged cuticles.

Something skittered in the rafters. Quartilla shrieked.

"You're not afraid," Cadogan informed her without opening his eyes. "You must have heard that a dozen times since you've been here."

"Of course I'm not afraid! I'm not afraid of anything. It startled me, that's all. I'm not used to vermin in the house, even if you are."

Ignoring the implied insult, he willed himself to lie still. Relax. Yet he could not stop the silent uproar in his whirring mind. Fear and frustration, remorse and regret jostled with one another in a bid for his attention. After a while he gave up trying to sleep and watched Quartilla covertly from under his forearm.

She was certainly no beauty, he decided. As bony as a fish and slightly cross-eyed, as if she were about to sneeze. Her prominent, high-arched nose could pass for Roman, but Cadogan suspected it simply had been broken at some time in the past. Her coppery hair was obviously dyed. The linen gown she wore might have been pleated once; it might even have been white once. Now it was as dirty as her sandals.

Her voice was the worst thing about her; a crime she compounded by sporadically attempting a Roman accent. When she drawled her vowels her speech was almost unintelligible.

Whatever possessed Dinas? Is the creature a discarded camp follower? No, a common harlot would never use that accent. Perhaps she really is a legionnaire's daughter fallen on hard times.

We've all fallen on hard times, one way or another.

A woman in the house. Would that be so bad? Admit it to yourself, Cadogan—you've been lonely. This is the first time in your life you haven't had other people around you, even if they were only servants. While you were building the fort you were too busy to notice, but since then you've sometimes longed for the sound of another human voice.

Not that voice, though.

The flame in the lamp guttered again and drowned in the last smear of oil. The room went dark. Quartilla put one arm on the table to cushion her head. Within minutes she was snoring.

Cadogan lay rigid with resentment.

So much to think about; I need a clear mind. Why does she have to be here now? It's too late to go to sleep and too early to get up. Too late for yesterday and too early for tomorrow. The ride to Viroconium was a waste of effort, it was all over before I got there. If only Dinas had brought the warning earlier . . . but that's Dinas, selfish to the core. After he dumped the woman on me I'm sure he never gave her another thought. He does what he wants when he wants and . . .

Cadogan's thoughts were interrupted by an unexpected sound from outside. The sudden, anxious neighing of a horse. He jumped to his feet and hurried toward the nearest window. In the dark he stubbed his toe and swore under his breath.

"What's wrong?" Quartilla asked groggily.

"There's somebody out there."

"Who?"

"How do I know?"

"What do they want?"

"They want to know why you ask such stupid questions!" Cadogan snapped. "Keep your voice down and be still."

"It's Dinas come back for me, I knew he would! Open the door for him at once."

"It's not Dinas. My horse knows his horse, they would have whinnied to each other. What I heard wasn't a greeting."

"Horses can't talk," said Quartilla. "Do you think I'm a fool?"

Cadogan wanted to throttle the woman.

Ignoring the throbbing pain in his toe, he peered through the narrow window. She crowded close behind him. He could feel her scrawny breasts against his back. Her breath fanned his cheek; an unpleasant smell, as if she had a bad tooth. "If it's not Dinas, who is it?" she asked. "What's happening? Tell me!"

In the gray light of dawn he saw a band of men approaching the house on foot.

"We're about to have company," Cadogan said grimly.

CHAPTER TWO

I love the smell of rain, and the scent of the sea. Moisture on a woman's inner thighs. Cedar branches laced with wood smoke. Ice on the wind from the mountains. Freshly turned soil in the midlands.

I can recognize the slightest scent, that is my gift.

And my curse.

Dinas rode with the effortless grace of a born horseman. Head high, shoulders back, spine supple as a willow. His strongly boned face was surrounded by a tangle of unkempt curls that stirred in the wind. From his attire it would be difficult to guess either his origins or rank. Beneath a beautifully cut but well-worn leather cape he wore a faded homespun tunic that came to midthigh, leaving his lower legs bare to allow maximum contact with the horse. His boots reached only to the ankle and were made of soft deerskin. Dinas wore no jewelry, not even a copper finger ring. His homemade saddle was little more than a large leather pocket stuffed with wool and strapped around the horse's belly.

The stallion he rode was the same color as his curls, a glossy brown so dark it looked black. The animal had an elegantly sculpted head, large, liquid brown eyes, and could canter for hours—all legacies from its desert ancestors. Dinas followed every move the horse made with his own body without even thinking about it. A casual observer might have trouble telling where the man left off and the horse began. They might even be mistaken for a centaur from mythology.

From time to time Dinas drew rein to take a closer look at a suspicious mound of disturbed earth or heap of stones. It was a habit of long standing. If he dismounted, the horse stood motionless until he vaulted onto its back again. He always took a careful look around before he rode on. A Noric knife was tucked in his belt and the scabbard at his hip held a shortsword modeled on the Roman gladius. The knife was designed for cutting meat, the sword for skewering men.

Woven woolen saddlebags containing everything else he owned— almost everything—were tied to the rear of the saddle by leather thongs.

Dinas had been born restless, unwilling to let the dust settle on him. Not for him the static existence of town and village. He was most comfortable in wild and secret valleys separated by trackless wastes. Heather and slough, deep lakes and impenetrable forest called to him. As soon as he was old enough to toddle he had wandered away from home at every opportunity. At first his mother ran after him. Then she sent one of the servants. Eventually she gave up and let him roam; any wild thing should be allowed its freedom. His mother was of the Cymric race. She knew about wild things.

That wild streak in Dinas had become an asset.

The loss of the legions had left the inhabitants of Britannia unprotected and increasingly vulnerable. The last Roman administrators had urged the Britons to arm themselves and promised to give them advice about manufacturing weapons and building fortifications. Their promises were worth no more than the air they floated on. In their panic at the end the Romans had departed too hastily, and in too much disarray themselves, to ensure a future for those they left behind.

The educated elite had struggled to maintain order for a while, but their efforts were doomed from the start. Their education had not been total, only what was sufficient for them to do their individual jobs. Each man knew a little; no man had a sufficient grasp of the whole. Civilization as they knew it began disintegrating. The political and mechanical machinery left by their conquerors was breaking down and they did not know how to fix it.

An ostensibly law-abiding society soon became lawless. No one trusted his neighbor anymore. Prosperous families sought to protect their wealth by burying it in Mother Earth. Hordes of coins and other valuables were being stashed throughout Britannia. A wild young man with few scruples and a wide-ranging horse might find treasure almost anywhere.

For several years Dinas had amused himself with this enterprise, but it no longer satisfied him. He needed something more challenging to occupy his mind. To replace the memory that tormented; the anger that burned and scalded and demanded.

The autumn morning found him at the westernmost edge of Britannia, only a few miles from Deva Victrix, once called the City of the Legion. Beyond Deva lay the broad estuary of the River Dee. Beyond that was the Oceanus Hibernicus; beyond that, unconquered Eire.

When he smelled salt on the wind Dinas halted the horse. He dropped the reins on the stallion's neck and sat immobile. Savoring the warmth of the sun on his bare head and legs. Smelling the pungent odor of the sweat on the stallion's flanks. A warm, animal smell, as familiar to him as his own.

He gazed across a reed-studded marshland to a faint line of yellow hills and wondered what lay beyond them. Reached for the reins; withheld his hand. Returned his eyes to the rustling reeds. He recalled hearing about a half-brained scheme to drain the marsh and create more arable land, but the plan had come to nothing when the local government collapsed.

"No tracks show in marshland," Dinas remarked aloud.

The stallion swiveled an ear to listen. Dinas often talked to his horse. He believed that people did not know how to listen, but a clever animal would detect the subtlest changes of tone and pitch and respond accordingly. The dark horse was clever. Interpreting his master's voice to indicate the possibility of forward motion in a direction he did not like, he took half a step back instead.

Dinas reached forward to scratch the base of the horse's ears, where the sweat gathered. "I hear you, my friend. You don't want to wade into that, eh? Don't trust the footing? Neither do I, but remember this place. This could be our escape route if we're pursued by fools who want to put my head above the gates. I've heard some strange tales about Deva."

The horse waited.

Dinas gathered up the reins. "I think we've scouted the territory long enough. Let's have a look at the town. Who knows what we might find, eh? Surely the bloody-boweled Romans didn't take everything with them when they left."

The dark horse felt the eagerness in his rider's body; the sense of expectation. Waited for the magic words that would release him to action. "Forward. Now."

He sprang forward.

For several days Dinas had been circling the City of the Legion at a distance. He had stopped to discuss the weather with farmers in the fields. Paid fulsome compliments to aging women drawing water from a well. Feigned astonishment at tales told by other travelers who loved to hear themselves talk. It was his habit to listen to everyone he met while divulging nothing about himself. A lean, sinewy man in shabby clothing, Dinas might have been any of the dispossessed who now wandered the countryside. Certainly not a person worth robbing. He would have drawn little attention except for the magnificent stallion he rode.

When Dinas was a boy their tutor had told them about the great black warhorse that carried Alexander of Macedon to victory. The relationship between the two was legend. "The horse was called Bucephalus," Lucius Plautius had told his two eager students. "After Bucephalus died Alexander could never hear his name without weeping."

Dinas had never named his own dark horse. He would have fought to the death to protect him, but if the stallion died he did not want a name to grieve over. He had no fear the animal would be stolen. If a stranger came too close, the horse pinned his ears flat against his head and gnashed his teeth until foam flecked his jaws. His hooves pawed chunks out of the earth. With eyes rolling and nostrils flaring, he looked ready to fling himself on the nearest victim. The most ardent admirer soon lost interest. "I'd have that brute killed if I were you," Dinas was sometime advised.

At night he pillowed his head on the warm silky neck of the dark horse.

Having made up his mind to enter Deva, Dinas followed the most direct route. The road to the northern gate was as straight as a spear shaft and broad enough for five men to march abreast. The closely fitted paving stones were set on a low causeway to facilitate drainage, and bordered with stone curbs. Dinas rode to one side, keeping his horse off the hard surfaces. Bare earth was easier on unshod hooves. Occasionally Dinas found part of an iron Roman horseshoe lying half hidden in the mud, and spat on it.

When Deva came into view Dinas halted the horse and sat very still, exploring the atmosphere with senses he could not name. They lay just beneath the surface of his skin. At the backs of his eyes. In the hair on his forearms.

They detected old dangers. And new possibilities? Perhaps. He could not be certain without a closer inspection.

Deva Victrix had been built as a statement of naked power. As such it was not a city in the defined sense; not a municipal center entrusted with civilian governance, but a large military garrison encompassing an array of auxiliary services. It covered over sixty acres and was bounded by an immense wall of rubble stone and flint, set at intervals with watchtowers. The pillars on either side of the gates were made of ruddy brick. The northern gates themselves, made of British oak, stood wide open.

"That old farmer with one eye told us they've blocked up the east gate completely," Dinas said to his horse. "So why is this one open? Could it be a trap?"

Through the man's buttocks and legs the stallion communicated his answer: The horse was alert but relaxed. Sensing no trap, he pricked his ears in the direction of Deva and waited.

Dinas shifted weight. "Forward. Now," he murmured. The stallion obeyed. Although horse and rider remained calm, they both knew Dinas could spin the animal on its haunches in the blink of an eye and gallop away.

As they approached the gates Dinas scanned the nearest watchtowers. They appeared to be unmanned. Part of the roof on the right-hand tower had collapsed. The ladder to the left-hand tower was missing altogether.

Through the open gateway Dinas could see two middle-aged men engaged in conversation. A shorter, somewhat younger man stood listening to them with his hands clasped behind his back. Dinas squinted, focusing on details. Knee-length homespun tunics over checkered woolen breeks identified all three as native Britons. The more animated of the talkers also sported a mantle sewn of otter skins. He and the silent listener wore their hair in the elaborate braids favored by men of the Deceangli tribe. The third man had no braids, only a sparse gray fringe that clung to his otherwise bald head like a highwater mark. A wooden cross depended from a cord around his neck.

"Aha," Dinas said under his breath. Recognizing the badge of a man who believed what he was told. A man who sought to be good and hoped to buy his way into heaven with coins laid on the palm of a priest. An almost imperceptible current ran through Dinas's body.

The dark horse gathered himself.

As they came through the gateway the trio turned toward them. With a disarming smile, Dinas addressed the wearer of the cross in formal Latin. "I wish you good morning, brother. I am a poor pilgrim on a pilgrimage."

The three stared up at him. Stared at his unruly mane of hair and his worn clothing. His magnificent horse.

"We don't get many pilgrims here," said the balding man. His Latin was colloquial; the accent rustic. His cheeks were chapped and his jowls were sagging but his face was friendly.

The man in the otter-skin mantle had narrow eyes peering from beneath an overhanging brow, like weasels peeping from their hole. "Deva is a bit out of the way these days," he remarked. "Even the Hibernian slave-catchers aren't coming this far inland—though of course we bar the gates at night. This is the only one we keep open during the day." He waved one hand toward the northern gateway.

The stallion flattened his ears.

Dinas raised one eyebrow—dark and sharply peaked—but maintained his friendly smile. "In my experience," he said in a polite tone, "any place worth visiting is usually out of the way. I understand you've converted the old Roman amphitheater into something you call a martyrium?"

The wearer of the otter skins gave him a hard look. "You know about that, do you?"

"I've heard of nothing else since I crossed the Severn."

The balding man fingered his cross. A beautifully carved wooden cross hanging on a leather cord. "Surely you exaggerate. Our small efforts here are not that noteworthy."

"Speak for yourself," snapped the other. "You know perfectly well how long and hard I've worked and how much I've accomplished." He turned back to Dinas. "You say you crossed the Severn? You came from the south, then? Where are you going?"

Dinas plucked a name out of the air. "Mamucium. I believe that is northeast of Deva? I've never been there before. Perhaps you can give me directions when I leave here?"

While he spoke, from his vantage point atop the stallion he was surveying Deva Victrix. Garrison no more, it was reduced to a dilapidated town inhabited by less than two thousand people. Once it had boasted a famous racecourse and a guesthouse with a hypocaust for the warmth and comfort of visiting dignitaries. Now whole areas were totally deserted.

Facing Dinas across a weedy parade ground was the former head-quarters of the garrison, an impressive building some two hundred and fifty feet square. Nearby was the armory, of almost equal size and designed to hold prisoners, hostages and booty as well as weaponry. Behind these stood a third structure with a central block of offices surrounded by corridors leading to a number of storerooms and workshops for the carpenters, smiths, masons, wheelwrights and other workers needed to keep the garrison functioning.

All unnecessary now.

Some of the materials used in constructing the headquarters complex and the commander's private residence had been cannibalized for less pretentious buildings. The wooden hospital and the granary had collapsed into heaps of rotting timber. Some of the long rows of timber barracks had been turned into housing but more were standing empty. Yet amid a welter of disorganization it was still possible to discern the former precise geometry of streets and squares.

Between two sheds a goat stood on its hind legs to chew clothes drying on a line. Nearby a miscellany of scruffy hounds lolled in the sun. Farther on, an old woman shook her fist at a half-naked boy who was chasing a flapping goose.

Not a pretty girl in sight, Dinas noted with disappointment. He dropped his gaze to the men below him.

The silent listener was a small man, but he had a large skull on which his ears stuck out like afterthoughts. His eyes were very blue. He edged closer to Dinas. "I like horses, I've always liked horses," he confided in a voice hardly louder than a whisper. "I am called Mera-doc. What do you call your horse?" He reached out to stroke the stallion's neck.

Dinas deftly reined the horse out of reach. "He doesn't have a name and he's not used to strangers. A stallion, you know. Difficult temperament. Stay clear of him for your own sake."

"Animals like me," the little man insisted in his soft voice. He approached the horse again.

Dinas did not move the stallion a second time. Let this fool learn the hard way, he thought.

"I am called Brecon, Brecon the woodcarver," said the balding man. "My friend here is called Ludno. I'm afraid we didn't hear your name."

"Dinas."

"Dinas? Is that all?" Ludno asked suspiciously.

"What more do you want?"

Ludno scowled. The clever retort he sought was eluding him. He settled for, "You ride a fine horse; is he yours?"

Dinas met his calculating eyes with a look of total candor. "This horse belongs to a man in Mamucium; I'm merely delivering him. A poor pilgrim must earn a few coins wherever he can."

"Oh." Ludno sounded disappointed.

Brecon said, "I would be pleased to show you around while you're in the area, Dinas. If you want to see the martyrium I can take you to the Coliseum."

"I can see it from here," said Dinas. The huge stadium was easily the most noticeable structure in Deva.

Gathering the otter skins firmly around his shoulders, Ludno stepped in front of Brecon. "I'll guide you myself," he announced. "My knowledge and understanding are extensive; my own ancestors were victims of the vicious games the Romans played."

"So were mine," countered Brecon. He pushed past Ludno, who pushed back.

While this took place Dinas was being distracted by Meradoc. The little man appeared to be spellbound by the stallion, and kept sidling closer and closer.

"How much do you know about the history of Christianity in Britannia, Dinas?" Ludno inquired.

Dinas pulled his attention away from the impending disaster. "As much as anyone else, I suppose. My parents were Christians."

Ludno's eyebrows came together like caterpillars mating. "You speak as if the faith were simply passed to you in your mother's blood.

It is not so easy as that. Faith is a challenge. One must work at it. Our Lord died on the cross for your sins, and good men and women have been slain so you could have the privilege of knowing about His sacrifice. You may not know this, but the teachings of Christ first reached these shores by way of *peregrini,* wandering missionaries from Eire. Their Celtic version of Christianity was a sophisticated religion that developed ten different computational cycles just for reckoning the date for Easter." Ludno glanced at Dinas to see if the other man was impressed.

How can a man be sly and pompous at the same time? Dinas was wondering.

Ludno plunged ahead. "At first the authorities tolerated Christianity as just another cult. The Romans had temples and shrines for so many: Serapis, Isis, Mithras and Astarte, to name but a few. Problems soon arose, however. Priests of the longer established religions grew fearful for their own power. They accused the Christians of cannibalism, claiming they 'ate the flesh and drank the blood of their god' during the Eucharist. The persecution of Christians became a popular pastime, particularly among the legions. That is why . . ."

Dinas stopped listening altogether. He had no desire to be lectured by the local fanatic and there appeared to be nothing worth having in Deva. The place was obviously impoverished. It was time to move on and see what lay beyond the horizon. There was always something better beyond the horizon.

He expected his horse to anticipate their departure and gather himself. The stallion remained rooted to the spot. Incredibly, Meradoc was circling around him with perfect confidence in his safety. The little man even patted the glossy haunches as he passed. Dinas braced himself for the mighty kick to follow.

Nothing happened.

As Meradoc came along his other side the horse arched his neck, displaying the impressive crest of a mature stallion. He flared his nostrils and made little whuffling sounds.

"Look out, you fool!" cried Dinas.

To his astonishment, the dark horse lowered his head for the little man's caress. "See? He likes me," Meradoc said shyly. He stroked the stallion's velvety nose. The horse gave a contented sigh that transmitted itself to its rider.

At moments like these, small moments indeed, lives are changed.

Dinas swung his right leg over the horse's withers with a catlike alacrity and slid to the ground. His scabbard clattered against his leg.

"Weapons of war are not permitted in Deva," Ludno warned.

"You can't expect me to leave a good sword lying outside the gates."

"Very well, bring it with you. Just don't wave it around."

"I never wave it around. This is a thrusting sword." Dinas took off his cape and folded it over his arm. He asked Meradoc, "Are you always so good with horses?"

The little man ducked his chin in embarrassment. "Not many horses come to Deva now. I never touched one until today."

"Pay no mind to him," said Ludno. "Meradoc is all right but he's a bit simple, if you know what I mean." He tapped his forehead.

I really do not like this man, thought Dinas. "No, Ludno, I don't know what you mean. My horse likes him, and my horse is an excellent judge of character. What is your occupation, Meradoc?"

By now the little man was rubbing the stallion behind the ears with his knuckles. The horse's eyes were half closed with pleasure. "I don't have an occupation. I just do whatever needs to be done."

"Then yours is the apex of occupations," Dinas told him. "It requires as much ability as all the others put together." Glancing toward Ludno, he was pleased to see the man's discomfiture at hearing a compliment paid to Meradoc.

"What does 'apex' mean?" whispered Meradoc.

Dinas whispered back, "The highest."

Ludno said sharply, "Do you want to see the martyrium or not?"

When Dinas felt Meradoc tug at his sleeve, he looked down. "It's worth it," the little man mouthed silently.

"I do."

"Then follow me." Ludno gave a peremptory wave of his arm—
and the dark horse flattened his ears.

Ludno and Brecon set off together, still arguing about who was
best qualified to guide, while Dinas followed, leading his horse. Meradoc walked at the stallion's shoulder. As the little procession made
its way through the town, people in the streets or standing in open
doorways watched curiously. Several men spoke to Brecon or Ludno,
but no one spoke to Meradoc. He would not have noticed anyway.
All his attention was on the dark horse.

What Dinas saw confirmed his initial impression of Deva. Although vast in area, the former garrison was little better than a prison
cell. Walls limiting space, roofs hiding sky. Dwellings crowded so
close together the occupants could hear one another farting. Un-
specified rickety structures slowly disintegrating. Air polluted with a
pervasive miasma; midden heaps covered with flies; open latrines
running with filth. Life always the same, day after day.

How could anyone choose to . . .

"Here we are," Ludno announced.

They had come to the large central square, from which four
streets radiated at right angles. The paved streets were swept clean,
but the little alleyways that ran between them were choked with
debris. Market stalls, more than half of them empty and with torn
awnings sagging, ran along two sides of the square. A few dispirited
women were picking desultorily over the meager merchandise.

There lies the future, thought Dinas.

Ludno cleared his throat to command attention. "Beyond the
square, and just outside the walls, you can see the great coliseum of
Deva, which was built entirely by the army. The military occupation
of Albion lasted for three and a half centuries, during which time
the Romans established and fortified a number of garrisons like this
one. They constructed twenty-eight cities and large towns and built
over seven thousand miles of roads. They built a wall twenty feet high
and over seventy-three miles long to protect the pacified southern part

of the island, which they called Britannia Superior, from the northern part, which they designated as Britannia Inferior. But the Picts
of Caledonia and their allies, the Scoti from Eire, were hardly inferior. The legions were never able to conquer them, which is why
Emperor Hadrian erected a wall to conceal his failure."

Dinás stifled a yawn. "I don't need a history lesson, thank you."

"You might as well hear him out," Meradoc whispered. "We won't
get any farther until he's made his speech."

Ludno cleared his throat again. "It is important to view our
Martyrium in context, Dinas. The Romans built the coliseum—that
means 'gigantic,' you know—to hold gladiatorial games for entertaining the famed Twentieth Legion, which commanded the entire
northwestern quarter of Britannia. Eight thousand spectators at a
time could be packed into the stands in our coliseum; it was and
still is the largest amphitheater in Britannia. Any living creature that
walked or flew was butchered in the arena for what the Romans called
sport. That includes human beings. Men and women and children
died in agony to provide amusement for their conquerors. Come, pilgrim. See for yourself." Giving a commanding wave of his arm, Ludno
set out across the square.

"He is a good speaker, you know," murmured Meradoc. "I get
chills when he talks about the martyrs."

They followed Ludno to an open gate set in the town wall. A
wide, paved walk, deeply grooved by chariot wheels, led from the
wall to an imposing archway. Before he entered the coliseum Dinas
paused to look up at the structure towering above them. It was even
larger than it appeared from a distance; thousands of tons of gray
stone scarred by chisels and roughened by weather. Implacable; indestructible. Built to stand for a thousand years.

Dinas was surprised by his horse's reluctance to walk through
the archway. Shadows gathered within that portal. Darkly suggestive
shadows, like old sins. When Dinas tugged on the reins the stallion
took a step back.

Meradoc made a low clucking noise. The horse took a step forward.

Once again Dinas raised a sharply peaked eyebrow. The skin around his mouth tightened imperceptibly.

The footing under the arch was gritty; the stone walls on either side were slimy. In the warm, damp air, a smell from the arena came to meet them. A fetid odor. The stallion snorted explosively. Every muscle in his body strained to turn and run.

Dinas tightened his hold on the reins.

Meradoc put one hand on the horse's shoulder. "Come now," he said softly. "Come now."

They stepped out of the shadows and into the arena. This time it was Dinas who wanted to shy away. The hairs rose on the backs of his arms.

The sandy earth that slaves had carefully raked before and after every event was no longer level, but as rough and pockmarked as old skin. On this killing ground captive wolves had been battered with spiked clubs. Captive bears had been baited by dogs bred for savagery. Captive gladiators had fought to the death while thousands of cheering, jeering men watched from the tiers above the arena, and the bright flags of Imperial Rome and the Twentieth Legion fluttered overhead. Centuries of blood had soaked into the sand. With those senses that he could not name, Dinas could still hear the roars and screams. Could feel the abject terror and the undying fury. And smell the blood. Smell the blood . . .

The amphitheater was hell.

In the middle of the arena, in the heart of that unyielding stone, stood a tiny wooden building topped by a cross. "There is our martyrium," Brecon said proudly.

Dinas could hardly hear him above the cries of the dead.

Ludno continued his lecture. "We built this chapel to commemorate the Christians who were tortured and slain in Deva Victrix. The timber was taken from oaks that were standing when Christ was alive. We men located and felled the trees; our women cut and shaped the wooden pegs that hold the building together. Even the smallest child had a job to do, if only bringing water to the workmen."

"I carved the cross on top," said Brecon as he outmaneuvered Ludno and opened the door.

CHAPTER THREE

A pale shaft of light slanted through the narrow window in the eastern wall. Cadogan's neck was stiff. He felt as if he had been sitting on the floor for days with his back pressed against the wall and his ears straining to detect the slightest sound.

Sometime during the night he had dreamed about his parents. Fragmented, disturbing dreams, mostly featuring his mother. He could not see her face but he recognized the flavor of her. The sweetness that surrounded him. He yearned toward her with every fiber of his being, even as she receded into a shadowy nowhere. Out of that same nowhere his father loomed toward him. Not sweetness this time, but a hard and bitter crust like that on a burned loaf of bread, which he could not break through.

Beside him Quartilla said in her knife-edged voice, "It's been quiet out there for a long time. Can't we get up now? I ache all over."

The dream evaporated. Cadogan did not know whether to be sad or glad. "Get up then. We have to sooner or later anyway."

With a dramatic moan, Quartilla stretched her legs in front of her. The stained gown she wore rode up to reveal thin thighs and dirty knees. Apparently she did not bother to use the washbasin.

Cadogan was disgusted. What does this woman have to whine about? She's spent the last ten days gorging on my food and sleeping in my bed while I sifted through wreckage.

"Who were they, Cadogan? Us? Or them?"

"Them, but I don't know which 'them.' My knowledge of the barbarian tribes is pretty limited. I couldn't get a good look at them, it was too dark. They might be Picts or Scoti, I suppose."

"Not Saxons?"

"I haven't heard about Saxons in this part of the country. Yet," he added. He struggled to his feet—he ached all over too—and peered through the window.

"What's out there?"

"Nothing. Grass and trees."

"Is that all?"

"See for yourself." He extended a hand to help her up but she ignored it.

Grunting and groaning, she scrambled to her feet unaided and rubbed her buttocks with both hands. "Sweet Mother Isis, I think I'm dead behind." Belatedly straightening her gown, she gave a cursory glance through the window. "I wonder why they didn't break down the door."

"I made that door strong enough to resist anything short of a battering ram," said Cadogan. "I also made sure the outside looks like nothing here is worth the effort to break in."

"That's what it looks like inside, too," Quartilla commented.

Cadogan went to the next window. Gloomily observed trees losing their leaves and grass turning brown. Pallid sky, threads of cloud hinting at rain. "I knew marauders would come sooner or later," he said over his shoulder, "so I tried to prepare for them. I knew what they had done in other . . ."

"What did you see in Viroconium? That is where you went, isn't it?"

He turned to look at her. She was sitting on the bed again, trying to comb a rats' nest of dyed red hair. "Didn't Dinas bring you from Viroconium?"

"No. I've never been there."

"Then where did you come from?"

She was not going to give him an answer, then thought better of it. For the time being Cadogan was her only protector. "Dinas found me hiding in the hills."

"Hiding from what?" he asked as he went to the next window.

"Them," Quartilla said simply.

Cadogan's voice sank deep in his chest. "Them. Yes. They'd already been to Viroconium by the time I got there."

"Was anyone killed?"

He was disgusted; Viola would not have asked that question so avidly. "A few of our servants were slain."

"Your *servants?*"

"Very well then, our slaves," he conceded. "In Viroconium we like to use more polite terms. Actually, a couple of them were indentured and might have paid their way to freedom someday."

Quartilla did not request elucidation on the topic; instead she wanted to know how the intruders entered the city.

"A handful of barbarians discovered an unguarded gate behind the theater," Cadogan told her. "Our house is one of those nearest the theater; it's a very desirable location. The raiders broke open a door leading to my mother's chambers—she used to love to walk in the garden without disturbing anyone—and ransacked her private rooms. The servants who came to investigate the noise were killed before the raiders fled.

"None of my family was in the house at the time, but Esoros, my father's steward, was there. When he realized what was happening he hid beside the furnace under the floor. He assumed barbarians wouldn't know about hypocausts and he was right. When I got there he was still cleaning up the damage. The rest of the servants were so frightened they'd run away, but Esoros has been loyal to my father for almost thirty years.

"He told me Father had gone to Londinium on business two weeks earlier. Thank God for that! If Vintrex had been at home he would have felt obligated to fight the barbarians himself, and they could have killed him in a blink. As for my mother, she died several years ago. Under the circumstances I'm glad of that, too. It would have broken her heart to have her jewelry and trinkets stolen."

Cadogan moved from one side of the window to the other, changing his angle of vision. "I don't see my horse anywhere."

The woman was struggling with an intractable knot of hair. "It must have wandered off," she said indifferently. The behavior of horses was not one of her interests.

"My mare would never stray, she's as loyal as Esoros." Cadogan stood indecisive for a few moments, then retrieved his smoke-stained cloak from its peg. "Stay here, Quartilla; I'm going to get her back if I can."

She jumped up and caught his arm. "Don't go, don't leave me! What if they're still out there?"

He pushed her away. "Throw the bolt when I'm gone. You do remember how to do that, don't you?" he added sarcastically.

When he went to the door she tried to prevent him from drawing the bolt.

Cadogan swore under his breath.

He opened the door on a sloping meadow studded with tree stumps and bordered by forest. The grass nearest the fort was badly trampled. Cadogan walked all the way around the building, studying the ground, while Quartilla clung like his shadow. When she saw the charred remains of last night's fire she pursed her lips.

"I almost wish those devils had broken in," Cadogan said. "If they had found any valuables maybe they would have left my horse." Putting two fingers into his mouth, he gave a piercing whistle.

Quartilla clapped her hands over her ears. "Stop that awful noise!"

Not as awful as your voice, he thought. He whistled again. Waited. Heard no answering whinny, no tattoo of trotting hooves. Hiding his dismay behind an expressionless face, he resumed searching for tracks.

"Was it a good horse?" the woman asked.

"*She* was a very good horse," he replied, deliberately stressing the feminine pronoun.

"There are plenty of other horses."

"Not like her. My uncle used to raise horses on one of his country estates; exceptionally fine animals. He even had two desert-bred stallions imported from Egypt to sire mounts for Roman cavalry officers. When the Romans left the business ceased to be profitable and he gradually sold off his herd. My mare is the last of his breeding stock. The horse Dinas rides is her son."

"That dark brute?"

"That dark brute. I told you they knew each other." Cadogan found the mare's tracks, leading in an erratic line away from the fort. There had been men on either side of her, and in several places a struggle had occurred. She had not gone willingly.

He swore again, loudly this time, and broke into a run.

"Wait!" shrilled Quartilla. He heard her pounding after him.

The trail extended the length of the pasture and into the forest. As Cadogan entered the shadowy realm of the trees he realized he had no weapon with him. He slowed to a walk, wondering whether to return to the fort for one or keep going. Before he could decide the woman caught up with him.

She bent over with her hands braced against her knees. "I told . . . told you . . . to wait!" she gasped.

"I didn't know you could run so fast."

"I can do anything," she said as she fought for breath.

"Turn around and go back. I'm going on."

"Then I'm going with you."

Plague take the woman! Cadogan thought. This time he did not repent. He broke into a trot, dodging trees and plunging through undergrowth. Let her keep up if she could.

She could. Moaning and complaining and gasping for breath, she stayed with him.

The second time he stopped, he knew he was defeated. If he outran Quartilla and left her alone in the forest the marauders might come back and find her. Or some other disaster could befall her. He had to choose between a woman and a horse and there was only one choice he could make.

"We're turning back," he said. "The forest is so dense it's impossible to find their trail, and they're long gone by now anyway."

"Are you sure? I can still . . ."

This time he interrupted. "No, you can't. Here, give me your hand and watch your footing."

As they walked he discovered they had gone farther than he thought. The trees loomed over them. The sun was climbing higher in the sky yet it seemed to Cadogan that the day had grown darker. It was cold under the trees.

"Londinium," Quartilla mused aloud. "Imagine your father going all the way to Londinium. I don't know anyone who's been there."

"He used to go at least twice a year."

"Really?"

"Yes, really." Did she think he was lying? Everything the woman did was irritating. "While he was still a relatively young man my father was appointed chief magistrate of Viroconium and its hinterlands by the provincial governor. He took his position seriously. After the Romans left he went on meeting his responsibilities: holding court, making judgments, meting out punishment for wrongdoers. He has a powerful sense of civic duty, my father," Cadogan added sourly.

A sudden crashing in the undergrowth made them both jump. A large red deer, as startled as they were, bolted past them and disappeared.

Cadogan gave a shaky laugh. "That's the last time I ever go out my door without a spear in my hand."

"If Dinas was here we would have had fresh meat tonight," Quartilla said.

"We can't be certain of that."

"You don't like Dinas very much, do you?"

Cadogan rubbed his chin. "I don't dislike him. We grew up together, we even had the same tutor, but we're not what you would call friends."

When a fallen tree partially blocked their way, Quartilla promptly sat down on it. Clasping her knees with both hands, she looked up at him. "Why aren't you friends?"

Cadogan sat down beside her. "Family trouble. You wouldn't understand."

"There's nothing I understand better," she averred. "Tell me."

By now he knew how stubborn she was. It would be simpler to tell her than to try to fend her off. "Our fathers were brothers," Cadogan began. "My uncle Ocellus was a lion in the house but a fox in the streets, and he made a lot of money early on. My father did well enough as a civil servant but there was always rivalry between them. However, they built new houses on adjacent sites in Viroconium; Dinas and I were raised shoulder to shoulder. At some time in the past my father Vintrex and Dinas's mother Gwladys became lovers. They managed to keep the affair a secret from both their families; I suppose only the servants knew about it. They know everything.

"Five years ago Dinas's father Ocellus gave him a yearling colt, large for its age and nearly black, the last and best animal he ever bred. Dinas was overjoyed. He threw his heart and soul into training that young stallion. When the training was completed Gwladys unexpectedly demanded that Dinas give the horse to me—to please her lover, I suspect. Dinas was furious, he has a hot temper at the best of times. He complained to Ocellus, who took his side. There was a terrible fight between his parents. Gwladys attacked Ocellus with a knife, and he broke her jaw with his fist."

Quartilla could not surpress a squeal of excitement.

"Gwladys came running to my father for protection. That was the first my mother—Domitia was her name—knew of their affair. Mother had never been strong; she took to her bed that same day and wouldn't see anyone but the servants. She wouldn't even see me, her only son. My married sisters came to the house and tried to advise her by shouting through the door. She insisted they leave her alone, so finally they did."

"What about Vintrex and Gwladys?" Quartilla asked breathlessly. "Did they run away together?"

"Of course not! Don't you understand? They were married to

other people. My father sent Gwladys back to her husband and forbade any member of our family to mention the matter again. A few weeks later Ocellus moved his entire household to one of his country estates, some fifteen miles from Viroconium. Dinas didn't go with them, however. While the porters were loading the baggage train he took the dark horse and disappeared. It was as if the earth opened up and swallowed them.

"In a misguided attempt to patch up things with my father, or perhaps just to placate his own conscience, Ocellus sent the bay mare to me. But it was too late, the damage had been done. The atmosphere was permanently poisoned.

"To make matters worse, Dinas and I had been spending time with two sisters, Viola and Aldina. When Dinas left he didn't say good-bye to Aldina. She decided, probably with some justification, that he loved the horse more than he loved her. She had to blame someone for what had happened, so she blamed my family. Viola sided with her sister and refused to see me anymore."

"Of course she did!" said Quartilla. "Any man who would choose a horse over a woman . . ."

"It wasn't me who did that, it was Dinas. I was innocent in the matter."

"No man is ever innocent," Quartilla stated with conviction.

Cadogan regretted having told her anything. He stood up and brushed himself off. In the excitement of the chase he had forgotten his weariness and the sleepless night, but now he felt exhaustion waiting for him like a lead cap on top of his head. "I'm going back to the fort," he said. "Are you coming?"

"Do I have a choice?"

I had a choice, Cadogan reminded himself sourly. I could have tried to save my mare and allowed this wretched woman to be stolen by barbarians or eaten by wolves. Leave it to me to make the wrong decision. "No, Quartilla, " he said, "you don't have a choice. Come on."

As they walked back toward the fort, with dead leaves crunching under their feet, he contemplated events he wished he could forget. The argument that had begun over a horse—so simple a matter as that!—had grown until, like a whirlpool, it had sucked into its vortex most of Viroconium society.

Viroconium, Cadogan thought with a wince of nostalgia. Sometimes his birthplace was still more real to him than the place he currently inhabited. If some unimaginable catastrophe wiped the city from the face of the earth he was confident he could reconstruct it stone by stone and street by street. In his dreams he often found himself there again; a living part of the Britannia that Rome had constructed. Part of a way of life that surely would last forever.

As chief magistrate of Viroconium and a large surrounding area, Cadogan's father Vintrex represented the law in the region. The peace and prosperity of an extensive municipality depended on his ability to maintain order. The magistrate's brother Ocellus was the largest landowner, a man who relied on the law in his frequent disputes over property. When the vicious quarrel broke out between them the brothers had been like two cats fighting with their tails tied together. No holds barred and nothing forgiven.

The inhabitants of Viroconium had enjoyed the feud between their leading families. No matter how Romanized the townspeople became, they were descended from Celtic warriors with the love of battle in their blood. Sides were taken and factions formed—even among the servants. Opinion was evenly divided. While women gossiped over garden walls, in the taverns and alehouses their menfolk laid bets on the outcome of the argument. They were distracted, for a while, from the larger problem looming on the horizon.

In the fourth century Jutes and silver-haired Angles had begun migrating to the temperate climate of Britannia from the colder region identified by the Alexandrian geographer Ptolemaeus as Germania Magna. Their numbers were swelled by Franks from Gaul, whose ancestors had been displaced by the Roman conquest. At first the authorities had tolerated the foreigners, seeing them as a possible addition to the labor force. But when hostile Picts and their allies,

the Scoti from the north of Eire, began marauding in the territory
of the Brigantes, the Roman governor of Britannia grew alarmed.
He could not afford to lose the goodwill of the Brigantes. Theirs was
a very large tribe, and collecting taxes from them required their willing compliance.

When the legions failed to defeat the invaders the governor had
sent a request to Aëtius, commander of the Roman forces in Gaul, for
additional military help. Aëtius had failed to respond. Fortunately the
Brigantes had proved up to the task themselves, driving their enemies back into the vast wilderness of Caledonia. A thankful Hadrian
had built his wall to contain the problem and the matter seemed to
be settled. For a while.

No sooner had the legions begun to pull out than more northern foreigners arrived. Many brought their families. They walked
along the roads like stray cattle looking for pasture, or followed the
rivers in boats piled high with household goods. The women had
clenched faces; the children had huge eyes and bloated bellies.

If they occupied land the Britons deemed unfit for farming the
immigrants were tolerated—at first. Alien settlements sprouted like
mushrooms in impenetrable forests or sodden marshland. Gradually
the newcomers established trade with their British neighbors, and
their customs and languages filtered into common usage.

The aggressive Saxons who plagued the eastern coast were a different matter. Seaborne marauders, they terrorized and disrupted shipping in the Oceanus Britannicus. A Roman official was given the title
"Count of the Saxon Shore" and empowered to deal with the problem, but the office was vacated when the holder was slaughtered by
the Saxons.

Many critical posts were abandoned by 410, when the last legion,
the famous Twentieth, departed.

In the decade that followed, civic government had continued to
function for a while, thanks to its elite cadre of Romanized Britons.
But inevitably, social discipline disintegrated. Episodes of domestic
violence became common. Young men from good families grew in-

creasingly unmanageable. The rate of robberies and burglaries rose alarmingly.

Native Picts and their allies, the Scoti from the north of Eire, came over Hadrian's Wall and began attacking isolated settlements. Worst of all, the Saxons had come ashore, seeking both land and plunder. Establishing settlements of their own. As their numbers expanded in the east the native Britons began to retreat westward. So did the Jutes and Franks and Angles. The old Roman roads offered easy mobility for native and foreigner alike. A perfect storm was bearing down on Viroconium.

Viroconium Cornoviarum was an administrative center, one of the civitates, or tribal capitals. The majority of its resident population comprised a middle class known as the curiales, members of the city council, their sons and relatives. Initially a rough frontier town during the Roman advance westward, Viroconium had served as a supply depot for Deva Victrix and Isca Silurum, then grown into a cosmopolitan city with a broad central avenue, the via principalis, lined with sweet chestnut trees imported from Iberia by the Romans. The avenue bisected a grid of paved residential streets that divided the city into sections of ascending prosperity. The amenities of urban life included a large civic complex with a marble courthouse in the Doric style adjoining a colonnaded forum; a lavish public bathhouse equipped for both men and women; a famous and well-subscribed theater; a hospital fully equipped with Athenian medical instruments; an assortment of taverns and alehouses; numerous shops and markets, and the customary brothels, all to a high standard. Viroconium's citizens were accustomed to luxury.

They lived in snug town houses, most of which were constructed of timber. To give a Roman appearance the exterior walls were often clad in brick, then plastered and painted in Mediterranean colors or made snowy with lime wash. Roofs were covered in red tile, which like the brick was manufactured locally. Clay pits were as profitable as stone quarries and just as hard on the slaves who worked in them.

At the higher end of the social scale residences sometimes were built of stone and mortar, and were exceedingly spacious. Each stood in regal isolation in its own walled garden. The formal hall was the primary area for entertaining, but usually a smaller lounge was available for more intimate gatherings. In addition there would be a dining room, from five to ten bedrooms, several multipurpose ante-rooms, a separate kitchen and a servants' wing. The latrine might be an earth closet in a corner of the garden, but an indoor urinal was provided for the master of the house and his male guests.

Some prosperous Romano-British families also owned sprawl-ing country villas several miles beyond the city walls to allow them to escape from the stresses of urban life. The term "villa" was under-stood to include both a magnificent residence and the vast acreage on which it stood.

All under threat now from an invasion of foreigners. Barbarians.

Vintrex had planned to enlarge the fortifications of Viroconium and establish a local militia. But before he could put his plans into action his family had been shattered by the revelation of his affair with his brother's wife. Domitia's death had followed within weeks. The emotional upheaval seemed to paralyze Vintrex. Half-finished sketches for raising the city walls and building watchtowers lay for-gotten on his drawing table. Incomplete lists of potential recruits littered the floor.

Cadogan recalled the exact moment he had decided to leave Viro-conium. Several days earlier, Vintrex had sent him to a stonecutter south of the city with instructions to order the marble for Domitia's tomb. "I cannot bear to do it myself," Vintrex had said.

When he arrived at the stonecutter's workshop Cadogan was told there were no samples to inspect. "Pure white marbles like Parian and Carrara are no longer available at any price," the young man was informed. "They were imported from the Roman colonies and that trade is gone now. I can provide a fine-grained limestone, if you want, though most of my customers say it's too expensive for the quality. Still, the only alternatives are . . ."

Cadogan had only half listened, standing under an awning while the autumn rain drummed above him and the stonecutter droned on and on, moving from a litany of complaints about the business climate to a recital of his mother-in-law's health problems. At last Cadogan said he must discuss the matter with his father before making a decision, then mounted his horse and rode back to the city.

He had made straight for the nearest tavern, where he was offered an inferior wine that had never known the advantages of a sunny Mediterranean hillside. He had drunk the sour liquid without really tasting it, while trying to block out the banal babble of the men around him. No one was saying anything important. No one ever said anything important.

Tied to a weathered stone hitching post outside, the mare had waited patiently in the rain.

At last Cadogan could no longer put off the moment. He had ridden through the streets at a walk, but even so, reached home sooner than he wanted.

Like a jewel set in its setting, the house where he was born stood against a backdrop of dark cedars. They provided a dramatic contrast to red-tile roofs and gleaming white walls. In a style introduced by the Romans, the main body of the house was composed of rectangular blocks enclosing a hollow square. The principal rooms opened onto the central court, known as an atrium, which was open to the sky and provided light and air to the interior. The exterior walls of the house had few windows and none at the front, thus eliminating street noise.

The private residence of the chief magistrate presented a deliberately blank face to visitors.

Bypassing the formal entrance at the side, Cadogan rode around to the servants' wing and the stables beyond. Whatever normal life remained in his father's house was to be found in the stables. Spirited horses and fragrant hay and rowdy stableboys laughing at bawdy jokes. Kikero, a splendid rooster with russet head and iridescent blue-green plumage on his back and wings, strutting around the place lording it over his harem of hens.

Vintrex was standing at the gate of the stable yard. He and his steward were discussing the proposed placement of Domitia's tomb. They looked up as Cadogan rode toward them. The two men were a study in contrasts. Vintrex, the carefully fed and highly educated product of ten generations of selective Romanization, had a noble forehead and refined features. But the years were not being kind to him. His gums were drawing back from his teeth; his flesh was sagging on his bones.

Esoros, on the other hand, possessed the wedge-shaped nose and deep eyes of a true Celt. His was a face that knew how to endure. Vintrex had once said of him, "My steward remembers everything and forgives nothing," but held him in the highest regard—a compliment Esoros returned by trying to speak like his master. The precise diction of the court and the forum sounded strange from his lips.

As Cadogan approached them, Vintrex had glowered at his son. "Who gave you permission to ride that ancient beast? She's an embarrassment."

"She's mine, Father, I don't need anyone's permission to ride her. She may not be young anymore, but she's still the best horse in the stable."

"Dispose of her!" Vintrex demanded. "I don't want to see her on my property again!" A vein throbbed visibly in his temple.

Cadogan had dismounted and handed the reins to a stableboy. "Take good care of her," he said under his breath, then turned to face his father.

The conversation that followed was not pleasant.

When Vintrex was told there was no white marble for the tomb, he was furious. He had berated his son in front of Esoros. "Did you even go to the right stonecutters? I seriously doubt it, I know a lie when I hear one. If you had any initiative you would have found the marble I sent you for, and at a decent price, too. But no; you prefer to drift through life with your nose in books. Wasting your time rereading dead words. How can I be proud of a feckless overgrown boy? What good are you to me at all?"

Stung by injustice, Cadogan had lost his own temper. Old wounds, the natural detritus of the relationship between father and son, were opened afresh. In the rising heat of their quarrel Cadogan eventually blamed his father for his mother's death. Vintrex countered by claiming Domitia's poor health dated from Cadogan's birth. The quarrel had come to an abrupt end when Vintrex shouted at his son, "While you are under my roof you will do what I say, when I say, exactly as I say, and nothing else! You are my *son!*"

"I am not your *property!*" Cadogan had shouted back at him. "Not anymore!"

After giving the matter deep thought for several days, one night Cadogan waited until everyone was asleep, then padded silently through the house. Collecting his personal belongings, including the things he had inherited from his mother and a list of household items he thought he might need. Before dawn he had loaded everything onto two packhorses and commandeered a porter to take charge of them. Before he rode out of the stable yard he had snatched up Kikero, bound his legs together and carried the surprised rooster with him on the bay mare.

Cadogan was drunk with a sense of freedom.

He had wandered the forested hills northeast of Viroconium until he came upon a sloping meadow skirted by oak and ash and alder. The land was unoccupied. There was adequate grass for his mare and a sparkling stream at the foot of the hill, and it was only a few miles to a small village. The first time he visited the village for supplies he could purchase some hens for Kikero.

Cadogan knew at once that he had found his sanctuary. A place where he could read, and dream, and commune with God, without being criticized.

When the packhorses were unloaded he had sent them back to his father with the porter. His final instruction to the weary servant was, "Tell Vintrex he will never see my mare on his property again. Nor me either."

Then he set to work.

Creating a home for himself proved harder than he anticipated.

At first he had envisioned a country estate in the Roman style. Like his parents' property in Viroconium, his house would be built around a courtyard open to the sky. The floors would be decorated with mosaic tiles. Cadogan planned to outfit a separate room for every household function, including a chamber for Christian worship, following the custom introduced under Emperor Constantine. In 313 Constantine had made Christianity the official religion and its Roman version the official version throughout the empire.

Cadogan's new home would have light and comfort and a place for God. In the quicksilver air of a forest clearing he almost sensed a Presence; in the shadowed silence of the trees he almost heard a Voice. Away from the bustle and distractions of the city he was certain he could find the tranquility he longed for.

The residence in Cadogan's imagination was very beautiful. Before he fell asleep lying on a blanket on the ground he talked in his head to Viola, telling her about the home he would build for the two of them. When she saw what he had accomplished, she would relent and return to him. In his dreams it seemed possible.

Reality did not conform to dreams. The stream that was to supply his water abandoned him. One morning it sparkled and sang. The following morning it was dry; the very stones in the streambed were dry. After some searching he found a trickle of water meandering off in another direction entirely. To his consternation, even that meager supply disappeared two days later.

When he went searching for an alternate water source he discovered that the nearest river was more than a mile away. He had no idea how to construct a viaduct. It was the sort of thing the Romans had known. In the end he had been forced to dig a well; three wells, in fact, before he finally struck water.

Nothing had worked out as Cadogan expected. Adapting to the

materials at hand was only the first in a long chain of compromises that gave Cadogan a sneaking satisfaction.

Vintrex would not have approved. He considered compromise a sin.

The elegant multiroomed stone-walled villa became a timber cabin with no inner courtyard, no reflecting pool, and no tiles on the roof. Only sod and thatch to keep out the rain. At night Cadogan had to bring Kikero and his small harem inside to protect them from predators, and he learned to be careful where he put his feet. Yet he was proud of his achievement. Sometimes, after Cadogan had completed a task, he reached out and touched the well-set log, the perfectly smoothed plank, and said, "There now. There now."

His home was not modeled on anyone else's ideas; it was shaped by its setting and his need. Its flaws and virtues were his own.

As he and Quartilla emerged from the forest and he saw the fort waiting for him, his heart leaped. At that moment he could think of nothing he would change. He broke into a trot, anxious to be under his own roof again.

He stopped short when the door creaked open.

CHAPTER FOUR

After handing his cape and the stallion's reins to Meradoc, Dinas ducked his head to enter through the low doorway. Brecon and Ludno followed, chanting in unison, "May the spirits of the martyrs be with us."

The room was dimly lit by one fat beeswax candle in a tall iron holder. It took a few moments for Dinas's eyes to adjust to the darkness. When he realized that Ludno and Brecon had dropped to their knees beside him, he knelt too.

Dinas had not prayed in years. He struggled to remember the words he had once known by heart; the forms he had forgotten when he decided to forget about God. Aware that the others might be watching, he bowed his head over folded hands and silently moved his lips.

The only sound was that of three men breathing.

Keeping his head down, Dinas covertly examined the interior of the chapel. There was no ornamentation of any kind. His parents, like other Christians of their class, had a special room in their home set aside for worship. A whole series of priests had conducted services in a dignified apartment plenished with the finest accoutrements the family could afford. Vessels of gold and silver were supplied for the Eucharist. Colorful tapestries depicting stories from the Bible were hung on the walls.

As a small boy Dinas had loved the vivid scene of Daniel in the lions' den, with bones and human skulls lying scattered about.

The interior of the martyrium of Deva was paneled with well-polished wood but there were no hangings on the walls. The only furniture was a narrow oak table covered by an altar cloth of bleached linen. The chapel contained nothing more except the candle in its holder, a carved crucifix on the wall—Dinas recognized the artistry of Brecon—and a faint, spicy fragrance, almost but not quite like sandalwood.

I was right, Dinas thought; Deva is far too poor to be worth my interest. If the local Christians owned anything of value their shrine wouldn't be so ostentatiously bare.

Ostentatiously?

The word caused an itch in his brain.

He unconsciously cracked his knuckles while he concentrated on clearing his thoughts. An image of the half-abandoned market-place slowly appeared behind his closed eyelids. Every detail was as clear as if he stood in the town square. There was nothing ostentatious about the poverty in Deva, it was real. The market was the proof of that. Yet from his own observations he knew commerce had not ceased. Someone always had something to sell; others always wanted to buy. Men like Ludno would find ways to make a profit.

Opening his eyes, Dinas surveyed the interior of the chapel again. He noticed a minute deviation in the color of the wood paneling behind the altar. His thoughts narrowed to a sharp focus. Like a man crossing a river on stepping stones, one at a time, he followed a series of seemingly unrelated facts to a single conclusion. Walked around it in his mind, looking at it from all sides.

And suddenly he was sure.

Afterward he would think of it as inspiration.

When he heard Ludno intone a pious "Amen," Dinas stood up. "I am deeply moved," he assured his escorts. "I must thank you for bringing me here, your martyrium is indeed a unique experience. Yet I wonder—how can you hold religious services in such a small space?"

"We only come a few at a time," said Brecon, "as the spirit moves us. I myself frequently pray here."

"But you don't celebrate the Eucharist in this chapel?"

Ludno's narrow eyes opened wide. "What made you think we did?"

"The altar."

"The altar reminds us of the sacrifice our ancestors made on this very spot," Brecon explained.

Ludno added, "For the Eucharist we would require holy vessels, and as you see, we have none."

"But you have an ambry, do you not? A concealed repository for holy vessels?" Dinas sounded very casual, as if the question were merely an afterthought. An equally casual gesture indicated the panel he had discovered. The plain wooden panel disguised as part of the wall.

Ludno said sharply, "The recess behind the panel is empty." He shot a warning look at Brecon.

"Don't tell me you were robbed!" Dinas sounded shocked. "Surely a holy place like this should be safe from . . ."

"We were not robbed," said Brecon. After another look from Ludno he added, "There was never anything in there to steal."

Ludno smoothly changed the subject. "Since an empty cubicle is of no interest to a pilgrim, I would be happy to entertain you with a recital of the martyrs of Deva. I am an expert on the subject, having memorized all of their details. I can tell you who they were—men and women as well—and when they lived and how they died. The latter is of particular interest. The Romans were very inventive in their methods of killing. I can enumerate at least seventeen different . . ."

A horse whinnied loudly at the door of the chapel, interrupting Ludno's lecture. Dinas bit his lip to keep from laughing; it was not the first time the dark horse had saved him. "I am sure your recital is most edifying, Ludno, but I'm being summoned. My horse thinks it's time to be on our way and I rely on his good judgment." Bowing to the crucifix on the wall, Dinas left the Martyrium.

Ludno and Brecon followed him into the daylight—or what now passed for daylight. While they were inside the blue sky had faded to a dirty white. A strong wind had sprung up, stirring the dust in the streets. Dinas put one forefinger in his mouth and then held it aloft to determine the direction of the wind. "Northwest," he announced, "and getting colder. Winter will be here soon." Taking his cape from Meradoc, he swirled the leather around his shoulders with careless grace.

"It's a long ride to Mamucium," Ludno observed, "and I should warn you that autumn storms are horrendous in this part of the country. No matter what your horse thinks," he added, barely disguising a sneer, "you would be wise to spend the night here. There are two inns in Deva. The one I own is far superior to the other and I will give you a reduced rate. Special for pilgrims."

"Or you can stay with my family," offered Brecon. "There's an extra bed in my workshop and my wife is a good cook. And I won't charge you anything."

Ludno glared at him.

Dinas weighed Brecon's offer against the plan already formed in his mind. This was better; an invisible helping hand. "Thank you for your generous invitation, Brecon. I accept for one night only; I am accustomed to sleeping under the stars. Now if you'll show me where I may stable my horse . . . ?" He reached for the stallion's reins.

Meradoc was slow to surrender his precious connection to the animal. He, who knew nothing of poetry, loved the poetry embodied in the horse. "Where are you going after Mamucium?" he asked Dinas.

"I don't know."

Meradoc cocked his head to one side. "If you don't know where you're going, how will you know when you get there?"

The question confirmed Dinas's hunch about the little man; there was more to Meradoc than met the eye. "I'll know I've arrived when I stop traveling, Meradoc. Would you like to travel with me?"

"Are you serious?"

"Don't tease the poor fellow."

"I'm not teasing him, Brecon, I mean it. Would your family object, Meradoc?"

"I have no family. I was left outside the gates when I was a baby."

Ludno exclaimed, "You can't just ride in here and steal him, Dinas!"

"Do you belong to this man?" Dinas asked Meradoc.

"We have no slaves in Deva," Brecon boasted.

"That is commendable and very Christian of you," said Dinas. "And I agree completely. No one can own another; spirits are always free. If this man is not a slave I'm not stealing him."

"Kidnapping him then," Ludno argued. "It amounts to the same thing."

"He's not kidnapping me," said Meradoc. "I want to go with him."

"But I expect you to gather firewood for my wife!"

"Meradoc, did you promise Ludno you would gather firewood for his wife?"

The little man hesitated, thinking back. "No, I didn't promise."

"Then it's settled." Dinas faced Ludno squarely, and for the first time revealed the steel in his voice. "Without a binding promise a free man can do as he likes." He turned to Meradoc. "Go now and gather the things you think you'll need. You can meet me at the northern gates at the first glimmer of sunrise. No later, mind you."

"Tomorrow night I'll sleep under the stars!" Meradoc exulted.

They made their first camp in a hummocky meadow traversed by a rock-ribbed stream, one of the tributaries of the Dee. In early spring the watercourse would have contained a rushing river. By midsummer the flow had slowed to a trickle winding down from the foothills to the west. Now it was torpid, like a snake on a cold morning.

Dinas drew rein. "While I see to my baggage you can unsaddle my horse and rub him down with fistfuls of grass," he told Meradoc, "but don't bother to tether him. He's free; he stays with me because he wants to. After you've taken care of him find a bit of level ground where we can spread our blankets, and a stand of trees to provide deadfall for a fire."

Handing the stallion's reins to Meradoc, Dinas untied his saddlebags and set them on the ground. He crouched down and began going through their contents. Clothing, blankets, a heavy winter cloak, food supplies, a drinking cup, a small cooking pot . . . and at the very bottom a bundle of lambskin, old and worn and as soft as silk. The bundle was tied with faded strips of wool that might once have been blue. Dinas stopped suddenly and looked up. Meradoc, busy with the horse, did not notice.

The pack Meradoc had strapped to his own back was much smaller, though it contained everything he owned. He did not expect the horse to carry it, nor did he expect to be offered a ride on the horse. The rigid class distinctions the Romans had bequeathed to Britannia remained in force.

This did not prevent Dinas from helping Meradoc to prepare the campsite. Working in a companionable silence, the two men cleared a sleeping area of stones and thistles and built a campfire. When Dinas produced a cork-stoppered water bottle from one of his saddlebags, Meradoc filled it from the stream. After they spread their blankets on the ground near the fire, Dinas took out bread, bacon and hard cheese, and sat down cross-legged to eat.

Meradoc was still standing. He shifted from one foot to the other.

Dinas glanced up. "Aren't you hungry?"

"I brought a hooded cloak and my other tunic and a blanket, but . . ."

"But?"

"No food," Meradoc admitted, ducking his chin in embarrassment. "I never thought about food. In Deva people feed me in return for my work."

"You're not in the town now, little man. Whatever we need out here we must supply for ourselves. I could give you some of my food but you wouldn't learn anything from that, except to rely on me. You must find your own food tonight."

Meradoc looked around. Grass. Trees. A few rocks. "Where?"

"What do you want to eat?"

Meradoc could not remember anyone ever asking him that question before. In Deva he ate what he was given, which was usually scraps. "Meat," he decided.

"Then untie your boots and give me the thongs."

Meradoc obeyed.

Dinas stood up and strode off across the meadow. "Come on."

Meradoc trotted after him. When they were some distance from the stream Dinas crouched down and skillfully turned the thongs into two snares, which he concealed in the tall grass. "Watch me," he instructed. Unnecessarily, since Meradoc was watching everything Dinas did, learning from the other man's body language just as he learned from the stallion's body language.

When the snares were in place they returned to the fire. Dinas resumed eating. Between bites he said, "This area is probably swarming with hares the legions imported to augment their food supply. Hares aren't stupid; they were clever enough to escape and have been breeding ever since. With any luck you might have one to skin and roast in an hour or two. In the meantime I suggest you fish. There are some iron hooks in my saddlebag."

"I've never fished," Meradoc admitted in a barely audible voice.

"Sweet smoldering Hades, man! I thought you said you could do anything."

"I can. If someone shows me the way you just did."

"Prove it." Dinas untied one of his own boots and handed the thongs to Meradoc. The little man perfectly replicated one of the snares he had made.

"Aha," said Dinas.

Although they checked the snares several times, no hares were trapped that night. But after a little coaching from Dinas, Meradoc caught enough fish to feed himself. When he had finished eating and licked his fingers he asked Dinas, "How did you know about the Romans bringing the hares?"

"I had a Roman tutor," Dinas said. "A most thorough fellow who stuffed our heads with irrelevant facts."

"Oh."

As they prepared to sleep, Dinas gave a low whistle that summoned the stallion from grazing nearby. The horse walked calmly to the blanket Dinas had spread on the ground and lay down beside it. To Meradoc's amazement, he stretched out his neck to be a pillow for his master's head.

That night two men slept under the stars.

Meradoc had thought he was too excited to sleep, but he was wrong. He awoke well before dawn, feeling better than he had in years. He slipped from beneath his only blanket and went looking for the horse, who was already up and grazing. The stallion gave him a friendly nudge in the chest with his muzzle. By the time Dinas stopped snoring the horse was rubbed down, the campfire built up, and four trout were sizzling on flat stones close to the fire.

"Remind me to show you how to construct a spit," Dinas said as he stood up and began stretching himself. He stretched like a cat, slowly and thoroughly. Meradoc resolved to start doing that too.

The two men ate without talking. Meradoc thought nothing had ever tasted as good as the fresh-caught trout. When the meal was finished he rinsed out their cups in the stream, emptied them onto the smoldering coals of the fire, and kicked dirt onto the hissing remains. Dinas strapped the saddle on the dark horse and tied the bags behind it, then vaulted onto the horse's back. "Forward, now." They set off in the same configuration as the day before: Meradoc walking at the stallion's shoulder.

Observing the location of the sun in the sky, the little man asked, "Are you sure we're going toward Mamucium?"

"We're not going to Mamucium."

"We're not delivering the horse to its owner?"

"I am the owner. He has no other."

Meradoc digested this information with a sense of relief. He did not mind that Dinas had lied to Ludno. He would very much mind being parted from the dark horse.

Dinas rode in silence with his eyes on the horizon. Sometimes Meradoc watched the countryside through which they were passing, sometimes he watched his feet take one step after another. At last he ventured, "Do you want to talk?"

Dinas replied without looking down from the horse, "Talk about what?"

"Anything. I want to listen."

"I don't want to talk," said Dinas. And that was that.

Too much walking made the dark horse fretful. He began tossing his head, shaking his heavy mane. Dinas reined him to one side and galloped him in a huge circle. Meradoc watched them dwindle into the distance with the stallion's tail streaming like a black banner. He maintained his steady pace until he heard the rolling thunder of hooves approaching again. He welcomed Dinas with a cheerful wave. "Don't ever hold him back on my account," he said.

"I won't," Dinas replied.

When the sun reached midpoint they stopped beside a shallow stream. The men drank upriver of the stallion, then walked away from the watercourse to relieve themselves.

The lack of another human voice was beginning to bother Meradoc, who was used to the babble of the town. "Why don't you like to talk?" he asked Dinas.

"I don't dislike talking, I can go on for hours under the right circumstances. But I think of words as coinage. I give what I need to get what I want."

"You talk to the horse, I've heard you."

"That proves my point. I talk to him so he will understand me better, which helps us both."

"I don't understand you, Dinas. Why did you invite me to come with you? You can take care of yourself very well without my help."

"Have you ever tasted anchovies?"

"What?"

"Anchovies. A small, bony fish, very salty, preserved in olive oil. Quite expensive, but worth it if you like them."

"I don't understand what you're talking about."

"Britannia is an island, did you know that? Anything we don't produce for ourselves must come to us by sea. Our markets used to do a huge trade in imported items like anchovies and figs and Persian melons. Olives and oil from Iberia, oysters and dates and coriander and . . ."

"I tasted dates once," Meradoc said dreamily. "They were sweet."

"Very sweet," Dinas agreed. "In the city where I was born, any host who failed to offer honeyed dates to his guests was considered a social outcast. After the Romans left there was no one to protect our sea-lanes, so now we have no more dates. No more anchovies. Yet merchant ships still sail the seas, dates still grow on palm trees, and fishermen still catch anchovies. Does that suggest anything to you, Meradoc?"

The little man was startled out of a pleasant reverie involving the taste of dates. "Suggest? To me?"

"I'm asking you to think," said Dinas.

No one had ever made such a request of Meradoc. Thinking was not one of the skills required of him in Deva. But it was not too late to start, so he spent the rest of the day thinking about Dinas. He had never met anyone like him before; a person who asked more of Meradoc than he thought he could do. People had always talked down to him. Dinas talked to him as if he had a good mind; as if he could learn.

And I can. If I can work with my hands I can work inside my head.

Thinking was challenging. One of Meradoc's more interesting thoughts concerned the difference between Dinas's flawless Latin and the Romano-British version commonly used in Deva. Dinas sounded even more educated than Ludno.

Why would a man like that wear shabby clothes but ride a splendid horse?

And why does he wander around the country alone, when everyone knows there are dangers beyond the walls? Does God protect pilgrims?

And if he is a pilgrim, is he a Christian? He said no prayers last night before he pulled his blanket over him.

And why is there anger in his face and sadness in his eyes, even when he smiles?

Thinking seems to produce a lot of questions. That's good. I like solving puzzles just as I like figuring out how things work.

I must do a lot more thinking.

CHAPTER FIVE

The man who stood in the doorway of the fort was considerably shorter than Cadogan, but with a wider frame. His torso was swathed in a curious garment woven of wool interspersed with hair from other animals—perhaps even humans. His hair appeared to be black, what one could see of it. The crown and area around the ears was plaited into countless tiny braids smeared with colored mud and twisted into an elaborate design.

Around his shoulders he wore a robe of wolf fur, fastened at the neck with a large tin brooch depicting animals in a most realistic manner. Above this work of art his upper face seemed startlingly primitive: low forehead, broad, flat nose, eyes so black there was no differentiation between pupil and iris. The lower part of his face was concealed by something Cadogan thought was a beard.

A vivid purple beard.

The intruder was gnawing on a strip of dried venison he held in one hand. As he stared at Cadogan and Quartilla his jaws slowly stopped working. He said something unintelligible and backed into the house. Cadogan followed him.

Quartilla went only as far as the doorway, where she stared in disbelief at the implausible beard. "It's a tattoo," she said in awe. "He's covered his face with tattoos! Hit him, Cadogan. Drive him out, drive him away!" As if the stranger were a serpent to be swept from a cold oven.

"Be quiet," Cadogan said with a calmness he did not feel.

The intruder stopped. Glanced from Cadogan to the woman at the door. A smile appeared like the sun rising above the purple shrubbery of his tattoos. He addressed himself directly to Cadogan in a serious but pleasant tone, like a man bargaining in the market-place. Once or twice he waved his strip of dried venison in the direction of Quartilla. Cadogan did not know his language but could guess its meaning—and the man's possible origin.

Quartilla said anxiously, "What does he want?"

"If I understand him correctly, he thinks you belong to me and he's asking for you. Very polite for a Pict."

She was horrified. "Kill him, kill him at once!" Her voice shrilled higher. "Kill him *now*!"

The stranger looked toward her again, then back to Cadogan once more. His black eyes, almost hidden within their full lids, were sympathetic. Cadogan recognized the universal expression of kin-ship shared by men in the presence of a difficult woman.

He smiled back at the man.

With this encouragement the Pict now launched into an intense monologue punctuated with flamboyant gestures. At one point he dropped his strip of venison. Without missing a beat he retrieved the meat from the dirt floor, ripped off another bite with his teeth and continued talking while he chewed.

Quartilla was on the verge of hysteria but neither man paid any attention to her. Establishing communication was more important.

As Cadogan watched in fascination, the stranger pantomimed an explanation for his presence. He had been a member of last night's raiding party. He became separated from the others when they were going through the forest. He had backtracked to the fort. He meant no harm to Cadogan and his woman, he was simply trying to make the best of his situation.

Quartilla seized Cadogan by the arm. "You maggot, you goat dung!" she shouted in his ear. "Why don't you act like a man? Why haven't you killed him already?"

Her interruption tore the frail fabric of understanding. "I'm try-ing to trade you for my horse," Cadogan said. He meant it as a joke, but as soon as he heard the words the idea crystallized. He motioned to the intruder and galloped his fingers in the air to suggest a horse running. Next he pointed at the woman. When the man did not respond he added a passable imitation of a horse's whinny.

The stranger still did not understand, but Quartilla did. Curving her fingers into claws, she tried to scoop out Cadogan's eyes with her broken fingernails.

The Pict hurled himself forward. Not at Cadogan, but at Quartilla.

He caught her around the waist and peeled her off Cadogan like peeling moss off a rock. She flailed and kicked but it was no use. He flung her to one side. When he turned back to Cadogan his voice rose in inflection, asking a question.

Cadogan could only shake his head.

Quartilla scrambled to her feet and leaped onto the stranger's back, clamping him with her knees like someone riding a horse bareback. She hooked one arm around his neck and tried to claw his face with the other hand, but only succeeded in ripping out a section of braided hair.

The Pict howled in pain.

The interlocked pair went careening across the room, crashing into tables and stools. At that particular moment Cadogan felt little compunction to rescue Quartilla, yet he could not help himself. He ran after them. As he tried to separate the combatants Quartilla sank her teeth into the stranger's ear. He lashed out with his fist and hit Cadogan square on the nose. Bone crunched. Cadogan cried out, and struck back. Now three people were floundering about the room, landing blows on whoever was nearest, all three sprayed with blood from Cadogan's nose.

Fighting the Pict was like fighting a swarm of hornets. The man was knotty with muscle and exceptionally agile; he easily evaded most of Cadogan's blows while successfully landing a number of his own. Quartilla confused the issue. She struck out at both men impartially with elbows to the diaphragm and knees to the groin.

When they blundered against the shelves at one end of the room the planks teetered, then showered them with tin pots and pewter cups and a great crashing of red pottery. Cadogan tried to catch a glass bottle the color of emeralds that seemed to fall toward him in a slow arc. His fingertips merely grazed the glass as an avalanche of scrolls cascaded over his head and shoulders. He shrugged them off and returned to the fray.

For a brief ecstatic time Quartilla might have been the Celtic warrior queen Boudicca facing the Roman legions, spending her body and soul in one wild exultant burst of action.

The tide of battle carried the trio to the other end of the room, where they hit the stone basin on its pedestal and almost, but not quite, dislodged it. The collision upset their precarious balance. They fell in a heap across Cadogan's bed, with Quartilla on the bottom.

The intruder laughed. He was the first to scramble to his feet, then extended one hand to help Cadogan off the bed.

Cadogan lurched over to the basin and thrust his face into the cool water. The water turned red.

The Pict was at his shoulder, chattering away like a man relating a blow-by-blow account of a glorious victory. When Cadogan straightened up the man gave him a comradely slap on the shoulder that almost knocked him down, and laughed again.

Never in his life had Cadogan felt pain to equal that of his crushed nose. His only experience of fighting consisted of the Greco-Roman wrestling matches favored by the noble youth of Viroconium. Highly stylized, closely refereed, they were more of an art form than a battle. The most he ever suffered was a bruise or two or a strained muscle. Now the center of his face was a throbbing agony that radiated outward like the sun. Blood streamed over his lips and chin and onto his heaving chest. When he tried to speak, the coppery taste of it in his mouth made him gag.

He became aware that Quartilla was sitting on the bed crying. Trying to put his pain aside, he went to see if she was hurt. She was very pale and looked shaken. When he bent over her the motion made his nose throb more violently. A fresh spate of blood poured down. Quartilla gave a little shriek and scrambled away from him.

"Are you all right?" he asked. The natural resonance of his deep voice caused a matching resonance in his broken nose.

"I was almost killed and you didn't care!" Quartilla accused.

He eased himself down beside her. "I tried to help you, but you kept hitting me."

"Because I hate you."

Cadogan noticed the stranger pawing through the wreckage of his possessions. "Leave those alone," he called. More resonance, more pain.

The man went on searching.

Cadogan stood up, intending to stop him—and suddenly was violently dizzy. There was a sickening ache in his groin where one of Quartilla's knees had done its damage. He bent over, cradling himself, and waited for the dizziness to pass. When it abated Quartilla was still crying—and the Pict was gone.

Cadogan stood in the doorway, gazing down the sloping meadow. Shadows were lengthening across the grass. "It will be night soon," he remarked. His voice was muffled by the cloth wrung out in water that he held over his nose.

"And we have nothing to eat," Quartilla said tartly. "How could you let that monster carry off all our food?"

" 'Our food,' as you put it, was almost gone anyway, thanks to you. All he took was the rest of the venison and one sack of the corn. You wouldn't eat dried venison if we still had any, and I don't feel like grinding corn to make flour. Unless you'd care to do it?"

She looked indignant. "What do you think I am, your servant? I'm no slave!"

"I don't have the slightest idea what you are, Quartilla. A while ago you were fighting like a barbarian."

"You're the barbarian, insulting me like that! I should leave right now."

"The door is open," said Cadogan. He resumed his gloomy perusal of the landscape.

"Where would I go if I left here? You said yourself it's getting dark. And what would I eat? For that matter . . ." A sly note crept into her voice. "What are you going to eat?"

"Nothing, tonight. A knee in the balls has an astonishing effect on a man's appetite. If I feel better tomorrow I'll go to the nearest village for fresh supplies."

"How far is that?"

"It was an easy ride on my horse. On foot it could be several hours."

"You were a fool to lose that horse, Cadogan."

He glared at her. "I wish to the good Lord that barbarian had killed you."

She began to cry. Hiccupy sobs, punctuated by blowing her nose on her sleeve.

He awoke in the middle of the night to find a woman curled up against him in the narrow bed, crowding him to the edge. For one heart-lifting moment he thought she was Viola. He almost reached for her. Then he remembered.

He did not remember going to bed, however, nor inviting Quartilla to join him. All he could recall of the evening was pain. When he shifted his legs a wave of nausea rolled over him. He lay still until it passed, then tried touching his nose with a tentative forefinger. He flinched.

The thought of a sneeze terrified him.

In the morning a temporarily contrite Quartilla made an effort to restore order to the fort. While Cadogan went to fetch water from the well she righted the stools and tables, returned the lamp to its place and the household utensils to their shelves. Among the broken bits and pieces on the floor she found several shards of emerald glass. She held the largest piece up to the light, then balanced it on one outstretched finger like a ring. Her pleasure was interrupted by Cadogan's return. He was carrying two brimming buckets. After he set them down she showed him the piece of glass. "What was this?"

"A container for perfumed oil. My mother's. She took it with her to the public baths."

"I've never been to the public baths." Too late, Quartilla realized how much that admission told about herself.

Cadogan filled the pitcher and basin and washed his face and neck, being careful to avoid his nose. Quartilla followed his example. Splashing lavishly so he would be sure to notice. After tidying her hair and smoothing her gown as best she could, she said brightly, "Are you going to get food now?"

"I suppose I must."

"Do you have money to pay for it? Money that monster didn't find?"

"I have money you couldn't find, Quartilla. Come along now, we'd best make a start."

"We? I couldn't possibly walk for four hours!"

"Eight hours," he corrected. "Four there and four back. You can do it; you walked all the way here from wherever Dinas found you."

"But surely you don't need me to go with you."

"I need you to help carry supplies," he said bluntly. "If you don't carry you don't eat. Of course I could leave you in the village, but I don't think they would feed you. Not unless I paid. Which I wouldn't. So make up your mind now." He started for the door.

She scurried after him. "You're a brutal selfish man and I hate you, Cadogan."

"We've already settled that," he replied.

There was no road to the nearest village. Cadogan's infrequent visits over the past two years had left no discernible trail to follow. He made his way through the forest by memory while Quartilla stayed close beside him, treading on his heels. She expected another horde of barbarians to spring out at any moment. If Cadogan shared her fear he did not show it. The ongoing pain of a broken nose and the lingering discomfort in his groin distracted him from larger worries.

They emerged from the forest into a ravaged landscape: an unfolding succession of barren hills scarred by extensive woodcutting during the Roman years. A few mighty oaks still lay where they had fallen when the last axes were laid down. Surrounded now by seedlings and saplings, the dead giants were both parent and nursery to the young trees.

The denuded hills offered no opportunity for an ambush. Quartilla relaxed a little, though she continued to complain about walking. To her relief, the hills gave way to moorland studded with sheep. "Why don't we take one of those, Cadogan? I'm fond of roast mutton."

"They aren't mine. They belong to the local smallholders."

"Surely they wouldn't miss one sheep."

He said in exasperation, "Is that how you propose to go through life, taking things that don't belong to you?"

"I have to survive!"

"That," he retorted, "is increasingly debatable."

His remark stung her into silence. For a while.

"Cadogan?"

"Yes?"

"Is it much farther?"

"We're about halfway there, why? Are you getting tired?"

"Are you?"

In truth he was. Not tired, but eager to give his nether parts a rest from the concussion of walking. "We can stop here for a while," he said, "but not for long, or we'll be going home again in the dark."

"Can't we spend the night in the village?" she asked hopefully.

"No."

While Quartilla reclined on the grass, Cadogan remained standing. Sitting down would hurt too much. But in spite of his discomfort he could think. Was cursed with a compulsion to think.

The words were blazoned across his brain. *Nothing will ever be the same again.*

Cadogan still could not fully comprehend, let alone accept, the changes that had come to Britannia. There had been warnings, of course, for years and years. At first they had consisted of subtle alterations, each no more than a slight annoyance. The quality of imported fabrics such as silk had declined. Exotic fruits no longer appeared in the markets. Other luxury goods to which the middle and upper classes had been accustomed became scarce and prohibitively expensive. Then one by one, they ceased to be available at all.

The women had been the first to complain. When the roads were no longer maintained to the usual standard the men began to take notice. Britons grew vociferous in their condemnation of the authorities. Senior officials offered complicated explanations. Gave elaborate excuses. Made empty promises. Then one by one, unnoticed at first but in increasing numbers, the Roman officials and their families began to slip away, taking with them as much of the island's resources as they could carry.

Why wasn't something done while there was still time? Cadogan wondered, as he had many times before. Men like my father must have realized what was happening. They should have demanded more legions, or at least kept the Twentieth. They should have made adequate preparations against the coming calamity. But no one expected calamity, not then. The inevitable was always in the future.

Then the future became now.

And here we are.

CHAPTER SIX

The morning found Dinas and Meradoc on their way again.

Inspiration had come to Dinas as he knelt in the Martyrium. One minute he had been bitter and confused; searching without a real sense of purpose. In the next minute he had the answer. Not in detail, that would come later. It was enough to have an idea so breathtaking in its audacity.

When he made camp with Meradoc that first night he had gone to sleep unsure of how to proceed. He awoke in the morning with the next step clear in his mind. He did not move, but continued to lie with his head pillowed on the stallion's neck while he thought. The dark horse knew Dinas was awake; had known even before he opened his eyes, but remained immobile, waiting for his master to make the first move.

Perhaps Meradoc is good luck, Dinas had thought to himself. A nice acquisition, that. I'll need more than luck, though. First, a company of strong, able men—clever but not too clever, so none of them will challenge me—who are willing to accept my authority without question. To lead other men I suppose I shall have to give up being a lone wolf. That could well be the hardest part. And then, there's the matter of organization—not my strongest point. No. I have the bones of the scheme but I'll have to have someone who can pull it together and work out the details.

I need a specific man with a certain kind of mind.

As they broke camp Dinas said to Meradoc, "You and I may do some interesting work together."

"Right now?" the little man asked eagerly.

"Not yet. I'll tell you when."

With no further explanation Dinas began saddling the dark horse. Seeing Meradoc watching him with an expectant look on his face, he said, "I have a cousin called Cadogan." He vaulted onto the stallion and gathered up the reins. As he rode away from the campsite he called over his shoulder, "Are you coming?"

Meradoc trotted after him.

They had been traveling for quite a while before Meradoc broke the silence. "You have a cousin called Cadogan?"

"I do."

"Are you and your cousin close?"

"We used to be the best of friends."

Meradoc waited again. Talking with Dinas could be hard work. "Used to be?"

"I don't know what he thinks of me now."

"Is he anything like you?"

"Hardly; we're chalk and cheese. You can judge for yourself when you meet him. That's where we're going now."

"I thought you didn't know where you were going."

"I didn't," said Dinas. "I do now."

Later in the day it was Dinas who began a conversation. "Do you know why you were left outside the gates, Meradoc?"

The little man ducked his chin. "Because I'm so ugly."

Dinas turned in the saddle to look down at him. "But you're not ugly; who told you that?"

"Everyone. My head's too big. As I grew it became less noticeable, but I'm still ugly."

"Meradoc, did you ever hear of Alexander the Great?"

He frowned. "I don't think so."

"You need an education," said Dinas. "To begin with, can you speak any language other than that imitation Latin?"

Another frown. "I don't think so." A pause. "A few words, perhaps. The language of the poor."

"The *poor*." Dinas poured scorn on the word. "You mean the

Britons who weren't fortunate enough to be subsumed into another race. Listen to me, Meradoc. Tyrants love simple language. Yes, no, stand here, run there, pay taxes, die. Latin is easily adapted to this purpose, but we Britons have another language. The tongue of our Celtic ancestors; subtle, complex, filled with shades of meaning comprehensible only to ourselves. The perfect weapon for resistance and subversion. As long as we retain it we can never be conquered. Overrun, perhaps, but not conquered. Bear that in mind."

Meradoc nodded obediently.

Dinas continued, "Now I shall tell you about Alexander. He was a prince of Macedon who conquered the world before he was thirty years old. During his campaigns he rode a horse called Bucephalus, which had the heart of a lion and was utterly loyal. Alexander gave the horse a lot of the credit for his success. Do you know what 'Bucephalus' means?"

Another frown. "I don't think so."

"In the Greek language 'Bucephalus' means 'big head.'"

"Oh," said Meradoc. And lifted his chin.

For a while they followed a Roman road that, Dinas explained, eventually connected with the highway linking Hadrian's Wall in the north to Isca Dumnoniorum in the south. Meradoc had never heard of Hadrian's Wall or Isca Dumnoniorum, but he stored the names in his mind. He was consciously storing a lot of things in his mind now.

The Roman road was beginning to show signs of neglect. Where it had been constructed on a causeway, there was occasional subsidence. Some of the paving stones had been taken away by locals to use for patching field walls. Stagnant water and dead leaves were pooling in blocked drains.

The road led past several villages that consisted of small groups of dwellings enclosed by an earthen bank or timber palisade. Apart from the villas of the Romano-British aristocracy, the houses of rural Britannia were constructed as they had been before the Iron Age.

The majority were round, with mud-and-wattle walls supporting a thatched roof. In larger houses the interior might be subdivided into compartments around its circumference. Where surface stone was common the walls were built of this material, which allowed for structures of varying shapes and sizes. But the basic concept remained unchanged. It grew out of the land. It suited the tribes.

In the countryside the harvest season was over. Beneath gray skies, people were hurrying to get the last crops in before the cold weather destroyed them. On either side of the road men in homespun tunics and breeks were swinging their scythes with tireless, repetitive grace. Their families were gathering up the sheaves amid pools of fragrant golden chaff. When the wind shifted, Dinas and Meradoc could hear the women singing a work song.

At one of the villages Dinas purchased goat's meat and cheese, which he divided with Meradoc. The little man refilled their leather water bags from the local well while Dinas admired a young woman who was sunning herself in an open doorway. He smiled, she smiled. He tightened his legs on the dark horse's sides to make the stallion prance. The girl's smile widened. An older man appeared in the doorway behind her and Dinas rode on.

The clouds parted; a golden sun peeped through for one last glance at the earth so soon to fall asleep. Birds responded by singing in a thicket; the hum of insects provided a counterpoint. Meradoc was in danger of dozing off as he trudged along, one foot after the other. One foot after . . .

"We turn here," said Dinas. They had come to a muddy trackway branching off to the east, toward a rise of hills.

The two men had not gone far along the trackway when the atmosphere changed. The light was still golden but a stillness came into the air; a weight. The stallion felt it too. His ears pointed rigidly forward, then swivelled back toward Dinas. A quiver of tension ran through his body.

Dinas dropped one hand to the hilt of his knife.

He could smell it before he saw it. Another village lay ahead, or what had been a village. With an exclamation of surprise, Meradoc pressed close to the horse.

No building was left standing, though there had not been many to begin with; only a few houses and a communal barn. Blackened timbers and scattered debris were all that remained. A pall of ash lay over the ruins, stirred by a rising wind. The bitter odor was compounded of burned wood and burned cloth and burned grain. Dinas flared his nostrils, trying to detect the smell of burned flesh, but mercifully there was none.

He noticed something unusual among the pitiful remnants of domesticity trampled into the mud. A small wooden cart and horse; a child's pull toy.

Dinas halted the nervous stallion and slid to the ground. After he pulled the toy out of the sticky mud he looked around for the child to whom it might belong. The only living things he saw were the crows picking through the wreckage.

With the sleeve of his tunic Dinas wiped mud off the toy, revealing faded paint beneath. Once the cart had been painted bright red. The horse had been dappled gray with a blue harness. When Dinas tried to spin one of the wheels with his thumb it would not turn. "Here, Meradoc, take a look at this. I had one like it when I was a boy."

The little man reluctantly left the stallion's side and examined the toy. "Good workmanship," he commented.

"Can you fix it?"

"Something's jamming the axle. Probably just mud, or a stone. Lend me your knife, Dinas."

"My knife!"

"Mine's at the bottom of my pack but yours is in your belt," Meradoc said reasonably.

"Very well, but be careful. The blade is Noric iron, it was expensive."

Meradoc began working the tip of the knife into the space behind the little wheel. "So you're not as poor as you say?" he asked innocently.

"I never said I was poor."

Meradoc gave the knife a minute twist. Nothing happened. He cocked his head and caught his bottom lip between his teeth. Twisted a fraction more firmly. Still nothing. Held the toy above his head to get a good look at the underside.

"What are you doing with that!" someone shouted.

Meradoc froze.

Dinas whirled around to see a man running toward them from the trees on the other side of the trackway. "Put it down!" the man cried.

Without taking his eyes off him, Meradoc crouched and set the toy on the ground.

"We meant no harm," Dinas tried to explain.

The man picked up cart and horse and cradled them to his breast as a mother would her child. He was tall and well proportioned, with thick hair turning silver. In his youth he must have been beautiful. His features still possessed a Grecian symmetry.

"We meant no harm," Dinas reiterated.

The stranger looked distraught. "I . . . you . . . I was afraid that . . ."

Meradoc put a hand on his arm. "It's all right," he said softly. "I am called Meradoc and this is Dinas. We were passing by and noticed your trouble. Can we help?"

"Yesterday you might have helped. It's too late now. This . . ." The man looked down at the toy held against his heart. "My . . ." He choked on the word.

"Did it belong to one of your children?"

"It belonged to me. My mother kept it all these years."

"Where is she now?" Dinas asked.

"She died. During the winter. It was a hard winter."

"Do you have a family?"

"One wife, three daughters. They died last winter, too. An illness came on the east wind. But I was too strong. Unfortunately." The man's eyes were tragic. Meradoc could not bear to look at them.

Dinas said, "What about the rest of your village? Where are they?"

"They . . . I don't know. Ran away, I suppose. We held out as long as we could." Abruptly the strength went out of him. His knees buckled and he slumped to the ground. His face was bloodless.

While Meradoc tended the stricken man Dinas searched the ruined village. Even where the ashes were deepest they were cold; the fire had burned itself out days earlier. The shocked survivor must have been wandering in confusion ever since.

Meradoc looked up as Dinas returned. "He says his name's Pelemos. He has several nasty wounds, including one to the head. What shall we do with him?"

"Why should we do anything with him?"

"Because he's alone and in trouble, Dinas. You don't intend to leave him like this, do you?"

"What can he do for me?"

"That's the wrong question," Meradoc said. "You should be asking what you can do for him."

"Why?"

"Because he's a man like yourself. Like me!"

Pelemos opened his eyes. They were the wondering, innocent eyes of a child. "Hello," he said, as if he had never seen either of them before.

Dinas snorted. "Listen to that, Meradoc. The man's simple, a liability if ever I saw one. We'd be better off with a milk cow."

Meradoc looked stricken. "Please, Dinas. Take another look at him."

"He won't have improved any," he said, but to humor Meradoc Dinas took a second glance. The injured man lay supine on the ground with Meradoc's cloak spread over the lower half of his body. A long tall body, Dinas observed, lifting one eyebrow. He bent over and examined the man more closely. The exposed shoulders were very broad;

the tanned arms were corded with muscle. The hands were large but well shaped, with sturdy fingers. The injured man was not young but obviously he was very strong. A body shaped by a lifetime of hard work.

Aha.

"No," Dinas said slowly, "I don't think we'll leave him."

They stayed with him for two days and nights; difficult days and nights during which Pelemos did not know who they were, or who he was, and called despairingly for someone named Ithill.

The two men consulted about the best way to care for him. "I never carry medicaments with me," Dinas said. "I'm so healthy you couldn't kill me with an axe, but my mother had some useful nostrums." Closing his eyes, he recited, "A dish of snails boiled with onions will improve general health. Eating goose tongue stimulates female desire. Pomegranate rind mixed with pine sap boiled in vinegar relieves constipation."

"None of that's any good here," Meradoc pointed out.

"No. All we can do is get some food into him and hope for the best. And pray, of course," Dinas added piously. Mindful of the circumstances in which he had met Meradoc.

"Do you think he's a Christian, Dinas?"

"How would I know? He's not wearing a cross."

When they tried to feed Pelemos he refused, insisting the food be given "to the others." His thirst was excessive. Meradoc found a well and an unburned bucket, and kept busy trotting back and forth with water. Dinas began to suspect Pelemos was suffering from the same illness that had taken his wife and children. There was a burial ground close to the village with several fresh graves. They were marked with little piles of stones.

Taking a blanket from his saddlebag, Dinas cut it into strips and soaked them in cool water. With Meradoc's help he wrapped the man's entire body in them. The wet wool dried out in a matter of minutes. They repeated the procedure. And again. And again.

On the third morning Pelemos awoke clear-eyed and hungry.

He devoured everything they gave him to eat and would have taken more if it were offered. Afterward he listened in frowning concentration while Dinas identified himself and Meradoc. "We are friends and travelers who came upon you in your distress and tried to help," he said. He did not go into any more detail, nor did Pelemos request it.

The unfortunate man still appeared to be dazed, but when Dinas asked him direct questions he was able to respond. With frequent prompting, he related a picture of rural life in Britannia that might have applied to thousands of people.

Five families had lived in his village; five interdependent households related in varying degrees by blood. They had farmed their land together, they had grazed their livestock on communal pastures. The life they lived was the life generations before them had lived. Roman eagles did not dominate their sky. Their allegiance was, as it always had been, to their tribal chieftain. Their education came at their grandmothers' knees. Their geographical knowledge did not extend beyond the market where they sold their surplus produce.

They were nominally Christian, but the Celtic version of Christianity that had been introduced by missionaries from Eire was not radically different from the pantheism of pagan Albion. In spite of the edict of Constantine, which had made the Church of Rome an official religion, Pelemos and countless other Britons continued to pray to the gods of nature as well as to Christ.

Their prayers had failed when the fever struck. They would never know its cause, any more than they knew how to fight it. The ancient remedies were useless. The men buried their old people and children first. Then their wives. When the few surviving men thought they could not suffer more, the raiders came.

"Who were they?" Pelemos asked his rescuers. "We never did them any harm, so why did they destroy the village?"

"I can tell you who they were," said Dinas, "but I can't answer your other question. Barbarians, that's what the Romans call them. Nomadic warriors who only love battle and booty. Angles and Jutes and Saxons from Germania, Franks from Gaul and Vandals and Goths and Ostrogoths from farther east. Visigoths from everywhere; some even gained official positions within the empire. For a while the Romans tried to negotiate with them, but they didn't realize the sort of people they were dealing with. Now the barbarians are running riot from the Rhine to Byzantium and everywhere in between."

"Can't they be stopped?"

When Dinas replied his voice was harsh with anger. "The first of them should have been turned back as soon as they reached this island—or slaughtered on the shore and left for the carrion birds, which would have been the better solution. When they started coming in large numbers, at first the authorities didn't realize what a threat they were to our way of life. By the time it became obvious, the legions that could have protected us were gone."

"What do you mean by 'our way of life'?" wondered Meradoc.

Dinas was anxious to be on his way again. No great effort was needed to persuade Pelemos to go with them. The man seemed almost relieved to turn his back on the ruins of a lifetime. His reaction was not unique. Throughout Britannia Superior people were struggling to find ways to deal with drastically changed circumstances. Some would flee, some would fight.

Some would try to pretend nothing had changed.

Dinas allowed Pelemos another day to rest and gather his strength, then the three men set out together. Dinas appeared to be more cheerful than he had been. Responding to him, the dark horse pranced and jingled his bit. Pelemos was quiet but that was to be expected. For him it was a victory to be able to keep going. Meradoc kept a watchful eye on him, prepared to help if necessary.

It was not necessary. The man was as strong as he looked.

Things are falling into place, Dinas told himself. First Meradoc, now Pelemos. What about Cadogan?

CHAPTER SEVEN

Cadogan and Quartilla had returned to the fort laden with food and necessities such as lamp oil. Cadogan carried the bulk of the supplies on his back, but Quartilla, to his surprise, willingly carried her share. He never knew what to expect of the woman. Nor what to do about her either. Foolishly, perhaps, he had hoped she might want to remain in the village, but from the moment they arrived she had been openly contemptuous of the simple thatched houses and the ordinary country people who occupied them. She clung to Cadogan like a burr to ensure he would not leave without her. When they arrived back at the fort she declared herself "delighted to be home."

Among Cadogan's purchases had been a thick pallet stuffed with goose down. A useful article in any case, but particularly useful for a man who was going to sleep on the floor. He knew he needed to sleep well; he would have to chop a lot of firewood.

The pair had settled into an uneasy domesticity. Uneasy on Cadogan's part, apparently satisfactory to Quartilla. The evening they returned from the village she had bustled about the place by lamplight, putting away their supplies and rearranging Cadogan's possessions. Neither wife nor servant, she was defining her position as co-occupier with equal rights.

It was not in Cadogan's nature to throw a woman out by the scruff of the neck, but he was not fooled by her clumsy attempts to ingratiate herself. He did not want her, nor did he want her in his house. Her presence only served to remind him how much he still wanted Viola. During all the long hard days he had spent constructing the fort, it was Viola he imagined waiting for him in the doorway. He refused to believe she was lost to him. The misunderstanding between Dinas and Aldina had caused her to take a stand that did not reflect her true feelings. When enough time had passed Viola would regret her decision, he was certain of it.

Almost certain.

For five nights Cadogan slept on the floor. On the sixth morning he awoke with such a pain in his back he had to get to his feet in stages. His stiff back helped to stiffen his resolve.

The woman was still sleeping soundly in his bed—most of the sound being her explosive snoring. He shook her, not too gently, by the shoulder. "You'll have to get up now, Quartilla, it's time for you to go."

She opened her eyes and stared blearily up at him. "Go where?"

"Back to wherever you came from."

She sat up, keeping a blanket across her naked upper body. "You don't know where I came from."

Cadogan was in no mood to play games with her. "Then you'd better tell me so I can send you home."

"I'm not a piece of baggage you can pack off on a mule!" she spat at him. "I'll have you know I am the daughter of a chieftain." Raising her chin, she pulled the blanket around her shoulders like a royal robe—as if indifferent to the fact that the movement uncovered her breasts. Two scrawny sacks hanging on a bony rib cage. "I was born and raised in a real fortress on a mountaintop, nothing like this pathetic hovel of yours."

"You said your father was a centurion," Cadogan reminded her.

"I never! I may have mentioned that my grandfather was a centurion, but you misunderstood." Her hauteur changed to belligerence. "That's so like you, Cadogan! If you'd been paying the attention I deserve, you'd know I said my father married a centurion's daughter."

Cadogan noticed beads of sweat on her forehead. She was not a good liar, so why did she keep trying? "British chieftains marry women of their own rank, Quartilla, so I'm surprised that one would marry a foreigner's daughter. Which tribe does your father belong to?"

She rolled her eyes. "He is . . . he was . . . a chief of the Iceni."

"The tribe of the warrior queen called Boudicca?"

"The same." Her confidence was coming back. She tossed her head and smiled at him. "I inherited my red hair from Boudicca."

If Cadogan had not been thoroughly sick of Quartilla by now he would have felt sorry for her, but this was a matter of survival. "Your red hair," he echoed blandly. Then he pounced. "Your *dyed* red hair."

Her face flamed. "It isn't dyed! Besides, Roman matrons dye their hair red to make them look like Helen or Cleopatra, and why shouldn't they?"

Cadogan had decided she was a pretentious peasant, yet she knew something about Helen of Troy and Cleopatra. That demonstrated a degree of education. But how? Where? Suddenly he was interested.

When he tried to question her she drew into herself like a snail into its shell.

"I hate you," she said.

Cadogan was halfway down the hill before he paused to wonder how she had driven him from his own home. She had not asked him to go yet here he was. Failing to communicate with her on any useful level, he had left the fort, calling back, "I'm going to the well for more water." But he had not brought any buckets. Had not brought anything except his own frustration.

The first spatters of an icy rain struck his face.

Perhaps I should do what Dinas did—wisely, in retrospect—and simply abandon the woman. Walk away without looking back, and start over in a different place. I've started over before, I can do it again, only better, with the knowledge born of experience. This time I'll find land near a quarry so I can build with stone. But first I must dig a real basement and put in a foundation. I'll need . . .

Concrete! The Romans often used concrete in place of stone because it could take any form. They mixed it themselves using . . . using what? Who still remembers? Someone must, I'll have to ask . . .

The rain began to fall harder. The air turned bitterly cold.

When the basement is finished I can install a hypocaust. Definitely, a hypocaust! Warm floors, warm water . . . But a hypocaust requires a furnace and slaves to stoke it. Perhaps not a hypocaust, then. I do want water piped inside, though, and good drainage. When I was living with my father I should have learned how such things worked, but that was left to the servants. Are the pipes tile or concrete? And how are they laid out, is it complicated? I'll find out. And I'll learn how to make concrete for the foundation and I'll buy tiles for the roof. Beautiful red tiles. I can do it. I can build . . .

For one heartbeat Cadogan's villa stood complete and splendid in his mind. On a high hill against a windswept sky. The home he would offer to Viola.

The vision was abruptly blotted out by a mental image of Quartilla.

Cadogan swore aloud.

If he abandoned her he knew he would never forgive himself. The woman would become a recurrent nightmare, spoiling any happiness he might find. His Christian conscience was not the only thing holding him back. Walking away was not practical. His most cherished belongings were in the fort, together with a substantial sum of money, cleverly concealed.

He turned and started back up the slope. He had only taken a few steps when he heard hoofbeats and a familiar voice shouted his name. With a sense of relief, Cadogan saw the dark horse emerge from the woods to the west and gallop toward him.

As Dinas drew rein Cadogan said, "I never thought I'd be so glad to see you."

Dinas slid down from his horse. "Same old cousin, affectionate to the end."

"It almost was the end between us. You told me about the danger to Viroconium and then rode away as if it didn't matter."

"It mattered, but there was little I could do about, so I got on with my life—which is the advice I gave you, Cadogan."

"You knew I would go anyway. You could have offered to go with me."

"Why?"

"Have you no family feeling, Dinas?"

For a fleeting instant the other man's expression changed. Then he went on the attack again. "What about your own family feeling, Cadogan? You left your home just as I left mine, only it took you longer to do it. Which reminds me—what did you do with the woman?"

"What woman?"

"I forget her name; the woman I left with you. Did you sell her or"—Dinas flashed his familiar sardonic grin—"did you eat her?"

Cadogan smiled too; Dinas could always make him smile. "She told me her name was Quartilla. A real problem, that one: too ugly to sell and too skinny to eat."

Dinas raised one eyebrow. "Don't tell me you kept her! You must have been desperate for a woman."

"Not that one," Cadogan assured him. "I'm glad you came back for her, she said you would."

"Oh no. No, no, no." Dinas was vigorously shaking his head. "I gave her to you as a present, you'd be insulting me if you returned her."

"But I don't want her, Dinas! Can't you understand?"

"I understand completely, I don't want her either."

"Then why on earth did you . . ." Cadogan broke off as he saw two more men come out of the forest. One was tall and unusually handsome, the other was short with unusually large ears. The dark stallion stretched his neck toward the short man and gave a soft whinny.

Cadogan said, "I thought he only liked you."

"He still likes me best," Dinas replied confidently. "But Meradoc seems to have a touch with horses."

"Meradoc?"

"The little fellow over there; he joined me in Deva. The other one is called Pelemos. We met him along the way."

Cadogan brightened. "You went all the way to Deva and then returned for Quartilla after all?"

"Of course not," Dinas said scornfully, "I have no interest in her. I came back for you, cousin. I could use your help with a plan I have in mind. If it works we'll both be powerful men. We can have anything we want."

Suddenly wary, Cadogan said, "I have enough for my needs already."

"You're too easily satisfied, cousin; you always were. That's why you settled for plain little Viola while I went for the prettier one. What was her name? I've forgotten that too." Ignoring the angry look Cadogan gave him, Dinas glanced toward the sky, then beckoned to Meradoc. "That rain is about to turn to sleet. Take my horse into the woods and find shelter for him, then you and Pelemos can join us inside." He handed the stallion's reins to Meradoc and ran up the hill to the fort.

"You could have waited for an invitation!" Cadogan shouted as he ran after him.

He entered to find Quartilla seated at the table with a heaping bowl of food in front of her, but she was not eating. She was staring openmouthed at Dinas.

"No warm welcome from you, eh?" Dinas said to her. "Enough of this lounging about. Obviously Cadogan hasn't trained you properly, but when guests arrive the servants bring fresh water to wash their faces and feet." When she continued to stare he struck his hands together like a thunderclap. "Now, Luculla! Jump to it!"

She jumped. As she ran out the door with a bucket in her hand Cadogan said, "What did you just call her?"

"Luculla. That's her name, I just remembered it."

"That's not what she told me. She said her name was Quartilla and her father was a centurion. Days later she claimed he was a chieftain of the Iceni. What did she tell you?"

Dinas laughed. "We didn't have much conversation; I don't believe in talking to women. Exchange a few pleasant words with them and they think they're entitled to ask for your time—or your purse. I found her squatting in the weeds beside a trackway south of here. She was furious because I saw her relieving herself, so to make up for it, I offered to take her someplace where she could get food. She followed me here and I left her with you. As a gift," he added.

"But weren't you even curious about her?"

"I'm curious about many things, cousin, but not about some stray woman I found in the road. From the look of her she was nothing and nobody. I did her a favor, that's all."

If what Dinas had said was true—and it probably was, it fitted with his character—he had treated the woman shamefully. "What about those two strays you have with you now, Dinas? Are you hoping to dump them on me, too?"

"They aren't strays, either of them; I've recruited them. I told you I have a good idea. After your woman serves us a hot meal I'll explain it to you."

"She's not my woman!" Cadogan sputtered.

Quartilla returned, red-faced and panting, with a brimming bucket carried from the well. In the doorway she almost collided with Meradoc and Pelemos. She hastily set the bucket down and stood staring at Pelemos as she had been staring at Dinas a few minutes earlier.

"Bring us some wine that's fit to drink and then prepare our meal," Dinas said. "Roast meat if you have it. Otherwise, cook something in a pot."

Awakened from her trance, she flared. "I'm not yours to command!"

"You're the only woman in the house," he replied in a reasonable tone, "and there are four thirsty, hungry men here. Do your duty."

Cadogan told his cousin, "I don't have any wine, just barley beer flavored with wormwood. And I don't know if Quartilla can cook."

"Jupiter and Juno, man! Have you been cooking for her? I got here just in time."

An hour later the four men were polishing off the remains of an adequate if not sumptuous meal of bread stuffed with pot cheese, venison stewed with dried fruit and juniper berries, and boiled apples flavored with cinnamon. The beer with which Quartilla filled their cups was a dark, musty beverage not to Meradoc's taste. When he set his cup aside Pelemos promptly drained it.

"Where did you learn to put cheese inside a loaf of bread?" Cadogan asked Quartilla.

"It is a great favorite in Egypt," she said.

Dinas lifted an eyebrow. "Been to Egypt, have you?"

"No." She would not look at him. Her eyes kept returning to Pelemos. But he remained oblivious to her, gazing into a faraway place.

"That good mare of yours, cousin," Dinas remarked. "I haven't seen her yet. Where is she?"

"Outside somewhere," Cadogan said with an airy wave of his hand. He would be embarrassed if Dinas knew he had lost the horse. "Grazing, you know."

"In this weather? You should take better care of that animal, cousin. There'll be no more like her."

While the woman cleared away the remnants of the meal the men gathered around the fire. A barrage of sleet was battering the roof; its chill seeped into the room. Meradoc took off his boots and set them to warm close to the fire. Cadogan rubbed his hands together, then blew on his fingers. "Now what's this idea of yours, Dinas?"

"In Deva I noticed that the market square was half abandoned, and the merchandise that was available looked like rubbish. Does that suggest anything to you?"

Meradoc lifted his head at the familiar question.

"Only that Deva is impoverished," said Cadogan.

"Under the Romans it was a major garrison stocked with every sort of merchandise, just as Viroconium was when it served as a supply center for the western frontier. The resources of this island were traded for valuables from the far corners of the empire, and that trade used the sea-lanes. The importance of Deva's neglected market lies in its implications, cousin. The imported luxury goods that brought such high prices are gone. *But the sea-lanes are still there.*"

"I understand now!" Quartilla cried. "You want to reestablish the luxury trade yourself!"

Dinas shot her a look that Cadogan found hard to read. "Aren't you the clever thing, Luculla? There is only one problem with that idea. I know nothing about merchandising."

"Neither do I," Meradoc interjected, "but I think I could learn."

Dinas turned to Cadogan. "Now you understand why I brought him along."

"I don't understand anything, Dinas. Is Quartilla right, do you intend to sail to Iberia and buy olive oil for import? Knowing you as I do, the idea is bizarre, but . . ."

Dinas laughed; a laugh intended to hurt. "You poor sad fool, you never see more than part of the picture, do you? I have no intention of risking my life on the sea, I'm too fond of living. Since I have to spell it out for you, listen closely so I don't need to repeat myself. Cargo is still being shipped through the sea-lanes but it isn't guarded by the legions. Commerce is wide open. Do you see the opportunities now? What I propose is this . . ."

CHAPTER EIGHT

They talked until late in the night; pausing only to add another log to the fire on the hearth. Meanwhile Quartilla lay snoring on Cadogan's bed. Meradoc was curled up on the floor at the foot of the bed. His eyes were closed. Pelemos, still awake but indifferent to his surroundings, sat on a stool, staring into his empty cup. The golden lamplight loved the planes of his face.

"This idea of yours," Cadogan said, "reminds me of the wild schemes you dreamed up when we were boys. You never thought anything through, Dinas; you never took things step by step. You rushed right in and expected me to back you up, and your half-baked notions invariably got me into trouble."

"Only because you couldn't run away as fast as I could."

"It would take more than speed to pull this off. You'd need a lot of men and a thorough knowledge of the western coast, Dinas, and you don't have either."

"You underestimate me. Since I left home I've traveled continually. I know the Ordovici and the Demetae almost as well as I know our own Cornovii. I've even received hospitality from some of the Dumnonii—an interesting people indeed. Their accents are almost impenetrable, and their kings are said to wear a heavy crown to hide their ears because their common ancestor mated with a donkey." Dinas burst into laughter. "That may or may not be true, of course; I never met their current king. But what I tell you next is true, Cadogan"—his voice sobered—"since the Romans left the old loyalties are breaking down."

"What do you mean?"

"New kings and chieftains are driving out traditional leaders and carving up their land to suit themselves. They're seeking allies wherever they can find them, even among the barbarians—who are also claiming land. Britannia's descending into chaos and confusion, and not just because of the influx of foreigners. We're doing a lot of this to ourselves.

"Cadogan, do you remember what it felt like to be fifteen years old and full of juice, bursting to do *something*? No matter what tribe they belong to, young men today are frantic to do something, anything, and without Roman control they're a seething mass of undirected energy. If a spectacular stag burst from the forest, some of them would even follow it. That's why I'm confident I can recruit as large a company as I want."

"I've never doubted your confidence," said Cadogan, "but . . ."

"I'm well prepared for this," Dinas insisted. "I've ridden the western coast from one end to the other; I know every beach and headland, I can tell you where every river and stream empties into the sea. I've explored the watchtowers the Romans built to protect the western shipping lanes and I know which ones are still usable. I've even found several possible locations for a stronghold."

Cadogan was shaking his head. "I don't understand where I fit into this grand plan of yours, Dinas. Or Meradoc or Pelemos, for that matter."

Lying on the floor, Meradoc heard his name. His eyes were closed but his ears were open.

"Meradoc is a treasure," Dinas said with a smile in his voice. "He can do anything, he's as handy as a little pot. When we get more horses—and we will need more horses—he'll have charge of them, but there'll be plenty of other work for him too."

"What about Pelemos?"

"Ah, my splendid stag!" Dropping his voice so no one else could hear, Dinas said, "Did you ever see anyone who looks more like a saint? Having him at my side will attract others."

"Is he as saintly as he looks?"

"How should I know? All he'll have to do is sit on a horse—I think we'll find a white horse for him—and look angelic. In a flock there's always a bellwether the other sheep follow, and Pelemos will serve that purpose splendidly. But it's the shepherd who's in charge. And I'm the shepherd."

"So you're just using him," Cadogan said coldly. "Using a poor unfortunate man who hardly seems aware of what's going on around him."

"Everyone uses everyone, Cadogan; don't you know that by now? But I promise you Pelemos won't suffer. He'll be a lot better off than if I'd left him where I found him. He'll share whatever we have and I'll look after him—just as I would look after you."

Cadogan held up his hands. "Oh no! Don't count me in on this, I want no part of it. What you propose is not only impossible, it's illegal. And it would imperil your immortal soul."

"Where have you been? Nothing is illegal anymore, cousin. The rule of law left with the Romans, and there is no such thing as an immortal soul."

"Of course we have souls," Cadogan retorted. He had long since learned to ignore his cousin's rebellious heresies. "As for the Romans, they'll be back. We just have to hold on and wait, they won't abandon us. Don't you remember what Lucius Plautius said? 'Their laws and their swords will always protect us.'"

"*Their* laws and *their* swords," sneered Dinas. "Not ours. In case you haven't noticed, we aren't Romans. We learned to wear togas and speak Latin and pay for a seat in one of the public toilets when there were perfectly good bushes all over the country. But in reality we remained a conquered people.

"Rome conquered us with envy, not armies. We were willing parties to our own enslavement, Cadogan. Have you ever tried to catch a magpie? If you hang something shiny in a tree the magpie will be so eager to seize the prize it never notices the net until it's too late.

The Romans seduced us with their own version of shiny things—
red wine and olive oil and underfloor heating—and we ran headlong
into the trap.

"Alaric and his Visigoths did us a favor by sacking Rome. When
they battered down those gates they set us free; free to be ourselves
again. Survival is nature's law, Cadogan, but I want to do more than
survive, I want to *live*. Freely, fully, in my own way, without anyone
else controlling me. I'm offering you a chance to join me and do the
same."

"A chance to behave any way I like without fear of retribution?
Because that's what you're talking about, Dinas. How can you rec-
oncile that with your Christianity?"

Dinas snorted. "Why should I try? My parents claimed to be
devout Christians, but between them they broke every command-
ment." Cadogan had never heard his cousin, who laughed so often,
sound so bitter. "They paid priests to worship in their houses and
thought that would be enough to save their souls. They never noticed that the priests only bowed their heads to count their profits.
At least I'm more honest than they were, I admit to being a thief. I
won't add hypocrisy to my sins."

Cadogan was taken aback. "You're a thief? My own cousin?"

Dinas raised one eyebrow. "How do you think I've been supporting myself? I left my father's house with nothing but the clothes
on my back and the horse I rode. Since then I've learned to sniff out
the treasure other men hide, and I'm good at it." Before Cadogan
could respond Dinas asked, "How do you support yourself, cousin?"

"Why, I . . . I mean . . . I have my own money."

"Where did it come from?"

"My father, of course. When I came of age he turned my entire
legacy over to me."

"Where did Vintrex get his wealth in the first place?"

Cadogan felt unaccountably defensive. "I assume he inherited
property from his father, and as a magistrate he also received a generous salary."

"Paid for out of taxes," said Dinas. "Taxes the empire collected from the Britons with or without their consent; hard-earned money taken from them by those with more power. The provincial government ostensibly served us, but in reality it was created to feed Rome's insatiable appetites. Legalized theft, Cadogan.

"People admire my father because they think he's a clever businessman. He's clever, all right. Ocellus knows a century of ways to get his hands on someone else's property, and it's always 'legal.' Legal because some magistrate says it is."

Cadogan bristled. "Are you implying that my father was complicit in . . ."

"Don't play the innocent with me. Figure it out for yourself."

"I don't believe you."

"That's your choice, cousin. If you want to believe the wealthy and powerful are that way because riches rain down on them from heaven, then do so. It's no more absurd than believing in God."

Cadogan was aghast.

Meradoc, lying silently on the floor, felt the world spin under him.

"Rome justified greed in the name of need and oppression in the name of discipline," Dinas went on. "Our class of people accepted that point of view, admired it even. Why? Because they wanted to be on top of the heap too, though they might never admit it. As long as Rome had the power they trotted after her like dogs following a bitch in heat.

"But we are not Romans!" Dinas burst out. "We have never been nor shall ever be Romans!" Jumping to his feet, he strode to the door and flung it open. He stared out at the slanting spears of rain, their silver illumined by the light from within the room. The popping sounds his knuckles made as he cracked them were like hail falling on stone.

Eventually he returned to the fire and stood looking down at Cadogan. "You may not remember this, cousin, but when I was a young boy Ocellus imported a pair of wolfhounds from Eire—Hibernia, as the Romans call it. Great shaggy beasts they were, long limbed and fearless. I loved them on sight and they went everywhere with me. I could walk through a forest as safe as if I were surrounded by a legion. Ocellus sold their puppies for immense prices. Men came from as far away as the highlands of Caledonia to buy our dogs.

"When the female was too old she had one last litter. Three big, robust males. They were too big and too robust, and she died giving birth to them. We also had a number of cats to keep the vermin down, and at that time there was a most unusual cat in the stables. She too was big, the largest cat I ever saw. Gwladys thought she was descended from Caledonian wildcats; she had their color and look about her.

"The cat gave birth to a litter at the same time as the hound, and in an effort to save the newborn puppies Ocellus put them with the cat to suckle. To everyone's surprise, she accepted them. She fed those puppies along with her own kittens, nursing them and washing them. The dogs lived, they even thrived. When the cat weaned the kittens the pups continued to follow her around, mewling and begging for milk. She lost her temper and slashed them with her claws but they wouldn't give up. At last the cat ran off into the hills to be rid of them."

"What happened to the young dogs?"

"They skulked about the stables for a while. Ocellus tried to hunt with them but they were no good with wolves, they would only chase mice. They weren't cats but they didn't know they were dogs. Finally Ocellus had them drowned. Stones were tied around their necks and they were thrown into the river." Dinas gave a sigh of regret. "If even one of those puppies had realized his true nature he could have avoided his fate. What about you, Cadogan?" he asked abruptly. "Do you know who you are?"

"I am . . . I hope I am . . . a decent Christian man."

"Is that all?"

"It is all I *aspire* to," Cadogan replied with dignity. "That, and a quiet life."

Dinas curled his lip in scorn. "Listen to me. Life is an opportunity, one single, amazing opportunity. Life is the sun and the stars, the wolves howling and the rain lashing and the thrill of danger around every bend. If you want to waste yours trying to be safe—though you will die in the end anyway, we all do—that's your choice. But I said it before and I'll say it again: Cadogan, you're a fool!"

In the morning they were gone. The three men had managed to slip away without waking either Quartilla or Cadogan—who had drunk too much beer in a vain attempt to keep up with his cousin. Now he was paying for it. His head was one gigantic throb. How does Dinas do it? he wondered. The man must have a lead-lined stomach.

Quartilla was bereft. "How could he go off and leave me behind?" she moaned.

"He wasn't interested in you in the first place," Cadogan told her. "It was all in your head."

"Not Dinas, you fool! I mean the other one, that gorgeous big man with the broad shoulders."

"Pelemos?"

"Of course, Pelemos! Don't be thick, Cadogan. From the moment he saw me he couldn't keep his eyes off me. He never said anything because he was so smitten, but I could tell. I can always tell."

Cadogan spent the day in a state of confusion. Part of him wanted to join Dinas on what would surely be the adventure of a lifetime—if they were not all killed. Another part of him was thankful to remain in the shelter and security of the fort—though that security already had been breached. A third part—no more than a niggling little voice at the back of his mind—said neither was the answer for him.

Quartilla accused me of hiding here and she's right. But I'm still a young man. If I spent the rest of my life like a hermit I would probably go mad. Should I return to Viroconium, try to patch things up with Viola and wait for my father to come home? What if he doesn't?

What if he does?

CHAPTER NINE

They were heading southwest. The land rose slowly but surely from the lush, damp midlands toward the distant mountains. Meradoc, who had never been more than a few miles from Deva before he met Dinas, observed every change in the scenery. If they flushed an unfamiliar bird he stopped in his tracks to watch it fly away. God made you, he said silently to the bird. He often thought of God, to counter the heresy of Dinas.

There has to be God. Who else could have made the dark horse?

Pelemos trudged along with his eyes on the ground. He spoke if spoken to, but that was the extent of his involvement with his surroundings. He continued living inside himself, in a place where his wife was alive. Ithill. Ithill. And the girls.

Sometimes he thought he could hear his daughters laughing.

If they passed a likely farmstead Dinas sent Meradoc to ask the farmwife for food. A bowl of fresh milk or a loaf of bread was usually forthcoming. Few women could refuse the soft voice and the innocent blue eyes.

Winter was a breath away. The fading sun slipped lower in the sky and a white haze hung over the distant mountains. Meradoc noticed that Dinas often fixed his eyes on them but never spoke of them, or of his destination. The trail he followed was old when Albion was young, and only visible to a few.

The only time Dinas mentioned it was when he remarked on the quality of a stream where they stopped to drink. "There will be better water than this where we're going," he said.

Although he was unaware of it, Pelemos began humming to

himself as he walked. Very softly, as if the music welled from his internal organs and was too personal for anyone to hear. Except for Ithill. All his songs were for Ithill. All his poetry was for Ithill, recited to her in the shadowy night as they lay with two heads on one pillow. She had called him her bard. "A bard is the memory of his tribe," she said.

Ithill, Ithill, with the stars in her eyes.

Meradoc concentrated on thinking and learning. Walking, he discovered, was a wonderful way to learn. When he filled his lungs to the very bottom with fresh clean air his head was clearer. He asked all the questions that occurred to him, and if Dinas was in a good mood he answered them. Some of the questions were about taking care of the horse, and Dinas always answered those. He gave Meradoc a small iron tool from his saddle bag, and showed him how to clean out the V-shaped cleft on the bottom of the horse's hoof, picking out stones and small debris.

The first time Meradoc tried this he asked, a little uncertainly, "Will he let me pick up his foot?"

"Of course he will," Dinas said, "if you don't startle him. Just act confident and he'll think you know what you're doing."

As they traveled the stallion continually tossed his head, making the reins carve patterns in the sweat on his neck. He resented having to adjust his pace to that of walking men. An occasional gallop in a large circle was not enough for him. When Dinas dismounted and walked with the others the horse relaxed a little, but not much.

Dinas came to a decision. "This isn't going to work until you two are on horseback. Meradoc—you've never ridden a horse before?"

"Not yet!" the little man replied hopefully.

"What about you, Pelemos?"

"I can drive a team of oxen."

"It's not the same thing, I assure you. We'll find mounts for both of you. Someone along the way will have horses we can buy."

A light flickered in Pelemos's eyes. "Buy? You mean with money?" He frowned as if trying to remember the meaning of the words.

"Don't worry about it," Dinas told him. "I never go anywhere without a little something tucked away out of sight." He patted his side, where a leather purse was strapped to his body underneath his tunic.

Meradoc had never thought about money before; about actually having money. Barter was the medium of the poor in Deva. "Are you very wealthy, Dinas?"

"No man answers that question honestly."

"But you wouldn't lie to me, would you?" The soft voice; the innocent blue eyes.

"No, Meradoc," said Dinas. "I wouldn't lie to you."

The following morning they saw two ponies grazing the stubble of a cleared field. Short, sturdy mares whose thick coats warned of the winter to come. "They're what we need," Dinas decided. "If you two fall off while you're learning to ride, it's not so far to the ground."

The owner of the ponies was not easily located, but eventually a scrawny boy who was out hunting with his ferret directed them to a barnyard comprising a huddle of wattle-and-daub sheds mired in a sea of mud, surrounded by wooden pens holding an assortment of cattle and goats. Off to one side, in a sturdy pen of his own, a red bull sang the last song of summer in hopes of one final mating.

Upwind of the barnyard was the farmhouse: a round dwelling built of mud and rubble stone that wore its thatched roof pulled tightly down around its shoulders. The farmer sat on a three-legged stool outside the door, sharpening an axe on a pedal-operated grinding wheel. Oblivious to the fate awaiting them, domestic fowl pecked in the dirt around his feet. As he concentrated on his task the man did not notice strangers observing him from the crest of a low hill.

Dinas told Meradoc to take the stallion out of sight. He and Pelemos went down to meet the farmer. The scrawny boy, who looked remarkably like his ferret, trailed after them, curiosity stamped large on his face. The farmer stood up as they approached. He resembled the scrawny boy, and thus the ferret. His gap-toothed smile was wide but his dark eyes were wary.

Following a lengthy exchange about the weather, the condition of the crops, and any relatives Dinas and the farmer might have in common—they discovered none—Dinas expressed a mild curiosity about the two ponies he had seen. The farmer extolled the many virtues of his ponies—his small, common, unimpressive ponies— concluding, with feigned reluctance, "I might be persuaded to take one solidus for such excellent mares, but you understand I'd be giving them away."

Dinas did not react. Emboldened, the farmer added, "One solidus each, of course. Two solidi for the pair."

Dinas threw back his head and laughed. Pelemos laughed too, more in imitation than amusement. "I enjoy a joke as much as the next man," Dinas said, "but I could buy a herd of horses for that amount. I'll give you exactly what your animals would bring in the horse market: one siliqua for the pair. That will save you having to feed them through the winter."

The farmer looked offended. "You know nothing about horses. Those ponies are fine breeding animals."

Dinas put two fingers in his mouth and gave a shrill whistle. Meradoc came running over the crest of the hill, leading the dark horse. The farmer watched in astonishment as the majestic animal trotted toward him. "*That* is a fine breeding animal," said Dinas. Taking the stallion's reins from Meradoc, he vaulted effortlessly onto his horse's back. "Now let's talk seriously."

The farmer gave him a long look, then turned to the boy with the ferret. "Go get the mares," he said.

During the negotiations Dinas insisted the farmer include bridles for the ponies. "You don't want saddles," he told Meradoc and Pelemos, "because you'll learn faster riding bareback. If you get in trouble you can simply put your feet on the ground."

Meradoc was ecstatic to have a horse—a pony—to ride. He

scrambled onto the little mare's broad, fat back and flung his arms around her neck. Pelemos was more cautious. He mounted gingerly and sat stiffly upright, holding the reins in one first and clenching the mane with the other. When Dinas was not watching he stretched one leg downward and discovered he could, indeed, touch the ground with his feet.

Even when Dinas held the dark horse to a walk, the mares had to trot to keep up with the stallion's long stride. Theirs was the hard, jolting trot common to most ponies. Dinas watched the neophyte equestrians out of the corner of his eye. From time to time he offered suggestions. "Loosen the reins a little, you're hurting her mouth. Don't lean forward. Look between your horse's ears to keep her going straight."

When they finally halted to relieve themselves Meradoc and Pelemos found it painful to dismount. Remounting hurt even more. Dinas rode away without waiting for them. They scrambled aboard as best they could and followed him. Onward and upward.

As the earth tilted toward the sky the scenery changed dramatically. They entered a region of moor and bog interrupted by large granite outcroppings. Thick white mist rolled down upon them from higher slopes, obscuring the view ahead. Armies of conifers spilled out of dark defiles on either side. The atmosphere was at once threatening and intoxicating, the air so sweet Meradoc could taste it on his tongue.

When the first flakes of snow swirled around them, Pelemos roused himself enough to ask, "Where are we now, Dinas?"

"The kingdom of Rheged in the land of Cymru."

Meradoc was puzzled. "Not Britannia?"

"Not according to the Cymri," Dinas said. "Many soldiers of the Twentieth died fighting in these mountains, but Roman authority was never recognized here. Cymru is a place apart. It's bordered on the north and west by the Oceanus Hibernicus, and to the east and south by the valley of Severn."

"What lies beyond the Severn?"

"Beyond the Severn . . ." Dinas paused for effect. "World's End."

Somewhat later, a vast dark shadow swept over the riders. Pelemos flinched, but Meradoc looked up in time to witness an immense golden eagle in full flight. His breath caught in his throat. "Did you see that, Dinas?"

"The lord of the mountains comes down to welcome us."

Us. Meradoc glowed.

As evening approached the snow began to fall in earnest. Meradoc was relieved when they came to a village located at the foot of a narrow pass leading into the mountains. Here a dozen small houses, roofed with slate, huddled together for comfort. He silently speculated on whether the houses were leaning against the hillside, or the hill was leaning on the houses.

When the villagers emerged to greet their visitors Dinas spoke to them in their own dialect, which sounded, thought Meradoc, like water running over stones. After a brief conversation Dinas turned to his companions. "We're welcome to stay the night here. We'll be well fed and sleep warm, but I warn you, each of us will have to pay for the privilege."

Meradoc and Pelemos exchanged worried glances. "We have no money of our own," Meradoc reminded Dinas.

Dinas laughed. "Who said anything about money?"

The meal came first, served in three different houses by three different women. Afterward everyone crowded into the largest house in the village. It belonged to the village leader; a knotty man with a face full of grudges. He met them at the door, asking, "You have the price?"

"I do indeed," Dinas replied. To the astonishment of his friends he held out his hands to the oldest woman in the room. In spite of her blushing protests, Dinas swung her into a long and sprightly dance while the other villagers clapped out the rhythm.

When the dance concluded everyone turned toward Meradoc.

During the dancing he had surveyed the room. In one corner he noticed a broken willow basket. Sidling over to it, he began skillfully reweaving the damage. When his turn came to pay he held up the mended basket with a shy smile. He was rewarded with ooohs and aaahs of appreciation, and a pleased nod from Dinas.

Pelemos came next. He too had been considering what he had to offer. As an anticipatory hush filled the room, he got to his feet and stood with his back to the fire.

Then he began to tell a story.

He spoke slowly, hoping they would understand, and used broad gestures to help make his meaning clear. The tale he told was taken from the history of his people. As he spoke, deities from the Celtic past slipped from the shadows to gather around him. He could not see them but he could feel them. Cernunnos the Shapechanger and Goibban the Smith; Epona of the Horses and Nematona, Daughter of the Trees.

The story lasted until the fire was reduced to glowing embers. Still held in thrall, the listeners went silently to their beds.

In the morning the village leader watched as Dinas saddled the dark horse. "We have a few mares we could breed, but no stallion. How much do you want for yours?"

"No amount would buy him."

"You tell a lie, my friend; everything's for sale."

Dinas tightened his lips. "Not this horse."

"You must be as rich as Croesus, then," the other man scoffed, "and you don't look it to me." Without warning he bent to run a hand down the stallion's foreleg. Without warning the horse clamped his teeth on the man's shoulder. Mighty neck flexed and powerful loin muscles rippled as the stallion sank back on his haunches. He lifted the hapless villager clear of the ground and shook him as a terrier shakes a rat.

The man screamed. Dinas barked a command. The dark horse dropped his bleeding victim.

As they rode up through the pass into the mountains Dinas said ruefully, "That's one place we can't go for hospitality again."

Meradoc said, "Who's Croesus?"

"The ruler of an ancient kingdom called Lydia. He was said to have all the gold in the world."

"Are you as rich as Croesus?"

Dinas laughed. "Nothing like it, little man. I have a bit of gold—and some silver and copper."

"In coins?"

"Some of it."

Urging his pony closer to the stallion, Meradoc subjected Dinas—and particularly his torso, with the faint outline of the purse visible beneath his tunic—to careful scrutiny. "Not on you, surely."

"No, Meradoc, not on me. Carrying valuables around is the best way to lose them. A woman in the mountains keeps mine safe for me."

Taking one hand from the reins, Meradoc pointed toward a distant massif barely visible through curtains of cloud. "Those mountains?"

"They are the peaks of Eryri, meaning 'land of eagles,'" Dinas said. "The first place God made, according to my mother."

Meradoc was delighted to think he had found another clue to the mystery of Dinas. "Does your mother live way up there? Is she the woman who keeps your money?"

Dinas sat rigid on his horse. He said nothing, but a muscle twitched in his jaw.

Meradoc was afraid he had gone too far. He allowed his pony to drift away from the stallion and concentrated on the mountains ahead.

What would it be like to live so close to heaven?

The pass was rapidly filling with snow. The thin air was not particularly cold, but the exhalations of horses and men formed little white clouds.

Pelemos began humming to himself; an undertone that had become such a part of the journey that the other two barely noticed it.

Sometimes the music was cheerful; sometimes it was dark and as bitter as tears. Today it was dark.

Dinas drew a deep breath. Nothing changed in his posture, but the horse felt the change in him. In a voice stripped of all emotion, Dinas said, "My mother doesn't live anywhere, Meradoc. She's been murdered."

CHAPTER TEN

Snow was falling. Tiny, powdery flakes, too small to be distinct but too thick to be ignored. They swirled through Viroconium like an invading army, softening sharp edges, blurring right angles. By late afternoon the tiled roofs and paved streets were white.

The hair on his father's head had turned white too, Cadogan noticed as Vintrex stepped down from a rather battered four-wheeled cart made of timber and wickerwork. The old man's shoulders sagged and his features were almost submerged in wrinkles, but the red-rimmed eyes that met Cadogan's were the eyes he remembered. Proud and remote.

Vintrex greeted his son with, "Why are you here? It is a little late to be remembering your responsibilities to this house and family! Did you come crawling back to ask me to change my will again? I wrote you out of it, you know. Everything will go to the sons of your sisters."

"I assumed that's what you would do," Cadogan said calmly.

His father glowered at him. "You *assumed* I am the sort of man who would disinherit his only son?"

"I assumed you would do what you thought was right."

"Are you saying that to impress me?"

"No, Father. I gave up trying to impress you a long time ago."

The conversation was taking a turn Vintrex could not control. He changed the subject. "The old emperor has died since you abandoned your responsibilities here, Cadogan. His death temporarily deprived the Empire of the West of a ruler. Not that Flavius Honorius was much of a ruler; a wiser man would have accepted the terms Alaric offered him and spared Rome the Gothic occupation."

Having delivered this announcement, Vintrex drew his travel-stained cloak about his body and stalked into the house. He left the cart and driver waiting outside the low brick wall that encircled his property.

Cadogan directed the man to the stable, then followed his father inside. He found Vintrex in the atrium, staring at the broken furniture and torn tapestries piled in what had been the reflecting pool. "Where did this wreckage come from?" he asked Cadogan.

"It was taken from the rooms the raiders ransacked."

The old man's face turned to stone. "Raiders? *Here?!* When?"

"A few days after you left for Londinium. Esoros didn't want to burn anything until you came back and decided what was worth mending."

"We do not mend trash," Vintrex said frostily. "Esoros should know that. Where is he now? Why did he not come to meet me?"

"He went to the market, but he should return soon."

"It was Alia's place to go to the market."

"Your housekeeper was killed by the barbarians during the raid."

Vintrex received the news stoically. "I see. I see that there is no new housekeeper and rubbish is piled up in the atrium. And you still did not tell me why you are here, Cadogan, or where you have been all this time."

"I was at home."

"At home?"

"The house I built for myself," Cadogan amended. "In the hills."

"I see."

"I returned to Viroconium three days ago because I was concerned about you."

"You only learned of the raid three days ago?"

"No, Father. In late summer Dinas visited me long enough to tell me barbarians were in this area. I set out for Viroconium immediately, but by the time I got here the damage was already done."

"You were frightened and ran away," Vintrex said.

"I didn't run away. I went back to protect my own home."

"Why would some shack in the hills need protection?"

"It's no shack, Father; I've put a lot of effort into it. Even Dinas said . . ."

"Dinas said? Don't believe anything Dinas says, he's as mad as a boxful of fleas. That's why his mother wanted to give the horse to you; she was afraid Dinas would ruin it. And from what I hear, he has. The stallion has a reputation as a man killer."

We're going to talk about that horse again, Cadogan thought. Everything comes back to the dark horse. "As far as I know he's never killed anyone, Father. Dinas likes to give that impression; he wants people to think only he could tame such an animal. But the last time I saw him he had a young man with him who could . . ."

"I order you to stay away from Dinas, Cadogan."

Dinas would say attack is the best defense. "Why were you gone for so long, Father?" Cadogan retorted. "Surely you had more than enough time to get to Londinium and back. Or was there a problem with your business—was the journey unsuccessful?"

His father's normally aloof expression was replaced by a look of confusion. "Business? Successful? I was . . . I was simply trying to uphold the law. But when we are overrun with savages who have no respect for the law, how in the name of our Lord can I be expected to maintain . . ." His voice trailed away. He ran his fingers across his forehead as if to collect his thoughts. The back of his hand was spotted with age; the thin fingers were trembling.

Vintrex steadied himself. "Unfortunately," he continued in a normal voice, "I was unable to conclude the matter which took me to Londinium. A most brutal murder had been committed in my jurisdiction by a person of high rank. The matter was sensitive for a number of reasons, and required special handling. To my dismay I discovered that no one remains in the capital with enough authority to deal with the situation. To all intents and purposes, Londinium has ceased to be a capital; it is like a disturbed anthill with the queen gone and the workers running in every direction. So that my journey would not be a total waste, I decided to travel on to Rome and make a personal plea to the emperor for more protection for my city."

Abruptly Vintrex sagged against one of the columns of the peristyle, the covered walkway surrounding the atrium. Cadogan feared his father was about to collapse, but the old man waved away his supportive arm. "I'm all right, leave me alone. Am I not entitled to a moment's rest? I have had very little rest these last weeks."

He straightened up with an effort. "There was a time, Cadogan, when a chief magistrate such as myself could have boarded a Roman trireme and been transported in comfort around Iberia and through the Mediterranean. Warships were expected to provide suitable passenger accommodations for officials of the empire. It was taken for granted. I never availed of the opportunity, though in my younger days I knew men who did. I used to wish that . . .

"But no more. I shall never envy any man who has spent one hour of his life on the open sea!" As Vintrex spoke these words his face took on a sickly pallor.

Ignoring his protestations, Cadogan hustled his father into the house and seated him on a cushioned bench in the hall. "You really are ill, Father. Stay here while I find someone to fetch Esoros."

Vintrex lay down on his side, drew his knees up to his chest and propped his head on one of the tightly stuffed cylindrical cushions intended as an armrest. There he lay like an ancient baby while Cadogan went to find help. He met Esoros rushing into the house. "Is he here?" the steward panted. "Is my master really here?"

"He's in the hall; he arrived a little while ago."

Esoros pushed past Cadogan and ran to the hall, which was a large, oblong room facing onto the atrium. The hall was painted in dark red and olive green, with a frieze of marbled panels divided by columns, and Roman statuary set in niches. In the center of the room stood a table made of highly polished dark shale, displaying a collection of silver and bronze figurines. High-backed couches provided for both sitting and reclining; a lady's basket chair with a silk cushion had been placed to give the best view of the atrium. Folding stools, padded footstools, small chests and cabinets inlaid with mother-of-pearl completed the furnishings.

When the house was new and Domitia came to it as a bride, she had spent many happy weeks decorating the hall to her taste. Every piece of furniture, every work of art had been carefully chosen by herself. She had berated the painters until they were able to mix the exact shades she wanted for the walls. She had commissioned an elaborate iron brazier to burn charcoal—which did not smoke and would not stain the walls and furnishings—and directed that beautifully shaped terra-cotta oil lamps were hung from the ceiling with bronze chains. No matter how cold and gray the British weather, her hall was warm and bright.

Since her death no one had changed a single item in the room.

Esoros dropped to his knees beside the couch where Vintrex lay. "You have returned safely, my lord! I shall offer a sacrifice of thanksgiving to—"

"No sacrifices," Vintrex commanded. "Control yourself, Esoros; you are a Christian now."

"Yes, my lord Vintrex. Forgive me. Sometimes I forget myself."

Cadogan entered the room in time to see Vintrex extend one hand and rest it on his steward's head; a fatherly gesture Cadogan could not recall having experienced in his lifetime. "You are forgiven, Esoros. Now tell me, where are my servants? Aside from yourself I've seen none since I arrived."

"Since the raid—you know about the raid, my lord?"

"I do; my son mentioned it in his own clumsy way. What has that to do with our servants?"

"Since the raid I have been unable to replace the servants we lost. The housekeeper and one of the porters were killed outright, and the remainder ran off. Two of the youngest girls eventually came back, I think they were afraid to be outside the city walls for long. But the others have melted away."

"The problem's not unique to this house," Cadogan interjected.

"More than half the slaves in Viroconium have fled the city. They prefer to take their chances with the tribes in the hills."

"But they are our *property*," Vintrex insisted. "They cannot run away, it is unthinkable."

"I'm afraid we have to think about it now, Father. Perhaps when things get better . . ."

"Just when is that supposed to be?"

"I don't know; I hoped you would. If you personally asked the emperor for help . . ."

The old man's shoulders sagged. "I never got that far, neither to the old emperor or the new."

Cadogan recalled his father's first words. "Who succeeded Honorius?" he inquired.

"The new emperor is a puling child they are calling Valentinian the Third. His qualifications are superb; his father was master of the horse under Honorius, who died childless. It seems there are no limits to which a horseman may not aspire these days," Vintrex added sarcastically.

Cadogan was determined to get off the subject of horses. "Did you reach Rome?"

"I made every effort, but our eastern ports are in Saxon hands now. In Londinium I was warned against making any attempt to deal with those savages, so I wasted a number of days traveling along the coast trying to find a Briton in possession of a boat that could carry me across the Oceanus Britannicus. I intended to arrange for overland transport in Gaul to take me on to Rome." His voice faded again.

"Esoros, bring wine at once," Cadogan ordered.

"I would, Lord Cadogan, but we have no more of the good—"

"At once!"

The steward returned with a sour beverage that the house of Vintrex would not have offered to a beggar in former times. The old man made a face, but he gulped it down.

Cadogan and his father had never been close; Vintrex was always too involved with his public life to show interest in his children, who knew him as an austere, aloof figure. So Cadogan was surprised at the depth of his concern for Vintrex. In his father's physical disintegration he glimpsed his own mortality.

"You should rest for a while, Father," he suggested. "We can talk about this later."

"I am perfectly capable of talking now!" Vintrex snapped. "What was I saying? Oh, yes—looking for a boat. In Durovernum I encountered a freedman who said he had a dugout canoe—a canoe, of all things!—which he claimed was capable of crossing the Fretum Gallicum. I had to offer him an extravagant sum to take me to Gaul, but you know me, I am not one to give up."

Both Esoros and Cadogan nodded in agreement.

"I left my driver and chariot in Durovernum with instructions to wait until I returned, no matter how long it took, and accompanied the boat owner to a private harborage at the edge of the sea. The man had a mast and sail for his canoe, but no covered accommodation to shelter a passenger. We set out on a most unpleasant morning, with a cold mist coming down. To my surprise we moved quickly at first. I began to think my plan had a fair chance of success.

"Soon a larger boat loomed out of the mist; somewhat like a great timber canoe, only broader. There was no sail. The boat was propelled entirely by oars manned by helmeted warriors. Their captain, as I assume he was, began shouting instructions to my fisherman in some coarse Germanic language. My fisherman not only understood the heathen tongue but was eager to comply. He seized me and bound me with rope, then helped transfer me to the Saxon warship, for that is what it was. The last I saw of the wretch he was laughing up at me from his canoe. With my money in his purse," Vintrex added bitterly.

"My dear lord!" cried Esoros, clasping his hands together.

"Fortunately I am not a total fool," Vintrex continued. "I still had a substantial sum concealed about my person, in places where I did not expect to be searched. When I discovered that the ship's captain knew a few words of Latin, I set out to impress him with my connections in the empire. As proof I showed him five gold double denarii minted in Rome. I do not know if he was aware of their value, but they gleamed persuasively. He handed them to another man who looked as if he might be his brother. This second man asked if I had any more. That was all I needed. I assured them that I would take them to a veritable fortune in gold if they would release me on the Gaulish shore.

"While this was going on we continued to move up the strait until in time we reached the open sea. There the weather was dreadful. Which worked to my advantage, in a way," Vintrex added with a glint in his bloodshot eyes.

He was actually enjoying this. The ordeal he had undergone was terrible, but in the telling it acquired a glamour he had not perceived at the time. His audience of two was hanging on his every word. "Is there any more of that wine?" he inquired.

Cadogan looked at Esoros, who shook his head.

"Beer, then," said Vintrex. "But be sure it's from the first brewing, when there's still strength to it. I am not a child to drink weak beer."

He kept them waiting while he consumed two large tankards of barley beer, then resumed his narrative. "The rolling and pitching of the Saxon boat made me violently ill. I vomited so copiously their captain feared I might die without taking him to my gold, so he promised to release me. It had the desired effect; I began to rally. I assumed he would take me east as I had requested, and braced myself for an unendurably long journey on rough seas.

"The journey seemed long and certainly beyond enduring, but when we made landfall I discovered we were in the territory of the Iceni! I tried to explain to the leader of the warriors that my gold was in Gaul, not Britannia, but the man's Latin was too limited and my knowledge of Germanic dialects was nonexistent."

Cadogan asked curiously, "Did you really have any gold in Gaul?"

"Of course not, that was only a ruse. I intended to escape as soon as we reached land and make my way to Rome."

"You thought you could escape from a boatload of Saxons?"

"I always do what I set out to do," Vintrex said coldly. "However in this case I did not get the chance. They were so angry to be thwarted of the gold they anticipated that they beat me half to death. After stealing everything I had—including my Tyrian purple magistrate's robe, which I would have worn for an audience with the emperor—they left me lying facedown on a muddy beach. When I finally came to myself, I crawled some distance inland and collapsed again. Several of the Iceni found me and took me to their village. When I was strong enough I returned to Durovernum on foot because I could not afford to hire any transportation." He gestured toward his feet, which Cadogan had not noticed before. Instead of Roman sandals or soft leather boots, his father's feet were bound in strips of dirty, bloodstained cloth. "Blisters," Vintrex said succinctly.

"I don't want to sound mercenary, Father, but what happened to that substantial amount of money you had on you?"

"I have no idea. Perhaps the Saxons found it while I lay insensate on the beach. Perhaps the Iceni took it while supposedly caring for me. At any odds, it is gone."

"At least you had your chariot and driver waiting for you in Durovernum."

The old man gave a harsh laugh. "You would think so, would you not? But they had disappeared, too—probably as soon as I was out of sight. No one in Durovernum admitted any knowledge of them. My own charioteer! And he had been with me for years."

"Then who brought you home, Father?"

"An avaricious scoundrel who made me promise to pay him an exorbitant sum as soon as we reached Viroconium. Which reminds me: Go out to him, Esoros, and see that he is paid. You know where my strongbox is."

"I know where it was," the steward replied bleakly.

"You mean it's gone!"

"The raiders took it."

Vintrex seemed to shrink inside his clothes.

"You may recall that I have money, Father," Cadogan said. "Until things improve it will be at your disposal."

If he expected his father to thank him for the offer he was disappointed. Vintrex was in no mood to be grateful for anything. "Who can say when things will improve? The highway between Londinium and Viroconium was thronged with refugees heading west. Men begged me to carry their household goods in my cart; mothers pleaded with me to take their infants. Where the highway cut through the forest they crowded into the center of the road, as if the pavement itself could protect them. Some of them were as bony as the Romans; they must have been starving for weeks. It was like being surrounded by ghosts. When at last I saw the walls of Viroconium my relief was enormous. Then I walked into my house and found my reflecting pool filled with rubbish." The old man's voice crackled with anger. "How could you do that to me, Esoros?"

If the steward was taken aback by his master's attack he did not show it. "Those things came from your wife's chambers, my lord."

At the mention of his dead wife, Vintrex briefly closed his eyes. When he opened them again he said in a more reasonable tone, "You should have burned them, Esoros, not left an unpleasant situation for me to deal with. Surely you know when to act on your own initiative."

Before Esoros could respond, Vintrex drew a sharp intake of breath. "What in Christ's holy name," he demanded, leveling a bony forefinger at the apparition entering the room, "is *that*?"

CHAPTER ELEVEN

Pelemos was fully aware.

His wakening had happened gradually, and against his will. Perhaps the process began when he sat on the pony and put his foot on the ground; on Mother Earth. It gathered momentum when they neared the mountains, and the sharp air lanced through his nostrils and into his numbed brain. It was completed on the night he told the story.

The following day he realized the trees marching up the slopes were not trees he knew. Fern and bracken were of unfamiliar colors. Soaring peaks in the distance astonished his eyes. He was in a different place, one that Ithill had never occupied. How strange to feel the *lack* of her presence!

Pelemos did not listen to the exchange between Dinas and Meradoc and therefore was unaware of the mention of murder. Yet he was aware that the atmosphere had changed, though his concentration was on the scenery. Swathes of peaty moorland were broken by rocky outcroppings. Abrupt cliffs thrust upward like swords through the thin topsoil. Great boulders were scattered at random, indifferent spectators to an ancient cataclysm.

Indifferent could be good.

"Cymru," he said aloud.

Dinas turned in the saddle to look at him. "What did you say, Pelemos?"

"Cymru is a beautiful name. Like music."

"It is," Dinas agreed.

"The kingdom of Rheged. And the peaks of Eryri."

"That's right. You know where you are."

"I do now," said Pelemos.

Every step was taking him farther away from pain.

Sometime in the future he would be able to think of Ithill again, of Ithill and the girls, because they were safe in the distance. Later still he would be able to look forward to them and not backward at them. He knew this though he did not know how he knew it.

The mountains, unlike the God he once had believed in, were here and now. He had a visceral sense of their immense weight. Their great age. He could almost worship their overwhelming presence. "I like the mountains," he remarked aloud.

Dinas turned to look at him again. "And the people?"

"I like the people too."

Dinas smiled, though his eyes were sad. "A Roman called Cato once described the Cymri as 'devoted to warfare and witty conversation.'"

They rode on and on. Up and up.

By the close of day the land was engulfed in purple shadows. One last flare of gold and crimson from the west, then darkness. Dinas drew rein. "Night in these mountains can be as black as the inside of a cow," he warned his companions. "Stay close to me now, we only have a short distance to go." He led the way beneath an overhanging shelf of rock, then onto a narrow ridge that climbed toward the sky.

A million stars blazed over them.

Pelemos caught his breath.

Dinas laughed. "Some people worship the stars as gods, or the eyes of gods," he said. "Others claim the stars are precious jewels hanging in the sky."

"What do you think they are?" Meradoc asked.

Dinas laughed again. "I think they are just stars."

The dark horse halted of his own accord in front of an earth-and-stone cabin tucked into the shoulder of a mountain. Dinas felt a pulse begin to pound at the base of his throat. It always happened, no matter how many times they met. Saba was a gliding walk, a laughing voice, wide-set gray eyes and a formidable jaw. She was all of that and none of it.

He gave one of his assortment of whistles—two low notes, followed by a trill. Moments later a door opened slightly and a wedge of firelight lanced through the darkness.

"It's me, Saba," Dinas called. "I've brought a couple of friends."

The door was flung wide and a woman stood there. Seen in silhouette with her back to the light, she was almost as tall as a man. Two dogs stood beside her, one on either hand. They did not wave their tails until she said, "You are well come as always, Dinas. You and your friends." Her voice was almost as low as a man's, but sweeter. "Put your horses in the lambing shed—you know where it is—then come inside and have a meal. There's mutton and barley in the pot."

"Saba always has mutton and barley in the pot," Dinas assured the other two as he motioned them inside.

After the darkness, the firelit cabin seemed wonderfully bright. Saba's mountain home was not as large as Cadogan's fort in the forest. It had only one door and two small windows closed with heavy wooden shutters. The thick walls were made of uncut stones fitted so tightly together that they required no chinking, creating a cavelike atmosphere of security.

Looking around, Meradoc recognized the work of a craftsman.

Skillfully plaited rush matting had been affixed to the underside of the steep slate roof to add a thick layer of insulation. At one end of the room was a stone hearth with an iron crane forged in a curvilinear Celtic design. The fire that blazed on the hearth was made fragrant by pine knots. A snug wooden bedbox carved with Celtic symbols filled an adjoining alcove. A matching table and stools were at one side of the hearth; a large loom stood on the other side, utilizing the light from the fire. On the loom was a half-finished woolen blanket containing all the colors of the rainbow.

The dogs, a shaggy pair of black-and-white sheepdogs, stationed themselves at the woman's feet and watched the newcomers with bright eyes.

Meradoc said shyly, "You have a good home here."

"It keeps the wind off," Saba replied. Glancing at Dinas, she said, "I'm not used to compliments on my housekeeping."

He raised one eyebrow. "Did you ever hear me complain?"

Saba laughed. Meradoc liked the way she laughed, tossing her hair back and exposing her full white throat.

Pelemos, to his surprise, liked her too. The first moment he heard her voice he had felt something stir in him that he had thought was dead. He was not ready to respond sexually to another woman; would not be ready in a long time, if ever, but it was reassuring to discover that he could feel again.

He was alive again.

When Saba gestured to him to seat himself, he drew a stool closer to the fire and sat basking in the heat. Only then did he realize how cold he had been since they entered the mountains. How cold he had been since Ithill died. How cold . . .

From the iron cauldron suspended on the crane, Saba scooped up steaming portions of meat, root vegetables and grain, which she served to the hungry men with black bread and cups of sweet, pure water. At first there was no sound in the room but the crackle of the fire on the hearth and three sets of jaws chewing eagerly. Soon, however, Dinas and Saba began the conversation of people who knew each other well.

"You're thinner than when I saw you last," she told him.

"And you are plumper."

"Sheep's butter," she replied, quietly pleased by his offhand compliment. "In the small pot there on the table; put it on your bread."

"No olive oil?"

"Not here."

"Didn't I bring you some once?"

"You did, but I threw it out . . . no, I tell a lie. First I rubbed it on my skin, but I didn't like the smell. That's when I threw it out."

"Waste of my good money," Dinas remarked. He drained his cup and mopped his bowl with a hunk of bread, then held both out to her for a refill. Said casually, "I thought we might stop here for a while, Saba. We'll do our share of the work. I'll hunt deer and wild goats and Meradoc will set snares, he's become quite good at it. As for Pelemos, he was a farmer, so he'll be a great help to you in lambing season."

Saba's jaw dropped. Lambs were not born until the end of winter, celebrated by the Celtic festival of Imbolc.

If her expression betrayed her surprise, her response was gracious. As she handed the refilled bowl and cup to Dinas she said, "You're welcome to stay as long as you like, all of you. I'd like to have company in the season of long nights. Pelemos, Meradoc, give me your bowls too. I'm sure you can eat more. Dinas devours everything in the larder when he comes to me, though until now he's never stayed for longer than half a moon."

"Half a moon?" Meradoc queried.

Dinas said, "About half a month in the Roman calendar. Time here is still measured in the old way."

"Like the animals and plants that sustain us," Saba elaborated, "we live according to the sun and moon. A year has two seasons decided by the sun: winter and summer. The moon divides those seasons into sections for shearing and for weaving, for planting and for harvesting, for work and for rest. Because those things never change we need no calendars."

"Some things change," Dinas remarked.

"Apparently they do, or you wouldn't be wanting to spend the winter with me."

"I have to think through a problem, and this is a good place for it."

"I've never heard you admit you have any problems."

"Things change," he repeated.

Her eyes searched his face, flicked a glance at the other two men and returned to Dinas. "I think I have enough fodder put by for your horses; ponies don't eat much anyway." She seemed to accept without complaint his disruption of her life.

Meradoc leaned over and whispered to Pelemos, "Are they married? Or what?"

Pelemos squinted at the couple in the firelight. "What, I'd say. But it's none of our business."

When the three men could eat no more, the bowls were wiped clean and the fire banked while Meradoc went out to the shed to make certain the horses were bedded down for the night. He broke the ice in the stone cistern and refilled their water buckets. He rubbed down the stallion and the ponies as well, paying particular attention to each animal's itchy places. The dark horse loved to be scratched behind his ears.

Upon his return to the cabin Saba directed him and Pelemos to a sleeping loft opposite the fireplace. It was accessed by means of a wooden ladder. Meradoc scrambled up first. The loft was surprisingly roomy; he could stand upright below the ridge of the roof. The goat shed in Deva where he usually slept was not nearly as dry, nor as pleasant. It had smelled of goat and other, less pleasant things.

The sleeping loft smelled of the armloads of clean straw thickly piled on the floor. Meradoc took a deep breath. And smiled.

As Pelemos started—with some trepidation—to follow Meradoc up the ladder, Dinas told him, "There's enough blankets up there to keep an army warm. If you want any more, just sing out. Saba comes from a long line of slaters, but she supports herself with her sheep and there's nothing she can't make out of wool. She even wove my saddlebags for me. This woman does all the shearing and washes the fleeces and spins the wool herself. Cross her at your peril, friends; she could break you over her knee."

Saba laughed.

Pelemos paused halfway up the ladder. Hoping to hear her laugh again.

While the other two made themselves comfortable in the loft and settled down for the night, Dinas and Saba took seats by the fire. They placed their stools in the way they always placed them; close enough for their knees to touch. The two dogs stretched out on the hearth beside them.

Meradoc tried not to overhear their conversation but sound carried upward.

He heard Dinas say, "When I leave this time I'll be taking my treasure with me, Saba."

"And here was me," she teased, "thinking you'd made the journey just to see my dimples."

"That too. But dimples won't buy horses and weapons."

Thick lashes curtained her eyes. Her thoughts hid behind those curtains, peeping out. "Your friends don't look like warriors to me."

"They aren't. But the fifty men I'm going to recruit will be."

"Fifty men," she said calmly. "As many as that. Quite a crowd for a man who boasts of being a lone wolf."

"I'll need at least that many if I hope to get my share."

Responding to a change in the tone of his voice, one of the dogs stood up and laid a shaggy head on his thigh. Dinas absentmindedly fondled the silky ears.

Saba said nothing. That was one of the things Dinas liked about her. Other women would pluck and prod at a man in an effort to plunder his thoughts, but Saba simply waited. She waited as Dinas would wait with a skittish horse and let it come to him.

"I intend to get my share, Saba," he repeated. "Why not? Isn't that what the strong always do? You may not realize this up here in the mountains, but Britannia is falling apart. We're almost entirely cut off from the continent now. Britons won't be paying taxes to Rome anymore but they will still pay taxes to someone. And the cleverest among us will find treasure amidst the wreckage.

"New kings are sprouting up like weeds, among Britons and foreigners alike. And what are kings—or emperors, for that matter— but scoundrels who stole and murdered their way to the top? 'Nobility' is a cloak their descendants put on to enforce their claim to privileges they deny to everyone else. I can be as big a scoundrel as any other man, and just as worthy a king. All that's required is to gather enough followers and seize enough land to provide for them. That's how the Romans came to rule the world, isn't it?"

"I wouldn't know," Saba murmured.

"The good farmland is already claimed, so I can't offer my supporters a fat living from grain and cattle. But there are other routes to prosperity. I know of several wild and empty places where I could carve out a kingdom for myself, and there are some abandoned watchtowers along the coast that would be useful in a pirate operation."

Saba had heard his flights of fancy before; heard them and often entered into them, responding to the boy still alive within the man. At the mention of pirates she cautioned, "There are pirates in the Oceanus Hibernicus already."

"Hibernian slave-catchers in skin-covered boats," he sneered. "The piracy I have in mind will be land-based. No matter how bad times are there will always be merchants who buy and sell, and considerable cargo is still being shipped through the western seaways. Much of it these days is tin; what the foreigners call 'the British metal.' The Syrians and Egyptians are buying large quantities of tin from the Dumnonian mines and sending it south to the Mediterranean, or shipping it north through the Oceanus Hibernicus to avoid the Saxon pirates. I'm told there's a great demand for tin in Germania."

"Strong as you are," Saba said, "you could never carry enough tin on your back to make the effort worthwhile."

Dinas raised a sardonic eyebrow. "I'm surprised at your lack of faith, woman! I don't want tin; I want the merchandise foreign traders bring to exchange for tin. Fragrant, full-bodied red wine from Gaul and sweet golden wine from Iberia. The only good wine to be found in Britannia these days is served in the halls of the Dumnonii. And whatever I may think about religion, Christianity is expanding since the Romans left and wine is an essential element of the Christian mass, which makes it even more valuable. But it's not just wine I'm after. Traders also bring Byzantine jewelry from Constantinople, or furs and amber from the Baltic . . . I could dress you in furs and jewels, Saba."

"And pretend that I'm a queen?" She threw back her head and laughed.

"I've even found the perfect setting for you," he said earnestly. "A fortress at the edge of the sea."

"Why the sea?" she asked. Playing along. "I'm a mountain woman; could we not build a palace in the mountains?"

He shook his head. "You don't understand how this will work. I'll station observers with fast horses along the coast. Cargo vessels have to put ashore to take on fresh water. When one of my men sees a likely vessel approaching, he'll light a signal fire and we'll all ride to meet the landing party. Seize the boat's crew, use their boat to board the ship, take what we want and then let the sailors go. Or we might hold the captain for ransom if that offers a better chance for profit."

From the hard glint in his eyes, Saba realized Dinas was serious. The boy in him had vanished entirely.

Dinas was saying, "Now you know why I need that treasure. It may not cover the entire cost of equipping my men, but I have something which might make up the difference. A couple of items I acquired in Deva recently. They may be very valuable or worth nothing at all, but . . . wait, I'll show you."

In one long stride he retrieved his saddlebags from the place where he always dropped them: on the floor beside Saba's loom. From one he extracted a leather bundle. The leather was lambskin, old and worn and as soft as silk. The bundle was tied with strips of wool that might once have been blue.

Dinas set the bundle on the table beside Saba. "See what you make of these."

She carefully untied the woolen strips and unfolded the bundle. Looked back at him with a puzzled expression.

"Take them out," he said.

The first object was an ordinary plate carved from olivewood. The wood had faded with time and was cracked down the middle. Saba ran her fingers over the damaged surface, shook her head, and set the plate on the table. Reaching into the bag again, she took out a bowl—or perhaps it was a cup—carved from a common variety of agate. She held the object closer to the firelight to examine it. Agates were lustrous when polished, but this stone was dull. A faint, dark stain remained in the bottom of the bowl. There was a jagged patch on the under side where something had been broken off. A foot, perhaps; a small pedestal.

The dog lying on the hearth lifted its head and whined.

Saba set the stone bowl beside the wooden plate. Opened the bundle flat. Held it upside down, shook it to make sure it was empty, then turned to Dinas. "Is this one of your jokes?"

"It's no joke, Saba. The men who were had these items were mightily determined to keep them a secret. At the time I assumed they were hiding a valuable gold chalice and paten—I'd heard some interesting tales about Deva. So I waited until everyone was asleep and helped myself. I didn't look into the bag until later, when I was safely away from the town."

"You must have been disappointed," she said drily.

"At first I was angry that I'd wasted my time. But then . . ." He did not finish the thought.

"You say these came from Deva."

"A shrine in Deva, yes."

"A Christian shrine, I assume." Watching his eyes, she added, "Surely not pagan."

"Does it make any difference?"

Some of the color drained from Saba's face. "If you stole from any sort of sacred place there could be terrible consequences for you. I thought you had better sense, Dinas."

"Being in a shrine didn't make those things holy," he argued. "Just look at them. Ordinary everyday tableware, and badly damaged at that. Would you offer such objects to a god? I saw possibilities in them, that's all. Remember the fellow who sold you the yearling ram with no balls?"

She was used to his sudden change of subjects. "Of course I remember him, Dinas, and I'm sure he'll never forget you. On the day we met I was trying to buy sheep from a man I thought I could trust. I was wrong. You appeared out of nowhere and rescued a gullible and inexperienced woman. I can still see the look on his face when you threatened to rip off his balls and put them on the ram."

Dinas grinned. "I was sorry he backed down and gave you a good breeding ram for next to nothing. I would have enjoyed putting action to words."

"Really?"

The grin widened. "We'll never know."

"I think better of you than you think of yourself."

"The more fool you," Dinas replied.

She knitted her fingers together in her lap. "That old cup and plate . . ."

He put his hand over hers and tightened the grip. "Do you know how many Christians claim to have a fragment of a martyr's robe, or a saint's finger, or tail hair from the donkey that carried Jesus into Jerusalem? There's a thriving trade in 'holy relics,' Saba. That's what we have here. A sophisticated fraud."

"It's not . . ."

"Of course not; don't be fooled. One of those men in Deva had a slithery quality about him. I know his type, he'd steal the feathers off a bird in flight. He wanted to charge me an outrageous price to spend the night in his leaky-roofed inn. He had these things hidden 'in a holy place' so he could produce them with great fanfare and sell them to some prosperous but credulous Christian. I didn't look prosperous and I'm certainly not credulous, so he didn't bother to show them to me. I know a thief when I see one, though, and I have no compunction about stealing from thieves . . ."

". . . and selling the stolen merchandise to someone else," she concluded.

This time when Dinas grinned he looked like a wolf baring its teeth. "Yes, if they'll pay enough for it."

Saba eyed the battered plate and lusterless cup. "I seriously doubt if anyone will."

In the loft above their heads Meradoc snuggled deeper into the straw and pulled his blankets around his shoulders. When he was warm and well fed it was easy to imagine himself having adventures. A tall watchtower, the windswept sea, brave men riding out on splendid horses . . . being with Dinas had opened doors in his mind he never knew were there. His last thought before he fell asleep was, What and where is Constantinople?

Long after his collected treasure was counted and assessed and Saba had fallen asleep, Dinas lay open-eyed in the dark, trying to reach out with his special senses. Listening for instinct and intuition. Seeking the nameless wisdom deep in his bones that had warned him of danger in the past. Something was happening; a coming together of forces he could not yet identify. Meradoc and Pelemos were part of it. But what part?

In the Cymric language the word "*hiraeth*" was applied to yearning for the indefinable, an amorphous longing for beginnings and conclusions. Dinas had an almost physical ache to discover landmarks in a shapeless life; to discover something he could hang on to when confronted by the terrible inner darkness that recently threatened to overwhelm him. Was he going about it the right way? Or had he already doomed himself to failure?

There were times when he felt an inchoate longing for the pagan religion the Romans had destroyed. The old ones knew things. Perhaps it was their voices that spoke to him in the night.

Gods; that was where the problem began. People needed to believe in deities wiser and more powerful than themselves. Yet the figures he had been taught to revere as a child had failed him. Christianity was a sham perpetrated by men who used it to their own advantage. Of that much he was certain.

As for the gods of the Romans, they were cast in human form with human vices. In the animal kingdom Dinas could name many noble creatures more worthy of godhood. Petty, greedy mankind could not be the pinnacle of being, any more than a world limited to five human senses could be the sum of all things. That would be illogical, and his education had taught him to be logical. But would a logical man steal from a holy shrine and expect to profit by it?

CHAPTER TWELVE

Quartilla had ignored Cadogan's orders to avoid the family's private apartments. Whenever the opportunity presented itself she surreptitiously searched his late mother's chambers. Domitia's broken furniture was piled in the atrium, but some small accoutrements of a fashionable woman's life had been overlooked and left behind. Half a stick of black kohl for lining the eyes. A tiny pot of lip stain. A few thin silk ribbons; an ivory comb.

Quartilla confiscated everything she found.

On the morning Vintrex returned she had spent a happy hour applying the dead woman's makeup. Peering at herself in a shard of broken mirror, wiping away mistakes and starting over. The room Cadogan had assigned to her was singularly lacking in a woman's necessities, so she set off in search of a decent mirror in good light. When she heard an unfamiliar male voice she followed the sound out of curiosity—forgetting about the cosmetics still smeared across her face.

When she entered the hall she saw an old man lying on one of the couches. His face was distorted with what might be pain. The grimace revealed long yellow teeth. She hated him on sight.

Raising himself on one elbow, he pointed a sticklike finger at her and demanded hoarsely, "Just what is that?"

Quartilla froze in her tracks.

The old man continued, "Surely it is the most extraordinary sight seen in Britannia since Emperor Claudius entered Camulodunum riding on an elephant. If that is an example of what you are buying to replace our servants, Esoros, you must return her to the slave dealer at once. You know I will not have an ugly woman in my service."

His words broke the spell.

"How dare you call me ugly, you scrawny old bear-bait!" Quartilla cried. She elbowed Esoros aside and bent over the figure on the couch. "This isn't your house, it's Cadogan's, and you can't give me orders. I'm nobody's slave, I'm as free as you are and a lot better looking!"

Her spittle sprayed his face. Vintrex shrank back against the cushions and rolled his eyes toward Cadogan. "You had better have a good explanation for this," he rasped.

"Father, this is Quartilla. She is . . . an acquaintance of mine."

"Someone you know socially?" Vintrex asked in disbelief.

"Not exactly. She . . . I mean Dinas . . ."

"Dinas again!" Vintrex was livid.

"The situation is complicated," Esoros said in a mollifying tone as he reached to place a cushion under his master's neck. "When you understand everything you will realize your son has acted out of compassion. He brought this poor woman here because she has no other home."

"This certainly isn't going to be her home!"

"Of course not, Father," said Cadogan. "It's only a temporary arrangement."

Vintrex became aware of a buzzing in his ears. It had happened before; had been happening with increasing frequency since he was captured by the Saxons. Or perhaps even before. Perhaps it began when she died . . .

The walls faded and disappeared into a mist.

"Your father has only fainted," Esoros assured Cadogan. "He is exhausted and hungry; I can take care of him."

"I'm sure you can, but I'm here now."

"I have always attended to my lord's needs," Esoros said frostily.

"I still would feel better if we had a physician look at him."

"Gratias has always been your father's physician, but he and his family left soon after the raid."

"I know they did. I went to their villa yesterday to see if Viola was there and found the place boarded up. A neighbor told me Gratias took his daughters to Athens so one of them could study the healing arts, but I think it was just an excuse to leave the city. I wonder if they even made it to Athens, the way things are now. My poor Viola. What might have happened to her?"

Esoros did not hazard a guess. Servants were expected to be unresponsive to their masters' private lives. "Gratias was the last of the physicians to leave Viroconium," he said, "and no replacement has been found. Now that the chief magistrate is back I am sure he will remedy the situation."

Cadogan was less sure. "Father's not ready to take up his office again. You can see how shaken he is, Esoros."

"He was upset by your woman."

"Don't be impertinent. And she's not my woman."

"No, Lord Cadogan. May I inquire what position the lady Quartilla does occupy?"

Was he smirking? Esoros could be an infuriating man. The steward of a great house ranked second only to his master, but he was still a slave—it would be well for Esoros to be reminded of that. Sometimes he gave himself the airs of a freedman.

Cadogan said coolly, "It is enough for you to know that I brought Quartilla to Viroconium. She is to receive every courtesy while she is under this roof."

"Yes, Lord Cadogan." But never "yes, my lord." Vintrex was the steward's only lord.

Damn his eyes, Cadogan thought, the man definitely *was* smirking. But I owe him no explanation. I brought Quartilla with me because I would not leave her alone and unprotected in the hills. I could not send her to her own people because I do not know where she came from. She never tells the same story twice.

I wish I could explain myself to myself.

Days passed and still Vintrex lay on a couch, or in his bed, growing increasingly thin and pale. He took for granted that Cadogan would stay and act as head of the family—under his strict supervision—until he himself was well again.

Quartilla took for granted that she would be treated as an honored guest in the extravagant Celtic tradition of the Britons until something better came along.

With his own money Cadogan hired the carter who had brought Vintrex from Durovernum to stay on as stable master. Not an arduous task, since there were only four animals in the stables including the man's team, but as a freedman he expected to be paid. It had taken him less than a day to ascertain that he had Cadogan at his mercy, since any sort of employee was scarce in Viroconium.

Meanwhile Esoros burned the broken furniture and searched the city for more servants. No one had any slaves to sell. He finally found a couple of old women past their strength who were willing to give the house an indifferent cleaning from time to time, a young girl who seemed to be terminally lazy, and a slatternly cook whose food tasted as bad as she looked.

When a meal was served that smelled like river mud, Quartilla rebelled. Throwing her plate onto the floor, she stalked off to the kitchen, where for an interminable time she made a great racket punctuated with vile language that, fortunately, could not be heard in the dining room used by the family. The meal she ultimately produced was excellent. Vintrex pronounced it "edible" and ate everything he was given.

Taking Cadogan aside afterward, he said, "This Quartilla person. I'm not saying I approve of her, but if you restrict her to the kitchen and servants' wing she can serve as cook until Esoros finds a better one. Then he can downgrade her to something more appropriate—cleaning the dishes, perhaps."

Cadogan was thankful that Quartilla was not present during this conversation. When he informed Esoros of his father's decision, the steward flatly refused to give Quartilla her instructions. "That woman is nothing to do with me, my lord. She is your guest. You tell her."

"But she's not my guest! I mean . . . if she is going to be a servant . . ."

Esoros shook his head. "I do not want her under my command, she is too arrogant. No good servant is ever arrogant."

Except you, Cadogan thought to himself.

He was left with no choice but to tell Quartilla himself, or explain her peculiar situation to Vintrex and leave the matter in the once-capable hands of the chief magistrate. He chose the latter. He waited until his father appeared to be in a relatively good mood as the result of a flagon of sweet wine Esoros had discovered.

Indifferent to the cold weather, Vintrex was sitting in a basket chair in the peristyle. The pool had been thoroughly scrubbed and refilled with clean water so it could mirror the sky once more. Although the sun was hidden by clouds, the light reflected from the water cast a sickly illumination over the face of the old man.

Cadogan seated himself on a stool close—but not too close—to his father's chair. "You look better today," he ventured.

Vintrex twirled his half-empty wineglass, an exquisite creation blown in the far-off and now dying empire. "The fresh air does me good, Cadogan. I am not as enfeebled as you would like me to be."

"What's that supposed to mean?"

"Only that I am not ready to have you take over as magistrate of Viroconium."

"I have no intention of usurping your office," Cadogan protested. "Even if I wanted to I don't have the authority. Magistrates have to be appointed by a Roman governor and . . ."

"And Britannia has no Roman governor at present," Vintrex finished for him. "Unfortunately for you."

"What made you think I coveted your position?"

"Esoros tells me you have been going through my private papers."

"This city is like a headless chicken now, Father. People keep coming to our door asking for assistance, and I can't just turn them away. They expect their chief magistrate to help them. There are no other magistrates left in this area, so I've been listening to their problems and handling them as best I can—in your name, always. Sometimes I have to look in your records to see how you've handled similar situations in the past."

"You have no ambitions for yourself?" Vintrex inquired suspiciously.

"To replace you? Of course not, Father. I'm not an ambitious man. And I certainly have neither the temperament nor the legal knowledge to fill your office."

"At least you have the humility to admit it. Call Esoros out here to refill my glass."

After the steward filled his glass and left the peristyle, Vintrex turned back to his son. "You did not come out here just to comment on my health. What do you want, Cadogan?"

"I want . . . I mean, I feel that I should . . . should explain about Quartilla, Father. I have let you draw certain conclusions about her which are in error."

Vintrex carefully set the wineglass on the little table at his elbow. "Enlighten me then."

Drawing a deep breath, Cadogan related as much as he knew of Quartilla's story—being careful to delete any references to Dinas. He was aware that his father's inexplicable dislike of Dinas had reached mammoth proportions.

Vintrex listened in stony silence. Yet behind his eyes every fact registered, every word and sentence was weighed and measured. For the first time Cadogan appreciated what it was like to face the chief magistrate in his official capacity.

"Is that all?" Vintrex asked when Cadogan finished talking.

"I . . . yes."

"You have not explained the circumstances of your first meeting with the woman."

"I thought I did. She was hiding in the hills, afraid of the bar-barians."

"And you found her there?"

Cadogan had great difficulty meeting his father's stern eyes. "I . . . I didn't find her myself, someone else did. He felt sorry for her, I suppose, and brought her to me because she had no place else to . . ."

"He? He who?"

Cadogan shifted uncomfortably on the stool. "Dinas. Dinas found her." Seeing the look on his father's face, he added hastily, "I didn't go looking for him. As I told you before, he came to warn me there were raiders in the area of Viroconium."

"And brought the woman with him?"

"Yes."

"What is she to him, his harlot?"

"I don't think so."

"Is she your harlot?"

"No."

"I see. So what is she, Cadogan?"

Cadogan shook his head. "I honestly don't know."

"What do you propose to do with her in your capacity as a quasi-magistrate?"

I will not let him goad me into losing my temper, Cadogan thought. "I'm hoping you can tell me how to find out about her family."

Against his better judgment, Vintrex was intrigued. "What good would that do?"

"I don't know who she is, Father, but I'm sure she isn't some cheap whore. When I first saw her she still had henna staining her finger-tips. She's heard of Cleopatra and Helen of Troy. She might have been a high-class courtesan or the daughter of a well-traveled mer-chant. Someone, somewhere, must be wondering what became of her."

"And would welcome her back?" Vintrex suggested. "Surely you realize we have much greater problems than returning a stray dog to its kennel."

"She's not a stray dog," said Cadogan.

"Then do as the Romans would do: hold burning bricks to her feet until she tells you the truth."

Beyond the sky a tiny shift took place on invisible scales. Cadogan's respect for his father, nourished by generations of a patriarchal culture, crumbled. "That suggestion appalls me, Vintrex!"

The older man stiffened. His son had never called him Vintrex before.

"If torture is one of your tools of governance," Cadogan went on, "I'm glad I shall never be a magistrate."

"As far as I can tell you're not anything much," retorted his father. "You say you have no ambition and I believe you. What have you ever accomplished?"

"Since I left here I've educated myself in the building arts and constructed my own home. No shack, but a sturdy little fortress that even offers a few refinements. And I enjoyed it more than you can imagine. Enjoyed planning it, and working on it, and would like to do it again. There is a satisfaction that comes from creating something substantial with your own two hands that you could never know."

"You do not know what you are talking about," Vintrex said. "I received tremendous satisfaction from having this house built."

"Having it built. Not building it yourself. If it was destroyed tomorrow and there were no slaves available to do the labor, how would you replace it?"

"You posit an impossible situation."

"Once you would have said the departure of the Romans was impossible."

Instead of answering, Vintrex reached for his glass and drained it to the dregs. As he set down the empty glass Esoros returned to the peristyle. The steward's face was ashen. He glanced at Cadogan, then fixed his eyes on Vintrex.

"There is a problem, my lord."

"So? Take care of it."

"I fear I cannot take care of this one by myself. The barbarians are approaching Viroconium."

"What?!" Vintrex rose to his feet with more energy than he had shown in days. He doubled his age-spotted hands into fists. "Raiders despoiled my property once, they shall not do it again."

The steward's expression was unreadable. "These are not merely raiders, my lord. They are an army."

CHAPTER THIRTEEN

Since the first limited attack on Viroconium there had been a spate of rumors about barbarian attacks elsewhere in the region. Bands of marauders were progressing from raids on isolated farmsteads and the wanton slaughtering of domestic livestock to terrorizing villages and towns. Population centers had become serious targets.

By winter half the inhabitants of Viroconium had left the city. More buildings were empty than occupied. Carefree citizens no longer strolled along the wide, pleasant streets, beneath chestnut trees imported from Iberia. The market squares were no longer thronged with shoppers. No speeches were being made in the forum; no Greek or Roman plays were performed in the theater. A tribe of feral cats had taken up residence in the forum, venturing out at night to hunt the rats that swarmed through deserted shops and houses.

The city walls Vintrex had planned to raise were still no higher than those of any other peaceful metropolis. The tall watchtowers Vintrex had designed had never been built. There was no trained and well-armed militia to occupy the unfinished guard posts, so the ordinary citizens of the town were taking turns standing watch at the gates, particularly the eastern gate, which was the main entrance to the city, and the southern gate, the commercial entrance.

On this day the shop owner on duty at the eastern gate had been the first to raise a warning. He rang the large iron bell hanging on one of the gateposts. The clamor annoyed a nearby group of women who lived near the east wall and gathered every afternoon to drink honey wine, boast about their children and complain about their husbands. They angrily shouted to the bell ringer to keep quiet. Startled, he dropped the bell rope. Then he remembered his duty and rang again. Longer. Louder.

Minutes later a second alarm bell had sounded from the south entrance.

Meanwhile, those who were nearest to the main gate had hurried to close and bar the heavy timber doors. Just before they shut tight, one of the men got a glimpse of what was approaching. He whirled around and ran through the city, bellowing at the top of his lungs, "The barbarians are coming! A whole army of them!"

This was the warning that alerted Esoros.

The remaining inhabitants of Viroconium soon poured into the streets. Men—and not a few women—snatched up whatever weapons they could find. Men and boys seized hunting spears and garden pitchforks; they pried stones from the cobbled streets to use as missiles. Women who once had bathed in asses' milk and anointed their flesh with oil of roses now drew the silver bodkins from their hair and prepared to do battle. They were Britons; they were Celts.

Leaning heavily on his steward's arm, Vintrex followed his son out of the house. Although his residence was a fashionable distance away from any of the gates, he could hear the roar of the crowd. Buoyed on a rising tide of belligerence. Inciting each other to combat. They were Britons; they were Celts!

There just were not enough of them.

Cadogan realized this as they entered the via principalis, the wide avenue that ran from the forum to the main gate. Some of the would-be defenders had turned around already and were heading back, looking frightened. It did not take long to discover the reason.

A mighty boom of thunder reverberated through Viroconium. Cadogan glanced upward. The clear sky was a cold winter blue.

"Battering ram," Vintrex said through tight lips. His voice did not sound like his own. Cadogan had never seen fear on his father's face before but there it was, clearly limned in every feature.

"What should we do, my lord?"

Vintrex did not answer Esoros. Instead he threw back his head and began marching toward the gate as if he thought he could turn back the others through sheer willpower. After a startled pause, his steward and his son went with him.

Dinas never goes anywhere without a sword, Cadogan recalled. What a good idea. Why didn't I think of it?

Too late now.

The men who were running away parted like a river to let the chief magistrate through. A few even turned to follow him. As they neared the eastern gate a second thunderous crash announced the mighty force pounding them from outside. The oak timbers bulged inward slightly; the massive crossbeam creaked, but did not give. A cry went up from the townspeople. Part anger, part despair.

Vintrex felt the assault on Viroconium as an assault on himself; an attack he personally could not hope to repel. But if he was going to go down he would go down fighting. He squared his shoulders and raised one fist in a defiant gesture.

In that moment Cadogan was proud of his father. He reached to put an arm around the bravely squared shoulders.

"Sounds like they're climbing the poxy walls!" cried Esoros, abandoning his efforts at formal diction. "Where'd those shitholes get any poxy ladders?"

"In the same place they found timber for a battering ram," Vintrex said testily. "Even my fool of a son knows how to fell a tree."

Cadogan's arm dropped to his side.

Recovering himself, Esoros urged Vintrex, "You must take shelter, my lord. They'll be on us in another minute."

Cadogan said, "Can we hide him below the floor?"

"With the furnace?" said Esoros. "No, it is winter now and far too hot down there for an old man."

"Who are you calling an old man!" Vintrex demanded.

The invaders began dropping down inside the wall.

Vintrex cried out in horror, "Saxons!"

Cadogan saw a swarm of thickset figures, taller than the Romans but shorter than the average Briton. Some of the Germanic marauders wore bronze helmets with noseguards and cheek pieces. All had full beards, though none was dyed purple. Absurdly, Cadogan thought, I should tell Quartilla—then realized she was still back at the house. With the Saxons coming.

Cadogan flung his arms around his father and tried to drag him away from the gates. With the aid of Esoros he got the old man moving, though every step was a struggle.

"I know he looks frail," panted the steward, "but my lord is really as strong as an ox."

"I believe you," Cadogan said through gritted teeth.

"Let me go!" cried Vintrex. Squirming, kicking, almost sobbing. "You must let me go!"

"To die? No, Father, we're taking you home."

When the first scream rang out Cadogan scooped Vintrex up into his arms and ran. He was surprised that he was not frightened. His brain was functioning coolly; analytically. Later he might feel fear, but for now he could trust himself to do what had to be done. That meant getting back to the house, gathering up all possible weapons, putting the women in the safest place and barricading . . .

The roar behind them mounted in intensity. There was more screaming, then the terrifying crash of gates made of solid British oak finally giving way. If they can climb over the walls, Cadogan asked himself, why do they need to break down the gates?

He and Esoros were not the only people who were running; everyone was running now. The inhabitants of Viroconium fled like rats being pursued by the cats from the forum. The Saxons pounded after them, whooping and laughing. Laughing! For some reason that added to Cadogan's anger.

"Let me go!" Vintrex was still shouting. "I can stop them!"

Lucius Plautius would say he was delusional. Dinas would say he was mad. They would both be right.

As they advanced into the city groups of Saxons broke off from the main party. Rampaging mindlessly, they began trampling gardens and ripping up small trees; kicking dogs who ran out to bark at them and knocking down any unfortunate child who got in their way. Like a river that had burst its banks, they raged without reason.

Others had a reason. With wooden cudgels and iron bars brought for the purpose, they forced their way into private houses and public buildings and began carrying out loot. Their reason for breaking down the gates quickly became clear. The Saxons had large carts on wooden wheels, some drawn by oxen, others pulled by themselves. As soon as the gates were open the invaders brought their carts into the city and began loading them up. They showed no discrimination in their choice of objects to steal. If they could carry it, they took it. If they could not carry it, they smashed it. Furniture, rugs, tools, even marble statuary were piled into the carts with reckless abandon.

A torch was put to the first of the plundered buildings.

The angry shouts of men and frantic shrieks of women filled the air.

Vintrex was muttering something. Cadogan tried to hear him. "What, Father?"

"Vandals, they are like the Vandals. They are not human, they are insane with the lust to destroy. The Angles were never . . ."

Cadogan shook his head and stopped listening. This was no time to discuss the differences in barbarian tribes; only time to run, to try to survive. He felt the responsibility for his father as a great weight on his shoulders. Yet also—and for the first time in his memory—as infinitely precious.

A large group of Saxons were gaining on them, howling like hounds out for blood. Esoros abruptly ducked into a narrow laneway at right angles to the avenue and Cadogan followed him, thankful to leave the via principalis. When the steward made an abrupt left turn Cadogan stayed close behind. It sounded like some of the Saxons had come after them, but he did not look around. Running with Vintrex in his arms took everything he had.

"Follow me!" Esoros called as he led the way into a veritable labyrinth of squalid alleys whose geography was unfamiliar to Cadogan. This was the realm of slaves: the man-made circulatory system

designed to maintain the less attractive functions of the city. Here
the sun never shone. A permanent twilight existed.

After a few minutes Esoros ducked under a low brick archway
into an alley littered with rubbish and bounded on both sides by a
high concrete wall. There were small drifts of dirty snow in the corners but the center of the unpaved alley was clear. Following the
steward's example, Cadogan slowed to a walk. The alley smelled as
if something had died there recently. Cadogan glanced down at the
man in his arms. Vintrex wrinkled his nose in disgust but said nothing. His face was livid.

They came to a long, low, tile-roofed building. The windows
and doors were boarded up and lime-washed plaster was flaking off
the brick walls, but Cadogan recognized something familiar about
the architecture.

At the far end of the building the alley opened onto a service
yard traversed by covered tile drains of varying sizes. On either side
of the drains were sunken, brick-lined pits. A distinct odor of decay
emanated from the pits in spite of their heavy wooden covers.

Setting Vintrex unsteadily on his feet, Cadogan asked, "Do you
know where you are, Father?"

"The bowels of Hades," the old man replied.

"I think this is the servants' wing of the house of Ocellus,"
Cadogan said, glancing at Esoros for confirmation. The steward
nodded.

Vintrex balked like a mule. "You cannot drag me in there, I will
never go into *that* house again!"

The Saxon roar was closer now; not in the alley but on the other
side of the wall. Very near indeed; then going past; going on
toward . . .

"My house! We must protect my house, Esoros!" cried Vintrex.
He bolted in that direction.

And Cadogan hit him. Hit him squarely on the jaw with enough
force to render the old man unconscious.

Esoros gasped. "What have you done?"

"Saved his life, I hope," said Cadogan. "Remove that cover over there and help me put him in the pit."

"You cannot put my lord in . . ."

"I can and will, whether you help me or not. It's one place the Saxons will never look for him."

The expression on the steward's face said more plainly than any words: I do not condone this and am no part of it. Yet he helped Cadogan double up the unconscious Vintrex and lower him gently into the pit. There he lay on a bed of decomposed vegetable matter and animal bones while the two men replaced the heavy wooden lid.

"Pull it slightly toward you," Cadogan told Esoros, "to let in some air. Not too far . . . that's better."

"What if my lord comes to and tries to get out?"

"He's not strong enough to lift the lid from the inside," Cadogan said. Hoping it was true. "Don't worry, I'll come back and get him as soon as we have his house secured. Am I right in assuming we're not far from there now?"

"Of course," Esoros replied huffily. "Why do you think I came this way?"

The two men continued down the alley, walking as silently as possible. In near darkness Cadogan tried to avoid the pipes beneath his feet but they did not seem to be a problem. "Just a little farther," Esoros muttered. Then, "Here . . ."

And there they were. At a brick wall twelve feet high, sealing off the alley. A ledge of snow topped the wall. At its foot was a pile of rubble left by the builders.

From the other side of the wall came a muted roar of Saxons.

Vintrex awoke with the worst headache of his life—and he was prone to headaches. He lay very still, trying to locate the source of the agonizing throb. Temples? Forehead? No. The pain was emanating from his jaw. Strange; he never had a headache in his jaw before.

Nor had he ever experienced a dream like the one he just endured.

He had dreamed he was being folded up like a woman's handker-chief and put into a box. Demeaning! He attempted to stretch his legs to prove that he was not in a box. With a jolt of alarm, he dis-covered he could not extend his legs.

His eyes snapped open in darkness. Not quite darkness; there was a triangular sliver of light somewhere above his head. When he reached out with his hands he felt, at arm's length, a curving sur-face of disgustingly slimy bricks. And what was this underneath him?

Bones!!!

Vintrex screamed.

"You've led us into a trap," Cadogan growled at Esoros.

The steward remained calm. "Not a trap, merely a slight diffi-culty. Shortly after his brother left Viroconium my lord had this wall erected between their insulae, though he was careful not to close off any drains."

"I don't understand."

"The wall was built over the sewer," Esoros explained. "You could not be expected to know that, Lord Cadogan. The houses in the theater district have their own sewer system."

Esoros searched through the snow-covered rubble until he found a large brick. Lying prone on the ground at the foot of the wall, he pounded on the earth with his brick until something under the shal-low layer of soil broke with a loud crack. The steward pounded some more, then got to his feet and began stamping on the ground. A hole the size of a man's head opened in the earth, the sides collaps-ing downward. By scuttling in the dirt like a hen giving itself a dust bath, Esoros soon was able to crawl inside. He disappeared under the wall. "Follow me!" he urged, his voice echoing strangely.

Cadogan crossed himself and cast a wild glance around. Hoping for a miracle.

There was no miracle, nothing to do but follow Esoros. Drawing a deep breath, Cadogan tried to squirm through the hole the steward had opened. It was too narrow for his wide shoulders.

"I can't make it, I'll get stuck," he called in an urgent whisper.

"Come or I'll leave you," the answer floated back.

Cadogan pawed frantically at the earth until he had enlarged the hole sufficiently to force his body through. He dropped head first into a large concrete sewer with a stream of viscous liquid running through the bottom. The smell was nauseating. Ahead he could dimly see the soles of the steward's feet.

"How do you know so much about sewers?" Cadogan wanted to know.

Esoros responded with a noise that might have been a laugh or a death rattle; an eerie sound that reverberated weirdly in the narrow confines. "When I was a boy," he said, grunting as he propelled himself forward with knees and elbows, "My job was . . . unh . . . cleaning drains. Small slaves are forced to crawl through them . . . unh . . . to keep them open." He paused to catch his breath. "That was the life your father rescued me from."

From somewhere behind Cadogan, a creature squealed. A shrill, malevolent sound, quickly answered by a second squeal. Then another, up ahead.

A living body slithered over one of Cadogan's legs. With an exclamation of disgust, he drew both legs under him and reached back to flail the air with his hand.

Something bit him. The pain was sharp and sudden; the astonishment lasted longer. "There are rats in here!" he cried out.

Esoros made that odd sound again. "Of course there are rats in here, this is a highway for rats. And slaves. Hurry up."

The presence of the rats added considerable momentum to Cadogan's efforts. As he crawled forward the stinking murk at the bottom was getting deeper. Wherever he put a hand he touched something slimy. Mud, feces, small dead animals. He was thankful that it was too dark to see anything clearly.

"Is the tunnel getting higher, Esoros?"

"It is."

"Why?"

"Ask the Romans," said the steward. "They were the only ones who really understood the drainage system. Can you see some light up ahead? That's at the inflow from your house. Your father's house," he corrected. "We just might be able to reach the laundry room in the servants' wing before they see us."

The steward's choice of words was chilling. Esoros spoke as if he knew the Saxons were already in the house.

CHAPTER FOURTEEN

Knowing that Cadogan disapproved of his idea—and perhaps of Dinas himself—Dinas still could not stop thinking about his cousin. He mentally made and remade his plans, always beginning with one more visit to Cadogan. He must persuade his cousin to help him whether he approved or not. The sort of practical mind Cadogan possessed was essential if the undertaking was to succeed.

Dinas wanted to make another visit to Viroconium as well. Much depended on what Vintrex had done. He was desperate to know—and dreaded knowing.

In unguarded moments Saba glimpsed the darkness lurking in his eyes. She wondered if he was frightened of the task he had set himself. The idea was so unlike him. Dinas was a man who cherished his freedom, who never wanted to be tied down. What could have prompted his sudden desire for kingship and all the responsibilities that went with it?

There was something else going on here, Saba decided; the unidentified problem he needed to think about. She would leave it up to him to tell her of his own volition. Their relationship was defined by the questions they did not ask each other.

Meanwhile she was enjoying her unexpected guests. They were totally unlike Dinas—and unlike each other—yet the three of them together reminded her of a three-legged stool, with each leg providing its share of the balance. Was that why Dinas had chosen the other two to be his companions?

Probably not. The Dinas she knew had always been a totally physical man, not given to analyzing himself or anyone else. Saba's intense inner life was the reason she lived alone with her dogs and her flock. Dinas had bounded into her life like a force of nature, a storm that swept over her from time to time and moved on, leaving her to her own contemplative nature. From the start he had recognized the rebel in Saba that had alienated her from her tribe. Yet he had never explored the reasons for her rebellion.

Seeing Dinas in the company of other men gave him a new dimension in Saba's eyes. With Meradoc he exhibited an almost paternal pride. The little man possessed an uncanny intelligence, not in his head but in his fingers. Anything he could touch, could hold, he could understand and repair or duplicate. By the time he had been with Saba for a few days everything in her house that needed mending was as good as new. He then turned his attention to her lambing shed and sheepfold.

When she tried to thank him he was so embarrassed he squirmed.

"The only fault I can find with your friend Meradoc," she told Dinas, "is the way he has seduced my dogs away from me. They still herd my sheep but when we come inside they lie down at his feet instead of mine."

Dinas laughed. "Let me tell you about my horse . . ."

Saba liked Meradoc but Pelemos intrigued her. He was undoubtedly male and exceptionally strong; using her axe, he cut a year's supply of firewood in a matter of days. Yet when she bathed her face and breasts in front of the fire he looked away. Should she try to lift a heavy object he insisted on doing it himself. If the snow was blowing hard enough to reduce visibility to a dangerous level and they used the night jar instead of going outside to relieve themselves, Pelemos tactfully retired to the loft while Saba used the jar.

Strangely enough, Dinas was less impatient and more polite when Pelemos was around. He told Saba, "I have a theory about Pelemos. I think he was a prince who was stolen by a devil and turned into a farmer."

She smiled, humoring him. "Are there such things? Devils, I mean?"

"If people can believe in gods they can believe in devils," said Dinas.

Most people never knew whether Dinas was being serious or not. Saba liked to think that she always knew.

She began to dread the passing of days that would take the three men away from her. She who welcomed every change of light, every fallen leaf or springing bud, closed her eyes to the heralds of the season. She tried to imagine the cabin as a bubble outside of time, holding the four of them warm and safe inside.

Some of the old people knew rituals that could control time. Half-forgotten stories were handed down from generation to generation; stories ignored by Saba's small self, the youngest child of a loud and boisterous family that had quarried slate in the mountains since before the before. The thoughtful little girl who hated noise and loathed everything to do with cutting stone, but preferred to play quietly in a corner and be left alone.

"Dinas said you are something of a storyteller, Pelemos. Is that true?"

"I just repeat what I remember from my childhood."

"That's exactly what I mean, Pelemos. Could you tell me some of those . . . memories . . . of yours? Perhaps in the evening, when we've finished the day's work?"

Pelemos was flattered by the request but afraid he could not live up to her expectations. The title of storyteller was, in the Celtic culture, the equal of a prince. "I'm only a farmer," he confided to Meradoc.

"Farmers can tell stories, all sorts of people can tell stories," Meradoc replied, thinking of Ludno and his pompous recitals.

"Can you? What tales did you learn from your parents?"

"None, I'm afraid. I never knew my parents; my earliest memories are of carrying water and emptying slops for people in Deva."

"Who raised you then?"

Meradoc cocked his head, considering. "I suppose I raised myself." The little man brightened. "But I once had a friend who was a cat."

"Cats are for catching rats."

Meradoc looked disgusted. "You say that because you think like a farmer with a store of grain to protect. But I tell you cats are for cats, just as Dinas said the stars are stars. Their purpose is simply to *be,* Pelemos. Cats and stars don't belong to us."

"What about horses, then?"

A dreamy look suffused Meradoc's face. "Horses belong to the gods."

"I thought you were a Christian."

"I am. But I believe in a lot of things."

"Either you're a Christian or a pagan," Pelemos said. "There are no other choices."

Meradoc, who was realizing that living involved innumerable choices, did not reply.

When the day's work was done and the bowls were scoured clean, they gathered in front of the fire to hear Pelemos tell a story. At first he was painfully self-conscious. Dinas and Meradoc had heard him before, but Saba was different. He felt as if he stood naked before her.

"Go on," Saba urged. "We're waiting."

Pelemos drew a deep breath and began to tell a tale.

About a place called Albion.

With the telling his confidence grew, until every word came sure and strong. There was a familiarity about them, as if they were permanently carved in his mind. The story developed its own momentum. Soon he was able to glance at his audience and gauge their reactions without losing the thread of the tale.

Sitting on the floor with his arms wrapped around his knees, Meradoc was listening with the openmouthed wonder of a child. For him, Pelemos included a magical cat in the story and made it seem absolutely real.

Dinas had been too distracted at first to settle down and listen, but finally was drawn in by a tumultuous battle fought between heroes. He dropped onto a stool, stretched his long legs in front of him and lost himself in deeds of high valor.

As for Saba, she watched Pelemos with intense concentration, as if she expected to hear a special word or phrase that would transform her life.

I am an ordinary man telling a story he once heard, Pelemos thought sadly. I cannot give you anything special, Saba. And you deserve something special.

He glanced at Dinas; measured the lean dark man as he had never measured him before.

If my daughters were still alive and old enough to marry would I give one of them to Dinas? What do I know of him? He rescued me, but was that a blessing? He has an education, but is that a good thing? He is wild and unpredictable. Is that a bad thing? Ithill said we should not judge other people.

When Pelemos thought of Ithill a light came into his face. He seemed to blaze from within.

Dinas straightened up on his stool. Stories! he exclaimed to himself with a sense of discovery. A man who can get people to listen to his stories will have them in the palm of his hand. I really must get that white horse for Pelemos. In the spring, when we leave here and everything begins.

CHAPTER FIFTEEN

In the cold sewer behind his father's house Cadogan was trying to pray. But the words would not come. What is an appropriate prayer for a man stuck in a sewer, anyway?

He felt an absurd desire to giggle.

"Esoros, are you sure you know what you're doing?"

"Yes, Lord Cadogan. There is a hatch here somewhere . . . ah, here it is. But . . . unh . . . it seems to be jammed. Squeeze in here beside me and help me push."

There was a time in his life—it seemed very long ago—when Cadogan would have been furious at a servant daring to give him an order. Now he simply wriggled and pushed until he was wedged into the pipe beside Esoros, and the two men put their shoulders to the hatch together. One heave. Nothing. A second. Possibly a fractional movement? On the third try a superhuman effort yielded a grudging response, and the iron hatch gave way, releasing a pent-up flood of dirty water.

Esoros said angrily, "How long has it been since anyone flushed out the washing tubs! I'll have to have a word with . . . Here, Cadogan, give me your hand." An iron grip closed around Cadogan's wrist and the steward gave a powerful grunt.

Moments later Cadogan was flopping around on a wet concrete floor like a fish out of water. "*Lord* Cadogan, if you please," he growled under his breath.

As the two men scrambled to their feet they could hear cries of distress coming from somewhere in the main body of the house. Cadogan gazed around in search of something he could use as a weapon.

The laundry was a dingy concrete cubicle with one small window and one closed door. Water was piped down from a cistern on the roof and heated in a copper cauldron over a brazier. Three deep stone tubs were set into the floor. In order to do the washing the servants had to kneel on bare concrete. Hanging on the wall above the tubs were wooden mallets of various sizes for pummeling the wet fabric, and a washboard for scrubbing it.

A mallet was the obvious choice, but Cadogan reached for the washboard first. Almost as long as his arm and studded with bronze bosses like a warrior's shield. Taking a mallet in his other hand, Cadogan pressed his ear to the door.

"What do you hear?" Esoros asked.

"Nothing now. It's all gone quiet."

"Is that good or bad?"

"How do I know, I can't see through the door. We'll have to go farther into the house, Esoros."

"I'm right behind you."

"You're going to be right beside me," Cadogan contradicted, "so you'd better grab a mallet."

"I'm not a warrior."

"Then try to learn fast. Let's go." Cadogan opened the door.

He stepped into a narrow service corridor almost as alien to him as the sewer. Walls and ceiling were unpainted. The concrete on the floor had been mixed with gravel to keep feet from slipping. Shallow shelves of roughly finished wood lined one side, while rusting tools and a tangle of worn leather sandals cluttered the floor. There was no window, only a distinct smell of mildew. At the end of the corridor a partially open door revealed a glimpse of the kitchen.

There would be knives in the kitchen.

Esoros had the same thought. They raced toward the open door but Cadogan reached it first, to find his progress abruptly halted by the appearance of a man brandishing an axe.

They stared in surprise at each other.

It was Cadogan's first close look at a Saxon warrior. He saw strong, florid features and a dirty blond beard that did not conceal a bull-like neck. Meaty shoulders sloped into powerful arms. A filthy outer coat made of bearskin was tightly strapped over a massive chest. Beneath this the raider wore a longer woolen undercoat and leggings that reached only to midcalf, skimming the tops of enormous boots. The overall impression was of a figure only slightly less formidable than a walking oak tree.

Cadogan took a hasty step backward, trampling on the toes of Esoros.

The steward yelped with pain.

The Saxon had not realized anyone else was with Cadogan. He stepped sideways, trying to get a look at the man who cried out. In that moment Cadogan darted past him and into the kitchen.

The kitchen was another unfamiliar territory. Most of the cooking was done on a gridiron over a charcoal fire kindled on a raised concrete platform. Shelves adjacent to the platform held an assortment of metal pots and pans, pottery jars and pitchers, a mortar and pestle, pastry cutters and a scale. In the center of the room was an oblong worktable whose deeply scored surface showed that it was used for carving. But there were no knives on the table or anywhere else, as far as Cadogan could see.

Two wooden cupboards stood against the opposite wall. Between them was a tall bread safe on legs. The bread safe was equipped with a slotted bottom to allow air to reach the loaves and prevent mold. Below this, a pair of shuttered doors fronted a large storage compartment for sacks of flour and meal.

No knives there either.

While Cadogan scanned the room the Saxon had his hands full with Esoros. The steward fought from a combination of fear and fury. Shouting profanities never heard in the front part of the house, he kicked and bit and struck out blindly with both fists. When all else failed to move the obstacle in his path he lowered his head and butted the Saxon in the midriff. The man exhaled a great "Whooof!" and sat down suddenly.

Something touched Cadogan's leg. He gave a start and glanced down. The shuttered doors at the bottom of the bread safe were ajar, and a hand was reaching out with a knife. Holding the knife up to him.

"Sssssst!" a voice hissed from within the cabinet. "Take this!"

He dropped the washboard, seized the knife, and plunged it into the back of the Saxon with an alacrity that surprised himself.

Cadogan had never stabbed a man. It was not as easy as he expected. The knife did not slide into the man's back like cutting into roasted meat; powerful living muscle was more resistant. The tip of the blade barely entered the skin. Cadogan put all his weight behind it and pushed, until he forced the knife into the flesh between the shoulder blades. The Saxon gave a mighty roar. Whirling around, he reached over his shoulder in a vain effort to grab the knife hilt.

Esoros seized the opportunity to close his hands around the Saxon's thick throat.

Locked together in mortal combat, the three men lurched across the kitchen. Crashing into the table and reducing it to splinters. Knocking over cabinets to an accompanying clatter of broken dishes. Grunting, cursing, sweating. When the combatants caromed into the bread safe it swayed dangerously, but remained upright. Blood sprayed everywhere as Cadogan plunged the knife again and again into whatever part of the man's anatomy he could reach, while Esoros held on like a dog at a bearbaiting and throttled him. It took both of them to kill him.

When the strength finally went out of the Saxon he fell facedown on the floor and did not move again. Gasping for breath, Esoros slumped on the floor beside him. Cadogan bent to feel for the pulse in the Saxon's neck but there was none. The man had died like a wild boar at the end of a long and cruel hunt, surrendering to a welcome death.

The wrecked kitchen looked like a slaughterhouse.

"I suppose you expect me to clean this up," said an irritable voice. Wrapped in a cloak that once belonged to Cadogan's mother, Quartilla scrambled out from the bottom of the bread safe.

"I've never been happier to see anyone," Cadogan said shakily. "You saved our lives."

She gave a sniff. "See that you remember it. Where did you come from, anyway?" She took another, deeper sniff. "You smell like a cesspit!"

"That's how we got in; through the sewer. How many Saxons are in the house?"

"I don't know, when they broke down the front door I ran here and hid."

Esoros said, "Did you bring anyone else with you?"

"Why should I? I knew there was only enough room in the bread safe for me."

"We had best go out there," Cadogan said reluctantly, "and see what's happening."

Esoros replied, "I do not think anything is happening. Listen."

All three listened. They heard nothing.

"That could be very good or very bad," Cadogan remarked. Bending over, he picked up the Saxon axe and hefted it experimentally. It was heavier than it looked, but well balanced and satisfying in its implicit cruelty. At that moment Cadogan felt like being cruel.

"Aren't you forgetting something?"

"What, Quartilla?"

"Your shield," she said mockingly as she handed him the washboard.

He took it.

"Stay here," Esoros told the woman as he opened the door leading to the main part of the house.

"I'll do no such thing! Why should I hide when I have two strong men to protect me? I'm going with you. Hurry up now." She gave Cadogan a shove that propelled him forward through the doorway.

They entered a corridor wide enough to allow two servants at a time to carry large trays. The walls were painted in lemon yellow to make the space brighter. A thick mat of woven grass silenced footsteps. Cadogan strained to hear any sound from the rooms ahead. There was none.

Is it a trap? Are the Saxons lying in wait? That doesn't seem likely, there's nothing subtle about their mode of attack. But still . . . I wish we had Dinas with us right now. He has an instinct for this sort of thing.

One careful step at a time, the three made their way toward the dining room. They entered through a small anteroom used for last-minute preparations. The only visible damage was a broken serving dish on the floor. "Perhaps we have been lucky?" Esoros suggested hopefully.

"We heard screaming," Cadogan reminded him.

The scene in the dining room was shocking. The invaders had overturned the marble banquet table, broken two of its carved pediments and hacked and slashed the surrounding couches. Velvet elbow cushions were ripped open, spilling their coiled woolen stuffing like intestines. The tapestry wall hangings that Vintrex had given Domitia as a wedding gift had been ripped from the walls and trampled underfoot. Anything of value was either destroyed or gone. But there were still no bodies; no blood.

Cadogan had a sinking feeling in the pit of his stomach.

The hall was next. Here they found what he had feared. The two old servant women lay in a single bloody heap with their heads bashed in.

Quartilla cried out involuntarily, then put her hand over her mouth.

The beautiful room, once Domitia's pride and joy, testified to the extent of Saxon violence. The smaller items, including the basket chair, were missing. The statues had been pulled from their niches and carried away, and someone had tried to hack the painted frieze from the walls with an axe. Everything remaining in the room had been battered to pieces.

There was human excrement on the floor. The whole room stank of it.

God alone knows what the Saxons eat, Cadogan thought in disgust. "Where's the other one, Esoros?"

"What other one?"

"The other house servant."

"That young one? Maybe she's hiding somewhere."

"You can look for her while I go back for my father."

"Are you going to bring Vintrex here?" asked Quartilla.

"This house is probably safe for now. They've finished with it and moved on."

"How can you be certain they won't come back?"

Cadogan gestured at the wreckage. "What for? You stay here with Esoros while I—"

"I'm going with you," Quartilla insisted.

"No, you are not," said Esoros. "You heard Lord Cadogan. We must obey his orders."

"I'm going with him!!!!" the woman screeched.

Esoros looked to Cadogan, who merely shook his head. "We might as well let her, she does what she likes anyway. But if you get killed, Quartilla, I won't bury you."

"Then I will not stay here either," the steward announced. "My place is with my lord Vintrex."

Cadogan gave a sigh. "I won't bury you, either."

The trio left the house by the servants' exit near the stables. Cadogan was glad they would not have to attempt the ghastly journey through the sewer again; there was no need. When they stepped outside cries and screams from the distance told them the Saxons had indeed moved on.

Once again Esoros, knowledgeable about the back ways of Viroconium, took the lead. Quartilla seized Cadogan's arm and clung like a limpet when he tried to shake her off.

They followed a circuitous route that led them through Domitia's medicinal herb garden, now gone to seed and weed, and into a fruit orchard belonging to a neighbor. They saw neither the neighbors nor their servants. Cadogan's little party reached the cobbled street and made their way to the former home of Ocellus without encountering any Saxons, either, though they could track the barbarians' progress by the tumult of their passing.

"They have entered the artisans' district," Esoros commented.

"Not much plunder there," said Cadogan. "Tinsmiths and potters."

"And jewelry!" Quartilla added enthusiastically. A moment later she released his arm. "Who lives in this big house, Cadogan?"

"Dinas did, for one. No, don't try to enter, we must go around to the back for my father."

"What's he doing there?"

"Sitting in a pot," said Cadogan.

The service yard was just as they had left it, with no sign of life. Cadogan was afraid Vintrex might have smothered or had a heart attack. He ran to tug at the heavy wooden lid. When he had displaced it enough to see inside, he discovered Vintrex glaring up at him. "As soon as I find a quill and something to write on I'm disinheriting you."

"You already did, Father," Cadogan reminded him. "Let's get you out of here now."

This proved more difficult than putting him in. Vintrex refused to help in the slightest, becoming a dead weight. The two men had to crouch down and haul him out by the shoulders. Cadogan muttered, "This must be what it's like to wash linen in a sunken tub."

"I would not know," Esoros replied stiffly. "I do not do laundry."

When they set Vintrex on his feet he began asking questions and making demands. Where were the invaders, who was watching the house, bring him a cup of beer at once, someone must fetch his heavy cloak. He was as authoritarian as ever though somewhat confused. Cadogan tried to reassure him. "Everything's all right, Father, we're going to take you home now. I'm sure we can find writing materials there."

"I'm not so sure," Esoros said, pointing. "Look."

Pale smoke was rising above the wall separating the two properties.

"My house!" groaned Vintrex.

"We left it only a little while ago," said Quartilla, "and nothing was burning then."

"We didn't see anything burning," Cadogan amended, "but we didn't go into every room. The raiders might have broken an oil lamp or else deliberately . . ." His throat closed, choking off his words. Stone walls might survive a fire, but he realized that the wooden interior of the house would burn.

Vintrex had the same thought. He made a wild lunge toward the wall he could never hope to climb, and almost tumbled into the gaping hole at its foot.

Esoros and Cadogan dragged him back.

The smoke visible above the wall was beginning to turn dark. Caught by a rising wind, it twisted in the air like a living being.

"We must leave here now," Cadogan urged. "If the flames spread, all the houses in this district could go. Perhaps that's what they want. They may be setting fire to the city; remember that the barbarians burned Rome."

"The public bathhouse won't burn," said Quartilla.

"What?"

"Is it not built of marble? And Roman concrete? With pools full of water and more water in reservoirs on the roof? Once we're inside the Saxons can set all the fires they like, but they'll only scorch the outside. We'll be safer there than anywhere else if we barricade the doors. They're made of bronze; they won't burn either."

Cadogan and Esoros exchanged glances. Sounding dubious, the steward said, "There is only the one entrance, through the courtyard. We could be trapped like rats."

"Nonsense," Quartilla retorted. "The public baths need a lot of servants, don't they? You know better than anyone that servants always have their own secret ways in and out."

"Like sewers," Cadogan said drily. "The baths it is, then. Come on, Esoros, give me a hand with my father."

The two men caught the protesting Vintrex under the shoulders again and began to run, closely followed by Quartilla. Avoiding any of the paved streets, Esoros guided the way through a different set of narrow lanes and alleyways. They came out near the public baths opposite the forum.

Only Quartilla looked back. Only Quartilla saw the smoke rising, thickening, billowing.

Built in the third century, the baths of Viroconium were considered a model of their kind. Entrance was through a large domed hall resembling the basilica of the forum. Once a client had paid the entrance fee he could sit in the hall for as long as he liked, watching young men boxing or wrestling, and being served refreshing drinks by solicitous attendants. Nothing was regimented; ease and luxury were the keynotes.

From the hall one entered the apodyterium, an antechamber where the clothes were removed by more attendants, shaken out, aired and cleaned if necessary. The room was lit by torches in wall sconces that revealed the full beauty of tile mosaics depicting a variety of sports. After the apodyterium came the frigidarium, where surface dirt was washed off with cold water. This was followed by the tepidarium and a second sponging with warm water, and then on to the caldarium, or hot room, where pores opened in the steamy atmosphere. Any deeply ingrained dirt was washed away by a flood of perspiration. The sweat was scraped off with an instrument called a strigil before the bather immersed himself—a separate sequence of rooms was provided for women—in one of several deep pools of hot water.

Afterward bathers retraced their footsteps until they reached the frigidarium to close their pores and be rubbed down with perfumed oils. The entire process usually was accompanied by conversation with friends, an exchange of spicy gossip, and music both vocal and instrumental.

When Cadogan's little group arrived there was no music; nothing but a babble of anxious voices. Quartilla was not the only person in the city who thought quickly in times of stress and seized upon the most probable sanctuary. A score of men and women, a few with children, already had gathered in the entrance hall. Cadogan recognized most of them as neighbors and acquaintances, people familiar with the amenities of the bathhouse.

When they saw Vintrex they rushed toward him, calling him by name and demanding that he do something. Cadogan struggled to keep them from overwhelming the magistrate. "Please, my friends, can't you see that my father is ill? Please step back, give him some air."

In their panic, no one was listening.

Quartilla drew a deep breath, opened her mouth to its fullest extent, and unloosed loose an ear-shattering scream that echoed around the dome of the hall like a summons from Hades.

The shocked crowd fell back.

Cadogan and Esoros hustled Vintrex into the apodyterium and sat him down on a bench.

It was almost twilight on a winter's day. Yet a lurid glow was growing in the sky to the east.

CHAPTER SIXTEEN

The atmosphere in the public bathhouse was permanently damp. A small army of slaves was dedicated to the ceaseless battle against mold and mildew. The warm rooms were vaulted with concrete rather than timbers as a precaution against steam. Hot air from the furnaces below the floors was circulated through flues lined with tile, while the furnaces themselves were safely ensconced in chambers carved from the living rock.

Quartilla was right; the baths would not burn.

Cadogan recruited several men to help him and Esoros seal the main entrance and ransack the surrounding chambers until they had a mountain of tables and benches to barricade the two massive doors. "If the Saxons try this they'll soon give up," Cadogan said with an assurance he did not quite feel. "They're ignorant barbarians; they'll go for the easier targets."

Seated on a bench in the apodyterium, under the watchful marble eyes of the goddess Fortuna, Vintrex began to shiver violently. The other refugees milled about the chamber like a herd of spooked horses ready to bolt.

"Fools," Quartilla commented. She gathered an armload of towels from the nearest table and wrapped them around Vintrex.

The old man looked up at his son. "My house," he said plaintively.

"I know, Father, but don't think about it now. Lives are more important than houses."

"Are they going to slaughter us all?" In his unwonted vulnerability Vintrex sounded almost childlike. Cadogan had an urge to put his arms around the old man but restrained himself. He knew his father. When the danger was over Vintrex would never forgive him for taking advantage of a moment of weakness.

"No, Father, they're not going to slaughter us," Cadogan said reassuringly. "I doubt if they'll even try to break in. A public bathhouse isn't much of a target for looting, not with so many wealthy houses in the area. But in case the fire comes close to this building, I'm going to take you to one of the pools as a precaution against the heat from outside."

Esoros hesitated. "I really do not think we should move from here. Let us take a little time and think about this. Perhaps . . ."

"Don't be an idiot," Quartilla said sharply. "At least Cadogan has a plan and that's what's needed. I'm with him. You will be too, if you have any brain at all."

Esoros was not immune to her insulting remarks; every one of them was marked and remembered. But this was no time for reprisals. "I'm coming," he decided. "Lead the way, Lord Cadogan."

When they left the apodyterium the light changed. Illumination in the bathing chambers was provided by oil lamps depending on chains from the ceiling. As Esoros explained to Quartilla, "In very moist air oil burns more steadily than torches."

The status Esoros enjoyed as steward to the chief magistrate allowed him access to many of the facilities the baths offered, and he was familiar with all the main areas. However, some chambers were off limits to all but the highly privileged. There were corridors he might glance down, but not follow. Esoros knew his place. As they moved through the series of bathing chambers he walked two paces behind Cadogan and Vintrex.

Quartilla walked beside them.

Most of the refugees followed, unwilling to be left behind. Their footsteps echoed hollowly on the marble floor.

Cadogan chose a room off the caldarium that contained a circular pool. He could not tell if any slaves remained below, stoking the furnaces, but the walls of the room were warm and a thin cloud of steam was rising from the water. Lamps were burning; towels were stacked on benches around the walls. Everything looked normal. Only an eerie silence argued otherwise.

The refugees hesitated at the doorway. "Come in if you like," Cadogan told them. "There's enough space here for a dozen or so."

Ten people accepted his invitation. The others, after an exchange of glances and some foot shuffling, went to seek a place elsewhere.

Cadogan padded one of the benches with towels for Vintrex and sat down beside him. The remaining benches were quickly filled by the others, including five men of varying ages. Esoros exchanged a nod of recognition with one of them, a great-limbed, ginger-haired individual in his middle years. There were also two women. One was a diminutive matron with gray hair and bony, imperious features. The other was a plump, pretty mother with three children; a boy of five or six and his little sister, plus an infant. The young mother uncovered her breast for the baby and then sat staring at the water, seeking comfort in the timeless communion.

No sound reached them from outside. Once there was something that might have been a crash in the vicinity, such as a wall falling. A slight shudder rippled the surface of the pool. Cadogan raised his head. "Esoros, do you want to go and . . ."

"No," said the steward.

Time passed without measure. People whose lives were governed by the daylight could feel the day dying; feel the night waiting. They unconsciously moved closer together.

Except for Quartilla. She took off her sandals and sat down on the wide rim of the pool, then began splashing her feet in the water. Esoros frowned. "You are a servant," he hissed at her.

"I am not," she hissed back to him. And kept on splashing.

The older woman spoke up. "This is the best place to be, otherwise the chief magistrate would not be here," she asserted. "We should give thanks for our good fortune."

"It's not my good fortune," said a paunchy man whom Cadogan

recognized as Talus, the owner of several alehouses. "I planned on going to bed with Orcadia the Dancer this evening. I was on my way to her house when those savages started burning the city."

Quartilla gave him a look. "So you rushed here to save yourself?"

"I did."

"What of Orcadia the Dancer? Did you bring her with you?"

"I . . . ah . . ."

"What of your wife then? I presume you have a wife? Did you bring her?"

Talus looked toward Cadogan. Indicating Quartilla with a jerk of his thumb, he asked, "Is this nosy bitch yours?"

"My wife?"

"Or your mistress."

"I would not have left any woman I cared about to burn to death," Cadogan retorted.

Talus bristled at the implied insult. "Magistrate! Does your son speak for you?"

With an effort Vintrex roused himself. "Of course my son speaks for me. Where is your wife, Talus?"

The small matron chimed in. "Yes, Talus, where is she? I trust you made sure of her safety before seeking refuge yourself."

Talus got to his feet and stalked out of the room.

The matron smiled, revealing prominent gums. "I apologize for not recognizing you sooner," she said to Cadogan, "but I have not seen you for years." Responding to his look of puzzlement, she added, "I am Regina Cassiodorus, the widow of Lentullus the Arbiter. Your dear mother and I were friends. What a fine figure of a man you have become! Domitia would be proud."

"Regina," Cadogan responded with a polite bow. Though he still did not recognize her.

Vintrex did. He made an effort to sit up straighter. "We have come together in difficult circumstances, Regina."

"Indeed we have, Magistrate. Perhaps it would be wise to put old animosities aside."

Vintrex sat even straighter. "You no longer blame me for Domitia's death?"

"With fresh death howling in the streets it seems futile to argue over old ones. Perhaps I was too hasty in my judgment at the time."

Vintrex's shoulders slumped again. "No, you were not. I blamed myself then and I blame myself now. But I thank you for your kind intentions, Regina."

"Then allow me to present my daughter-in-law, Pamilia, and my three grandchildren." Regina gestured toward the young woman nursing the infant. She blushed at the attention directed toward herself and hastily covered her breast. Though her pale blue eyes were unremarkable, she had a glory of light brown hair braided to form a coronet atop her head. Her little boy was darker, with a petulant mouth, but her daughter was the image of herself.

"What a beautiful family," Vintrex said gallantly. "And your two sons, Regina; what of them?"

"I wish I knew." Some of the strength faded from the woman's face. "They went to Venta Belgarum seven weeks ago to sell some property we own there, and have not yet returned. Petros left Pamilia and his children with me for safekeeping, ironic as it seems now."

"They will be safe with us," said Cadogan.

Regina responded with a tiny bow. "How very kind of you."

Their formal manners annoyed Quartilla. They spoke as if they were strolling through the forum on a lazy afternoon. "We can't be responsible for you!" she burst out.

Cadogan said, "Of course we can. Didn't you hear her? They're old friends of my family."

"She never said that. And Vintrex said she blamed him for—"

"They are friends of the family," Vintrex interrupted with as much force as he could muster. "If my son says so, they are."

Cadogan was stunned by his father's abdication of authority. If he had been worried about the old man before he was twice as worried now.

Alerted to a change in the balance of power, the four remaining men approached Cadogan. The big, ginger-haired man, who had a strong Caledonian accent, introduced himself as Godubnus the Ironmaster. Esoros studied his face, then said, "I think we've done business before . . . at the house of the chief magistrate, in fact. Remember?"

"That was some years ago," Godubnus replied. "Is my ironwork still satisfactory?"

"If it were not, you would have seen me long before this," said Esoros.

"What I make will outlive us all," Godubnus boasted. "These three men work for me. Nassos, he's from Ratae, and Karantec and Trebellos, who are Silurians." The latter explanation was unnecessary; the Silures were noted for their swarthy skins and curly locks.

"We were delivering the parts for a new furnace for the baths when the alarm sounded," Godubnus went on. "It's a big order and worth a lot of money. I knew we could never get the fully loaded wagon back to the workshop, so we drove it around behind the baths. I only hope the thieving Saxons don't find it. They'd steal my iron and eat my mules."

Cadogan told him, "They won't steal a furnace, they won't even know what one is. You could be right about the mules, though."

"I hope not," said Godubnus. "There aren't many mules left since the Romans pulled out. My team is over twenty years old but still strong. I don't know how I could replace them."

Pamilia unexpectedly spoke up. "Can you not breed more?" the young mother timidly suggested.

Nassos said, "Mules are usually sterile."

"Sterile? Barren, you mean? Why is that?"

"A mule is the offspring of a mare and an ass," Karantec told her, "and they are two very different kinds of animal. Breeding them to each other is like . . . like . . ."

"Like crossing a Celt with a Saxon," said Quartilla.

The remark provoked a ripple of nervous laughter. It ceased

abruptly when one of the lamps around the pool dimmed. No solicitous attendants were hovering nearby to replenish the oil. The night
was hovering instead.

Quartilla withdrew her feet from the pool and strapped her sandals on. "I don't want to sit here in the dark, Cadogan."

Dark.

A Stygian blackness engulfs me. Lucius Plautius would say I am
depressed. He could be right. Dinas would say there is no such thing
as depression. He could be right, but I don't think so.

I don't want to sit here in the dark either.

"Come with me, Esoros, and we'll find some lamp oil."

"Please, no stinking herring oil," Pamilia protested in her whis-
pery, diffident voice. "They must have perfumed oil here somewhere."

Since I left Viroconium I've grown used to the smell of burning
fish oil, Cadogan thought with surprise. When did that happen?

The two men began a fruitless search. They discovered the others
from the entrance hall huddled in a service chamber, gobbling re-
freshments meant for the clients of the bathhouse. In another chamber they found shelves stacked with towels and boxes of sponges, and
cabinets filled with salves and ointments. But nothing to burn in the
lamps. "They probably keep their expensive oils in the basement," said
Esoros.

"Do you know how to get down there?"

"No, Lord Cadogan. Those passageways are well concealed;
clients must never see what goes on below."

Furnace stokers were like sewer cleaners: invisible. The Romanized luxuries of Viroconium had simply appeared as if by magic.
Until now.

They returned to the pool room to discover that the walls were
cool to the touch. The water was growing cold and another lamp had
exhausted its fuel. The chamber that had been warm and welcoming
had become a place of shivers and shadows. Pamilia's exhausted
children were crying fretfully. Vintrex was huddled in the same po-

sition he had been in when Cadogan left. The face he lifted toward his son might have been the face of a dying man. "No oil?" he asked querulously.

"We couldn't find any, but it doesn't matter. We'll be safe enough here, Father, and the Saxons will be gone by morning."

"How can you be sure?"

"It stands to reason. The barbarians aren't urban, they won't stay in the city. They'll take their plunder and leave."

"Move on to their next victims, more like," said Godubnus. "With my mules in their bellies."

Regina spoke up. "Any plan is better than no plan. What we must do now is accept our situation and make ourselves comfortable for the rest of the night."

Vintrex struggled to his feet. "Allow me to assist you," he said gallantly.

The night was interminable. The dark stole the light little by little, as each exhausted lamp surrendered and died. At last the children fell asleep. From time to time the adults spoke to one another in hushed voices to be certain they were not alone. After an eternity Cadogan thought he heard footsteps outside, but they faded away. Another eternity and more footsteps. Going . . . gone . . .

Quartilla was shaking his shoulder. "Cadogan!" she said in a loud whisper. "It's light outside."

Swimming up through layers of wool. Layers of clouds. The cushion of unconsciousness. Don't want to wake up. Don't want . . . "I'm awake, Quartilla. Did you say it's light outside?"

"I did."

"How do you know?"

"You fool, I went and looked, of course. The sun's just coming up, and . . ."

He was fully awake now, skin prickling with alarm. "And what?

What else did you see?" He leaped to his feet and began adjusting his clothing.

"Wait for me," said a gruff voice as Godubnus heaved himself off a bench.

Before the two men reached the entrance hall they could smell what waited outside. Viroconium stank worse than burning fish oil. A pall of smoke hung over the city; the air was thick with ash and soot. As Cadogan and Godubnus left the bathhouse a layer of carbonized detritus crunched under their feet.

The ironmaster said, "Should we go back for the others?"

"Not until we know what we're facing," Cadogan replied grimly. "They've finally fallen asleep; let them have a few more moments of peace."

It did not take long to discover the source of the crash they had heard. In some unimaginable fashion the Saxons had succeeded in dislodging, though not fully toppling, one of the marble columns that were the pride of the civic complex. This had rendered the pediment above unstable, until the whole structure collapsed into the porch of the courthouse. The Doric capital atop the column miraculously had survived its fall and lay to one side; a thick square abacus, not as elaborate as the Corinthian style, yet beautiful in its way.

Cadogan stared down at it. "I'm surprised the barbarians didn't smash that."

"Why would they?"

"It's what they do."

The two men walked on.

Cadogan was right; the Saxons had left Viroconium—or what remained of Viroconium. But not before making the city unlivable. In some districts anything that could burn had burned. Many buildings had been reduced to scorched walls, their interiors devoured by fire. Even the precisely pruned trees in the residential insulae had been charred beyond recovery.

"I didn't realize so much of Viroconium was built of timber," Cadogan remarked. "I always thought of the city as brick and plaster."

"And iron," added Godubnus. "You'll notice that the iron posts for the streetlamps are intact. Last forever, these will." He reached out to touch one and snatched his fingers back. "It's still hot!"

The amount of debris strewn across the streets and down the laneways was appalling. At first the two men paused when they saw an intact article and picked it up—a blackened bowl, a single shoe miraculously unburned. They carried the objects for a short time and then dropped them again. There was too much and they had no idea what to do with it. Salvage must come later, if at all. On this smoke-stained morning it was all they could do to take measure of the catastrophe.

Some districts appeared to have escaped the fire but not the looting. There was no observable pattern. The Saxons had run back and forth, some dragging their carts, others attacking whatever caught their eye, wreaking havoc at one location and hardly touching the next. They had rampaged through the city like mindless animals. In their wake, the sense of order that had characterized Viroconium was totally destroyed.

Dazed survivors had begun wandering through the city. Some recognized Cadogan; spoke to him, expressed relief that he was still alive or asked about his father. Others ambled past him, blank-faced. The disaster was ongoing for them. Their morning had not yet come.

Over all lay the smell of the fire. And cooked flesh.

"There are people in those ruins," Godubnus said.

"I know."

"Should we start pulling them out?"

Cadogan shook his head. "Once we begin we'll have to keep on, and the two of us aren't enough to make a difference. First we need to organize a search team and see what conditions are like in the hospital. It's going to be . . . it's all such a . . ." He waved his hand in a helpless gesture.

But he could not afford to be helpless. He was no longer one man alone in a fort of his own construction. He was one man at the heart of an unfolding nightmare, and the only way out was through.

Cadogan turned back before they reached the house of the chief magistrate. He could not bring himself to see it yet. To see a broken smoldering ruin, with the fire's red eyes still peering balefully out from piles of rubble.

CHAPTER SEVENTEEN

In the depth of winter they celebrated the Feast of Christ's Birth in the cabin on the mountain, though Dinas did not pray. Saba filled the room with candlelight from a store of beeswax candles she had saved for the purpose. They ate roast mutton and boiled vegetables from the root cellar and sang Christian songs of joy, though Dinas did not sing. Soon Saba and Meradoc fell quiet too, content to listen to the pure, clear voice of Pelemos.

"He might almost be an angel," Meradoc whispered to Saba.

"If people can believe in devils they can believe in angels," she replied. She glanced at Dinas but he had not heard the exchange. He sat wrapped in thoughts he did not share. When she reached out and lightly touched his arm he gave a start, looked around, forced a bright smile. "Sing some more, Saba."

"It wasn't me, it was Pelemos."

"Oh. Yes."

Then he was gone again; gone into that place in his head where she could not follow.

Later, as Pelemos was helping Saba to bank the fire, he said softly, "Why do you love Dinas?"

The question startled her; she had never asked it of herself. After a pause she said, "I guess I love Dinas because he makes me . . . uneasy. He is a fleeting shadow on the mountain, neither one thing nor the other."

Pelemos was not enlightened.

The following morning dawned cold and bright. The late-rising sun cast a roseate glow on the snow. The air was so sharp it hurt the throat. When animals and humans had been fed Saba suggested, "Walk with me, Dinas. This is the sort of day I love best."

He raised an eyebrow. "Enjoy freezing, do you?" he asked as he reached for his hooded cloak. The heavy winter cloak she had woven for him.

When she whistled for the dogs, they left Meradoc reluctantly and slouched out of the cabin behind Dinas and Saba.

Skirting the shoulder of the mountain, they angled their way downslope, crunching through brittle, thigh-deep heather, not dead but asleep in the snow. The sheepdogs were content to follow the trail the humans broke for them until they came to a narrow valley with a frozen lake in its lap. The dogs set off to the explore the area; to discover who or what had been there recently. The head of the valley was blocked by a tumble of gray boulders. They had been thrown there long ago by the ancient gods, according to the old people. Saba selected one, pushed the snow off, and beckoned to Dinas to sit down beside her. As she always did.

As he always did, Dinas lifted his head to gaze toward the highest peaks of Eryri.

"I feel humble here," he said. The first words he had spoken since they left her cabin.

"Kings aren't humble," commented Saba.

"I said I felt humble," he said testily. "I didn't say I am humble."

"No." She gazed out over the frozen lake; at the deep blue shadows lying on the snow. Chafed her bare hands together. "It's very cold this morning."

Dinas said, "You know I never feel the cold." He caught her looking at the goose bumps on his forearms. "Did I tell you that a man called me a liar recently?"

"I hope the poor fellow had lived a full life before he made his fatal mistake."

"It wasn't fatal. My horse tore a chunk out of his shoulder, that's all. He won't be using his right arm for a long time."

Saba clucked her tongue. "No wonder you have such a fierce reputation."

"Do I?" he asked innocently. Pleased.

"Perhaps I should say your horse has a fierce reputation. When you leave here you had best go by a different route."

"I was planning on it anyway. We'll take the pass of Llanberris; I should be able to find more recruits in that direction."

"You never made plans before; you always went where the wind blew you."

"For which you should be grateful," said Dinas.

Saba's eyes were following the contours of the valley. Every inch of it known to her, as familiar as her own body. Softened by snow now, but waiting to burst forth in spring to the summons of the sun. "King Dinas," she mused. "King. Dinas. How strange that sounds. It must be exciting for you."

"I'm not doing it for the excitement. The past is gone and there's no point in thinking about it, so I'm making plans for the future."

"You never did that before, either." Saba blew on her hands and rubbed them together again.

Dinas reached out and imprisoned them in one of his own.

They sat shoulder to shoulder then, watching the dogs. One had discovered some tiny mammal under the snow and was trying to dig it out. The other joined in enthusiastically. They were a team.

Dinas said, "I have my reasons, you know."

"I'm sure you do."

Anger flickered across his features like summer lightning. "What do you want of me, Saba? Should I go back to Viroconium and wait for the barbarians like an ox waiting for the axe? Or do you expect me to stay here with you until my muscles turn to strings and the teeth fall out of my head?"

"No," she said in a low voice. "I don't expect that."

It would be a relief to tell her, Dinas thought. Part of him had wanted to tell Cadogan; his cousin was the sort of man to whom one might make such a confession. But could Cadogan possibly understand the storms that swirled through him night and day?

Saba at least was familiar with his passions.

"I could be a good king," he said. Testing the waters. "And you would be a splendid queen."

She turned to face him. "Long ago we agreed that we were content the way we were; me raising sheep on the mountainside, you roaming the land in search of treasure. You never spoke of being a king then, and I never asked to be a queen."

"Things change."

She could hold back no longer. "Stop it, Dinas! That's no answer. You come riding in here with two strangers and tell me you're changing your life from top to bottom and want to change mine too. I won't be picked up and shaken like a lamb that refuses to breathe! Tell me what's going on or you can just ride out the way you came in."

He tried to make a joke of it. "Not that way, surely. I'd have to go through the village where my horse attacked a man."

"I mean it, Dinas. And turn loose of my hands! You're always grabbing my hands."

"Maybe I'm holding on."

"Why? Because change frightens you? Don't look at me like that, everyone's afraid of something. I am; I'm afraid of leaving here. I was born here and I want to die here when my time comes, and be buried with my people. I don't belong in a place with roads and towns and comings and goings. I don't want to learn a different way of living. Nothing ever changes here except the seasons and the shadows of the clouds on the mountain, and that's the way I like it. That's all I want."

He said reproachfully, "I thought you wanted me."

"Sometimes I do."

"Listen to me, Saba. I'm offering you a chance to—"

"No," she interrupted, "you're running away from something

and trying to make me go with you. Perhaps I will and perhaps I won't, but first I have to know what it is."

Dinas knew when he was beaten. It had not happened very often. When he spoke again the look on his face was so intense it frightened her.

"Last spring," he said, "I found myself riding across some of my father's land; the farm where he used to raise horses. You might say I was blown there by the wind. Ocellus had made the estate his permanent residence some years earlier and I hadn't been there in a long time. When no watchmen challenged me on the approach road I thought my parents must be away, and I was glad. It meant I could ride on by without seeing either of them.

"Yet I didn't ride on by. Perhaps I was just curious, I wanted to see what had become of a place where I spent many happy days as a boy. But as I approached the villa I felt uneasy. Everything looked the same as I remembered it—yet not quite. I tried to halt my horse. He seized the bit in his teeth and wouldn't obey me. He felt like he was about to turn and run away. Suddenly an intense cold flooded my belly. Then the stallion began to tremble under me, and I knew."

Saba knew too. There were horrors coming, but she could not stop her ears.

Dinas continued, "The front gate to the grounds around the villa was ajar, which was unusual in itself. Ocellus always kept that gate closed. The stables and outbuildings looked deserted. There was not a person to be seen anywhere; no servants, not even any dogs barking. The very air seemed frozen. I had to force my way through it. I didn't want to enter the house, yet I could not help myself. I tied my horse to a post and went in.

"The villa was more than empty. It was brimming with emptiness, crammed floor to ceiling with an awful absence. Nothing was disturbed, all the furniture was in place, there were even half-filled pitchers on one of the tables. I could not hear my footsteps on the tile floor. All I heard was the thunder of my heart.

"In spite of the climate Ocellus insisted on having an atrium in every house he owned. The principal rooms opened onto it. When I stood in the center of the atrium I could look into them, one after another. I saw her in the last one, the marital . . . bedchamber." Dinas stumbled over the word. When he spoke again his voice was utterly flat.

"My mother was lying on her back on the bed. Her head was hanging over the side with her dark hair streaming onto the floor. Her blood had streamed onto the floor as well. So much blood. Her throat was cut open like a gaping mouth. Her eyes were open too, looking at me. Upside down, looking at me."

Saba wanted to throw her arms around him but dared not. Dinas looked as if he would shatter like glass.

"I knew who had killed her," he continued in that same toneless voice. "I could still smell him on her. I sat beside her for a long time. Then I bathed her and dressed her in her finest gown and jewels and buried her in the garden."

"But . . . no funeral? No priest, no burial rites?"

"Gwladys gave Christianity lip service, but she had other gods. I put her at the foot of an oak tree, which is where she would want to be, and I said the things she would want said. To the gods she knew. Then I rode to the nearest village and sent a messenger to inform the chief magistrate of Viroconium that a murder had been committed in his jurisdiction."

Saba was finding it very hard to take all this in. "Why didn't you report to the magistrate in person?"

"He's my uncle Vintrex, the man responsible for destroying our family. I gave him the name of the murderer, that was enough."

"I'm surprised you didn't hunt the murderer down yourself."

Dinas lifted his head. His eyes were unreadable. "Even I would not kill my own father."

"But why would he . . ."

"He never forgave her infidelity. Ocellus is incapable of forgiveness. After they moved to the farm it probably ate at him and ate at him until it exploded in his guts."

"And he killed her."

"Yes."

"And you expected the law to avenge her death."

"Yes. At the time . . . yes. I still had some belief left in the law, and I thought Vintrex of all people would gladly crucify Ocellus. After several days had passed I began to worry that Ocellus might have escaped—he's always been too cunning by half—so I forced myself to go to Viroconium and learn what was happening. When I reached the city I discovered the magistrate was away; his steward said Vintrex had gone to Londinium on business. Business! Obviously the miserable maggot had forgotten all about my mother. That's when I knew the truth of the world, Saba: No one cares. Nothing matters and no one cares."

CHAPTER EIGHTEEN

Godubnus was proud of his men. In the distressing aftermath of the raid on Viroconium they worked unflinchingly to pull bodies from the wreckage and help bury the dead. The bloody, battered, the sometimes roasted dead. Mercifully the Saxons had not mutilated anyone, they simply slaughtered those who got in their way. But their methods of slaughter were messy in the extreme.

At first the ironmaster and the other survivors looked to Vintrex for leadership, but it soon became obvious that the old man was incapable. Cadogan did his best to help his father retain a semblance of dignity, though it was no use. Like a child, Vintrex trailed along behind his son, leaning on his steward, waiting to be told what to do.

Cadogan, who never sought the role and did not want it, became the tacit leader.

He quickly learned not to examine the corpses. Not to recall their names, not to imagine the pain they had suffered nor to agonize over their fate. None of it could be undone. He could function only if he thought about what to do next and planned the next step, no matter how insignificant it might be.

Because the wells were polluted—whether by accident or Saxon intent, no one knew—clean water was the first necessity. Cadogan organized teams to go in search of drinking water, and other teams to find food and cloth for bandages and bring back whatever medicaments were left in the hospital stores.

The barbarians had rampaged through the hospital, destroying everything they did not understand. Which was almost everything.

During the days immediately following the attack, many of the survivors left to seek sanctuary among friends or relatives in other towns. A large cadre of the remaining citizens talked about rebuilding. "Viroconium will rise from the ashes better than before," they assured one another. "Just as soon as spring comes." But none of them took the first preparatory steps toward rebuilding. Beneath a blanket of snow and ice they met in lean-tos fashioned from the rubble of their homes, and made bitter jokes in the Roman fashion.

Vintrex made no jokes. Still leaning on Esoros and with Cadogan at his side, he took an abbreviated tour of the city. "Tragic," he said in summation. "Two hundred years of irreplaceable architecture reduced to rubble."

In the fire-scorched ruins of their house Cadogan found a blackened silver cross that had belonged to his mother. For as long as he could remember it had hung over her bed. It was the only memento he carried away with him.

Vintrex prayed at Domitia's tomb in the garden. Then he paused beside the snowy mounds of earth beneath which lay three female servants whose names he never knew. Afterward he let Cadogan take him back to the temporary command post in the entrance hall of the baths, where Quartilla was dispensing supplies people asked for and advice no one wanted.

"This is not my city anymore," Vintrex said gloomily. "I should be entombed in the garden with my wife and her pet dog."

"Nonsense, Father, you have a lot of life ahead of . . ."

Vintrex waved his hand for silence and eased himself down onto a bench. "Do you know how old I am, Cadogan? Fifty years. Fifty; half a century. Appalling number. Yet I have heard it said that among our Celtic forebears men sometimes lived twice that long. Thank God I won't. Bring me a drink, Esoros; one that will burn all the way down. There is frost in my marrow."

As the steward hurried away Vintrex continued talking. "When I was a child it was always morning. I looked away for a moment and afternoon crept in. Now I sense the night approaching. How did that happen so quickly, Cadogan? In full possession of my youth and strength I assumed they were permanent. People grew old through carelessness, I thought; it could never happen to me. But it did. Now my back aches all the time and my teeth are rotten. Sometimes there is blood in my urine. Sometimes I cannot urinate at all. I am trapped in the web of my years so that I cannot escape punishment for my sins."

"Don't talk like that, Father."

"Ah, but that's how I think. Since I have nothing left to look forward to but death, I am becoming a philosopher."

The remark was the last thing Cadogan expected of his father. His surprise showed on his face.

Quartilla, who had been watching them from across the hall, abandoned her self-imposed task and drifted over to eavesdrop.

"When I was a boy," Vintrex continued, "I was taught that the Greeks became philosophers when the Romans supplanted them as a military power. My tutor said the life of the mind is the last retreat of a defeated warrior." He tapped on his forehead with his fingertips.

"You mustn't think of yourself as defeated," his son protested.

"I know exactly what I am, Cadogan. Self-knowledge is the Philosopher's Stone. Even as a lad I knew I could never settle for a mundane existence like my father's. You may not know this—I am sure I never told you—but he spent his adult life as the underpaid scribe of several minor officials in a shabby little office. My father's first duty every morning was to empty any night soil left from the evening before. I was disgusted by the way he was treated and even more disgusted by the way he accepted it.

"It was my ambition to become a highly respected priest and eventually a bishop. But there was a problem. As the oldest son I was expected to do my duty by my parents and provide them with comfort in their old age. In addition, I had a younger brother who would need help to get a start in life. The stipend Rome provided for priests was small indeed; anything more than a bare subsistence depended on local donations. Viroconium was prosperous in those days, but wealthy people are much less inclined to give away their money. A bishop would be better supported but it would be years before I could hope for a bishopric, and in the meantime my parents would grow old in poverty. I could not bare the shame.

"In the way that such things happen, a chance encounter in the public baths opened up another road for me. I was introduced to one of the Roman administrators, who was in the city to prepare for the next regional census. I did my best to make a good impression on him, and before he returned to Londinium he offered me employment. Within a year I was supervising the census in Viroconium."

An image leaped unbidden into Cadogan's mind. His father as a handsome youth in the company of an older and dissolute Roman . . . he struggled to push the image aside.

"After five years," Vintrex was saying, "I was appointed assistant to the chief magistrate. I studied every aspect of the law and made the right political connections, so that when he died I was given his office. Of course there were some problems along the way. Like your mother."

Although he was aware that Quartilla was listening avidly, Cadogan could not help asking, "What about my mother?"

Vintrex did not want to answer that question; was sorry he had even mentioned Domitia. But he no longer seemed able to control his tongue. Perhaps his secrets had become too heavy to carry. "In her youth," he said slowly, dragging the words out of the caverns of memory, "your mother was a beautiful woman who attracted favorable attention in some high places. Unfortunately her antecedents were . . . shall we say . . . a trifle common. Too *Celtic,* if you take my meaning. Her most prominent admirer could not marry her himself, but after showering her with gifts and seeing that she was well educated, he arranged a suitable marriage for her."

Cadogan drew a sharp breath. "To you, Father?"

Vintrex would not meet his eyes. "To me. Yes."

"And that boy who wanted to become a bishop; what happened to him?"

The old man's voice dropped to a near whisper. "He built a house and had a family. And when his hair was turning gray he fell in love for the first time in his life."

Cadogan could fill in the rest. "Fell in love with his brother's wife."

"Yes."

Enraptured by the romance of it all, Quartilla clasped her hands together and cried, "I knew it!"

Vintrex rounded on his son. "What's that infernal woman talking about? Did you tell her my private business?"

Before Cadogan could defend himself his father's face turned an alarming shade of purple. Vintrex gasped, shuddered, and fell full length on the floor of the hall.

CHAPTER NINETEEN

Spring would not reach the peaks of Eryri for many weeks, but Dinas knew when it began in the midlands. Knew by the angle of the light; knew by the singing in his bones. The old restlessness took hold of him again. No matter how warm the cabin, no matter how tender the arms of Saba, only action could satisfy him.

Pelemos was fully occupied with the sheep. Long before lambing began he had learned how to wash the wool, boiling the fleeces from the previous winter in a great cauldron until the thick grease floated to the surface and could be ladled away. Saba strained some of this and used it to protect her face and hands from the cold. She had shown Pelemos how to separate the clean strands of fiber again and again until they became almost as light as down, ready to be woven into the softest woolen fabric. She had even taught him the language of the weaver, with an unfamiliar name for every tool and method.

Meradoc kept almost as busy with the horses, though their care was less demanding. He brushed the stallion and the two little mares every day with a tool he made himself, using stiff straw and brambles with the sharp points filed down. He painted their hooves with some of Saba's wool grease to keep them from splitting, and rubbed a little more around their eyes to protect them from the wind. He taught the ponies to pick up their feet on command, one at a time, and to pluck bits of bread from between his lips. He did not attempt to teach the stallion any tricks. That, he thought, would be undignified.

Even during the worst of the winter Dinas had ridden the dark horse every day to keep him fit. He had leaped and plunged in the deep snow and would have unseated a lesser rider, but Dinas merely laughed and urged him on. He also encouraged Meradoc and Pelemos to ride their ponies daily so they would not grow soft. The only way the ponies could get through the deep drifts was to follow in the trail the dark horse broke for them. Seeing the little procession making its way along the mountainside, Saba had smiled to herself. At a distance they might almost be a father with his family.

After the restlessness seized him, Dinas rode alone. He set out in the icy pink dawn and did not return until the sky was Tyrian purple and laced with stars. During lambing season, when Pelemos really proved his worth and Meradoc became a welcome assistant, Dinas was somewhere else. Somewhere inside his head, living his dream, shaping and reshaping it until it was more real than reality to him.

Not King Dinas; I've decided I don't want a crown. Julius Caesar wanted to be a king, or an emperor, or some other fancy title, and look what it got him. Stabbed a score of times by his supposed friends and left to welter in his own blood. Titles are dangerous. Stars and mountains have no titles, they just are. Stars. Mountains. Infinitely powerful and instantly recognizable.

I shall simply be Dinas. That name will stand for everything I am. Names are more important than titles anyway.

My horse has grown such a massive winter coat that Saba calls him "the bear."

The bear. Arthfael in the Cymric tongue, Ursus in the Latin. The Great Bear in the night sky is Ursus Major. That would be a splendid name for a horse if I were going to name my horse. Which I'm not.

Some things must never be changed.

Returning earlier than usual from one of his solitary rides, Dinas made an announcement. "We've taken advantage of your hospitality long enough, Saba. We're going to leave in the morning."

Meradoc and Pelemos reacted with mixed feelings. The prospect of resuming the adventure was exciting; the prospect of leaving the cabin was painful. Over the winter both men had come to consider the place almost as their home, and Dinas and Saba as their family. In Meradoc's case it was a dream come true. For Pelemos it filled a gap he had thought could not be filled.

Saba had known their departure was inevitable, but still it was a blow. She could accept Dinas leaving—if she was honest with herself, and she was, the sporadic nature of their love was one of its attractions—but Pelemos and Meradoc had become her friends. In the solitude she thought she wanted, she had undervalued the human need for friends.

"Do you have to take them both, Dinas?" She was breaking the unwritten agreement about questions but she could not help it.

He raised an eyebrow. "Want to keep one of them as a pet?" he said teasingly.

She laughed to keep the mood light. "To replace my dogs? I think not, the dogs would never understand. But having help has made a great difference this winter; I never realized how hard I was working until other hands eased the load. With one or two men I could . . ."

"Or two?" he queried.

"I could buy more sheep and harvest more wool." Her voice warmed with enthusiasm. "The women from the villages below could share in the weaving, Dinas. Life is harder for them than for the men, and it would be a help if they had blankets to sell."

"You could build a kingdom of your own up here in the high pastures," Dinas said with a smile. "I never thought of you as being so generous."

"I've been generous to you," she replied tartly.

The unexpected display of ambition on the part of a woman had caught Dinas off guard. He attempted to look contrite. "You've been more than generous, and I'm grateful."

"We all are," Meradoc chimed in.

"If she needs one of us to stay," said Pelemos, "it should be me.

My poor skills would be no use in ambushing ships, but farming is—"

"Is out of the question," Dinas interrupted. "I need you, Pelemos; I need both of you."

"It was just a thought," Saba said coolly.

Dinas smiled again to conceal his confusion. Was her indifference real, or feigned? He had no idea. His relationship with Saba had lasted so long because she never demanded his understanding. She allowed him to come to any conclusion he liked.

He had chosen to think she was very much like himself.

Saba caught and held his eyes. Dinas infuriated her with his smiling lazy mockery. She thought he was doing it deliberately to hurt her. Or—and this was worse—perhaps he didn't know the effect it had on her. Or care.

Suddenly she was very tired. Let him go, then. Let them all go.

She stood in the doorway of the cabin and watched them ride away. For the first time he could remember, she did not wave farewell to Dinas when he turned in the saddle and looked back. She simply closed the door.

"I could still stay with her," Pelemos offered. "I would not mind."

Dinas said sharply, "She didn't want you, she wanted me."

"Then you stay with her," suggested Meradoc.

"Don't be ridiculous." Dinas tightened his legs on the dark horse and galloped away. They had to push the ponies to their utmost to keep up with him.

The pass of Llanberris proved more challenging than anything they had yet encountered. The peaks looming above were gaunt, primeval, shrouded with an icy mist too bitter to breathe. The wind moaned around crags and buttresses formed in the dawn of time. Boulders as large as cottages loomed out of blowing snow, then as suddenly disappeared.

Light played tricks on the eyes.

Near the foot of the pass the riders were confronted by snow-drifts as high as the stallion's withers. They had to retrace their steps until they found another way down. No trail was safe; none was level. The slopes were littered with ubiquitous scree that could slide unexpectedly under a horse's hooves and send animal and rider plunging to their doom.

Wolves could be heard howling in the distance, though it was hard to believe anything could survive in such a landscape.

While they sheltered in the lee of a cliff to catch their breath, Meradoc said, "Does anyone live up here at all?"

"More than you would expect," Dinas told him. "They've been grazing their sheep in the high pastures for centuries—or quarrying slate, like Saba's people. It's a hard life but it's what they know. The old ones would never leave, but in the tail of winter we may find some youngsters willing to talk about it."

"Talking is one thing," Pelemos remarked. "Changing your life is another. I never knew anyone who willingly changed his life."

"I did," said Meradoc. "And so did you."

"I'm not sure I did. In fact I'm not sure how I came to be here at all."

"Perhaps you're under an enchantment," Dinas remarked.

Pelemos swept his eyes over the scene around them. The eternal mountains, the ephemeral mist. Anything might come riding out from behind a boulder with a blast of silver trumpets and a rainbow of ancient banners.

"Perhaps I am," he said.

As they made their way down from the pass they caught glimpses of bleak, lonely farmhouses tucked into isolated valleys; they encountered tiny communities of slate miners working in nearby quarries; they could not help seeing the abandoned dwellings of those who had failed to make any living from the infertile soil. Dinas never lost his way, but rode with calm assurance. When they saw anyone he always stopped for a talk, which inevitably became a drink of something that burned the throat, and a night's sleep under a roof.

Dinas had an unerring instinct for finding those whose spirits were not permanently rooted in their native soil. He could talk to them in a language they understood. By the time they reached the foothills he had recruited eight young men with fire in their bellies and hunger in their eyes. Dafydd, Cynan, Hywel, Cadel, Bleddyn, Iolo, Docco and Tostig—whom the others called "Otter" because he had short arms and legs but an extremely long torso.

Before they set off on their first morning as a company, Dinas appointed Meradoc captain of the horse. "Everything to do with the horses, except for my own, is your responsibility. As an officer, you will ride just behind me. And one other thing—keep an eye on my saddlebags. Don't let anyone touch them. If they aren't with me they must be with you, understand?"

By now Meradoc knew what Dinas had in those bags, down to the last gold coin and fishhook. And leather bundle. Knew and did not judge. He had thrown in his lot with Dinas and the dark horse and that was that. "I understand," he said.

Dinas told the recruits, "You are infantry now but that's only temporary. What we need is cavalry. Every one of you who stays with me and proves his loyalty will be given two good horses. In the meantime, follow Pelemos. His pony walks at a pace you can keep up with. Don't come near my stallion though, he doesn't like other people."

Dinas made sure the dark horse pranced and rolled his eyes in a way guaranteed to ensure respect.

The first thing a leader must have is the respect of his men.

In the first flush of excitement the little band did not question where Dinas was leading them, but when they made camp a husky former stonecutter called Tostig asked him, "Why are we going east? You said our stronghold would be on the western coast."

"We aren't setting up a permanent base right away," Dinas replied, "because I want to get the horses first. That's why I'm going to the territory of the Cornovii; they breed the best animals. While we're there I plan to add a cousin of mine to our number, and also visit Viroconium about a personal matter."

"What personal matter?"

Meradoc shook his head at Tostig. "Dinas doesn't like to be questioned."

"Why? What's he trying to hide?"

Dinas kept his face impassive and pretended he had not heard.

Leading may not be as easy as I thought. But I can do this.

He envisioned himself at the head of a well-equipped private army, arriving unannounced at Cadogan's fort and creating such an impression his cousin would beg to join them. With Cadogan as one of his officers he could approach Vintrex and demand justice for his mother. If justice had not already been done. Which he doubted; there was very little justice left in Britannia. But with an army at his back he would have a better chance.

At night when they sat around a campfire with their bellies full, belching and farting and talking about women, Pelemos told stories.

His tales were about a place called Albion that no one believed in anymore, during a time no one remembered. Later some would claim he never repeated a story, but he did. He could tell the same one over and over, changing names and small details, and make it fresh and new every time. Pelemos could go from comedy to tragedy with a subtle change of voice, and be equally convincing. He might put stress on a certain incident one time and hardly mention it the next.

There were some constants. Meradoc discovered the stories always included six recurring characters. He began secretly putting names to them: Warrior, Priest, Druid, Warrior Woman, Friend, and Bard. They might be of either gender, with the exception of Warrior and Warrior Woman, but they were always recognizable. If one paid close attention.

Dinas also listened closely, displaying an attentiveness that was out of character with his restless nature. He began to long for the wild, free Albion the Romans had destroyed. A partly fictional Albion in which memory and imagination competed for primacy, shaping and reshaping a history that never was.

Dinas was aware of this. But he chose to believe anyway.

One day Meradoc asked him, "Where does Pelemos get the tales he tells?"

"Storytellers are inspired, I suppose."

"Inspired by what?"

Dinas gave an uncomfortable laugh. "You ask too many questions, little man." Then he changed the subject.

I once told Meradoc I wouldn't lie to him, but failing to answer a question isn't a lie. Besides, what I know of inspiration defies explanation. A few minutes spent in a Christian shrine, pretending a piety I did not feel—did the martyred saints inspire me that day in Deva?

Are there such things as saints? Or angels, or sorcerers, or gods. Or God.

Do I care?

Equipping and training a company of inexperienced warriors—and it was warriors Dinas wanted, not merely followers—presented some large problems. Finding twenty-one suitable horses was not going to be easy. They had to be sound in wind and limb and less than ten years old. Every man should have two, one to ride and one to lead, and Dinas was including a backup for the dark horse in that number. He preferred to have geldings, which were less trouble, but he would accept a good mare if he found one.

The dark horse would be the only stallion.

When they entered the territory of the Cornovii Dinas sought out horse breeders his father had known. To his chagrin, only two out of fifteen still had any animals. The other farms had been sold or abandoned. After five days of hard negotiation Dinas succeeded in buying only half a dozen horses. The best of the lot was a lop-eared, big-headed gelding whom the seller swore was descended from Sarmatian stock.

"The Romans recruited the Sarmatians as mercenaries," Dinas told Meradoc. "Their cavalry horses were famous for their speed and agility. But I'm afraid you and Pelemos will ride ponies for a while longer."

"I don't mind. I like my little mare."

Dinas, who could be stingy with compliments, gave him an appraising look. "You've developed a good seat. And soft hands. You deserve a good horse."

"I suppose good horses are very expensive."

Dinas smiled. "You learned that from Saba."

"Learned what?"

"To ask a question without asking a question."

It was Meradoc's turn to smile.

"Just so you know," Dinas said, "when I find the right animal for you I'll buy him. I have enough money; trust me."

"I do," said Meradoc.

Cadel pleaded to be given the Sarmatian horse. He claimed he had had some riding experience and therefore deserved the best mount.

"What riding experience?" Dinas challenged. "Your background is the stone quarries."

"We used donkeys in the quarries," Cadel replied, bristling. "And I rode them."

Since there were more men than horses, Dinas devised a plan he called "ride and tie." Each recruit was given a number. One through six mounted the available horses and the rest followed them on foot. When the person with number one reached a certain point he dismounted and tied his animal, leaving it for a walker. Number two repeated the maneuver, then number three, and so on. The exchanges continued throughout the day. By sunset every man had spent considerable time on horseback.

Dinas asked Meradoc to keep an eye on them and help where necessary. "As my captain of the horse, when we make camp it will be your job to set up picket lines for the horses. They need to be able to reach enough grass to feed."

"You never tie up your horse at night," Meradoc remarked.

Dinas smiled. "I don't need to."

The following day Dinas decided to proceed directly to Cadogan's fort. His cousin might know where to buy some good horses, though he would be unlikely to suggest a good armorer. He also possessed the one animal Dinas wanted as backup to the dark horse. Cadogan would need persuading to part with the mare, of course.

Dinas trusted his skills of persuasion.

As they went deeper into the territory of the Cornovii they saw increasing evidence of the barbarian invasion. Not just an occasional burned-out homestead, but little bands of refugees carrying everything they still possessed on their backs, and telling frightful tales of plunder and pillage and rape.

Rape. Two or three of Dinas's recruits began to speak nervously of returning to the mountains to protect their womenfolk.

"There's no need for that," Dinas assured them, "the barbarians won't go as far as Eryri. One look at those peaks will turn them back."

That night while Meradoc was rubbing down the dark horse with bunches of dead grass—paying particular attention to the itchy, sweaty spots where the saddle had been—Pelemos approached him. "What about Saba?" he asked in a worried voice. "She's alone up there in the mountains. She doesn't even have a small boy with a sling and some stones to defend her."

"You heard Dinas," Meradoc replied without missing a stroke. The stallion was already shedding his winter coat. A cloud of dark hair lay on the ground around his hooves. "He said the barbarians wouldn't go that far."

"I didn't expect them to come to our village, either," said Pelemos. "One day we were preparing for winter as we did every year, and the next . . . Meradoc, could you find our way back to Saba?"

Meradoc stopped grooming the horse. "I couldn't," he said flatly. "And if I could, I wouldn't. We can't desert Dinas."

"He deserted her."

Meradoc gave Pelemos a pitying look. "She's his woman, not yours. And we don't know what passed between them. I do know Dinas, though; if he thought Saba was in danger he never would have left her."

Pelemos folded his arms and stood watching while Meradoc finished rubbing down the stallion, then raked up the loose cloud of dark hair with his fingers and folded it over and over again until he had a thick soft mat.

"What are you going to do with that?" Pelemos asked.

"Make a pillow for my head."

"Meradoc," Pelemos said gently, "the horse is his, not yours."

Saba had been on Dinas's mind too, but a woman who wanted no part of his plans could not be allowed to interfere with them. To keep from thinking about her as he rode, he thought about the stronghold he would build. There were several possible locations along the coast that would serve his purpose. Yet one by one he had dismissed them. This was too near a town, that was too far from the sea-lanes.

He knew all along there was only one place for him.

The far southwest corner of Britannia Superior was the kingdom of the Dumnonii. A peninsula shaped like a clenched fist, pointing a long finger out into the cold abyss that was the western ocean. The name of World's End was well deserved.

Like most tribal leaders, the Dumnonian kings had no permanent residence. Instead they held a series of courts, moving from one to the next whenever they exhausted the local hospitality. One of their feasting halls had occupied a rugged coastal promontory overlooking the ocean. The location, midway down the western side of Dumnonii territory, was convenient, the aspect majestic. Earlier kings had made it a principal site for tribal assembly. More recent leaders had abandoned the place, leaving only tumbled ruins atop a pinnacle rising from the sea.

Wind and weather had sculpted the site into a natural fortress, uniquely defensible. The only connection to the adjacent cliffs was a narrow neck of land. The bay below the promontory had a shingle beach and was sheltered from the ocean breakers, but the coastline on either side was too rugged to permit landing from the sea.

Dinas had discovered the deserted peak on a day of lowering skies and howling wind. No sane man would have ridden a horse close to the edge of the cliffs on such a day. No sane horse would have permitted it. Dinas and the dark horse had gone to the very brink. There they halted.

To gaze at the lonely, storm-wracked majesty of Tintagel.

CHAPTER TWENTY

"The trick," Cadogan explained to Nassos, "is to fell the trees before the sap rises. If we wait too long the sap will keep the wood from drying out enough to use, and sap rises early in birches. You can tell because they get their leaves early."

"I thought we were going to build with oak," said Nassos, who was carrying a large axe on his shoulder. He had spent part of the morning sharpening the axe head. Running his thumb along the edge until at last blood spurted, and he was satisfied.

"The walls and beams will be oak, but birch is soft wood, and we'll use a lot of soft wood in the interiors," Cadogan told him. "Birch has sprung up wherever the Romans cleared the land. There are stands of ash and hazel, too, that we can coppice and use for making charcoal."

"You know how to make charcoal?" Nassos asked in surprise.

"Not yet, but I know where there is a family of charcoal makers who can teach me. Regina says that none of our women know how to cook on an open fire."

"Not many city women know how to cook at all," Nassos said. "They always relied on their servants. My mother now, she could cook the best food you ever tasted over a roaring blaze or on a flat rock. She made me the man I am today."

Cadogan gave a wry smile.

Nassos, the youngest member of the ironmaster's crew, was a bony, round-shouldered man who looked as if a breeze would blow him away. His looks were deceiving. He could wield a heavy ham-

mer all day long, beating red-hot iron into any shape required. Like
Karantec and Trebellos, Nassos possessed impressive strength.

It would be needed.

Six weeks earlier, the surviving heads of the leading families of
Viroconium had gathered in the ruins of their forum to take a vote.
At Cadogan's suggestion they were following the democratic pattern
of the Athenians. He could think of no other way to resolve the argument between the majority who wanted to stay in the city, at least
for the time being, and the few who claimed they never wanted to
see it again. Until the issue was settled they seemed determined to
waste their time and energy on quarreling.

Cadogan did not want to be in charge; it was a position they
kept forcing upon him as the chief magistrate's deputy. But his protests were too polite. No one listened. His problem was the fact that
he had sympathy with both sides. He could understand people who
had spent their lives in the city and could not, or would not, accept
anything else. He could also understand those like his father, who
felt trapped in a nightmare and longed for escape.

The stroke that felled the chief magistrate had paralyzed his left
side and damaged his speech. Vintrex still managed to convey his
feelings, though the only one who could understand him was, amaz-
ingly, Quartilla. She had nursed him untiringly. The medicaments
taken from the hospital were mostly unfamiliar to her, but she knew
how to concoct any number of potions and poultices out of such
diverse elements as dogs' urine and balsam. By the time the vote was
taken and seventy-two men, women and children were planning to
leave Viroconium, Vintrex was able to sit up with support from Esoros, and was aware of what was going on around him. There was only
one word he could say clearly but it was unmistakable. "Go! Go! Go!"

The Saxons had not left a living horse, pony, or donkey in Viroconium. Godubnus had found his big wagon where he left it, but
the traces had been cut and the mules were gone. Under his instruction the component parts of the furnace were removed and carried

into the public bathhouse for storage. Then the damage inflicted on the wagon was repaired by Cadogan, while Godubnus and his men made a hasty trip to their workshop to stock up on weaponry.

Cadogan had examined the timber vehicle thoroughly, measuring the interior dimensions. He concluded that the wagon was large enough to contain Vintrex on a pallet, plus the oldest refugees and the smallest children. Any remaining space would be filled with foodstuffs and cooking pots, and a clanking hoard of knives and axes from the ironmonger. Cadogan was not happy to carry so many dangerous weapons; they spoke of terrors to come. But he understood their necessity.

He had repeatedly issued stern edicts against transporting the luxuries people thought of as necessities. No charcoal braziers: "There isn't any charcoal where we're going." No cedar chests specially fitted with dowels for storing Egyptian bed linen without creasing it: "Forget about fine linen. What we need is enough blankets to keep everyone warm."

He had relented in the matter of toys, allowing one favorite to every child.

When all was ready the eight strongest men had been strapped into the mule harness Cadogan had reconstructed to fit them, and the procession left Viroconium by the eastern gateway.

Those who had chosen to remain in the city closed and barred the gates behind them.

Not knowing what else to do, Cadogan planned to take the refugees to his fort temporarily. He could house the most vulnerable inside for a night or two and help the others set up shelters nearby, until they decided what to do next.

At the back of his mind he was aware they might want *him* to make that decision, might even expect it.

Oh no. No no God no.

One thing at a time. Let's get there first and then they can nominate a leader. British tribes have always elected their chieftains.

But just not me.

When the refugees set out on a bitterly cold morning, several of the women could not stop crying. Some of the men were stony faced with anger—or grief—but the overall atmosphere was one of stunned silence. They followed the Roman road for only a short distance before turning off and heading northeast. Across ice-spangled grassland. Toward dark forests and unfamiliar hills.

As he jolted along in the wagon Vintrex had lain with his eyes open, staring up at the bleached winter sky. He was so quiet he might have been dead. Quartilla had insisted on riding with Vintrex to take care of him—which meant that someone who really needed to ride was forced to walk—but she had cushioned his head on her lap. She frequently assured an anxious Esoros that his master was still breathing.

The first time they stopped for the night there had been little conversation. A fire was built and food portioned out. People ate because they knew they would need to, not because they were hungry. Afterward, Regina and the other women had put the children to bed beneath the shelter of the wagon and surrounded them with blankets. The adults made themselves as comfortable as possible and lay fighting the cold; fighting their memories. Fighting their fear of a barbarian attack at any moment.

Cadogan had posted guards around the camp. He took double turns standing watch himself.

In the dark, the dark.

When the sun rose, the refugees had been astonished to find themselves still alive. Cold, stiff and hungry, they began to grapple with the reality of their situation. One of the men had asked Cadogan the question that was on everyone's mind: "Where we're going . . . will the Saxons attack us again?"

Cadogan decided it was best to be honest. "I'm taking you to my place for now. Since I left Viroconium I've been visited only once by foreigners and they weren't Saxons. They took my horse but they didn't steal my chickens. The Saxons are after valuable plunder, they won't bother with sparsely furnished forts in the wilderness."

Several women went pale at that word. After countless centuries, "wilderness" was still the terrifying heart of darkness. Since the first man lit the first fire and pushed back the shadows by a critical fraction, humanity had been struggling to escape from the wilderness. The thought of returning voluntarily chilled them to the bone.

A young mother clasped her husband by the arm. "I can't do that!" she cried. "Oh please, let's go back to the city. I don't want my children to be raised like wild animals. Or *eaten* by wild animals!" The terror on her face was heart-wrenching. And contagious.

That day the number of refugees had been reduced to fifty-three, plus Cadogan's group and the men from the ironmonger. Nineteen had headed back toward Viroconium, carrying a generous portion of the supplies. It would be a long, cold walk for them.

As they disappeared from view Regina had uttered a heartfelt, "God help them."

The second day of the journey to Cadogan's fort had been harder than the first. The third day had been almost unbearable. When the refugees emerged from the forest on the fourth afternoon and saw the lonely cabin on the hillside, several women began to cry again.

Kikero had greeted the return of humans to his home by standing as tall as he could, stretching his gorgeous wings and crowing with delight.

Cadogan had ushered the refugees into his cabin and tried to make space for all of them. "You'll be warm soon, just sit here . . . stand over there . . . don't worry, we'll have heat, I'm going to bring wood in and light a fire . . . yes, there will be fresh water, I promise . . . put those children on the bed and don't worry . . ."

He felt as if he had been saying "Don't worry" nonstop since Viroconium.

I wish someone would say that to me. And make it sound convincing.

Once the fire blazed into life, its warmth combined with the body heat of sixty people crammed into a small space soon made the atmosphere intolerable. "Take down the planks over the windows and prop the door open," Cadogan had said to Esoros.

Esoros looked offended. "I am not your steward. This is not my lord's house and I take no orders here."

"But you've been helping me ever since . . ."

"Whatever I do," Esoros said loftily, "I do for my lord Vintrex."

Cadogan was dumbfounded.

He had noticed Quartilla watching him and pushed his way toward her. "Did you know Esoros would let me down like that?"

"I could have predicted it."

"Why?"

" 'Whatever I do, I do for my lord Vintrex,' " she mimicked, sniggering. Then her expression turned serious. "That's who Esoros *is,* Cadogan," she said earnestly. "Don't you understand?"

In reducing Esoros to his essential core Quartilla had, for one fleeting moment, left herself open. Cadogan sensed it and seized his opportunity. "And who are *you*?" he asked her.

She opened her mouth to answer—just as a fight broke out and a man fell into the firepit on the hearth.

There was a frantic scramble to pull him clear, slap the flames from his clothing and assign blame. A new fight began at once. Cadogan was drawn into the vortex of the conflict and spent an inordinate amount of time trying to restore order among people who had been through too much, and could not control themselves any longer.

Afterward, Cadogan would remember that night as one of the worst in his experience. Barely contained grief and fear and anger finally had boiled over. Men fought men, husbands fought wives, women fought everyone. Shouting and cursing, pots thrown, pottery breaking, people knocking each other down, children screaming in terror.

Lucius Plautius would call it hysteria.

In total frustration, Cadogan had fled outside to fill his lungs with clean air and gather himself before returning for one more futile attempt to establish peace. He was sickened by the actions of the very people he had been trying to help.

Just walk away, he had counseled himself. Not for the first time. But he knew he could not do it.

As he headed back toward the open door, Godubnus emerged. "There you are!" the ironmaster had called cheerily. "You left just when the fight was getting good."

Cadogan shook his head. "There's nothing good about it, they've gone mad and I can't stop them."

"When there's an uncontrolled explosion in the smelter I can't stop it, either," Godubnus said. "Let it burn itself out; it will. Then we'll pitch in and clean up."

"Are you serious?"

Godubnus chuckled. "That's what Morag used to say to me."

"Are you serious?"

"Not that; what Morag always said was, we have to pitch in and clean up." He let out a great sigh. "By all the blood in me, I miss that woman."

Cadogan appreciated a tiny respite from what was waiting in the cabin. "Was Morag your wife?"

"My fourth," Godubnus had replied. "I like delicate women—a great big man like me—so I married three delicate flowers, one after another, and every one of them died in childbed. Then I found Morag, a strapping big girl though as bony as a Roman. Morag was made for me. Best year of my life was spent with that woman. She even worked the bellows at my forge."

"Where is she now?" Cadogan had asked, fearing the answer. "Surely you didn't leave her back in . . ."

"Och no, she's buried in the highlands of Caledonia. A wild bull gored her," he said matter-of-factly. "I came south over Hadrian's Wall to start over. Now it looks like I'm going to be starting over again."

As Godubnus had anticipated, the emotional explosion burned

itself out. By the following day the chastened refugees had been willing to consider their future in more reasonable fashion.

First Cadogan had insisted they repair the damage done to his fort. He put the ironmaster and his crew to work rehanging the door—which somehow had been wrenched off its hinges—while Regina assigned cleaning and tidying chores to the women. Perched on a stool near the center of the room, she had issued her orders in a voice accustomed to being obeyed.

"You there!" she called to Quartilla, who quickly looked around to see who else she meant. "Yes, you with the rusted hair and the big nose; why are you standing around doing nothing? Find a broom and sweep the breakage off the floor. Anything that is not broken, put to one side."

Quartilla had goggled at her. "But I . . . I have no . . ."

"If there is no broom, make one!" Regina snapped. Swiveling on her stool, she addressed her next command to the next woman she saw, who happened to be her daughter-in-law. Pamilia was given her orders in the same peremptory fashion as Quartilla. Pamilia responded languidly, casting a shy, sidelong glance at Regina, but Quartilla jumped to obey.

Cadogan could hardly believe his eyes.

Karantec and Trebellos were equally prompt to respond when Regina sent them for more water. They were halfway out the door when she called them back. "Have either of you any experience with hunting?"

The two Silurians nodded in unison.

"Cadogan, are those hunting spears over there against the wall?"

This time Cadogan nodded.

"Then you two take those spears and bring back all the game you can kill. Do not dare to return here with empty hands. I do not care what you bring us as long as it is meat. We have a lot of mouths to fill."

Within a week, Cadogan and Regina between them had turned the urbanites of Viroconium into several reasonably competent work parties. All but Vintrex and the infants were given jobs within their capabilities. Even Esoros, albeit with bad grace, was doing the sort of menial labor he had long considered beneath him.

Their first imperative had been shelter. The entire group could not remain in the little fort, even for a short time, but the hasty lean-tos they threw together from branches with blankets draped over them were not sufficient in wintry weather. The skills that Cadogan had developed in building his own house he began to teach to others. Soon he was envisioning half a dozen similar structures rising on the hillside.

Some were unwilling to share his vision. Viroconium as it used to be was still home for them. Nothing else could be good enough.

"We can't create another Viroconium," Cadogan had tried to explain, "because it took centuries to develop that city. But it must have begun with a tiny village; a small cluster of houses like those we're going to build here. Your ancestors made that beginning and we can make another."

He could feel the resistance in them, the still smoldering anger in them, but the only way he knew to deal with it was to ignore it. As the first oaks in the forest were selected for felling, the thaw set in. Men who had hung back stepped forward to drag the logs back to the site. Women whose eyes were still red with crying discussed where they wanted their hearthstones set.

And as Cadogan said to Nassos, "The trick is to fell the trees before the sap rises."

CHAPTER TWENTY-ONE

Above the headwaters of the Dee they came upon a filthy, blood-stained man staggering through the dead bracken. When he saw Dinas and his band he broke into a shambling run. After a few steps he gave up the struggle and turned, like a stag exhausted by harrying wolves, to meet his doom. His swollen face was a patchwork of bruises.

In spite of them Dinas thought he recognized a former neighbor and leading citizen of Viroconium. "Tarates, is that you?"

The man gaped at Dinas and rubbed his reddened eyes. "Dinas, son of Ocellus?"

"The very same. But what happened to you? You look half dead."

Tarates collapsed as if the air had gone out of him. He sank onto the ground and held up a pleading hand. "Save us, in the name of God!"

Dinas hastily slid off the dark horse and took the proffered hand in his own. "Save you from what, man?"

"The Saxons." His voice faltered. "The Saxons," he repeated in a gravelly whisper. And began to sob, the helpless sobs of a grown man at the very end of his strength.

Embarrassed and confused by such naked anguish, the recruits could only stare at him.

Pelemos shouldered past Dinas and gathered Tarates into his arms. "You're safe now," he said gently. "Don't be afraid, you're safe with us."

Dinas took a step back and watched. Watched Pelemos cradle the broken man as a mother cradles her child. Observed the tension leaving the exhausted body; saw peace stealing over the ravaged face. There was no doubt of it; Pelemos had a gift. "Everything will be all right," he murmured over and over. "We can protect you, no harm will come to you. Rest easy, you're safe with us." It hardly mattered what Pelemos said. The reassurance was in the sound of his voice.

When Tarates was calmer, Meradoc brought water for him to drink. Cynan offered bread and cheese. Tarates crammed the food into his mouth with both hands, gulping frantically, only to spew it up again. "Take a small bite or two and then wait for a while before you try to eat any more," Pelemos advised.

Tarates made a visible effort to get control of himself. Shrugging Pelemos away, he propped himself up on one elbow. His eyes were glassy.

"You said 'save *us,*'" Dinas pointed out. "Are there more of you around here?"

Tarates said eagerly, "Did you see them?"

"No. Only you."

"There were more. I know there were. A score of us at one time. You did not see them?"

"No, I'm afraid not," Dinas repeated. With a crisp gesture he ordered his band to search the area, just in case. "What happened to you, Tarates? How were you injured?"

"Am I?"

"There's blood on your clothing."

"Oh." The man looked down at himself. He ran his tongue over his cracked lips. "Strangers," he said. "Strangers attacked us. At the full moon."

"Saxons?"

Tarates licked his lips again. "No, Britons. Like us. Not our tribe though. Not Cornovii. I do not know . . . what was I saying?"

"You were attacked by some Britons," Meradoc prompted.

"Ah. Yes. They beat us senseless. They stole our supplies."

"What about the Saxons?"

Tarates shuddered. "That was *before.*"

"I think he's had enough questioning for now," Pelemos told Dinas.

Now that Tarates was talking he was reluctant to stop. He struggled to capture the random fragments of memory flickering through his head. "The Saxons were *first,*" he said carefully. Pinning it down. "The Britons attacked us *later.* When we were trying to go somewhere . . . but we became separated . . . When was that?"

"Tonight's the last night of the full moon," Dinas told him, "so either it happened recently, or a month ago. By the look of you it might have been a month ago."

Tarates reached up to touch the back of his head with tentative fingers, and winced. Pelemos was staring, appalled, at that part of his anatomy. Meradoc moved around behind him to have a look.

"We walked and walked," Tarates was saying. "We were so lost. When we saw strangers we hid. I do not really remember what happened, or when."

Dinas said firmly, "Begin at the beginning. You know that much, don't you?"

Tarates could not make his eyes focus. "Viroconium? It started with Viroconium?"

"You don't sound certain."

"I am certain. I was there when the Saxons came. Both times."

Dinas tensed. "What do you mean, 'both times'?"

"The second time, they burned the city. I remember that. Flames as tall as trees. Afterward . . ."

"Afterward?"

"It's all a blur. No . . . wait. Cadogan said . . ."

Dinas leaned forward to put a hand on his knee. "My cousin Cadogan? Was he with you?"

"He was with his father."

"The chief magistrate?"

Tarates groaned. "My head hurts."

Meradoc said in an awed voice, "His skull's been bashed in. I don't know how he walked at all. Let him rest."

"In a moment." Dinas skewered Tarates with his eyes. "What happened to Cadogan and Vintrex?"

Tarates began to weep again. "They are dead. The Saxons burned the city and killed the people and they are dead. We were the last of them. We are dead too."

That night the full moon rose. Swimming up out of a sea of dark trees. The trusted guide of travelers, inspiration of poets and stimulus of lovers stared down at the earth with a celestial indifference that unhinged human minds and set the wolves in the hills to howling. Urbanus and rusticus alike cowered beneath that cold blue light. Men asleep in their beds were tumbled into nightmare. They awoke disoriented and made dreadful decisions. Some murdered their wives. Some went to war on their neighbors. It had always been so.

Dinas sat late by the campfire, thinking about the citizens of Viroconium, slaughtered by barbarians. And about Tarates and his party, attacked by Britons.

Barbarians. From the Latin "barbarus," meaning foreign; strange; not speaking our language. But what is our language? Not the formal Latin that Cicero spoke in the forum. We took the Latin we learned from our conquerors—a mixture of the coarse speech of the legions and the stilted phrases of officialdom—and blended it with the dialects of many British tribes. To this we added borrowings from Caledonian and Pict, Cymri and Erse. And now Angle and Jute and Saxon, making a strange brew indeed.

Strange. Are we barbarians now, we Britons?

So be it.

The following morning, leaving his band in camp and charging Pelemos to care for Tarates, Dinas and the dark horse crisscrossed the surrounding area in search of a healer. He approached every farm and smallholding with a friendly smile on his face. In spite of this, he could hear bars being conspicuously slammed across doors. When he tried shouting a request for help it was ignored. Two or three men even threatened to turn their dogs on him.

At last his nose led him to a tanner at work over his pits. The acrid smell was unmistakable. With no door to hide behind, the solitary tanner was forced to confront his uninvited visitor. A grudging conversation followed. "Country people used to offer help when asked," Dinas remarked rather bitterly.

"That was then," the man said.

"What has changed?"

"Everything."

"I don't understand."

"Where have you been?"

"In the high mountains."

"If you're smart you'll go back there."

Dinas repeated, "I don't understand."

"Stay here much longer and you will."

"I can't go anywhere right now, I have a badly injured man to care for first. Surely there is at least one healer around here."

The tanner looked past him, scanning the area. "Anyone with you?"

"Only my horse. The injured man I told you about is back in my camp."

The tanner gave a noncommittal grunt. Scratched his head. Blew his nose on his sleeve. Finally said, "There's an old fellow who lives in the bole of a tree in the woods over there, where I get my oak bark. If he'll talk to you at all—and he may not—he's the person you want."

Dinas thanked the tanner and offered him a small copper coin, which he refused. "We still help," he said. "But we have to be careful."

The dry, rotted heart of the ancient oak was just large enough to house a human being. There was no doubt of someone's being there; Dinas could hear him breathing, but he did not respond to a greet-

ing. After calling aloud several times and pounding on the tree
trunk with his fist, Dinas was about to ride away.

Then the dark horse snorted.

A grizzled head immediately popped out of the aperture in the
tree. The man regarded the stallion with his right eye. A greenish-
gold eye as bright and glittering as a fox's. "I hear you," he said to the
horse.

"Are you Bryn the Healer?"

The man turned his head so he was looking at Dinas from his
left eye. "I might be and I might not. Who's asking?"

"I am called Dinas."

"I do not know anyone called Dinas. Who sent you to me?"

"He said his name is Rogan."

"I know three Rogans. Which one?"

"Rogan the Tanner."

"Ah." Bryn gave Dinas the benefit of both his eyes. "That's all
right then." He stepped into the daylight. A wizened, graying individual with a ragged beard and skin the color of tanned leather.
"What do you need of me?"

After Dinas explained the situation, Bryn asked only for enough
time to pick the herbs he would need. "I won't say I can help the
man, but I won't say I can't. A broken skull is not easily mended, but
if the fellow's brains are showing I can apply a poultice of master-
wort and oil of melilot. The bared surface will become firm in time,
almost callused."

"Will he still be in his right mind?" Dinas wanted to know.

The healer's eyes danced. "As much as he ever was."

When they reached the camp Bryn gave Tarates a long and involved examination that included looking down his throat and tasting his urine. Dinas and his band watched curiously. "Is he a druid,
do you think?" Cadel asked Bleddyn.

"I can't say, I never saw a druid."

"You wouldn't know one if you saw him," Bryn remarked over
his shoulder as he prepared a poultice.

Iolo cleared his throat. "I think my father's father was a druid. He could whistle up a wind."

"Why would anyone do that?" Docco wondered. "There's far too much wind already."

"In the mountains there is," Hywel agreed, "but if you were in a boat with a sail you would need wind."

"I'm never going to get in a boat," Dafydd said. "I'm a dry land man, me."

Out of the corner of his mouth Dinas told Meradoc, "That's the very first man I'm going to put into a boat."

Bryn continued with various treatments until sunset, when he changed the first poultice for a second and instructed Tarates to get some sleep. "I am afraid I will never wake up," the injured man said.

"You will," Bryn assured him. "And you will feel much better."

Tarates reached tentative fingers toward the back of his head, now encased in layers of cloth and clay and herbs. "I feel . . . I think I feel a little better already," he said with surprise. "You must be a sorcerer."

"A druid, I told you!" Cadel hissed to Bleddyn.

"Druids and sorcerers are not the same thing."

"Of course they are. Even the birds in the trees know that."

It was taken for granted that the healer would stay the night in camp. After eating an inordinate amount of food for such a shriveled man, he regaled the others with an assortment of bawdy stories. For once no one asked for Pelemos to tell a tale by the fireside. He stood leaning against a tree with his arms folded, listening without comment.

Meradoc sat down beside Dinas. "Are druids and sorcerers the same thing?"

"How should I know?"

"You carry the blood of the Cymri, do you not?"

Dinas gave a faint smile. "Through my mother. Her mother was born on Mona, the sacred island of the druids." The smile disappeared. "The Romans slaughtered every living thing they found on

Mona and burned the sacred trees. *They* thought the druids were sorcerers and enchanters." His nostrils flared with contempt. "It was not druid magic that frightened the Romans, though. It was druid wisdom, which in their ignorance they mistook for magic."

Meradoc phrased his next question carefully. "Was your mother very wise?"

Dinas phrased his answer carefully. "My mother had all the gifts," he said.

Later, pillowing his head on the neck of the dark horse, he whispered to the stallion, "Just like that and they are gone. Gwladys and Vintrex and Cadogan. And Ocellus too, if there is any justice left in the world."

Closing his eyes, Dinas tried to picture Cadogan's face. One last time.

CHAPTER TWENTY-TWO

In the morning Tarates awoke with clear eyes. "The pain is gone!" he cried in astonishment. "That healer of yours has worked wonders, Dinas."

When Bryn bent over him to feel the pulse beating in his neck, Tarates jokingly asked, "Will you marry me?"

The healer grinned. "I'm open to all offers."

At his instruction the injured man was helped to sit up. He was given a cup of broth that he drained to the final drop, then he managed to eat three or four bites of hard cheese and a small piece of smoked eel. He lay down again with a satisfied sigh.

Watching him closely, Bryn said, "Are you dizzy?"

"A bit, but not much. I do not want to be any trouble."

The healer turned to Pelemos, whom he perceived as a natural caretaker. "Feed him lightly for the next few days and give him all the water he'll take. Before I leave I'll show you how to make fresh poultices for his wound. You'll need to change them every two or three days until the exposed brain forms a film on the surface, almost like a callus. After that he should wear some sort of cover on his head for protection."

"For how long?" asked Dinas.

"The rest of his life, I should think."

Tarates turned ashen. Dinas did not look very pleased either.

After the healer had enjoyed a second hearty meal in the camp, Dinas offered him a silver denarius for his services. Bryn peered at the coin with his left eye, then handed it back to him. "That's of no use to me."

Behind his hand Tostig whispered to Dafydd, "The old fool's holding out for gold."

Bryn heard him. "Gold is no more use to me than silver," he said. "It's all just metal. What I value are food and friends and fire and water."

Aha. "Stay with us, Bryn," urged Dinas, "and I can promise you all four. A man with your skills will be a valuable addition to our company. As for you, Otter"—he turned narrowed eyes on Tostig—"if you want to be one of us, never again call any man a fool. He might be dead tomorrow. Then you would have the rest of your life to regret your words to him."

Tostig, embarrassed, stared at the ground.

"I might as well join you," Bryn said. He sounded like a man accepting an unavoidable but not unpleasant fate. "My tree is going to come down in the next storm anyway."

Tarates soon was fast asleep. A pale, wan sky loomed overhead. Grass was beginning to grow but the wind was still cold. The unspent day stretched ahead with no shape; no certainty.

Since joining Dinas, the young men comprising his company had grown used to being on the move. Immobility rested heavily on them. They slouched about the encampment, gnawing bones, throwing stones at birds, staring into the distance looking for something to look at. Before long a chance word excited resentment and the first fight broke out. Dinas promptly put a stop to it but he could feel their restlessness simmering under the surface. Like his own.

He took Meradoc aside. "We'll allow Tarates this one day, then we're leaving tomorrow at sunup. Heading south. Be sure the horses are ready."

"But I thought we were going to . . ."

"The two people I needed to see are dead," Dinas said bluntly. His face revealed nothing of his feelings. "We're on our own now."

Meradoc looked puzzled. "I thought we always were."

The problem of Tarates had to be faced. When Dinas tried to

question Bryn about his condition, all the healer could tell him was, "That man feels much better than he really is."

"You said he would be like this for the rest of his life. How long will that be, exactly?"

"Until he dies," said Bryn.

"Can he travel?"

"Not on foot, and I wouldn't put him on a horse. He might get dizzy and fall off."

Dinas hit his own thigh with a clenched fist. "Plague take the man! We can't leave him here, and from what he says, there is nothing left of Viroconium, so I can't send him back there even if I could spare a couple of men to take him. Meradoc," he called out, "you'll have to rig up something so we can carry Tarates with us until I figure out what to do with him." Under his breath Dinas added, "Perhaps he'll die along the way and we can bury him under a stone."

He saw Pelemos watching him from across the camp. Although the other man could not possibly have heard what he just said, Dinas bit his lip.

Meradoc spent the rest of the day devising a litter. Hywel was dispatched to find and cut two long, straight saplings. Bleddyn and Iolo were put to work tearing every bit of spare cloth into strips and plaiting it into ropes. The others watched the process with a great deal more interest than they normally would have shown.

They had nothing else to do.

When Meradoc had finished, the litter was, everyone agreed, a triumph. He had constructed two sets of harness for the ponies. A hammock made of blankets stretched between the saplings was attached to the harness and slung between the ponies. Docco volunteered to try it out. Dafydd and Iolo led the ponies in a circuit of the camp, while Docco lay in the hammock, laughing and shouting bawdy encouragements. "It's the most comfortable way to travel in the history of the world!" he assured Tarates afterward.

"You have never ridden in a sedan chair, then," said Tarates.

Meradoc asked, "What's a sedan chair?"

The following morning, when Pelemos and Meradoc mounted their ponies, they were careful not to dislodge the makeshift harnesses. For once the ride-and-tie technique was unnecessary; all would be kept to the walking pace necessitated by the litter. They broke camp shortly after dawn beneath a sky filled with clouds like clotted cream. "At least it's not raining yet," said Cynan, who always had to comment on something.

"It will," Bryn informed him.

Led by Dinas on his stallion, they headed south toward the valley of the Severn. The men on foot walked on either side of the horses. The allegedly Sarmatian horse, who had a tendency to kick, brought up the rear, behind the ponies and litter.

The clouds rode the wind but did not ride away over the horizon. Instead they thickened. Darkened.

Being forced to a walking pace upset the dark horse. He arched his neck and danced sideways until the strength of his rider's legs forced him forward. His discontent rippled down the line, infecting the others. Ears went back, heads were tossed, reins were snatched from the rider's hands. The animals balked or bolted, depending on their dispositions. The recruits cursed or cajoled, depending on theirs. Meradoc was frustrated in his attempt to call out instructions because no one was listening to him.

Dinas rode on ahead, his thoughts elsewhere.

The morning was almost over before he drew rein. "Halt here long enough to water the horses in the river. After that the walkers can ride for a while." The walkers, who had been watching their companions struggle to control their mounts, were less than enthusiastic at this.

Dinas dismounted at river's edge and let the dark horse drink before he did. The stallion eagerly sucked up the water, swallowing in greedy gulps. Dinas looked around for Meradoc and saw him busy with the ponies, so he used the edge of his cloak to wipe the nervous sweat from his horse's neck. Then he slaked his own thirst and went to check on Tarates.

The injured man's first words were, "Where are we?"

"There's no point in asking, you wouldn't know the place," Dinas said irritably. The injured man was costing them time and he was anxious to reach his destination. Thinking about it helped to block out the other thoughts trying to crowd in. But the dark horse could feel them through the reins Dinas was holding; could feel the tension gathering in his rider's body. When Dinas gave the command, "Forward, now," the stallion almost shot out from under him.

Clouds as purple as a bruise began to leak rain. Fingers of lightning danced along the horizon.

When Dinas ordered his band to mount up, there was a sudden skirmish. Cadel took the Sarmatian gelding while several others tried to claim the gentlest horse. The horse in question panicked and tried to run backward. "Meradoc!" Dinas shouted, but the little man was fully occupied already. The lightning and subsequent crack of thunder had upset both ponies. Meradoc was afraid Tarates would be spilled from the litter.

Cursing, Dinas turned the stallion and galloped back along the line. This brought him within range of the Sarmatian horse, who had not yet assumed his place at the end. The big-headed gelding wheeled around, unseating Cadel in the act of mounting, then lashed out at the stallion with both hind legs. The kick struck the dark horse full in the ribs with a sound like thunder—a hairsbreadth away from Dinas's knee.

With a scream of rage, the stallion rose on his hind legs and pawed the sky.

Cadel cowered on the earth beneath him.

Dinas clamped his fingers around a lock of mane as his horse plunged toward his adversary. The gelding refused to give ground; being a warhorse was in his blood. Both animals reared again while Cadel desperately tried to scramble clear. The horses towered like titans above the mere mortal. In their passion they were indifferent to humanity. Dropping to all fours, they turned in unison, then, as if on a prearranged signal, they kicked each other almost simultaneously with the full force of their powerful hindquarters.

Meradoc imagined he could hear something breaking. Not the dark horse! Perhaps he cried out. He did not know. He slid from his pony and wrapped his arms around her neck. He wanted to close his eyes but could only stare.

The two horses whirled to face each other and began jockeying for position. Darting, feinting, striking out with one foreleg and then the other, rhythmically grunting with concentration. Theirs was a deadly dance. One was going to die that day; the horrified spectators were certain of it.

"Stop them!" Meradoc cried to somebody. Anybody. But even Dinas could not stop them, all he could do was hang on. To fall between them might be fatal.

The stallion screamed again. The Sarmatian tried to match him, but being gelded had robbed the horse of his full vocal power. This added to his anger; he redoubled his efforts, fighting with a savagery compounded of cunning and naked fury.

What happened next was almost too quick for the eye to follow.

The Sarmatian dropped almost to his knees and his big head snaked forward, reaching with bared teeth for the stallion's slender foreleg. Seeking to crush the bones. At the same moment the dark horse went up for a third time. Balancing on his hind legs, he slammed one front hoof squarely between the gelding's eyes.

The Sarmatian dropped like a rock. Dead before he hit the ground.

Dinas was fighting the stallion to a shuddering halt when, as a last act of conquest, the dark horse lifted his tail to drop a steaming pile of dung on his fallen foe.

Most of it fell on Cadel.

The sudden end of the battle left everyone shaken. The dark

horse could not stop trumpeting his victory through distended nostrils. Dinas slid from his back as Meradoc came running up. "Is he all right? Was he hurt?"

"I almost lost my knee," Dinas said, sounding aggrieved.

Meradoc plucked the reins from his cold fingers and led the stallion forward a few paces, watching his legs to ascertain if he was sound.

"I almost lost my knee," Dinas repeated to no one in particular. They were all talking, not listening, as each man gave his own breathless version of what just happened. Only Cadel was silent. All he had seen of the battle was the massive bellies of the two horses fighting above him. He could see nothing now through the brown dung plastered over his face.

"I hate horses," he remarked.

Dinas gave orders to pile some earth over the carcass as an act of respect to a warrior; he did not want to waste more time digging a hole big enough to bury him. But by the time they got Cadel cleaned up and the excited horses calmed down it was almost sunset. They made camp a mile away and spent a restless night. The horses were not the only ones who had been overstimulated.

Once again, Dinas could not sleep. He sat staring at the campfire until the air around him resounded with snoring.

He had a gift for uncovering hidden treasure. It had been proved again in an unexpected way with Meradoc and Pelemos, and now, Bryn. All three possessed special talents that would be useful to him. But what possible use could he make of Tarates, who was, at best, a stone around his neck? Dinas still thought he could abandon the man and never look back, but it would be a mistake to reveal that side of his character to his men. Let them see him act with compassion. Like Pelemos, whom they all admired.

Although he was unaware of it, the lone wolf was changing.

Getting to his feet, he went to see if Meradoc was asleep. Sometimes a conversation with Meradoc unearthed the answer to a problem. The little man was snoring in a series of rippling whistles, but Tarates was awake. Lying on his litter under a blanket pearled with raindrops.

"The pain," he explained as Dinas bent over him.

"Do you want Bryn to . . ."

"That won't be necessary, Dinas. I am growing used to it, and it is much less than it was. Do you know what I would like, though? Sit here with me for a while. The night will not be so long if I have company."

With a sigh, Dinas sat down cross-legged on the damp ground.

"Is there a problem?" asked Tarates.

"A problem? I have a handful. My most recent disaster involved my losing one horse and gaining two men. I really needed that horse."

"I am sorry you consider me a disaster," Tarates said stiffly.

"You misunderstood me."

"Perhaps. I knew you as a boy, Dinas, when no one understood you. You gave no more light than marsh gas: a flicker here, a flame there, and gone again. Your cousin was the steady one."

"Yes," Dinas agreed, "Cadogan always was the steady one. If you know that much it means your memory's coming back."

"Considering the state of me, I might be better off without it. Who wants to recall a nightmare? It could ruin my sleep for the rest of my life. Tell me, Dinas, do you ever have trouble sleeping?"

"Sometimes. Like now, when I have a lot on my mind."

"Worrying about the men with you?"

"Not worrying, no. But they're part of it."

Tarates said suspiciously, "What are you up to now?"

Meradoc had stopped snoring. Now he started listening.

"What makes you think I'm up to something?"

"I knew you of old, Dinas, remember?"

"Perhaps I've changed."

"Oh yes," said Tarates. "And perhaps the sun will rise in the west tomorrow."

"One's as likely as the other," Dinas told him. "To be honest, I'm happy the way I am."

"Do you never get lonely?"

"Lonely? I'm as free as the wind and have everything I want."

"What about women? Have you no wife, no . . ."

"No," said Dinas.

Tarates pressed on. There was a pain rising in him and he sought distraction. "Are you saying you don't feel the need of female company?"

The chill turned to ice. Polite, but ice. "You ask a lot of questions, Tarates. I already have one man who does that and I'd rather not have two. I'll tell you this, though. A woman is warmth and scent and texture, which I enjoy very much. But have you ever listened to a gaggle of females talking? They twitter like birds in a tree. Beautiful, of course, but you can't understand them."

As they were saddling the horses the following morning Meradoc said to Dinas, "You lied to Tarates last night, I heard you. You have Saba."

"No one has Saba," Dinas replied. "She's as free as I am."

CHAPTER TWENTY-THREE

The work was unremitting; nothing came easily. They were trying to wrest a home and a living from an unforgiving wilderness. The years Cadogan had spent in the endeavor had toughened him, but the new pioneers, the urban elite, had soft hands and undeveloped muscles. Only Godubnus and his three men, Esoros and—perhaps—Quartilla had had any experience of real labor.

If asked to help Esoros invariably declined unless the request came from Vintrex. Which rarely happened. Vintrex seemed content to spend his days in a half-aware dream. He slept a lot. He ate a little. He watched the activity around him as a man might watch the busyness of ants.

As for Quartilla, sometimes she would work as hard as a man and sometimes she was, as Cadogan wryly remarked to Godubnus, "the queen of Egypt."

"Women do what women do," Godubnus replied.

"Was your Morag like that?"

The ironmaster scratched his head; considered the question. "I think they're all like that. But then I've only had four wives and a random sampling of casual women, so I'm no expert."

Cadogan, whose experience of women was considerably less, envied him.

The dream of offering Viola a fine house built by himself; the dream of a country life with her and their children; the dream of having time to read and think in peaceful seclusion as the years drifted past . . . so many dreams had been blown away.

Where do dreams go? Cadogan wondered. Do they descend on

people who had different dreams and pull their lives out of shape? Who is living the life I wanted, and unhappy about it?

But he had little time for pondering. Every minute of daylight and much of the night was fully occupied.

When Pamilia bemoaned the lack of servants to do her menial work, Regina lost patience with her daughter-in-law. "If you grieved half as much over my son as you do over your maids, I might have some sympathy for you."

"I weep every night for my husband," the young mother protested. "You just do not hear me." She turned to Cadogan. "Why did you not bring some servants with us?"

"We brought the people who wanted to come. You can't blame the servants, Pamilia; they saw a chance for freedom on their own, and they took it."

"They may all be dead by now!" she wailed.

"Perhaps."

"When this is over can we look for them and reclaim them?"

Regina was disgusted. "This is not going to *be* over, you simpleton," she told the girl. "It already *is* over; it ended when they sacked Viroconium. We have a new life and we must learn how to live it. You can start by washing your own clothes in the river."

Pamilia was aghast. "I had rather die."

"Die, then," said Regina. "Die in dirty clothes and that is how we shall bury you."

After some sniffling and a few feeble protests that Regina ignored, Pamilia gathered up her soiled garments and those of her children and headed for the river.

Cadogan had known it would not be easy dealing with the disparate personalities of the refugees. Mistakenly, he had expected the recalcitrant Esoros to be his aide and ally. Instead the position was ably filled by a small grandmother who tolerated no nonsense. Regina had little physical strength but great mental energy. She was the first one awake every morning and the last to go to bed at night. During the day she knew where everyone was and what they should be doing, as well as what they really were doing. Any person who shirked was given an embarrassing tongue-lashing.

Cadogan assigned the tasks; a challenge in itself. Some of the men he put to work at construction were unable to perform simple carpentry. They could not see how the pieces must fit together, and only recognized a mistake after things fell apart. Others were too impatient and insisted on forcing the materials, which resulted in considerable breakage. Any person who claimed he knew exactly how to do a job had to be watched closely. Braggadocio usually disguised ignorance.

Recognizing his own early mistakes, Cadogan had a sneaking sympathy for all of them. But there was more to be done than building cabins. Even as he worked his mind was busy laying the foundations for the next step, the next series of actions that seemed inevitable to him if to no one else.

He formed the habit of talking things over with Regina at the end of the day, after the children had been put to bed and before the fire was banked for the night. At his invitation Regina and her family had remained in his house after the others moved out. Vintrex, Esoros and Quartilla were also sharing the house—Vintrex had been given his son's bed—but Cadogan wanted someone he could talk to; someone with an orderly mind. Regina listened intently to his ideas, asked intelligent questions and offered constructive criticism. Best of all, she made valuable contributions.

"The number of people you brought here would populate a sizable village," she observed. "Did you not say the Saxons are targeting towns? Is it wise for us to live so close together?"

"It's the obvious thing to do," said Cadogan. "We can look after one another and share the work."

"Who said obvious is better? There will be no work to share if a horde of Saxons swoop down and slaughter us all at the one time. Could we not spread out a bit?"

Cadogan immediately saw the wisdom of her suggestion. He could envision a handful of cabins scattered seemingly at random through the forest, well out of sight of one another. "We won't look anything like a town," he told Regina. "We won't even have roads. We'll only use the trackways the deer use."

Regina agreed enthusiastically. But when Cadogan tried to explain the idea to the others he was showered with arguments. They could not visualize how it would work. Everyone saw something wrong with the plan; no one could see anything right. At last, exasperated, he selected one of his treasured books, unwrapped the scroll of papyrus, thrust the end of a thin stick into the ashes until it was covered with soot, and began drawing a detailed map on the back of the precious manuscript.

"Your houses will be spaced well apart in a sort of giant wheel, with a hub of cleared ground at the center where we can grow grain. The greater our self-sufficiency the less likely we'll be to attract attention. It would be madness to troop off to the nearest town to buy supplies in any great number.

"The houses should be as inconspicuous as possible. This is hilly country, so we can tuck them into the contours of the land. They'll be built low to the ground and surrounded by timber stockades like this, see? From a distance a house will look like part of a woodland. Their exact location will depend on the nearest water supply. People are too vulnerable if they have to travel a long distance for water. We'll dig wells and divert water into ponds when we can. We'll also need sheds and pens for livestock"—he was warming to the topic as he went along—"because we should have at least one milk cow for every family, and a couple of pigs. And oxen for the plows. And hens for eggs and meat. We should plant orchards and . . ."

"Where will we get seed for an orchard?" a man wanted to know.

A woman protested, "I have never milked a cow in my life!"

Another pinched her nose with her fingers. "Pigs. How very disgusting. What do you think we are, peasants?"

"We are now," Regina said in a voice that brooked no argument. "But at least we're *living* peasants. If we want to go on living we need to make intelligent plans."

Reluctantly they gathered around Cadogan and watched as a sooty stick traced the outlines of their future. Barns and sheds and workshops and storehouses. Livestock pens. Pits for tanning leather. Pits for burning charcoal.

"You are talking about a large expenditure here," a man warned. "Who is going to pay for the cows and pigs and oxen and plowshares? Unless I am mistaken, not all of us got out of the city with our money."

There was a rumble of agreement. No one wanted to admit they had any money with them.

Including Cadogan.

Why does everything come down to money? he wondered. Is that our heritage from Rome? If so, it's a blighted heritage.

I know the people who followed me from Viroconium. Some have been guests in my father's house. Others have appeared before Vintrex in his official capacity. I can't help knowing aspects of their lives that they would not like to have made public, and there's not a man among them of whom I could say with certitude: He would not steal my money if he knew where it was.

Sometime during a sleepless night—and Cadogan was growing used to sleepless nights—a solution came to him. There was one person whose money no one would dare to steal.

In the morning he explained the idea to Vintrex, who roused enough from his torpor to listen. Cadogan was pleasantly surprised when his father approved. "You want to tell our friends that I am lending them money to buy what they need? I had no idea you were so clever, Cadogan. How can I object, since you will not really be using my money anyway, but your own. I assume you have it here someplace?"

"I have enough here, yes."

"You were always financially prudent, whatever your other failings," Vintrex said. "Of course you learned it from me." The old man's rheumy eyes gleamed with a telltale smugness. Cadogan knew

that expression of old. His father used to wear it after he had been
with Gwladys.

When he had a chance to speak with Esoros alone, Cadogan
asked, "Does my father have money hidden away that no one else
knows about?"

The steward's face was a closed book. "My lord Vintrex does not
tell me everything."

"But you are privy to his personal finances. Is that not one of the
responsibilities of a steward?"

"Are you questioning my ability to discharge my responsibilities?"

The steward was deflecting and Cadogan knew it. The man's re-
fusal to answer was an answer in itself. "I would not insult you so,"
Cadogan said politely. Leaving Esoros and the fort behind, he walked
out into the forest. The trees.

Thinking, in peace among the trees.

In the dying years of the empire unscrupulous officials stole everything that was loose. My father proved he had no scruples when he
seduced his brother's wife. If he did amass a dishonest fortune in
those days, he would have been far too clever to keep it at home. But
where then? Not in the city, where everyone knew everyone else's
business.

A place like this, perhaps. Remote but not too remote.

Before they quarreled, my uncle's country estate would have
been the perfect hiding place.

Suddenly Cadogan smiled.

Dinas has been roaming the countryside for years, sniffing out
buried treasure. Suppose the first hoard he discovered had belonged
to the chief magistrate of Viroconium?

The irony was delicious to contemplate.

Cadogan asked Godubnus to accompany him when he went to purchase livestock. The ironmaster, who had lived outside the walls and

was never a citizen of Viroconium, was easier to trust than the urbanites. He was rough and ready and spoke his mind, but Cadogan was almost certain he did not say one thing and mean another.

Still, one could not be too careful.

The day before they were to set out Cadogan waited until the others had left the fort, then quietly barred the door. Using one of the andirons, he pried up a hearthstone. Beneath it was only innocent earth, as blank as a baby's face. Anyone else would have put the stone down again. Cadogan used the sharpest point on the andiron to scratch a hole in the earth, into which he thrust two fingers and a thumb. He felt around until he caught hold of a tightly woven string. A little twitch; a firm tug . . .

The carefully prepared soil fell away to partially reveal a sheet of scratched and battered tin the length of a man's forearm. An abandoned object of no value. Lying flat on the floor, Cadogan ran his fingers along one edge of the sheet until he found a tiny catch. A flick of his forefinger and the catch released. The tin lid opened wide on concealed hinges, revealing a hidden vault containing a timber box bound with iron.

He sat up long enough to brush himself off, then knelt and reached down with both hands. It took considerable strength to open the chest that contained his personal fortune: a gleaming hoard of gold and silver coins, most of them Roman, enough to support a man for several lifetimes. In the world as it had been.

In that world Cadogan had prepared his treasury carefully, still trusting—almost trusting—that such precautions would be unnecessary.

Now he knew that no precautions would be enough.

The following morning he met Godubnus and Trebellos at the edge of the forest. Both men had packs strapped to their backs. "I thought we'd need an extra pair of hands," Godubnus explained, indicating his companion. "Did you say we're going to a market a half day's walk from here?"

"A fair up in the hills," Cadogan corrected, "and if we're fortunate we'll ride back. I hope to purchase a couple of horses, an ox and a milk cow to start with."

Godubnus turned to Trebellos. "You can ride the cow," he told the Silurian.

Twice a year, in the spring and the autumn, a great fair was held at major crossroads in the hills. The purpose of the fair was to attract people from afar to purchase local produce, and to bring items for sale that were not available in the area. It was also a wonderful opportunity for a festival.

When farmers drove their animals a long distance to sell them they hoped to get a good price, so they brought their best livestock. If Cadogan was going to find a replacement for his stolen horse, the fair would be the place. Unless, by some miracle, he might find the mare herself.

Perhaps the barbarians didn't eat her after all.

Before they set out the three men armed themselves from the ironmaster's supply of weapons. Godubnus took an axe, plus four knives of various sizes that he thrust through his belt. "You bristle like a hedgehog," Pamilia teased him. An unsuspected sense of humor was beginning to surface in the shy, quiet young woman.

The Silurian's weapon of choice was a butcher's cleaver capable of dismembering an ox, which he strapped to the pack on his back.

Cadogan chose a knife long enough to qualify as a shortsword. "Kill a man with one thrust to the belly, that will," Godubnus assured him.

"I don't want to kill anyone. I actually don't like to fight."

"You had better get over that," said the ironmaster.

"I'm hoping these weapons will be deterrents if we run into any trouble."

"The only way to avoid *that*," Karantec remarked, "would be to stay right here. But then we wouldn't have any livestock."

"So sooner or later we would starve to death," Nassos added helpfully.

The entire population of their little settlement gathered to see them off. Smiling and waving; anxious and worried and trying not to show it.

The youngest children cried.

Cadogan and his companions had to walk for several miles to reach the road that led to the fair in the hills. There were no signposts to guide them, no landmark features. Only moorland and woodland and bog. Wind-ruffled grass, smell of pines, hum of insects. Spring pregnant with the summer to come. "I know the way," Cadogan told the other two, "because I often went to this fair as a boy. My uncle used to breed fine horses. If he took some to the fair to sell, my cousin and I rode them for him."

"So you're an equestrian!" Trebellos exclaimed.

"Hardly that. An equestrian was a knight; an officer entitled by birth or appointment to ride a horse in the service of the emperor. I just enjoyed riding. My uncle liked me because I wasn't always trying to show off the way my cousin did. Dinas could have a horse in a lather before he got out of the stable yard." Cadogan gave a reminiscent smile. "In my memory of those days at the fair, the sun was always shining. When I sat on a horse and the crowds looked up at me I felt ten feet tall."

The other two made no comment. There was no response to such unimaginable privilege, so casually voiced.

The hills rolled on and on like a green sea, climbing toward a particularly dense belt of forest. After they entered its cold shade the little party stopped to catch their breath. Godubnus said, "Are you sure we're still going the right way, Cadogan?"

"See where the moss is growing on those tree trunks? That's the north side, and we're headed north."

"How do you know about moss?"

Cadogan laughed. "You would be surprised what I've learned since I left Viroconium."

"Do you never regret it?"

"Leaving the city? No," Cadogan lied.

"It was either a very brave or a very foolhardy thing to do," the ironmaster said. "You had everything a man could want there."

Cadogan decided it would be a good idea to be frank about the situation. Starting a new life together, they would learn about one another anyway. "What I had was a father who demanded total control," he told Godubnus. "He had a hundred sayings he kept hammering into us. 'Duty above all else,' 'Compromise is cowardice,' 'Absolute obedience is the most noble virtue.' We were expected to live by those aphorisms every day of our lives. The smallest misstep resulted in a furious tirade. He was as stern with us as he was with the miscreants who appeared before him in his office as chief magistrate.

"My mother suffered him in silence for the most part, though I recall a few times when she tried to stand up to him—usually in defense of one of her children. Father insulted and humiliated her until she backed down. At last my sisters escaped the old tyrant by marrying, but the only way I could escape him was by running away."

"The chief magistrate doesn't seem like a tyrant to me."

"That's because you're not his son. Besides, he's ill."

"And you feel sorry for him," Godubnus guessed.

"Perhaps I do. Sorry for him and for myself. Running away didn't do any good, I'm stuck with him now in spite of it."

"I don't know if we ever escape anything," said Godubnus. "Our fate is our fate."

"Are you sure? My cousin Dinas would argue the point with you. He thinks we have a right, almost an obligation, to take our lives into our own hands and shape them for ourselves."

The ironmaster looked skeptical. "You believe that?"

"I would like to believe it. My cousin certainly does."

Trebellos said, "Your cousin must be a heathen, then."

Cadogan laughed.

When at last they came to the road they sought, it was not a road in the Roman sense at all. A wide, weed-fringed, foot-beaten trail through the forest, deeply rutted with cart tracks, never straight because it followed the contours of the land, consisting of numerous curves and bends that could conceal an ambush-in-waiting.

As he walked Cadogan heard again the voice of Dinas: "Life is the sun and the stars, the wolves howling and the rain lashing and the thrill of danger around every bend." And what was the rest of it? Ah yes. "You will die in the end anyway, we all do."

Is that the secret of courage, then? Accepting you are going to die no matter what, so you might as well take a risk? If it's as simple as that I might as well have gone with Dinas.

But if I had, what would have happened to the people I brought away from Viroconium? What will happen to them anyhow?

How can one ever *know* when making a decision? Or is every decision as potentially dangerous as the forest, dark and full of violence. The smallest mischoice could lead to . . .

I wish I didn't have to think.

Look at Godubnus and Trebellos. Striding along without a serious thought in their heads. I'm sure they don't ask themselves questions they can't answer. They simply accept whatever the day brings. How I envy their simplicity! Lucius Plautius would call it wisdom.

Is this constant turmoil in my mind a legacy of my Roman education? I wonder . . . unlike the Greeks, the Romans sought knowledge but not wisdom. Then, as if knowledge were quantifiable and their stores were complete, they abandoned any interest in intellectual pursuits and devoted themselves to the search for material wealth and the prizes of conquest. Like Dinas.

Perhaps they were right. In seeking wisdom I've discovered my own ignorance. If I had the chance to . . .

Cadogan's thoughts were interrupted by a shout from Trebellos. "I think I see a banner through the trees!"

The three men began to trot forward.

In a valley surrounded by hills, the fair was spread out like a handful of colored baubles thrown into someone's lap. For a moment Cadogan felt the thrill of excitement he had known as a boy. The tents and banners of the various clan chieftains, the swirling throng of ordinary people dressed in their finest, the herds and flocks and whinnying and bellowing, the giddy shriek of children and warm laughter of women, the racecourse marked off in the grass, the whole brilliant panorama of tribal society come together to buy and sell, to compete and make wagers, to lust and love and fight and befriend. To celebrate life.

Yes!

Cadogan broke into a run. The other two pelted after him.

As they drew nearer Cadogan's pace slowed. Seen close up the fair was not as he remembered it. It was smaller, shabbier. Fewer tents and faded banners. The finery of the ordinary people was not finery at all, but patched and faded remnants from better days. There was not as much livestock as before, and it was not of the best quality.

Cadogan paused long enough to extract a purse from his tunic; a small purse containing only a few coins for food and drink. He began to worry that there would be no need for the rest of the money he brought.

Everyone is older, he observed. Of course they are; I am too. But none of them are smiling the way I remember; even the children look dull. Or was it always like that and I've forgotten?

"I don't see any oxen," said Godubnus.

Trebellos added, "Or pigs either."

"Perhaps they're beyond those tents," Cadogan suggested. Angling to his left, he made his way through the crowd. Except it was not a crowd, just a score of people who reluctantly moved aside to let him pass.

Didn't the clan chieftains used to paint their tents with the symbols of their families?

Were there not vendors who moved through the crowd, selling hot morsels of roasted fatty meat, fresh off the spit?

Where are the wine merchants?

Noticing a sullen, potbellied man standing beside a wooden tub and a stack of battered tin cups, Cadogan held up three fingers. The man's dour expression gave way to a snaggle-tooth smile. He ladled thin yellow beer into three cups, but did not give the cups to his customers until money changed hands.

"Smells like sheep piss," Godubnus remarked, though he did not hesitate to gulp the beer down. Trebellos also drank thirstily. Cadogan touched the cup to his lips, then set it down again. "Where did this come from?" he asked—trying not to convey his disgust at the musty taste.

"My own barley," the brewer boasted. "It's the best drink you'll have today."

Cadogan gave a faint smile.

As he led the way between two tents, hoping to find better livestock on the other side, a man stepped out in front of him. His features and hairstyle were those of a native Briton, though Cadogan did not recognize the tribe. An otter-skin cape and colorfully embroidered tunic identified him as being more than simply a clan chieftain; around his neck he wore the heavy gold torc of a tribal king. A pair of spear carriers stepped up beside him. Heavy-set, sallow-skinned individuals dressed in goat-hair coats and wide leather trousers. In a guttural voice one warned Cadogan, "Strangers not welcome here." His thick accent was hard to understand, but the look in his icy eyes made his meaning clear.

The other man hefted his spear and pointed the iron tip straight at Cadogan's heart.

CHAPTER TWENTY-FOUR

There are places that speak to men's souls, thought Dinas. If they have souls. Cadogan would know better than I—especially now. Hail, cousin! Floating up there above the clouds. I hope you were right about your God and your heaven.

I would rather have Tintagel.

The journey to Tintagel was an arduous one. Speed was sacrificed to the requirements of the injured man, which meant Dinas and his company must proceed at a walk. Day after day. The dark horse never submitted to the forced pace; he tried his rider's patience with his constant prancing and head tossing. When Dinas dismounted and led him it was worse, the stallion tossed his head so violently he almost pulled the man off his feet. Dinas could feel the dark fire of his own hot temper flickering just beneath the surface. He had never lost his temper with his horse, nor in front of his men. But it could happen.

Dangerously, it could happen. He knew from past experience that if he really lost his temper he could not control himself at all.

Meradoc made a suggestion. "I can lead him, Dinas. He'll be quiet for me."

Dinas quelled a sudden flare of jealousy. "If he won't settle down for me he certainly won't do it for you."

"Let me try, at least? What have you to lose?"

"If you're leading him, what do I do for a horse to ride?"

"Take your choice of the others," Meradoc replied.

Dinas preempted the gray gelding Tostig rode, demoted Tostig to Meradoc's place with the ponies and litter, and handed the reins of the dark horse to Meradoc with a warning. "Don't let him get away from you."

Meradoc stroked the stallion's neck. "Are you ready?" he whispered.

The dark horse rolled a liquid brown eye toward him.

"Right then. We're off." Meradoc strode forward.

The stallion lowered his head and walked obediently at his side.

Dinas scowled.

"That's ridiculous," commented Cadel, who was on foot. "The best horse of the lot and no one's riding him. What if someone sees us? What will they think?"

"Wipe the horse manure out of your eyes," Dafydd advised. References to dung now accompanied almost every remark to Cadel. "Who's paying any attention to us?" Dafydd was correct. The broad valley above the Severn was lush and green with the burgeoning spring. On the fertile farmlands every able-bodied man, woman or child over the age of four was fully occupied with the demands of the season. Plowing, sowing, planting, herding, milking. No one had time to stand and gawk at a troop of itinerants passing by.

"When we make camp there should be good foraging around here," said Docco.

Iolo asked him, "Why are you always thinking about your stomach?"

"Because my stomach is always hungry."

Bleddyn laughed.

Placing one hand on the withers of his horse, Hywel raised himself off the animal's back. "I think there's a town up ahead," he reported.

Dafydd said, "Cadel, why don't you ask Dinas to let you sit on his stallion so you can make a grand entrance?"

Cadel ignored the remark.

Dinas had already sighted the timber walls and cluster of roofs

standing out against the sky. That should be Glevum, he thought.
The old legionary fortress at the crossing of the Severn. Like Deva,
Glevum had shrunk and faded into a rustic country town. From his
last journey in this direction he knew there were the remnants of an
armory here, and weapons for sale. Horses too.

"We'll make camp earlier than usual," he announced. "While the
rest of you get settled I'm going on a shopping expedition."

Meradoc reluctantly surrendered the reins of the dark horse.
Dinas vaulted onto the saddle, paused only to check that his saddlebags were firmly fastened on behind, and cantered away.

He was very late returning.

The campfire had been built up and died down again to a cooking heat; the horses had been rubbed down and hobbled to graze.
The foraging party had found a number of local edibles to add to the
meal and everyone had had enough to eat—even Docco.

Pelemos was worried because Tarates had no appetite. When he
expressed his concern to the healer, Bryn said, "It's to be expected.
The poor man's been jiggled and joggled all day and must have swallowed a bellyful of dust."

"We've all swallowed dust—except for the men on horseback
who ride above it. Dinas promised there would be two horses for
everyone by the time we reached our stronghold, wherever that is.
Do you think he'll keep his word?"

"Dinas always keeps his word, Pelemos," Meradoc interjected.

Bleddyn sucked the last of the grease off his fingers. "You're quite
his champion, aren't you, Meradoc? Yet he won't even let you ride
his horse."

"I never asked to ride his horse."

"You're obviously better with it than he is."

"That's not true. I'm just good at calming horses, that's all. Dinas
is too . . . too . . ."

"Too what?"

"Too full of fire to quiet a horse down when it gets excited."

The other men laughed.

A moment later they heard the distant thunder of hoofbeats approaching; too many hoofbeats for one horse. Meradoc leaped to his feet. "They're back!"

They were indeed. Mounted on his stallion, Dinas rode into the encampment leading four saddled horses who kept colliding with one another. Two of them had large packs lashed to their saddles; packs bristling with weaponry. Adding to the confusion was a mare running loose with a foal at her side. A colt not even weaned yet, with ludicrously long legs and a stiff little tail like a bottle brush.

The recruits scattered in every direction to avoid being trampled. Meradoc ran forward to take the four snarled lead ropes from Dinas. Seeing the little foal, he gave a whoop of joy. "Is he ours too?"

"You can eat him for all I care," Dinas growled as he dismounted, which was awkward; the stallion was so agitated he would not stand still. With an effort and a considerable amount of cursing, Dinas and Meradoc began securing the four saddled horses to a picket line. All the while the loose mare raced around them, calling to her colt, who was trying his best to stay near her, and responding to the constant neighing of the stallion as well.

At last the saddled horses had been securely tied and unloaded, their burden of weapons laid on the ground. The recruits reconvened to have a look. The new horses were sturdy geldings, short in height but heavy boned, with manes hogged in the Roman style. Animals that could carry a man or pull a wagon or race against each other at a fair.

The mare running loose was different altogether. Lean and leggy, with a fine head: wide between the jowls and tapering to a small muzzle. The four geldings still had shaggy remnants of their winter coats but she was as clean as polished wood. Her rich chestnut coat gleamed in the firelight. "She must have cost a lot of money," Meradoc breathed in admiration.

Dinas gave a noncommittal grunt.

He ordered the recruits to encircle the mare and gradually close in, but his horse kept whinnying to her. Distracted by the stallion and anxious about her foal, the mare was impossible to catch. Every time they thought they had her she bolted. "Lead my horse so far away that they can't hear each other," Dinas said to Meradoc. "She's in season; it's making him crazy."

"But the little colt . . ."

"We'll take care of it, just get my horse out of earshot, will you?"

This time Meradoc found it very difficult to calm the stallion. He kept wheeling around and trying to look back at the mare. They were carrying on a fevered conversation in the night that excluded everything but themselves. At last, by a combination of pulling and cajoling, Meradoc was able to lead the dark horse away from the camp, but no matter how far they went the stallion could still smell the mare; hear the mare; want the mare.

Meradoc knew that Dinas could always control his horse from the saddle, no matter how excited the stallion was. "Would you let me ride you?" he whispered to the dark horse. A tentative whisper, hopeful yet astonished at its own presumption.

The stallion leaped and plunged and whinnied. The world he currently occupied had no place in it for mere humans. It was all about the mare, the mare. The ancient and overriding imperative. He stood on his hind legs and pawed the sky and screamed for his mate.

At last Meradoc gave up, tied him to the strongest tree he could find and sat down to wait.

No one slept in the camp that night. The mare could neither be caught nor silenced. She would hardly stand still long enough to nurse and her foal grew increasingly frantic. Soon his baby squeals of protest pierced the darkness. They upset the restive horses on the picket lines, who threatened to break free. Eventually Dinas ordered every man to go to a horse and be responsible for keeping that particular animal under control.

None of the recruits knew how to manage an overexcited horse. They learned that night, beneath the indifferent stars.

By dawn men and horses alike were exhausted. The horses were now tractable, however, and the stallion had relaxed enough to be led back to camp. Although the mare and her foal were still loose, she was willing to allow the infant enough time to nurse.

A weary peace greeted the rising sun.

"Now is the best time to try out your new horses," Dinas announced after the men had eaten a meager breakfast. There was some grumbling; horses were not a favorite topic at the moment. Dinas assigned horses to them anyway.

Cadel refused to take one. Bryn also insisted on remaining afoot, which was just as well, Dinas thought. They now had a total of nine horses, not counting the mare and the stallion, and nine men to ride them: Dafydd, Cynan, Hywel, Bleddyn, Iolo, Docco, Tostig, Pelemos and Meradoc. The two ponies could be designated as backup. Dinas would take the chestnut mare as his own second horse once he caught her. All he needed now were nine more horses and enough weaponry and . . .

Is it only because I'm tired that this begins to look so difficult? he asked himself. Perhaps we'd better stay in camp another day. Or two.

In his mind's eye Dinas saw Tintagel receding into the distance.

No! It would not be allowed. The overwhelming passion he had experienced the first time he saw the peak rising from the sea came back to him in full measure.

Hold on tight. Keep going. We can do this thing.

Pelemos approached him wearing a worried expression. "I don't like the way Tarates looks, Dinas."

"I've never liked his looks myself."

"That's not what I mean. His color is very bad and there's a smell of decay on his breath."

"Talk to Bryn, he's our healer."

"I already did. He sent me to you."

"I'll have a look at him," said Dinas, "but I don't know what you expect me to do."

While he was bending over Tarates, who really did look awful, he felt a tug at his arm. "I don't want the horse you assigned to me, Dinas. Every time I try to mount he kicks out at me."

"Then trade horses with one of the other men, Iolo. I'm sure that one of . . ."

"I tried that. No one else wants him either."

"Meradoc is the man to deal with this, he's captain of the horse."

"Meradoc has his hands full already," Iolo said. "He's been trying to catch that crazy red horse before she injures herself."

Cynan hurried up to them. "Come quick! We were beating out the campfire when the wind blew some sparks into the dry grass and now . . ."

Dinas gave a weary sigh.

If Cadogan were here he would create order from chaos. What was it my mother said? "Dinas for dreams, Cadogan for practicality." Yes. Gwladys preferred dreams. What dream did Vintrex embody for her, I wonder?

The day presented one problem after another. Just when one fire was extinguished a fire of a different sort broke out. And then another. Horses fought, men quarreled. When Dinas sent Tostig and Cadel in search of game to augment their rapidly dwindling food supplies the two came back empty-handed. "We didn't see so much as a hedgehog," Tostig reported.

Meradoc—in a sour mood because he still had not caught the mare—told Dinas, "We need more substantial food than nuts and berries and a few crumbs of dry bread. You could ride back to that town where you bought the horses and buy some meat and cheese."

"I don't think so."

"Why not?"

Dinas looked around to be certain no one else was listening. "The problem is this, Meradoc: I didn't buy the horses—not all of them. I bought and paid for the four geldings, who were seriously overpriced, by the way, and started for camp. Then I noticed a fenced paddock where a man was turning out a mare with her foal. Even from a distance I could tell their quality, so I stopped to watch. You don't see horses like that anymore.

"The man who put them into the paddock fastened the gate and walked away. He didn't even look back. The mare ran up and down along the fence, stopping to snatch a mouthful of grass and running again. My horse began calling to her and she answered. I decided it was time to ride on. I didn't expect her to jump the fence and join us."

"So you stole her?"

"Not exactly, though it might have looked that way. When she jumped the fence she left her foal in the paddock and the little fellow went crazy, trying to get through the fence and go after her. I was afraid he'd hurt himself. I couldn't catch her to put her back in, so I opened the gate to let him out." Dinas gave a rueful smile. "You can understand why I'd rather not go back there."

"But you'll keep the mare." A statement, not a question.

"If you can catch her, Meradoc, I'll keep her. And the foal will be yours."

Meradoc glowed.

Bryn found Dinas glowering over the depleted contents of his saddlebags. The geldings had cost too much. Everything was costing too much. Following the collapse of empire, people with anything to sell were demanding ridiculous prices.

"I'm baffled," Bryn reported. "I don't think the problem with Tarates is his head wound. That's healing as I predicted, yet he's in a lot of pain. I gave him a strong infusion of willow and he said it helped, but I don't believe him. There's something seriously wrong inside of him."

"An injury?"

"Or an ailment that had nothing to do with the attack. I can't treat it until I know what it is."

Dinas followed Bryn to where Tarates lay. The man's condition had visibly worsened. His discolored face was covered with a slick of greasy perspiration and he seemed to be mumbling incoherently. Dinas bent closer.

"The end of the world," Tarates was saying. "The end of the world."

Dinas gave an annoyed snort. "It's no such thing, Tarates."

"The end of the world. I am dying. Please God I am dying. This hurts too much. The end of the world."

Dinas stood up. "He certainly will die if he keeps on like that."

"He will anyway," said Bryn.

Dinas—who had casually wished the man would die—now was determined to keep him alive. He demanded the healer save Tarates no matter what it took, and sent a scouting party to find herbs and roots and other necessaries for more of Bryn's concoctions. While the battle of life and death was being fought Dinas paced around the encampment, angry at his own impotence. Late in the afternoon he set off on foot to try to catch the chestnut mare himself.

The rest of his band felt as helpless as he did, and found ways to keep themselves busy as far from the sufferer as possible. Only two or three, including Meradoc, were driven by pity to visit him again and again.

When Tarates began to writhe with pain and his eyes rolled back in his head, Meradoc could stand it no longer. "I'm going to get some water for him," he told Bryn.

"Water's no good to him now."

"He can't drink," Pelemos interjected. "It's as if his jaws are locked. Just look at him; he's out of his head, he doesn't even know what's going on."

"I'll be right back," said Meradoc.

He returned carrying a stone cup brimming with water from the nearest stream. By this time Tarates was spasming like a half-crushed earthworm. Pelemos was whispering Christian prayers over folded hands. Bryn was muttering incantations to elder gods.

Meradoc knelt on the earth beside Tarates.

"He won't take it."

"I know, Pelemos, but let me try anyway." Cradling the cup between his hands, Meradoc held it to the man's lips. Which had turned blue and were tightly pressed together.

At the touch of the cup Tarates gave a low moan.

Meradoc pressed the vessel more firmly against his mouth.

The lips slowly parted.

Meradoc tilted the cup.

Tarates swallowed convulsively. Almost choked; caught his breath. Took another swallow, a little easier this time. Then another. His lips caressed the rim of the cup. His eyes resumed their rightful place in their sockets; cleared and were aware. With a sigh of ineffable relief, he smiled up at Meradoc.

And died.

As if a gentle hand had passed over his face, the agony faded. Only the smile lingered.

When Dinas returned to the camp leading the chestnut mare they told him about Tarates, and showed him the dead man. Still smiling.

"I ordered you to save him!" Dinas burst out.

"We did everything we could," Pelemos assured him. "The poor fellow was hurt worse than we knew."

Bryn nodded in agreement. "When a man reaches the edge of the cliff there are only two ways to go: step back or step forward. He stepped forward."

The recruits dug a grave deep enough to put Tarates well beyond the reach of predators and lined it with leafy branches. Though he was not of their tribe, they lowered him into the earth with great tenderness. Standing around the grave, the entire company said Christian prayers for a Christian man. Celtic Christianity had taken root in the high mountains from which the recruits came, but the Roman version had not. The ritual they recited was in the ancient tongue. The language of Albion.

Afterward they built a stone cairn over the grave and rode away.

CHAPTER TWENTY-FIVE

Trying not to look at the spear leveled at his heart, Cadogan said, "Call off your dogs. You have no right to insult a visitor to the fair." As he spoke Godubnus and Trebellos stepped up beside him, mirroring the other man's spear carriers.

"I have all the rights I claim," replied the man with the gold torc. "Call off your own dogs."

Cadogan made a slight but perceptible gesture to indicate to his companions that they were to hold their position. His heart was pounding so hard he thought surely everyone could hear it. Yet he managed to say, in a tone borrowed from the chief magistrate of Viroconium, "From your appearance you are a Briton, but from your accent you are not one of the Cornovii. This is their tribal territory—and mine. You are the outsider here; identify yourself."

The other man's eyes glittered with amusement. "You have not heard of me, then? But you will, I assure you. I am called Vortigern. *King* Vortigern."

The name meant nothing to Cadogan. "King of what tribe, what territory?"

"That remains to be determined," Vortigern replied smoothly. "Now it is your turn to identify yourself."

To his surprise Cadogan heard himself say—exactly as his father would have done—"I am called Cadogan, citizen of the Roman Empire."

Vortigern blinked. It was an unintentional reflex, but enough to reveal a chink in his armor. Cadogan quickly pressed home his advantage. "Kings in Britannia are elected by their tribes, Vortigern, and they rule with the consent of the emperor. Which tribe elected . . ."

"Which emperor?" Vortigern interrupted. "The Emperor of the West or the Emperor of the East? The child Valentinian in Rome, or Theodosius the Second in Constantinople?"

Be very careful, Cadogan warned himself. This man is not only clever but knowledgeable. "The empire is being ruled jointly as a matter of expedience, but it is still one—"

"One nothing," Vortigern interrupted again. "The West has collapsed under the weight of its own corruption and the East is busy rediscovering its Greek heritage. Neither of them knows nor cares what happens in an insignificant backwater such as Britannia."

"Who told you that?" Cadogan asked. His curiosity was piqued. Vortigern was arrayed as a king, but aside from wars with their neighbors, British kings rarely left their own territories. He was surprised that Vortigern knew anything about the forces that were ripping the empire apart.

"My information comes from Hengist of the Jutes," said Vortigern, jerking his thumb at one of the spear carriers. "The man aiming his weapon at your heart is Hengist's brother, Horsa. These two led a large band of Saxon settlers to Britannia, and at my invitation are going to bring an army north to defend my borders from the Picts and the Scoti."

This time Cadogan made no effort to hide his astonishment. "*Your* borders? I told you before, this is the land of the Cornovii!"

"And I explained before," Vortigern stressed, "my territory is where I say it is. I say it runs from here to Hadrian's Wall, and I am prepared to fight for it with the aid of my Saxon friends."

Cadogan was dumbfounded. This naked landgrab was so unexpected he could think of no appropriate response. "But what about . . . what about . . ." To his dismay, Cadogan's numbed brain refused to supply him with the name of the king of the Cornovii—a man whom he had met many times in Viroconium.

"Ogmeos," whispered Godubnus.

Cadogan shot him a grateful look. "What about Ogmeos?"

"He is willing to cede his office and titles to me," Vortigern replied smugly. "So many Picts and Scots are flooding into his kingdom that he is unable to cope with them. Rather than admit defeat, he and the other chieftains have accepted me as their new king provided I drive the invaders back over the Wall. Hence, my two generals here."

Cadogan glanced from Hengist to Horsa. Horsa was the taller, Hengist the more battle scarred, but there was no doubt they were warriors. As was Vortigern himself from the look of him. His face was set in the implacable lines of a man determined to have his way at all costs.

Cadogan recognized the expression; he had seen it before on Dinas. Its familiarity steadied him. "I assume you have confirmation of this from the proper authorities?"

"What proper authorities? The only authorities in Britannia now are the sword and the spear, and I am well equipped with both. Tell me, Cadogan, citizen of the empire: Have you come to pay tribute to your new king, or to buy and sell merchandise to enrich my treasury?"

"Perhaps we should discuss this in private," Cadogan suggested, "as befits men of equal rank."

Vortigern blinked again. "Equal rank?"

"You have not heard of me, then?" Cadogan was pleased to repeat his own words back to him. "I am the son of Vintrex, chief magistrate of this entire province. For the duration of his current illness he has appointed me to serve in his stead. So as you see, there is still authority after all."

Horsa lowered his spear.

Vortigern said, "I don't believe you."

"That is of supreme indifference to me," Cadogan replied, gaining strength from the other man's uncertainty. "Whether you believe me or not the authority is mine. If you doubt me ask your friend Og-meos, who knows both my father and myself very well. He has dined in our home on more than one occasion."

Both Hengist and Horsa were now looking directly at Vortigern.

The self-proclaimed king shifted his weight from one foot to the other. He has strange eyes, Cadogan thought. You can almost see him making calculations behind them.

Vortigern cleared his throat. "Perhaps you are right," he said. "We should be discussing this between ourselves. Allow me to offer you the hospitality of my tent." Without waiting for Cadogan to accept, he took hold of his elbow to guide him.

Cadogan subtly pulled away. Just enough to establish his independence; not enough to be a rejection. Turning to Godubnus, he said, "You two wait here for me. If I do not return soon, you know what to do."

Godubnus nodded. "We know what to do," he echoed.

Hengist and Horsa looked at each other.

Vortigern's tent was the largest on the fair grounds. Fifteen cattle hides had gone into its making, augmented by strips of red deer hide and yellow wildcat fur. Its design was British; Celtic British. Wolf-fur robes were piled deeply on the ground inside, and the air was redolent with the bloody remains of a meal. When the two men threw back the flap and entered the tent a young woman jumped to her feet and ran out, carrying a piece of meat in her hand.

"One of my wives," Vortigern commented. "I appreciate some of the old customs."

Cadogan tried not to look shocked. "I assumed you were a Christian."

"Oh, I am. When it suits me. But a king should be able to impress his people with his virility—among other things. Hence I have three wives. Well-satisfied wives," he added with a grin.

"Now down to business, Cadogan. You know my intentions and I assure you I am able to carry them out. Is there any reason why the provincial magistrate or his deputy would disapprove? Under the circumstances, I should think that anyone who is able to turn back the tide of invaders would be considered a hero."

"There are suitable rewards for heroes, but they do not include giving them entire provinces."

"Come now, Cadogan. You speak like an educated man, surely you have studied history. The ultimate reward for a hero has always been land. When we are successful here I plan to give large tracts to my two generals as their reward."

"You will turn back the Picts and Scots yet give more land to . . ."

"To the Saxons. Yes. In my opinion they cannot be stopped anyway; there are too many. Is it not better to make friends of them rather than enemies?"

"A lot of people won't see it that way, Vortigern. Especially those whose land you give to the foreigners."

"There may be trouble," Vortigern agreed. "In fact I am sure there will be trouble. But change happens anyway. I intend to ride the tide rather than be swept under by it."

"You don't happen to know my cousin Dinas, do you?"

"I don't think so. Do I need to know him?"

For the first time since they met, Cadogan smiled. "There is always that possibility."

As Cadogan and his companions were returning to the fort Godubnus remarked, "I'm glad to be going home with my head on my shoulders. When you said 'You know what to do' back there, I had no maggot's notion of what to do."

Trebellos added, "I thought you meant for us to attack those two bodyguards of his. We would have been slaughtered."

"I didn't want you to do anything," Cadogan told them. "I just wanted the others to think there was something you *could* do; something they might not like."

"How did you leave things with Vortigern?"

"I have no doubt he will ask Ogmeos about me, but Ogmeos

will back me up. He's always had great respect for my father. No one really knows who has any authority in Britannia now. Or how much. Vortigern seems to be new at this business of making himself a king; he's causing a lot of noise but treading carefully. I can't prevent his usurping a kingship; what I can do—I hope—is ensure our safety within his territory. That's what we talked about. We came to an agreement that the refugees from Viroconium would be allowed to settle and farm without interference, and if necessary, his warriors would protect us. In return I promised him that neither Vintrex nor myself would oppose his kingship."

"And Vintrex will agree to that, will he?"

"I'm not going to tell him about it."

"He'll find out sooner or later," Godubnus warned.

"You know the condition my father's in; he may never be able to understand what's taking place. Anything could happen before then. As I understand it, Vortigern's arrangement with Hengist and Horsa won't be complete until they drive the northerners back across the Wall. In the meantime Ogmeos and the other chieftains may decided to rebel against Vortigern. He's impressive but it takes more than that to make a king. If those two Jutes fail . . ."

"Did you see the way they looked at me? They knew I was a Caledonian."

"But they didn't attack you, Godubnus," Cadogan pointed out. "That means hostilities haven't begun yet. We have a little time to get ourselves settled."

"You mean, get ourselves dug in."

"That's another way of putting it."

"What about the livestock we came for? We didn't buy a single animal."

"I thought it best not to let Hengist and Horsa know we had any money on us. We'll find pigs and cows somewhere else."

"Or live on roots and berries," Trebellos muttered to himself.

———

The work on the settlement continued. Cadogan pushed the others harder than ever, anxious to have as many as possible under a snug roof before the winter came. Building was only a part of it. Without anyone to teach them, they had to learn long-forgotten skills such as making charcoal and brewing beer and tanning leather. For some of them it came easier than for others. It was as if the blood of their ancestors spoke to them.

There was a social dimension to be considered as well; one Cadogan had not thought about before. Among the group there were four men for every grown woman.

While everyone was desperately busy it did not seem to be a problem. Cadogan was only vaguely aware of fleeting glances, occasional touches. Simmering rivalries. The time would come when those things began to matter.

Meanwhile Vintrex grew increasingly irascible. Esoros withdrew into a hard shell of negativity, like some old turtle caught on a sand bank. And Quartilla's mannerisms were maddening. Yet whenever Cadogan needed something urgently, she was there. Unfortunately she was also there when he wanted to be alone. She had an unerring sense of those times when he retired into contemplation to work on a plan or solve a problem, and would interrupt at the crucial moment, shattering his thoughts like windblown seed.

None of the men showed any interest in her, though she boasted of imagined conquests. Cadogan would have been delighted for anyone to take her off his hands. He began to think of offering a dowry with her.

"Godubnus, have you ever thought of marrying again?"

"After four tries? No thank you. I struck lucky with the last one; that means it's time to quit."

"Nassos, you're a sturdy young man. Surely you feel the need for a wife."

"Who do you have in mind?"

"Quartilla would do for you, she's a—"

"I don't think so."

"Karantec, what about you? I assure you Quartilla is the best cook in—"

"No," Karantec said firmly.

"Even if she came with a dowry?"

Karantec narrowed his eyes. "How much?"

"Let's say . . . a gold denarius?"

"And where would I spend it? Better I remain celibate. You should marry her yourself, Cadogan."

"I don't have time for a wife," Cadogan said hastily.

There had been a time—how long ago it seemed now!—when the leaders of Viroconium society had ordered their servants to load a wagon high with delicious edibles and potables, soft blankets and folding stools, and had driven several miles out into the country to enjoy "a rustic feast." Which lasted only until the first drop of rain or the first wasp sting.

Those pleasant pastimes now seemed like fantastic tales invented to entertain credulous children. Members of the former upper class were becoming intimately acquainted with the realities of rustic nature. Bathing only rarely, in icy streams populated with things that squirmed or bit. Squatting uncomfortably behind bushes in the rain, with only leaves to wipe their buttocks. Eating whatever they were given without asking what it was or where it came from.

The forest that had looked so picturesque in the distance, so invitingly cool on a summer's afternoon, consisted of living trees that held on to life with a tenacity to match that of human beings. Every axe blow meant to kill an oak left human muscles aching. And it was not enough just to fell a tree. Smaller trees were used whole, as logs for the walls, but larger trees had to be debarked, their branches removed, and their trunk sawn into planks. In the beginning this basic task took a team of neophyte woodcutters several days. Clearing an entire site for building could take weeks.

The necessity to have water close by eliminated a number of

otherwise excellent sites. More than one woman set her heart on a house on a hilltop, only to learn she was going to have to live in a valley.

It was not enough to have a cleared site. The ground where the house would stand had to be leveled before construction could begin, and provision made for drainage. Cadogan showed the others how to pour buckets of water into the center of the space and watch how it ran off. If it simply formed in a puddle, channels had to be dug, filled with pebbles and then covered over before the walls went up.

Men began reminiscing about drainage tiles in the way the women spoke of peristyles and reflecting pools.

Thatching roofs was another challenge. In retrospect Cadogan knew he had made a botch of his the first time, but he had tried again and again until he discovered the secret and made it watertight. Sod had to be cut, dried, netted—which necessitated weaving grass ropes—and secured to the roof timbers to support the weight of the thatch. He was forced to use cedar for the cross beams because cedar was lighter than oak and easier for one man to lift. He discovered that the downward slope from the rooftree had to be at a precise angle, steep enough to allow water to run off but not so steep as to encourage the thatch to slide off. Reeds from the river were good at turning water, and the air within their hollow stems added insulation, but they had to be cut, gathered and transported.

Cadogan demonstrated the art of thatching to the men. And commiserated with fledgling thatchers when they tumbled off a roof.

Women learned to plait grass ropes and to cut and gather reeds; children learned to chink log walls with mud. Everything had to be learned. Everything was hard. Men and women looked at Cadogan— or rather at his fort—with new respect. Knowing what he had accomplished by himself was a challenge to the other men.

More than one woman flirted with Cadogan when her husband was not around.

He was scrupulously careful not to respond to them in any way that could be misunderstood. With every day that passed he was more aware of his responsibilities, his unwanted, unasked-for responsibilities. They were such a small community and their existence hung by such a fragile thread.

Houses began to rise in the forest; a thatched timber rectangle on each cleared space. To the citizens of Viroconium they might be huts, but they were snug and solid. Expectations were being scaled down. The nature of "civilization" was changing. Civilization meant living with like-minded people who respected and helped one another.

When he had a rare few moments to call his own and was not fully occupied with planning or building or sorting out arguments between his fellow settlers, Cadogan liked to wander in the forest. Among the trees. Occasionally, in the precious quiet of solitude, memories of the past would pop into his head like isolated jewels. Himself as a small boy, crying over a skinned knee, and Domitia gathering him into her arms and comforting him. The tenderness of her kind face smiling down at him.

A slightly older version of himself racing his cousin Dinas through the columned splendor of the forum. The light slap-slap of his sandaled feet on the smooth paving stones, and Dinas laughing. Dinas who always won their races, swift as quicksilver; Dinas darting out of sight a moment before one of the civic councillors appeared to chastise the rowdy children. Cadogan standing there with his head down, taking his punishment—until Dinas hurled a pebble from his place of concealment and drew the man's attention long enough for Cadogan to make an escape.

Dinas. Laughing. Perhaps dead now. Like Domitia and who could say how many more?

It did no good to summon up the past, Cadogan decided. Nothing could be gained by it, nothing could be changed; that task was done. Concentrate on the future.

In the arboreal peace of the living, breathing forest, Cadogan wondered what sort of civilization would come to Britannia with Hengist and Horsa.

When the settlers gathered at the end of the day to share a meal and discuss the next day's work, they sometimes spoke of Viroconium. Without actually saying so, they were aware that the city's wounds had been mortal. No one could have continued to live in those noisome ruins for long.

"The other survivors are probably scattered throughout the territory by now," was Regina's opinion.

Esoros said glumly, "Or they may all be dead."

"I doubt it," Godubnus told him. "Likely they're doing what we're doing, trying to stay out of the barbarians' way."

"Would they not try to rebuild the city?" asked Nassos.

Cadogan said, "The Romans built Viroconium, not us. Our people wouldn't know how."

"But we're learning how to build now," he heard one man whisper to another.

Sitting among them, staring into the fire, Cadogan was beginning to dream a new dream. He saw himself rebuilding Viroconium. Not as it had been; he admitted to himself that times had changed. Strength had become more valuable than luxury. He would employ a design of his own, combining half-remembered technology with Celtic resourcefulness. Houses would be adaptations of his own fortress. On the foundations of the courthouse he would erect a great timber meeting hall, rectangular in shape, with the walls curving upward to a vaulted and thatched roof. Not Roman. British.

Quartilla nudged him with a sharp elbow. "What are you thinking about?"

"Nothing."

"That's a lie, you can't think about 'nothing,' any more than you can see 'nothing.' Were you thinking about me?"

"Why would I think about you?"

"Because you're a man. All the men think about me, I can see it in their eyes."

"You must have remarkable powers of vision, Quartilla."

"I do. I can even see the future."

"Then tell me what you see."

"In my future?" she asked brightly.

"No, in ours; all of us here."

She pursed her lips and tried to look thoughtful. Suddenly she laughed. "You believe I can see the future? Cadogan, you fool!"

Stung, he replied, "No, I never believe a thing you say, Quartilla."

"Good. That makes you a bit less of a fool."

As so often before, her reply left him speechless.

"No one can see the future anyway," she said after a few moments. She began to fumble with her hair. The red dye had almost grown off, leaving greasy brown locks with crimson tips, as if the hair had been dipped in blood.

"I know a woman who can see the future," Cadogan claimed.

She released the lock of hair. "Do you? Really?"

"Yes, really. My cousin's mother."

Quartilla asked breathlessly, "Are you talking about Dinas?"

"I am. When Dinas and I were little she used to send us out looking for owl scat; little pellets of dung with bits of undigested bone and fur in them. She held them in the palm of her hand and told us all sorts of things."

"Did they ever come true, the things she told you?"

Cadogan smiled. "Always," he lied.

He glanced up to find Esoros watching him the way a man might watch a snake.

CHAPTER TWENTY-SIX

The blunt summit known as Tintagel Head was littered with the detritus of habitation. The collapsed feasting hall of the Dumnonii; broken amphorae that stored wine in an early Celtic monastery; the ruins of tiny stone huts built by a tribe that had ceased to exist before the before. When Dinas dug his toe into the topmost layer of soil he turned up a small steel plate broken from a piece of Roman body armor.

Aha.

Dinas stood alone on the summit, gazing at the foaming surf below. He raised his eyes to the distant purple line where sea met sky; watched the clamorous seabirds swimming on the wind. Surveyed the tumble of broken stones and the few surviving pieces of salt-rotted timber. The scarred earth, trodden by how many feet over how many generations?

Tintagel exists outside of time and space, he thought. That is something Gwladys might have said.

Dinas drew a deep breath and filled his lungs with air from beyond the edge of the world. It was cold and sharp and impossibly pure. Turning, he looked toward the men watching from him the cliffs. The mainland, he called it in his mind, divorcing himself from it. Becoming part of sea and sky instead.

"How's the view?" Bleddyn shouted into the wind.

Dinas pretended not to hear.

Tintagel, Tintagel, he whispered. As a man whispers the name of his beloved.

When he was still a little boy Gwladys had told him, "I can see you up in the sky."

"Really?" he cried excitedly. "Am I flying?" He began to flap his arms.

Her smile was fond and tender. Gwladys understood about dreams. "Almost, little man. What I see is a pinnacle of rock with men staring up at it. You are on the very top, riding a horse in the sky."

Dinas had assumed she meant a peak of Eryri, where she had lived as a girl. Eryri had featured prominently in all the tales she told her child. When he was grown Dinas had visited the high mountains repeatedly, seeking the locale of her vision. In time that quest had led him to Saba.

But the peak in his mother's vision, he had realized the first time he saw it, was Tintagel Head.

Now he stood there. Now everyone was staring up at him. Meradoc and Pelemos and Bryn and the recruits. His men; his band. The foundation of his army.

He wanted the moment to last forever.

Realistically, he knew that of the eleven, only eight could be considered warrior material—nine if he counted Meradoc, which was doubtful. Of those men, one, Cadel, had made it plain he would never mount a horse again. So Dinas had a possible cavalry of seven or eight and one foot soldier. Not an auspicious beginning.

Yet on an afternoon in early summer when the sun was blazing fit to split the stones and the wind off the sea was like an invigorating slap in the face, Dinas knew he could do anything.

Meradoc was holding the reins of the dark horse, who had grown impatient to be with Dinas and was pawing the earth. "How long is Dinas going to perch over there like a frog on a log?" Cynan wondered aloud.

"No frog would be pacing back and forth the way he is now," said Docco. "I know a lot about frogs, they make good eating."

"Perhaps he's planning the layout of our stronghold," Hywel suggested. "Deciding where the walls will go and all that."

"Or pens for the horses," said Dafydd.

"He'll call us when he's ready," Meradoc told them.

"I'm ready now," Cynan growled. "It's rotten cold out here."

"It will be just as cold over there; that's the wind from the sea you're feeling."

Iolo leaned forward to catch a glimpse of the angry surf breaking against the foot of the cliff. "I'm not sure I like the sea."

"You'd better learn to like it," Tostig advised. "We're going to make our living from it."

Cadel, who also was gazing with trepidation at the sea, said, "That's going to be a lot harder than quarrying."

"Don't be ridiculous," Bleddyn told him. "It can't be anywhere near as difficult as a cold winter in the high mountains."

They had been assigned to tend the horses, who were gathered into a little herd on the cliffs. Both horses and men grew restless while Dinas paced and gazed and measured and planned.

And saw the future growing.

"Are we going anywhere or are we just going to stand here?" Docco shouted at last. He had been put in special charge of the chestnut mare, who as usual was skittering about and making the others nervous. Although Dinas and Meradoc working together finally had succeeded in catching her and putting a head collar on her, no one had yet tried to ride her.

Dinas was not thinking about horses now. From his vantage point atop Tintagel Head he could see what his men could not. A group of people were coming toward them from the east. When Dinas raised a hand to shade his eyes he could make out twenty or thirty men, but no women or children. Two of the men were on horseback. The rest were afoot, walking briskly and with purpose.

A muscle twitched in Dinas's jaw. Raising his arm, he silently pointed in the direction of the approaching men. Tostig was the first to react. He turned to look. Saw nothing. Mimed a large shrug.

Dinas shook his arm emphatically and pointed again.

This time they all looked. Docco cried out, "It's an army!"

His shout startled the chestnut mare. She jerked the lead rope out of his hand and galloped away. Her colt, who was growing fast but as yet unaccustomed to a head collar, raced after her.

On Tintagel Head, Dinas swore a combination of pagan and Christian profanities.

Meradoc had his hands full trying to hold on to the dark horse. The stallion was determined to follow the mare. Cupping his hands around his mouth, Dinas shouted, "Come over here now, all of you, and bring the horses with you."

Immediate chaos followed his command, but they were beginning to learn discipline. After a frantic scramble, eleven men and all of the horses except for the mare and her foal joined Dinas on Tintagel Head. The horses were relegated to the large artificial terraces; aprons of level land where monks had once grown their crops of peas and beans.

As the strangers drew nearer Dinas could make out details. The two riders wore mantles trimmed with seal fur. One had a sword on his hip. Some of their followers were carrying weapons—mostly hunting spears or farming implements—but there was no sense of an organized army. This was simply a collection of tribesmen hastily summoned to investigate an incursion into their territory.

Dinas dispatched his largest men, including Pelemos, to meet them at the neck of land that connected Tintagel to the cliffs. A brief conversation ensued. The two riders dismounted. Accompanied by five of their followers carrying spears and two with pitchforks they made their way along the natural causeway and onto the pinnacle, where Dinas met them.

The horsemen wore masses of jewelry to identify their chieftainly status. Large brooches set with roughly cut gemstones, elaborately twisted earrings, silver and copper on their fingers and wide bronze bracelets halfway up their arms. The older of the two also wore a massive gilded chain around his neck. An even more massive ornament depended from the chain: a gleaming brass eagle that once had topped a Roman standard. As he walked it swung heavily against his belly.

Seeing the direction of Dinas's glance, he said emphatically, "Mine. Mine by right."

"I'm sure it is," Dinas replied. "I was just admiring it. It must take a strong neck to carry that."

The eagle wearer's stern features softened ever so slightly at the compliment. "A chieftain's neck," he said. "And your rank, stranger? What gives you the right to occupy Tintagel?"

Dinas had expected such a decisive moment, though it had come earlier than he liked. It would have been far better to greet the first challenge with a stronghold already built and fully manned. Instead he had eight or nine untrained warriors and a pile of ruins at his back.

But he was ready. He began by introducing himself as "Dinas of Tintagel."

The other two exchanged surprised glances.

"And your names are?" Dinas inquired politely.

In a grudging voice the eagle wearer said, "I am called Kollos. This is my brother Geriotis."

The three men nodded to one another, following the ancient tradition. Dinas promptly launched into the speech he had composed many weeks ago; during the long nights beneath the stars. "I am Dinas of Tintagel because I have claimed and occupied this place. Abandoned land belongs to the man who is strong enough to take it. That is the way in Britannia now."

"Britannia?" queried Geriotis. "You are in the kingdom of the Dumnonii. We recognize no authority but our own."

Dinas directed his reply to Kollos. "Yet I see you take pride in displaying the symbol of Roman authority."

The eagle wearer hesitated. "Are you claiming to have Roman authority?"

His question confirmed what Dinas had suspected: The inhabitants of this remote corner of the island remained unaware of events beyond their own borders. For all they knew, Rome still had its foot on British necks.

Instead of answering the Kollos's question, Dinas told him, "What you see here is an advance party only. There will be more coming, of course. Under my *direct* command," he added, wanting the Dumnonians to infer that Rome knew about and sanctioned the expedition.

Geriotis gestured toward the group that had accompanied them, and was now strung out along the edge of the cliffs. "We have more than thirty men with us," he boasted.

Dinas responded with an easy laugh. "Thirty men; as many as that? I have a hundred within two days' march, and more on the way."

The bejewelled Dumnonians exchanged glances again. "Will they be bringing their women with them?" Kollos wanted to know. His voice betrayed his eagerness. At the end of the world too many women died in childbirth.

Aha.

Dinas let his laughter subside to a knowing smile. "What army travels without women?"

Geriotis cleared his throat. "We are famed for our hospitality," he said rather stiffly.

"So I understand. We shall not abuse it; we only wish to establish a settlement of Britons; Celtic people like the Dumnonii. Our women are very beautiful," he added as if it were an afterthought.

"So this is not a hostile invasion?"

"Of course not, we are suffering from hostile invasion ourselves. Tribes of foreign barbarians," Dinas elaborated, dropping his voice to a sinister near-whisper. "They're crowding our people off their land; that's why we need to settle elsewhere. Among our own kind," he emphasized. He raised his voice. "Bryn, step over here! Just look at this man," he said to the Dumnonians. "What invading army puts scrawny old men in its front rank?" Another smile.

"Dinas is pushing his luck," Pelemos murmured to Meradoc. "I don't like this."

"Bryn doesn't like being called a scrawny old man, but look at him. He's standing there and taking it because he trusts Dinas. And I do too."

"Let's hope your faith is not misplaced, Meradoc."

"I played on their distrust of foreigners," Dinas explained to his men after the Dumnonians departed. "The Dumnonii tribes sell their tin to foreigners, but apart from that they keep themselves to themselves. I learned that the first time I came here. Living at the end of the world has made them suspicious of outsiders. So I convinced them that we are, if not brothers, at least Celtic cousins. With women into the bargain. That's what did it."

"We don't have any women," Iolo said peevishly.

"Not yet. Give me time."

Pelemos asked, "What will happen when the Dumnonians realize we've tricked them?"

"We haven't tricked them; I told the truth about foreigners invading our territory, I just didn't go into details about my plans. Did you see how cooperative they became when they understood the situation?"

"But they don't understand the situation," argued Hywel. "I don't understand the situation. Are we going to found a settlement or waylay merchant ships or what?"

"We're going to establish a kingdom," Dinas said. With a light in his eyes.

"That's all right then," Bleddyn told Iolo. "There will be women, you won't have to amuse yourself at night anymore."

Cadel sniggered.

Their immediate need was to set up camp. There would be many more nights of sleeping on the ground in all weathers before they had a proper stronghold with walls and a roof, but now they could see the tangible background to Dinas's dream, it was easier to wait. They busied themselves with locating places to sleep, sheltered from the wind by tumbled ruins, and penning the horses on the terraces below the pinnacle. Then it was time to go looking for firewood. There was nothing on Tintagel to burn. The few pieces of ancient, rotting timber that remained from earlier occupations were so suffused with salt they might have been made of stone.

Meradoc did not need an order from Dinas to know he was expected to recapture the mare and her foal. Preferably before dark; she might be miles away by morning. He took his pony to ride on the search rather than the horse he had been assigned. He preferred familiarity in a strange place.

Privately Meradoc thought Tintagel was an exceedingly strange place. The wind eddying and shrieking among the ruins sounded like a chorus of ghosts.

The first night that Dinas spent in possession of Tintagel he did not expect to be able to sleep, though as always he brought the stallion to stand by his blanket. At his command the dark horse lay down and stretched out his neck to pillow Dinas's head.

"We're here," the man said softly.

The horse responded with a gentle snort through silken nostrils.

Dinas laced his fingers over his chest and looked up at the stars. "We're here, Saba. You should have come with me."

Then he dropped into a slumber so deep it was as if the darkness opened up and swallowed him.

He was not the only man to think about women—or a woman— that night.

Wrapped in his blankets with his head pillowed on a mossy rock, Pelemos was thinking of Ithill. She had begun tiptoeing back into his mind whenever he let his guard down. He was not ready yet—he tried to tell her he was not ready—but that was just like the woman.

Plump and pretty Ithill with the stars in her eyes.

He had hated her. How long ago that seemed, the first time he realized he hated her. For making him so vulnerable. In his youth he had believed he was invulnerable; neither cold nor hunger nor anything else could hurt him.

Ithill could hurt him. With a single careless remark she could make him suffer for days.

There had been times during their life together when he hated her so much he wanted to kill her—which would have given her the ultimate victory. Because he knew that if she died, when she died (and in their early years he was certain she would die before him, in childbirth, with her narrow hips, because she did not know the secret all Roman women knew of preventing conception and he could not teach her, did not know the secret) when she died it would cause him more pain than anything else could. More pain than he could bear. And she knew that.

She knew it when she smiled at him with her eyes but not her lips. Her lips that could smile at any man and it meant nothing. Only her eyes smiled at him. Her lips folded themselves so sweetly around his penis. The sensation was incomparable. Nothing in his imagination had prepared him for it. And he hated her because she could give him such incomparable pleasure and then take it away again.

If she died. When she died.

And then, she did.

Ithill. Ithill!

Tostig was dreaming of a girl called Angharad from his home village. She had never called him "Otter," and on summer days she sometimes came to the quarry to watch him at work. When no one was looking she let him put his hand between her legs.

In the morning, Tostig promised himself, I shall ask Dinas about those women we're going to have with us. Perhaps he'll let me suggest a few.

————

Bryn the Healer also had women on his mind. There had been so many of them in his life—young and old and in between, healthy and dying and in between there too. Women who came to him seeking help—on their knees, some of them—and a few, a very few, who helped him. I should have kept one of them when I had the chance, Bryn told himself. Sleeping close to a warm woman on a cold night would be good medicine for an old man. Why did I not foresee the day when I would need that kind of medicine? The nostrums I concoct don't take the ache out of my bones or improve my eyesight. What is the secret for capturing youth? Could I steal a bit of it from a young warm body? Where am I going to find a young woman now? Even if I did find her, one of this lot would take her away from me.

Cold nights. For the rest of my life.

The healer shivered under his blanket.

Meradoc was not thinking of women at all. Early in his motherless, sisterless life—so early he did not even remember it—he had come to the conclusion that women occupied a different sphere from his own. The comforting virtues they embodied—or he thought they embodied—were not for someone like him. He was, he had concluded, a crumb picker. Allowed to gather the crumbs from beneath other people's tables. He was fortunate that the possessors of well-supplied tables were willing to feed him and let him sleep in a shed with the goat.

Meradoc had told himself these things and thought he believed them. Until he saw the stallion Dinas rode. The living symbol of a wild free life, and of beauty beyond his dreams.

For Meradoc it was enough to know the dark horse and to live in his realm.

CHAPTER TWENTY-SEVEN

"What am I going to do with her?" Cadogan, at wit's end after his most recent confrontation with Quartilla, was seeking advice from Regina.

"What do you want to do with her?" the woman replied. "Strangle her? I would be happy to provide the cords."

It was the end of a long day and he had recently returned from a long ride. The westering sun was shooting spears of reddish gold through the trees. Cadogan ached; ached in every bone and muscle. He longed only for a meal and his bed. Instead he had just endured another verbal duel with Quartilla that served no purpose and re-solved no issues. When she flounced out of the house he had turned to Regina. Seeking sanity.

As always at this time of day, she was visiting the tiny shrine he had set up in one corner of the house. Domitia's silver cross, cleaned and polished to a fine luster, hung on the wall. Two curving lines that intersected to form the outline of a fish, the symbol for Christ, had been deeply inscribed into the earthen floor below the cross.

Because Regina was finding it hard to kneel on the bare floor, Cadogan had made a cushion for her. The result of his handiwork was lumpy and shapeless, so he had made the mistake of asking Quartilla to sew a better one. With predictable results. Hence the most recent altercation between them.

As he held out his hand to help the Regina to her feet, Cadogan said ruefully, "I'd like to strangle Quartilla, believe me I would. At least that would solve one problem. We have eight houses completed now—nine if you count this one—and more underway. Would you not think that at least one of the men who has no wife would be willing to take Quartilla off my hands? She's strong, she's still young enough to bear children, she can even cook. What's wrong with her?"

"What's right with her?" Regina countered. The creaking of her knee joints as she stood up embarrassed her.

"Ah. Yes. It's hard to pin down her virtues, I suppose. She doesn't . . . I mean she hasn't . . ."

"Exactly. And the more time a man spends around her the more obvious her faults become. What we need is a stranger who is only passing through on his way to some distant place. Unfortunately we are so well tucked into the hills that random travelers do not come our way."

"Your description fits my cousin perfectly," said Cadogan. "But as he's the one who unloaded her on me in the first place, I'm sure he would never take her back. Besides, I don't know where Dinas is or even if he's alive. I don't expect to see him again; not with things as they are in Britannia."

"Things as they are," Regina echoed.

The gray sound of defeat in her voice—her suddenly old voice—set alarm bells ringing for Cadogan. Regina couldn't be old! How had the years crept on her without his noticing? He only realized how much he relied on her when he heard the whisper of mortality.

"They aren't so bad here," he said briskly, trying to bring back the woman she always had been. "They're better than last year. And last year was better than the one before. Now we have two healthy new infants in the group and another on the . . ."

"What do those children have to look forward to?" Regina eased herself onto a stool and gazed up at him. Her eyes, he discovered to his distress, were faded and rheumy. The whites had turned the yellow of old ivory. "What, really, are their expectations, Cadogan? When I was a child growing up in Viroconium I could look forward to a pleasant life among comfortable surroundings and cultured, congenial people of my own station. What do we have to offer these children?"

"They can have a good life here, even if they have to work hard," Cadogan asserted, "and we're not uncomfortable. We've even become a real community—you commented on that yourself only the other day."

"A community of rusticans living hand-to-mouth in the wilderness," she said, with unexpected contempt. "The children may not know how much we've lost, but I do. God help me, I do. Deep inside, I always believed this hiatus was temporary, an adventure, if you will, and in the end we would go home."

"*This* is home now," Cadogan insisted. "Remember what you told Pamilia three years ago? I've never forgotten it. 'We have a new life and we must learn how to live it,' you said. I was impressed by your words, Regina; I thought you understood the situation better than anyone else. Was I wrong?"

She lowered her eyes and would not look at him. "It is easy to be resilient in a temporary situation. But a permanent change of such magnitude . . ." Lifting her head, she gazed toward the open doorway and the rosy sunset light. "I am forced to accept that I shall be buried here. Among these hills, in a place that was never my choice. When my husband was entombed on our property in Viroconium, I expected to lie beside Lentullus for eternity. *That* was my choice."

"I'll take you there when the time comes," Cadogan promised, eager to lift her mood.

She reached up and put her liver-spotted hand on his arm. "It would serve no purpose to take me back, dear friend. I have nothing to go back to. The Saxons broke into the tomb and stole my husband's grave goods, then they desecrated his remains and scattered them about the garden." Her voice was as dry as dust. "I saw it happen while we were making our escape. The barbarians were too preoccupied with their . . . sport . . . to notice me sneaking away with Pamilia and the children. When I returned to what had been our home, there was nothing left but rubble and ashes."

"Surely some of those ashes are . . ."

"Lentullus? I think not. As a Christian I believe that the important part of Lentullus has long since gone to be with our Lord, and I cannot see myself crouching in the dirt to scrape up anonymous ashes. No, Cadogan; when the time comes, bury me here. The important part of me will be gone by then, anyway."

He did not try to comfort her. He realized she was past comforting; Regina had come to terms with life in her own way. Cadogan envied her. Such peace of mind eluded him.

The dream of returning to—and rebuilding—Viroconium was alive inside of him. Growing in him. Becoming an obsession. He could envision a great timber hall rising on the foundations of the old courthouse. Walls curving upward to a vaulted and thatched roof. He could almost smell the cedar beams and the thatch. Would he even need to use cedar? Could he summon a large enough workforce to build the hall entirely from oak? And construct new houses on the sites of the old ones, built in a new style; a British style . . .

The dream tugged and pulled at Cadogan as his dream of Viola had once tugged and pulled at him. Viola. Almost forgotten now; a wistful presence that occasionally drifted through his thoughts for a moment or two, only to be displaced by something more immediate.

Desire what you can have, he told himself.

As Cadogan went outside to fetch firewood for the night, Pamilia emerged from the edge of the woods. She had lost weight since leaving Viroconium and there were lines in her face that had not been there before. "Is Regina inside?" she called out. "I've come to ask her to take supper with us. Godubnus has slain a fat roe deer and it's been roasting all day."

"For an ironmaster, your husband has become an uncommonly fine hunter," Cadogan remarked as she came up to him.

"Godubnus is thorough at everything he does," said Pamilia. Patting her mounded belly.

"Are you smiling or blushing? I can't tell in this light."

"Both," she admitted with a laugh. The formerly timid, diffident woman laughed easily now.

"Your husband is a lucky man."

"We were lucky that you consented to marry us."

"Since there is no priest among us, I only did what I thought right."

"You always do what you think right, Cadogan." Pamilia paused, then confessed, "Godubnus was not my first choice, you know."

He chose not to understand. "You could not have done better than Godubnus."

"I know that now. I have everything I want. Now . . . about Regina? And perhaps you would have supper with us as well?"

"I usually eat with Vintrex."

"And Quartilla and Esoros, I know. Oh, forget about them for once, Cadogan, and join us! You will have a much better time; the children are eager to see you again."

It was not difficult to persuade him.

The path through the woods to the house of Godubnus was familiar to him, though less so to Regina, who rarely visited her former daughter-in-law. In the velvet dark beneath the trees Regina took Cadogan's arm and held on tightly. Pamilia walked beside them, carrying a torch and chattering happily. "Ours is the best house so far," she told her former mother-in-law. "With every house he designs, Cadogan thinks up new refinements. We have two fire pits, one at either end, to keep us warm in the coldest weather. My children no longer sleep in the bed with us, they have a bedbox behind a timber screen. And there is a cradle waiting for the new baby, too, in a snug little recess. Godubnus is wonderful, he's so anxious for his son!"

The fingers clutching Cadogan's arm tightened almost imperceptibly. It was not easy for Regina to hear praise heaped on the man who had replaced her own son as father to her grandchildren.

Nothing was easy anymore. Every step was difficult. How much harder must it be for poor Vintrex, who could hardly see, much less think? We are too old, Vintrex and I, Regina thought sadly. We should not have lived this long. I could lie down right here in the leaves and wait for the wolves to come.

But she knew she would not.

The meal Pamilia served to her guests bore little resemblance to the banquet her servants would have prepared in Viroconium. Food that would have been only partially eaten; nibbled at and cast aside because there was always too much and it was too rich. Here in the hills they ate and enjoyed much simpler fare. Nothing was swimming in butter or cream because the settlers had only two cows among them, and milk was reserved for the children. There were no spices to disguise the taste of spoiled meat because meat was eaten fresh, usually on the day it was killed. No exotic dainties waited to tempt jaded palates, because people who had been working hard from sunrise to sunset had excellent appetites.

The oak table Godubnus had constructed with his own hands was piled with food. In three years the women had learned how to grind grain into flour; the men had learned how to build stone ovens. Steaming hot slabs carved from the deer's haunch were served on thick trenchers of crusty dark bread, soaked with meat juices. The deer fat had been roasted separately to form a crisp crust, then cut into strips and passed around to season boiled root vegetables. Pamilia had pounded hazelnuts to a paste that she sweetened with honey to make a delicious cake. There was a choice of beverages— barley beer or spring water—but no one complained about the lack of wine.

Every crumb was eaten; every drop drunk.

Watching them, Cadogan felt a quiet pride. His people had suffered so much and learned so fast, most of them. Those who refused to learn, and there were two or three, had been forced out of embarrassment to catch up. In spite of their achievements he knew they were not safe. No one was safe anymore—but was life ever safe? They at least were equipped with the basic skills of survival and, more importantly, with a newfound confidence in their own abilities.

Cadogan had acquired a degree of confidence in his own abilities as well. He had devised a method for dealing with seemingly insurmountable problems. Building his first little fort had taught him that lesson. For someone who had never fastened two sticks together before, the idea of building an entire house had seemed ridiculous at first. Then he discovered that the trick was to concentrate on one job at a time, however small. A man could not do everything at once but he could do one thing. Concentrate fully, work carefully, get it right, and move on.

Strangely enough, Cadogan had begun with his door. It seemed logical at the time; it would be impossible to have a house without a door to enter. The task had taught him a lot about woodworking. He made four doors before he had one that was straight and true. Then the completed door required a frame to hang from, and the frame demanded a wall, and the walls a roof . . . and in the end the door frame was wrong and had to be rebuilt . . . But the finished product was greater than the sum of its parts. Like this new settlement in the hills.

Godubnus noticed the expression on Cadogan's face. "You're looking rather pleased," he commented, startling Cadogan out of his reverie.

"Am I?"

"Did you hear some good news?"

"When?"

"This morning. When you rode away on that scraggly horse of yours."

The two women looked at Cadogan with sudden interest.

He told Godubnus, "That scraggly horse, as you put it, is a treasure; a tough little gelding who was born and bred in rough country and can handle any kind of footing. When I bought him at the last autumn fair I had to outbid three other men, and two of them Saxons."

Regina gasped. "You never mentioned seeing any Saxons!"

Cadogan instantly regretted his words. "I didn't want to worry you."

Pamilia stood up abruptly. "I had best put the children to bed."

"Leave them be," her husband told her. "They're old enough to know."

"Know what?" Regina's voice quavered, but her face was set in determined lines.

"You'd better tell the women what you did," Godubnus said to Cadogan. "Even if they don't like it."

"They won't like it," Cadogan replied, "and neither will my father. That's why I don't intend to tell him. And I don't want anyone else to tell him, either," he added with a meaningful look at Regina. "Do you remember the first time I went to the great fair to buy some livestock—and came back without any?"

She nodded.

"That was where I first met the man who calls himself King Vortigern. I didn't know what to make of him until I realized he reminded me of someone else; my cousin Dinas. Dinas can be impressive but a lot of that is bravado. I suspect the same is true of Vortigern. He's attempting something that's nearly impossible and disguising his vulnerability with a cloak of arrogance. He might just succeed, though; in fact I'm counting on it."

Regina and Pamilia looked puzzled.

Cadogan continued. "A few years ago Vortigern realized there were no truly strong leaders left among the tribes of southern Britannia. The Roman authorities had always discouraged their development. Vortigern—who's still a young man—decided to return to an earlier era when Britons were their own masters. To that end he's building a confederacy of tribes who will accept him as overlord. And he's hired an army of mercenaries to protect himself and his supporters."

"Mercenaries!" Regina's hand flew to her raddled throat.

"The Romans used mercenaries against the Britons," Cadogan reminded her. "Why should Britons not use paid killers to protect themselves? That's Vortigern's argument as he put it to me. In his case, though, it's something of a calculated risk. His mercenaries are Saxon warriors led by a pair of Jutes called Hengist and Horsa."

Regina looked so appalled Cadogan feared she might faint. But he plunged on. "I don't know if Vortigern can control his Saxon forces and I suspect he doesn't know, either. Who can tell what Saxons are really like? I guess we'll find out soon enough. The truth is, they can't be stopped in any case. They're pouring into Britannia like water through a sieve. There are hundreds of Saxons—perhaps even thousands—in the east already. Soon there may be more of them than of us."

Regina did not faint. Her face was dead white and her eyes were like two holes burned in a blanket, but she held her place, watching his lips with a dreadful fascination.

"As I see it, we have two options," Cadogan went on. "First, we can retreat into the high mountains and hope the foreigners won't want to follow us. Other tribes of Britons fled into the far west during the Roman occupation. It wouldn't be easy for our people, though. We'd be living among strangers in an unfamiliar territory, and the skills we've mastered here might not be enough to keep us alive there.

"Secondly, we can stay where we are and keep what we've built. The barbarians will arrive soon enough. But if Vortigern wins his gamble our position will be strengthened because I've made an arrangement with him; a sort of compromise. He has agreed that we can keep our settlement and his Saxon mercenaries will protect us from other foreigners . . . if we accept his kingship and look to him as overlord."

"An arrangement," Regina said in a harsh whisper. "If we accept."

Pamilia reached out and gave her a comforting pat. "What do you think, Godubnus? Will this Vortigern person keep his word?"

The ironmaster shrugged his heavy shoulders. "I work with my hands, I don't know anything about politics. And it's all politics, this business of kingmaking and agreements. We have to trust someone who understands it. Cadogan comes from a political family, I don't, so I'll go along with whatever he decides."

Suddenly Cadogan was very tired indeed. The food he had eaten—the roasted deer, the boiled vegetables and sweet cakes—sat in his stomach like rocks. Groaning under the weight of a responsibility he had never wanted.

Regina drew a deep, shuddering breath. "I think . . . ," she began.

All eyes, even those of the children, turned toward her.

"I think . . . Cadogan, are you sure the number of Saxons is growing?"

"I am. Since I bought the horse I've been able to gather quite a bit of information. Farmers and traders tell me what's happening in this territory, and refugees bring news from farther away. It's not like the old Roman network of mounted couriers but word does filter through, even if it's shouted from one hilltop to another. At first the Saxons were only interested in plunder; now they're building settlements and raising children. They're here to stay. And they're spreading westward all the time."

"I see." With an effort, Regina gathered herself. Her aging spine was permanently bowed, but she sat up as straight as she could, drawing upon reserves of energy she willed herself to possess. When she spoke again she forced her voice to be steady. "We do not have two options, Cadogan. We have three. We can flee to the west, we can stay here and assimilate—or be assimilated—by the Saxons, or we can fight."

"Fight?" He could hardly believe what he was hearing. "We have nothing to fight with, Regina! The Romans pulled out and left us with no standing army and hardly any weapons. I'm no fighter anyway, that's why I made an arrangement with Vortigern."

She said coolly, "Shall we eliminate that option, then?"

"Dinas would vote for it," Cadogan admitted.

"I won't see my children slaughtered!" cried Pamilia.

Regina was not finished. "Going into the mountains means running away. We ran away from Viroconium because the barbarians took us by surprise, but we know what we are up against now." She looked smaller, older, frailer than ever. But she lifted her chin as she said, "I for one do not intend to be driven out again."

Later, as they were walking back through the forest to the fort, Regina asked, "When were you planning to tell the others what I heard tonight, Cadogan?"

"Not until I had to. If I had to."

"And leave us open for a nasty shock? Sometimes I forget how young you are. You still think trouble will go away if you ignore it."

"I'm not that foolish; I was trying to protect you."

"No one is protected by ignorance, Cadogan."

My mother was, he thought. For a while she was. How much does Regina know about my father's infidelity? How much did anyone in Viroconium know about it? It seemed everyone was aware of the scandal, but what about the details? Who started the affair? Why did it go on for so long? Neither of them was young; it's hard to blame their behavior on hot blood.

Regina's voice cut through his thoughts. "Hold that torch higher, do you want me to stumble over a tree root and fall on my face?"

"Sorry." He raised the torch. "Regina, you were my mother's friend. What did you think of my father in those days?"

"Why are you asking me this now?"

"Perhaps I'm tired of being left in ignorance."

She gave a sniff. "I can tell you this much: He was a cold man. And a stern disciplinarian by all accounts, though Domitia told me he was as hard on himself as on anyone else. Esoros is the one to ask about Vintrex, though; he has been the shadow to the chief magistrate's sun for many years. No one else knows Vintrex so well."

"Esoros would never discuss my father, or anything else, with me. At best there's an armed truce between us."

"As there is between Quartilla and myself," Regina replied. "Three years under the same roof and I still do not understand the woman."

"Nor do I. All I know for certain is, you can't believe anything she says about herself."

"I know more than that, Cadogan. Whatever her background, Quartilla was no servant."

"How can you be sure?"

"I have had numerous servants, from the cream to the dregs. I know how the unfree think and what they can do. The skills Quartilla possesses, and she has a considerable array, are the skills of a free-born woman who grew up among educated people. In Viroconium," Regina reminisced, "we knew who everyone was and their station in life. We knew it from their features, their accents and their demeanor. But Quartilla . . . if she chooses not to tell you, you may never solve her riddle, Cadogan. I suspect she is not unique; there are others like her now and there will be more. We are being pulled up by our roots and dispossessed."

"No." Cadogan spat out the word as if it burned his tongue. "We will not be dispossessed, Regina. It's decided. We're staying right here."

CHAPTER TWENTY-EIGHT

Fortune was with them at the beginning. The first ship they robbed was a Syrian merchantman laden with wine and slaves, plus some perfume from Capua and ornaments made of Corinthian bronze. It came in too close to Tintagel Head and grounded on a reef. Dinas and his men gleefully waded into the surf to offload the merchandise, which they stored in the tower. The slaves were released to make their way to freedom—or what freedom they might find in Dumnonia. Thus lightened, the Syrian vessel was refloated and sailed away.

The success had come just in time for Dinas. He had very little gold left in his saddlebags.

Taking Meradoc and two packhorses with him, he rode inland. He was able to sell some of the wine, and buy grain and fish oil lamps and hard cheese. He also added a few more coins to the little hoard in the saddlebags. When they returned to Tintagel he counted the money carefully a second time and made sure the bowl and the plate were still intact. Against his better judgment he was becoming superstitious about them. He was glad he would not have to sell them.

That earliest venture had proved so easy—late in a warm summer when the sea was calm and the weather benign—Dinas thought it would always be easy. Buoyed by success, he and his band threw themselves into the task of completing a stronghold before the weather turned. From the tumbled ruins on Tintagel Head they scavenged enough usable material to build a fortified tower and a dozen stone huts for barracks and storage.

The tower was accessed by a flight of steps cut into the stone. On the day the work was finished Cadel stood on the bottom step and looked up admiringly. "Are the walls straight, Dinas?"

"Of course they are, as straight as a poplar sapling." Holding both hands open in front of him, Dinas sawed them up and down through the air to indicate the straight sides of his tower . . . just as Dafydd approached.

It was too good an opportunity for an inveterate prankster to ignore. "Ho, Dinas!" Dafydd called out cheerily. "What are you going to do about that wall?"

Dinas turned to face him. "Which wall?"

"The one that's leaning out, of course. It looks to me as if it's about to fall down, I'm glad we spotted it in time. No, don't walk around to the other side, it might topple onto you!"

Dinas scowled. "You must be joking."

"Would I joke about something so serious? Cadel, wipe the horse manure out of your eyes and have a look, will you? You should be able to see the problem from where you're standing." As he spoke Dafydd gave a surreptitious wink.

Cadel resented the remark about horse manure, but he enjoyed a joke as well as the next man. "There's definitely something wrong, Dinas," he reported. "We must have used larger stones on one side than on the others."

"I don't see what difference that would make."

"There's Cynan and Otter, let's see what they think." Cadel beckoned the pair over; Dafydd greeted them with another surreptitious wink. "We're talking about the new tower, lads. Cadel and I think it's leaning but Dinas doesn't agree."

"There's nothing wrong with it," Dinas insisted. He remained where he was while the four recruits surveyed the tower from various angles with much nodding and muttering.

Impelled by curiosity, Pelemos ambled over to see what was going on.

When Tostig felt the time was right, he caught Dinas by the

arm and led him forward a few steps, to the very base of the tower. "Now tilt your head back and look up," he said.

Dinas stared up along the stone shaft. Suddenly he caught his breath and staggered back, raising his arms to shield his face. "Sweet Christ, Otter, it's falling on me!"

The four recruits howled with laughter. Cynan gave himself hiccups.

Dinas failed to see the humor in it.

"It's only a trick of the eyes," Tostig tried to tell him. "We discovered it when we were building the tower. It isn't falling at all, it only seems that way if you stand close to the base and look straight up."

Pelemos had a different explanation. "The problem is the height of the tower, it's too tall. It profanes the heavens to build something like that. You should knock the top off of it, Dinas."

"I certainly will not! It's a splendid structure, fit for a king."

"All right. But don't say I didn't warn you."

Thereafter the tower was referred to as "the famous falling tower" by everyone but Dinas. "I don't think it's funny," he complained to Meradoc—who thought it was very funny but did not say so.

As the days grew shorter the band attacked two more ships, though not with the success of their first undertaking. The crew on one vessel were well armed and ready for them. Dinas ordered his men to turn back rather than risk their lives. The other ship had sold its trade goods and was carrying only tin ingots, which Dinas scorned. "We'll do much better in the spring," he assured his men.

The dying of the summer brought a change to the land of the Dumnonii. As the nourishment faded from the grass near the sea Meradoc and the recruits began taking the horses farther afield in search of good grazing. Thus they discovered that wars were being fought inland. Small wars on a small scale, but violent nonetheless. Individual chieftains maintained their status and enlarged their holdings by fighting one another. Like the Celts of old, they defined themselves in battle. War was their sport and their religion. As the days began to grow shorter they initiated conflicts with increased urgency, anxious to consolidate their wins before winter and mud made warfare unproductive.

Meradoc reported this to Dinas with some amusement. "It's like stepping back in time," he said. "We Britons used to live like that, I suppose. Before the Romans invaded."

"If we had been better at it the Romans never could have conquered us," Dinas replied. "I think we had best start having weapons practice."

With the change of seasons the recruits learned the major difference between life in the high mountains and life on the edge of the ocean. Autumn brought gale force winds that came roaring over the rim of the world to batter the helpless land with waves as tall as trees. Giant crests of white foam leaped and curvetted like silvery horses, tossing their spumey manes. The nights were bitterly cold and the days not much warmer. Men had to shout as loud as they could in order to be heard over the wind. The wind, the wind, the omnipresent, salt-laden wind with all the force of the ocean behind it.

Dinas loved it. He climbed to the top of his tower and bared his teeth to the wind, daring it to do its worst.

"He has an iron spike in the wall up there to hold on to," Bleddyn confided to Iolo, who never climbed to the top of the tower.

The winter surpassed the autumn for savagery. The horses had grown heavy coats, but even so they used up their reserve fat in keeping themselves warm. The recruits took turns spending an entire day with them while they grazed on sparse, frozen grass, which gave little nourishment. They only brought the horses back to Tintagel at night when wolves could be heard howling in the distance.

As soon as the sun went down the men sought their stone huts and did not emerge until morning. Even Dinas did not sleep in the tower at night. He tried it for a while, but there was something in the voice of the wind that disturbed him. At first he shrugged it off. He loved everything about Tintagel, he told himself. It was the realization of his wildest dreams.

Then Bryn claimed that the promontory was haunted. "Something's alive here that has never been alive," were his exact words.

"What are you talking about?" said Dinas. "A ghost from the past?"

"Or the future," Bryn replied. "Either is possible, you know. Or maybe you don't know. Young people these days . . ."

At night Dinas began sharing a hut with Meradoc and Tostig. He explained that he slept better close to the ground. Which was true.

No merchant vessels dared the Oceanus Hibernicus in the dead of winter. The supplies Dinas had purchased with the stolen wine would be almost gone by Christmas. "I should have rationed our food from the beginning," he said to Bryn. "I don't suppose you know of any edible roots and herbs we haven't found yet?"

"If I did, I would have eaten them by now," the healer admitted.

Dinas and Meradoc set out again with packhorses and saddlebags. They visited three separate Dumnonian villages without finding anyone who wanted to buy the Capuan perfume. The women wrinkled their noses. "It stinks like a farting fox," one haughtily informed Dinas.

After examining the Corinthian bronze ornaments with grave suspicion, the patriarch of a fourth extended family chose to be insulted. "You offer me the figure of an ass!"

Dinas took back the brooch and looked at it himself. "That isn't an ass, it's an embossed horse. It may not be a very good representation, but I promise you, that's what it is. A horse is a noble emblem indeed, you should be honored." Using flattery and guile in equal measure he eventually persuaded the man to buy two brooches for a fraction of their value. A she-goat and a straw basket filled with birds' eggs. As they were riding away Meradoc said, "You told me those bronze things were fancy cloak fasteners."

"They are," Dinas confirmed.

"But you told that man they would keep his prick stiff all night if he rubbed them on it."

Dinas raised an eyebrow in mock surprise. "Did I? Who knows; maybe they will. Stranger things have happened."

Meradoc laughed. "Now that *is* funny."

In appalling weather they crisscrossed a sizable portion of Dumnonii territory. They did not meet the two chieftains who had greeted them upon their arrival at Tintagel, nor did they find anyone as hospitable. Some helped them out of pity; some shouted at them and threw stones. At last, when nothing was left in the saddlebags but the wooden plate and the stone cup, they made their way back to Tintagel.

"We can survive on what we have," Dinas assured his men, "if we go hunting every single day and bring back anything we can find. Even vermin."

"I didn't think the Saxons had come this far," said Tostig the Otter.

On the coldest days of winter the entire band crowded into the tower to hear Pelemos tell stories. Although their bellies were cramping with hunger, his words filled the dark chamber with sun and summer. Disheartened, discontented men who had been talking about leaving decided that things were not so bad after all. They felt part of something almost mystical; a brotherhood of heroes extending back into the distant past.

Albion.

Standing off to one side, Dinas tried to fathom the power of the bardic art.

Does everyone dream of a secret Albion; a place in the heart, not the head? Is that what a true leader gives his followers?

If he knows how.

I wish I knew how. But at least I have Pelemos.

Strange to think that I came upon him by accident. I didn't even want to bother with him at first because I thought he was simple. And he is, though not in the way I meant then. There's nothing wrong with his mind. His simplicity is his strength. He uses it to lighten the burdens of others, while his serenity lifts their spirits. With Sa-

ba's lambs he showed a totally masculine tenderness I had never seen
before. I envy it, as I would envy someone who hears music I can't
hear. Pelemos is the quietest of men; he lives in a world of his own
most of the time, yet the less he says, the more he is admired. People
are drawn to him like iron filings. My men speculate on his saintli-
ness.

I, who believe in nothing but myself, am amused by ordinary
men crediting sainthood to another ordinary man—though their
delusion serves me well.

Then Dinas stopped speculating altogether and lost himself in
the story Pelemos was telling. A story about a band of courageous
men who performed many wondrous deeds. In the shadowy tower
of Tintagel, it seemed plausible.

The winter dragged on. Dinas was the only one of the men familiar with eating shellfish; to the others the armored denizens of the
deep were creatures out of nightmare. However hunger was a quick
teacher. Soon they were scouring the rocks in search of crabs and
barnacles.

The sparse grass atop the cliffs was rimed with ice, it crunched
when the horses tried to crop it. But they learned too. Although men
and horses grew thin, no one actually starved.

Yet still it was winter. Dark and cold and relentless.

One day Docco suggested they might have to eat the horses if
things got any worse. "They're no good to us anyway," he said. "We
can't gallop along the coast in search of ships when there aren't any
ships. One horse would feed us for at least . . ."

The look Dinas gave Docco contained more ice than the winter
wind. "One man would feed us almost as long," he snarled, "and be
more tender. You, for example. You have more fat on you than anyone else."

After that there was no talk of eating the horses.

Then one morning there was a perceptible change in the angle of
the light. A few days later the omnipresent wind swung around and
began to blow out of the south. The horses stopped trying to tear

nourishment out of the reluctant earth and lifted their heads, sniffing through distended nostrils.

The dark stallion whinnied to the chestnut mare. She answered
with longing to equal his own.

Spring was in the air. It sang through the veins like red wine.
Men who were weak with hunger began to believe they would be
stronger soon. And they were.

With spring the tin trade resumed. Ships began to appear along
the coast again. Most had sails of various descriptions, from square
to triangular. Some were exotic in outline. "Byzantine, I think. Or
eastern anyway," Dinas remarked to Tostig. A few of the ships were
broad-beamed timber vessels like those known to be used by the Saxons, totally dependent on oar power. Dinas made no effort to attack
those.

He realized their first success had been a fluke. The task of
seizing and boarding ships was both dangerous and complicated.
The horses were useful for hurrying men to landing sites, but then
someone had to hold them during the action, which tended to ex-
cite the animals. Once or twice they broke away and their chagrined
riders had a long walk ahead of them.

The men they were trying to rob were also uncooperative. Dinas
and his band soon discovered they were not the only pirates at work
along the southwestern coast, and merchants from the east had begun arming themselves. "I suppose it was inevitable that others would
have the same idea I did," Dinas admitted to Meradoc. "I just wish
they had waited a little longer, until we had more men and arms
ourselves."

"Perhaps we should have waited until then," Meradoc suggested.

Dinas glowered at him. "I'll take care of the thinking; you take
care of the horses."

He put Dafydd in charge of what he called "seagoing opera-
tions." When a landing party had been waylaid, captured and securely bound, Dafydd and the other recruits would take their boat

and return to the ship, where they captured and bound the crew and then helped themselves to the portable merchandise.

It only worked once the way Dinas had envisioned. Next time out, Docco got violently seasick in the rough swells and almost fell out of the boat. Dafydd took pity on him and headed back for shore, which gave the crew on board the merchant ship adequate time to prepare to repel them. They seized Dafydd and Cadel as they climbed up the boarding net and threatened to cut their throats unless their sailors were released at once.

Dinas was furious.

"You couldn't have done any better if you'd been there," Cynan told him.

"Someone has to wait on shore to oversee the operation!"

"Then let me do it and you go in the boat."

"I am your commanding officer," Dinas said with fire in his eyes, "and I . . ."

"You what? If we leave can you do this by yourself?"

Dinas had not anticipated mutiny. He took it badly. He tried bluster but it did not suit him, and the recruits, having survived a very hard winter, were not easy to bluff. In the end he promised them a larger share of the spoils when there were spoils, and agreed to take his turn in the boat.

On the next occasion the boat they seized capsized shortly after they left land, headed for the ship. The recruits had to swim for their lives—mountain men who did not know how to swim. Tostig lived up to his nickname by paddling frantically until his body understood what was required. Together he and Dinas dragged the others to safety.

Except for Hywel. He was last seen only a short distance from safety. A round head with wet hair plastered over it; one arm upflung in entreaty. Then he was gone. They set up a vigil along the cliffs, watching for his body, but nothing came ashore.

This was different from the death of Tarates. Hywel was one of their own. The recruits could have accepted a death in battle, as they had accepted the frequent deaths involved in quarrying in the mountains. But to have a comrade die in the cold, alien sea appalled them. They were stunned speechless. Even Cadel made no comment.

Bryn retreated to the tower and communed among the shadows with his own gods.

Meradoc groomed the dark horse over and over and over again, until the stallion pinned his ears back and demanded to be left alone.

That night Pelemos thought about Hywel, and the arm upflung in supplication. Thought about dying.

Thought about Ithill.

When she was dying he had laid his head on the straw mattress beside her and pressed his cheek to her temple. Her feverish temple where the hair clung in damp ringlets. He had sought to dream her dream; to dream into death with her so they would never be separated.

It was thus, as he clung to her like a conjoined twin, that he had felt something go out of her. As ephemeral as a shadow yet as real as a flame, it had fled from him to a far place.

He had cried out and clutched her with all his strength. But she was gone.

Yet there had been a single moment—he was convinced of it then, and would be so for the rest of his life—a tiny slice of time when he might have interposed himself between her and the force that was drawing her away. He might have kept her forever.

Forever.

Was that not where she had gone? Into forever?

He had willed himself to follow her but his traitor body would not release him. His heart had kept beating, his lungs had kept breathing. Why? For what purpose?

Surely not to lure others to their deaths.

The following morning Pelemos sought out Dinas and asked for a quiet word alone with him. Dinas nodded assent. The lines in his face seemed deeper than they had been the day before.

The two walked down to one of the terraces where another rectilinear hut was being built. The work was temporarily postponed due to bad weather. "I for one think we've followed your dream far enough," Pelemos began as they sought shelter from the wind behind the half-built hut. "Creating your own kingdom . . . a man has a right to attempt that, Dinas. But not to spend the lives of other men for it."

Dinas raised an eyebrow. "How else does one acquire a kingdom?"

"I never thought about it before. Did you? Do you really know how hard it would be to create a *kingdom*? When I was a boy I dreamed of having my own farm, and even that was incredibly hard.

"You're not a bad person, Dinas, and I don't condemn you for a bit of piracy. We might all have profited if things went the way you planned. But I see no profit in this, only danger and death. The crewmen we waylaid last time told me they had done their trading already and were heading back to the north. The only cargo they had on board their ship was tin ingots; a heavy load of ingots. What would we have done with those? Who would have bought them from us, the Dumnonians? It was their tin in the first place.

"If we were lucky, Dinas, we might have had two or three profitable years here, but merchants don't like being robbed. Either they would find new shipping lanes or start fighting back. Either way . . ."

"Either way," Dinas repeated glumly. He stared at his hands. Cracked his knuckles. Looked up with a forced smile. "Suppose we had more men; a hundred, say, or even two hundred—"

"Remember how hard it was to recruit these," Pelemos interrupted.

"You helped me gain their trust, Pelemos."

"And look what it did for Hywel: He's dead. No, Dinas, this life isn't for me. For a while I was like a man asleep, I just trundled along behind you. I'm awake now, and I can see that I don't belong here."

"What will I do without you?" Dinas asked, trying not to sound desperate. "I can't inspire the men the way you do."

Pelemos shook his head. "I'm sorry, Dinas. Truly I am. But . . ."

"But what? Where will you go?"

"I have a place in mind."

"What would persuade you to stay? What can I offer you that—"

"There is nothing you can offer me, Dinas. Not gold, nor silver, nor anything cold. I'm like Bryn in that respect."

"I don't understand."

Pelemos said sadly, "I know you don't. I . . . wait, there is something I would ask. As a favor; not as a bribe to get me to stay because I cannot. But would you let me take the pony you gave me? And perhaps the horse?"

Dinas was glad of an excuse to lose his temper. Part of his temper; holding on tight to the deep rage within him that could be tapped in an emergency. "Do you think I'm a fool!" he shouted at Pelemos. "You announce that you're deserting me and in the next breath you demand two valuable animals?"

"I'm not demanding," Pelemos said mildly. "I'm only asking. The pony in particular would be handy where I'm going, but I can walk if I have to. I've walked everywhere all my life, riding is new to me."

"Handy? A pony? Exactly where are you going?"

Pelemos met Dinas's eyes and held them. "Eryri," he said.

CHAPTER TWENTY-NINE

"He's lost his mind," Dinas told Meradoc. "If Pelemos wasn't mad to begin with, he is now."

"If you think he's gone mad why did you let him take the horse and the pony?"

"I doubt if he would get where he's going without them. He may not anyway, but at least he'll have a better chance of reaching the high mountains."

Meradoc's jaw dropped. "Is that where he's going? To *her*?"

"You knew about this?"

"Not really. But a long time ago he asked me if I could find my way back up there. I didn't think he was serious."

Dinas shook his head. "I know one thing about Pelemos, Meradoc. He is always serious."

"And you just let him go? I can't believe it. She's your woman, isn't she?"

Dinas kept his face impassive. "No one can own anyone else, Meradoc, spirits are free. And freedom is the greatest gift of all, my mother taught me that. She abhorred slavery in all its guises, including the domination of women by men."

"But Saba could come with you if she wanted to?"

"She could," Dinas said tightly. "She didn't."

Meradoc thought it would be tactful to change the subject. "What about horses? They have spirits too, don't they? Yet we say we own them."

"The stallion is as free as I am," Dinas replied.

———

The recruits were already upset about the death of Hywel; Dinas was careful in his choice of words when he told them of Pelemos's departure. "Our friend has a calling to a very different life," he said. "I sent him with my blessing, and a horse and pony. It was the least I could do when he's been so good to us."

He was not sure they believed him. Looks were exchanged; mutterings were heard. Iolo speculated that Pelemos had gone off to become an anchorite. But no one mentioned the word "desertion," and when Meradoc backed Dinas up, a possible crisis was averted.

There were more immediate matters to worry about. No matter how much he might struggle against it, Dinas knew the truth when he heard it. And Pelemos had told him the truth.

This isn't working. If I had more men in the beginning . . . If I had chosen a different territory . . . If I had Cadogan with me . . .

There's the problem, I didn't have Cadogan. With his tidy mind he would have spotted the problems before they arose. He would have planned out the whole thing: how many men, how many horses, where to get them, how to use them . . . Cadogan knew that a man with no experience of the sea should not attempt what I've attempted here.

But I wanted Tintagel. God help me, how I wanted Tintagel! Dinas, you half-aborted ass, what were you thinking? How can it be that a man wants something so much it blinds him to everything else?

Saba.

Too late for that now.

I hope Pelemos finds her and makes her happy. I really do.

I hope he falls off his horse and breaks his neck.

None of this addressed the problem at hand. Pelemos had drawn Dinas's attention to the fact that he had real responsibilities to the recruits. If he called everything off and sent them home—though he knew his pride would not allow that—they would be disgraced.

They had left the quarries and their families with such high hopes. To come back slinking like dogs, with their tails between their legs . . . he could not do that to them.

Nor could he continue trying to subsist on inept piracy while ostensibly creating a kingdom.

What would Cadogan do?

Take over an already existing kingdom, perhaps?

Not the entire territory of Dumnonia, that would be impossible. For now.

But one of the petty kingdoms that made up the whole—that could be done. Not all at once, though. First he would need to ingratiate himself with the current chieftain and . . .

Having a new dream to dream increased Dinas's appetite and put a spring in his step.

"Does that mean we won't have to go out in a boat anymore?" Dafydd said hopefully when the plan was presented to the recruits.

"We won't need boats," Dinas assured him. "We shall continue to be based at Tintagel, but we'll turn our attention inland. In less than half a day's ride from here there are at least seven Dumnonian clans that continually fight with one another. And beyond that, who knows how many others? The region is underpopulated; no chieftain has what might be called an army, so no chieftain ever wins a decisive battle."

"What about the king of Dumnonia, doesn't he have an army?"

"Not like the Romans did, no. What the king has is underkings—chieftains—who profess loyalty to him. They pay him taxes—grain and cattle—and in return he promises to protect them from outside invasion. If he needs an army to defend the borders of the kingdom he calls on the chieftains to send him their warriors. When the battle's over they go home again, and the king goes back to feasting and enjoying women. The chieftains return to fighting one another to keep their battle skills in order."

"I begin to understand why you want to be a king," said Cadel. "What I don't understand is why we've been trying to be pirates."

"I thought it would be a good way to raise enough money to equip an army of my own," Dinas told him. "But it's too slow and the profits are too uncertain, I realize that now."

"He's just seeing it *now*?" Cynan muttered to Iolo.

Ignoring him, Dinas continued. "Men like Kollos and Geriotis command fifteen or twenty warriors each; thirty at the most. What I propose is to offer ourselves as a private fighting force to the chieftain with the *smallest* army. We'll help defend his people—for a price. Then we'll assume more and more power until we're able to take over his land and extend our control outwards. By that time others will be eager to join us; a winner has no difficulty attracting followers."

Tostig told Bleddyn, "He makes it sound easy."

"He made it sound easy the first time," Bleddyn reminded him.

And for a time, it was.

That first summer only a few battles took place. Dinas and his band augmented an "army" of but ten men, none of whom were well armed. The shortswords and lightweight javelins Dinas brought from Tintagel impressed them mightily. Their opposition was impressed too. A temporary truce was soon arranged and the two chieftains sat down together for some serious mead-drinking and flirtation with each other's womenfolk. Dinas was invited to join them because he had been foremost among the fighters, the quickest, ablest of the lot, nimble with a knife and swift with a sword. He fought as if each man he faced were a personal enemy. He did his share of the killing.

By autumn he was the one doing most of the talking as well, planning the next season's campaigns. An alliance was formed; the taking of spoils was discussed at length. When one of the chieftains made a clumsy effort at speaking Latin, Dinas interrupted him. "Use the tongue you learned at your mother's knee," he insisted. "Show that you are a free man. I've heard too much Latin."

The Dumnonian was happy to comply.

Dinas and his men retired to Tintagel for the winter. They divided their winnings from the first season of warfare: a few bits of jewelry, some weapons, and a handful of Roman and Greek coins. Dinas gave the jewelry and weapons to his men and put the coins in his saddlebags.

Fine weather lingered late that year. The recruits, who considered themselves hardened veterans by now, devoted much of their time to weapons practice. Bryn endlessly brewed potions and medicaments in anticipation of battle injuries that might never happen. On sunny days Dinas rode the stallion several miles along the cliffs to a slope that led to the sea. They cantered in the surf with the white spume flying. Alternatively he amused himself by teaching the dark horse to climb the tower steps to the very top. From there the two of them could gaze out over the dark sea and the shifting fog banks of autumn.

Britannia—or the idea of Britannia—had become as amorphous as fog. Stability was a thing of the past; borders and boundaries changed constantly. No man could predict what might happen tomorrow. Less than a generation after the departure of the last legion, what had been a peaceful, almost tranquil outpost of the Roman Empire was riven by warfare. Battles had become commonplace between native tribes, foreign tribes, rival chieftains, sons and brothers and anyone with sufficient ambition and weapons.

Strangers began to appear more frequently in Dumnonia. Refugees fleeing the upheavals elsewhere in Britannia; outlaws searching for a place beyond the reach of any law; slave traders seeking white-skinned merchandise to sell in the Byzantine markets. Such men often gave no names and revealed nothing of their backgrounds. In the general collapse of society they found a sort of freedom.

There were also a few who had crossed the Severn for legitimate purposes. If they strayed into Dumnonian territory they were slain as intruders by militias similar to the one Dinas had formed.

His were not the only mercenaries at World's End. The situation was provoking the rise of fighting men as decaying manure provokes the growth of weeds.

Dinas kept busy negotiating positions of advantage for himself and his band. Sometimes this involved switching sides. Loyalty had become a debased coin. From one season to the next it was impossible to predict which chieftains would be in the ascendancy. And which would lie, bloody and beaten, beneath a cairn of stones.

Some warriors—though not his, he strictly forbade it—were reverting to the ancient custom of taking the heads of fallen enemies and putting them up on poles.

Bleddyn went like that. In a senseless battle between two petty chieftains who were both dead within the year anyway. Dinas did not realize what had happened until he saw the young man's head raised on a pole outside the tent of a chieftain who wanted to hire him.

They were all young men. Cynan who died in courageous combat with a Dumnonian almost twice his size; Iolo who suffered what seemed to be a minor injury to his arm, but saw the entire arm blacken and rot in spite of all Bryn could do; Docco who was speared on a pitchfork and died in agony.

Others were recruited along the way to fight beside Dafydd and Tostig and Meradoc. They were not fighting for a kingdom; that goal had been abandoned. Dinas could not even remember when he had given up on it. Perhaps it was the day he saw Bleddyn's head on a pole. Perhaps it was the day he encountered a tin merchant who reported that Londinium was in danger of turning into a wasteland. Whole areas in the center of the city were roped off where houses were becoming unstable and a passersby could be killed by falling masonry.

"Londinium!" Dinas said wonderingly to Meradoc. "The capital city of Britannia Prima, the Western Empire, falling down. Who would have believed such a thing possible?"

Meradoc asked, "Were you ever in Londinium?"

"Once. Almost. I rode around the walls but never passed through any of the gates."

"Why not?"

Dinas tried to remember. So much had happened since then. What had seemed a monumental decision at the time was trivial now. "The city was too big for me," he said at last. "I could hear a lot of noise and see crowds streaming in and out and it made me uncomfortable."

"But you grew up in a city."

"Yes."

"Would you ever go home again, Dinas?"

"Would you?"

The two men looked at each other. After a long pause, one of them said, "I am home."

The next outsider Dinas and his men encountered was, in Bryn's words, "an exotic bird." They were returning to their base at Tintagel at the end of a long season of warfare. The band numbered fifteen at the moment, the largest it had ever been, though they had only five rideable horses plus the stallion. The chestnut mare's first colt, a leggy bay, was yet to be trained to the saddle.

As they approached the cliffs Dinas saw a ship far out at sea; a long narrow vessel with a triangular sail. Driven by the prevailing wind from the west, the ship was skimming toward land. Dinas drew rein. "See that, Meradoc?" he called over his shoulder to the little man riding the chestnut mare.

"I do. It's a pity we're not still in the pirate business . . . or are we?"

Dinas smiled. A thin, bitter smile; the only kind he ever smiled now. "Let's wait and see what the gods are bringing us."

He led the way onto Tintagel Head.

It was the first visit to Tintagel for three newcomers to his band. They approached the natural fortress with a degree of awe. No Pelemos had inspired them; they had joined Dinas because of the reputation he had acquired. Leader, warlord, wild man. Wild as the wind was wild, unbeatable and unpredictable. It was the sort of reputation that attracted a young man.

While Tostig was getting the rest of the men settled in, Dinas made his way down to the shingle beach below the peak. He carried a round wooden shield on one arm and a sword on his hip. He was more curious than worried. When the ship was close enough to make out details he could tell that it was not rigged for battle, nor heavy enough to carry much cargo. A rare sight in these waters.

The rowboat that landed on the shingle beach held five men. Four burly sailors who, from the scimitars in their belts, were obviously bodyguards as well. The fifth individual was a short, swarthy man with a divided beard and eyes like polished jet. He was swathed in yards of colorful fabric shot with gold thread, and wore a turban of crimson silk.

By the time the strangers had clambered out of the boat, Tostig and Meradoc had made their way down to the beach to stand beside Dinas. Other members of the band ranged along the downward path, weapons at the ready, while Bryn watched from above. Advancing age had not dimmed his curiosity.

Dinas drew in a deep breath, inhaling unfamiliar scents. The wearer of the turban smelled of rich spices and musky perfume. Dinas forced himself to recall his Latin, which had grown rusty with disuse. Once he had condemned Latin as the language of the conquerors. He was glad of it now. Rome had enforced a common language for the sake of trade which simplified situations such as this.

Meradoc and Tostig listened as hard as they could, trying to catch some hint of meaning, while Dinas and the man in the turban carried on a long, occasionally testy, conversation. Dinas stood with his feet planted wide apart and his arms folded. The stranger chattered like a magpie and constantly gesticulated. When their talk was concluded the foreigner returned to his boat and his crew pushed off. Dinas stood watching while they rowed back to their ship and prepared to sail away.

"What was that about?" Meradoc asked as they climbed back up the peak.

"Later," Dinas said tightly.

He did not explain until the three of them—himself, Meradoc

and Tostig—had retired to their hut for the night. "There's no need for the rest of them to hear this," Dinas said. "They know little or nothing about our earlier enterprise, which is just as well. The man who was just here is an agent from Constantinople. He represents a cadre of merchants who deal in tin."

Meradoc was impressed. "Syrian?" he asked. "Or Egyptian?"

"You remember everything you hear, don't you?" Dinas said approvingly. "I'm not sure just which it is, Meradoc; that's not important anyway. Here's the heart of the matter: An effort is underway to reestablish the Byzantine trade network that once included the Western Empire. Our visitor's mission is to warn people like us against interfering with shipping around the coast."

"But we haven't done that in years!" Tostig protested.

"I know it and you know it, but he didn't seem to. I tried to convince him."

"Did he believe you?"

"Perhaps." Dinas gave a sigh. "Of all the crimes I've committed, it's ironic to be blamed for one I've given up."

Meradoc said, "He warned you? What kind of warning?"

"Veiled threats, mostly. I suspect they're flexing their muscles now they no longer have to deal with Rome. By comparison we're very small fish. That's why Constantinople is sending this emissary, or whatever he is, with so little apparent military support. It's the sort of thing the Romans did at the height of their power to show their contempt for ordinary people. I know their tricks and I'm not impressed."

But although Dinas tried to sound confident, the encounter had upset him. In a few years life had shrunk from an unlimited horizon to a series of petty wars he sometimes won and sometimes lost, and which never seemed to represent any advance. His world had become very small indeed. Now a bolt of lightning from a far distance had singled him out. For what purpose?

That night Dinas left the hut and sought out the dark horse. At the familiar command the stallion lay down and allowed him to pillow his head on the warm and silky neck.

"What are we doing here?" Dinas wondered aloud.

The horse had no answer for him.

There aren't any answers. Once I thought I knew them all until . . . the unavenged—unavenged!—murder of Gwladys left me with a rage I can neither throw off nor satisfy. What I should have done in the beginning was hunt down Ocellus and kill him with my bare hands. But I didn't. Couldn't. Not my own father. It's too late to find him now; he might be anywhere. He could even be dead. Would that make me feel any better?

Would anything make me feel any better?

He had no answer for that question either.

Spring brought another battle season: two men killed, little booty taken, but a new alliance formed with, of all people, Kollos, the chieftain who had greeted them on their arrival at Tintagel. Kollos and Geriotis had quarreled and now Kollos wanted to seize his brother's land. He would pay, of course; he understood the mercenary business.

It would be the last campaign of the summer, Dinas promised his men. But first they would return to Tintagel for a few days' rest and to prepare their weapons.

More importantly, the horses needed rest. The chestnut mare was in foal again, carrying the second offspring she would bear to the dark horse. The stallion had been slightly lame off and on all summer. When they reached Tintagel Bryn said the problem was a sprain in the shoulder muscle, and treated him with evil-smelling poultices. Meradoc insisted there was damage to the knee joint, though Bryn could not detect any swelling. Their constant fretting over the horse began to irritate Dinas.

"Whatever's wrong, you're only making it worse," he told them. "I know him better than either of you. All he needs is a long canter in the sea to tone him up again. Have him ready for me in the morning, Meradoc."

Morning dawned crisp and clear. The seabirds were more raucous than usual, which indicated a possible change in the weather.

Before taking the stallion for his canter Dinas and the other men went to gather firewood while it was still dry. The nearest trees were some distance inland, but by using the horses they could carry back enough wood to last for weeks.

When they had gone, Bryn retired to his hut to steep and strain and simmer. Meradoc massaged the stallion's knee with a concoction of his own made of rancid butter and salt water, then gave him a thorough rubdown to have him ready for Dinas. He put on the saddle and bridle and tied on the saddlebags. Whenever Dinas rode the stallion he always carried the saddlebags with him, though they currently contained little more than a spare cloak, the stone bowl and the cracked plate. There had been few spoils from the summer to add the clink of coin to his hoard.

When everything was ready Meradoc led the dark horse to the foot of the tower and stood waiting. He would wait for half a day if necessary, he had done it before. Even if there was nothing important to do Dinas would be in a hurry when he returned. Lately he always seemed to be impatient.

But for what? Meradoc wondered. Their days had become almost predictable, one following the next in a similar pattern. Faces changed, however. And Dinas was getting silver threads in his hair. At least the dark horse remained the same. Meradoc reached out to stroke the silken neck and check the belly band that held the saddle in place. He might as well loosen it if they had a long wait.

That was when he saw them. Coming up the narrow path from the bay. Stooping over as they ran, agile as cats, some with knives held in their teeth.

Meradoc gave a shout of warning. There was no one to hear except Bryn in his stone hut. Bryn stuck his head out the doorway, took in the scene at a glance, then ducked back inside.

The attackers were not Britons; the most cursory glance told Meradoc that much. They were bearded, swarthy men wearing outlandish clothes. They must have been watching for their chance from the bay, or a ship out at sea . . . and there were so many of them! They swarmed onto Tintagel Head shouting to one another. One ran into Bryn's hut. Meradoc heard a scream, then silence.

The stallion was plunging wildly by now. He tore the reins from Meradoc's fingers as one of the attackers struck the little man on the side of the head. Meradoc instinctively rolled with the punch. Down onto one knee, twist sideways, up again with fists at the ready. But too late. The invaders had already formed a circle around Meradoc and the horse. One man drew a huge curved knife from his belt and brandished it in the air, laughing. The others urged him on with barbarous cries as he tried to catch the stallion's reins. What he meant to do was obvious to Meradoc. Whoever they were, they intended to slaughter every living thing on Tintagel.

With a defiant cry Meradoc flung himself at the stallion. Miraculously, the horse stood still for him. He scrambled onto the saddle and clutched the animal's mane with both hands.

The circle around him tightened. Jeering. Bloodlust in their eyes.

For the first and last time Meradoc felt the power and spirit of the horse beneath him. He clamped his legs against the stallion's sides and drove him toward the tower steps; the only avenue of escape open to them.

Up, up they went. The attackers did not try to follow. Instead they stood at the base of the tower, watching in amazement.

Up, up to the very top.

Only then did one of the invaders—he with the scimitar in his hand—put a foot on the bottom step.

Meradoc cast a despairing glance toward the land. He saw Dinas and the others approaching, but they would not arrive in time to save anyone on Tintagel.

How quiet it has become! he thought. He could feel the wind blowing around him but he could not hear it. Yet he saw everything with a marvelous clarity, as if for the first time. He felt strangely at peace.

The man with the scimitar was taking two steps at a time. Grinning. A white slash of teeth in a black beard. In a few moments he would reach them. He was already waving his weapon. Man or horse, he did not care which he struck first as long as the blood flowed red and hot.

Meradoc looked down toward the rocks far below. They waited at the very edge of the sea. The way to freedom.

Freedom is the greatest gift of all.

Bending over, Meradoc murmured in the ear of the dark horse, "Forward, *now!*"

CHAPTER THIRTY

On a bitterly cold day in the dead of winter a man was riding through the forest. His face was haggard and he slouched awkwardly on his horse, a leggy bay colt who wore no saddle. In one hand the man clutched the lead rope of a chestnut mare. A dark brown yearling trotted loose beside her.

When he came to a hillside given over to pasture the rider drew rein. The bay horse snatched at the bit, eager for a mouthful of the winter-killed grass. The man sat looking up the slope to the cabin at the top. More than a cabin; a small fort with smoke rising from a hole in the thatched roof. The man drew a deep breath, trying to inhale the warmth of the smoke. But it was too far away.

He almost rode on. Hesitated. Urged the bay horse up the hill instead.

Outside the cabin he drew rein again and gave a shout. Not really a shout; more of a croak, but someone inside heard him. The door opened and Cadogan peered out. He challenged the huddled figure on the horse. "What do you want?"

"A kind word would do," the man replied hoarsely.

Cadogan gaped at him. "Dinas? Is it really you?"

"What's left of me." The statement was literal, for in the next moment he swayed and almost fell off.

Cadogan leaped forward to steady him. "Quartilla! Help us!"

She emerged from the house already complaining. "It's Dinas," Cadogan told her. The complaint died on her lips and she ran to help him. Between them they eased Dinas from the horse and helped him inside.

He was pale, unshaven, shivering from the cold. His face was so deeply lined that Cadogan would not have recognized him except for the eyes. It was hard to believe this was the same vibrant man he had last seen five years earlier.

"Put more wood on the fire, Quartilla, quickly! He's freezing."

For once she did not argue. While she fed the fire, Cadogan sat Dinas on the nearest stool and wrapped one of his own cloaks around him. Dinas hunched on the stool with his head down, staring at the floor. Cadogan noticed that his cousin's hair was thickly frosted with silver.

"Are you hurt?" he asked.

"No."

"Hungry? Thirsty?"

"No. Look after my horses, will you?"

"I will of course, but . . . where did you come from?"

"Everywhere. Nowhere." Dinas looked toward the bed. "Can I sleep there?"

"Of course you can, but first . . ."

Dinas shrugged Cadogan off and stumbled over to the bed. He fell onto it like a tree falling and was asleep between one breath and the next.

"He's an old man!" Quartilla exclaimed with horror. "Are you sure that's really Dinas?"

"I'm sure. God only knows what's happened to him. Let him rest as long as he likes, then have plenty of food ready for him. He'll tell us about it in his own good time."

"Shall I send for—"

"No, just let him be. He would hate to have anyone else see him like this."

Dinas slept until the following evening. He awoke ravenous and ate everything he was offered—after reassuring himself that his horses were being well tended. When Cadogan asked about the stallion the expression on his cousin's face made him drop the subject. Instead Cadogan told Dinas something of his own recent

history: the escape from Viroconium and the building of the settlement.

"You'll see some of the others when you're feeling stronger," he
promised. "We have houses all through this area now. We raise everything we eat and even have a little left over for barter."

"I thought you had money."

Cadogan said, "Money's not worth much these days."

"No," Dinas agreed. "Money's not worth much." Nodding toward
Quartilla, who was sewing at the other end of the room, he asked in
a low voice, "What about that one?"

"I married her."

"Surely not."

"Regina—you remember Regina, the widow of Lentullus the
Arbiter?—she disapproved of my having a young unmarried woman
in my house."

"Why didn't you throw her out, then?"

"Who, Regina? She was my good friend, I don't know how I
would have gotten through the first few years without her. She only
died last autumn."

"Why didn't you throw the other one out?"

"No one else would take her in," said Cadogan.

Dinas raised an eyebrow. "You sleep with her, don't you?"

"Occasionally," Cadogan admitted. He added with a shy smile,
as if still surprised by the discovery, "She's wonderful in bed."

Dinas raised both eyebrows.

"And you, Dinas. Have you no family?"

"Does it look like it?"

"What about your two friends: Meradoc, I think his name was,
and Pelemos?"

"Pelemos may have a family by now, at least I hope he does. He
left me and went to live in the high mountains."

"Ah. And little Meradoc?"

Dinas closed his eyes. When he opened them he noticed the
little shrine in the corner. "Do you still believe in God, Cadogan?"

"I do. When my father was dying he called out the name of Jesus Christ."

"So Vintrex looked for redemption at the last moment, did he? How like him."

"You sound bitter, Dinas. Do you still blame Vintrex for the affair with your mother?"

"I never blamed him, they were both in it together."

"That's Christian of you," Cadogan said.

Dinas gave a harsh laugh. "Greater sins have been committed since that one." He continued to look around the room, noticing details. A pallet rolled up and tucked into a corner; three tin cups hanging on pegs beside a water pitcher. "Does someone else live here with you?"

"Only Esoros, my father's former steward, but since Vintrex died he spends a lot of his time in the village on the other side of the forest. It's too quiet for him here. He'll be back soon, though. I let him take the pony and cart to bring supplies for Godubnus, our blacksmith."

"You have a pony?"

"A pony, a horse and an ox," Cadogan said proudly. "The pony's a surefooted Saxon beast that—"

"*Saxon?*"

"Things have changed," said Cadogan.

Dinas could not help glancing at Quartilla, who caught his eyes and gave him her most seductive smile. He looked away again. "Some things never change," he remarked.

The wind was rising; Cadogan could hear it rattling the shutters he had closed when the sun went down. "Esoros didn't make it today but he'll probably be back tomorrow. Are you tired, Dinas? Would you like to go to bed now?"

"I'm not too tired to unroll that pallet over there and let you and what's-her-name have your bed back."

"Quartilla," she called across the room. "My name is Quartilla."

"And you're the queen of Egypt, I assume," Dinas muttered.

Cadogan tried not to laugh.

In the morning Dinas was awake before anyone else. When he went outside to relieve himself the dark yearling came up to him and nuzzled him, seeking bits of bread. He rubbed the yearling behind the ears for a while, then went back to the house.

He found Cadogan waiting for him at the door. "I wanted to be certain you're all right."

"Of course I'm all right," said Dinas. "I'll be moving on in a few days, when the horses are thoroughly rested."

"Where will you go? You're welcome to stay here, you know."

"And do what, farm? I think not. Does that woman of yours have anything cooking on the fire?" He brushed past Cadogan and strode into the house.

For Cadogan the morning passed quickly enough. He was busy as he was always busy, even in winter when there was no planting or plowing. Wood had to be chopped and thatch repaired and a hundred other small details seen to; the details that kept life going. From time to time he went back to the fort and found Dinas lounging by the fire, poring over one of Cadogan's precious manuscripts. He seemed in no mood to talk, so Cadogan left him alone. By afternoon his work was done, an icy rain was falling, and he could retire to the comfort of his own fireside. Dinas seemed glad to see him. "What are we going to do now?" he asked brightly.

"I don't know about you, but I'm going to sit down and put my feet up."

Dinas nodded. Stood up and went to the door. Stared at the rain, cracked his knuckles, paced back and forth, and cracked his knuckles some more until Quartilla shouted abuse at him.

He's like an animal in a cage, Cadogan thought.

Dinner was simmering in an iron pot on the hearth when Esoros arrived. Cadogan heard him first; he had been listening for the creaking of the cart wheels. A few minutes later the door opened and the erstwhile steward came in, shaking ice from his clothing. He stopped in midstride. "We have a visitor?" he asked in surprise.

"My cousin Dinas," said Cadogan. "You may not remember him but he—"

"Dinas. Son of Ocellus," Esoros said through stiff lips.

Dinas nodded. "The same. I assume you are Esoros?"

The other man was watching him with dreadful fascination. "We thought . . . Cadogan thought . . . you were dead."

Dinas raised an eyebrow. "Did he? My cousin is often mistaken."

Esoros fumbled for a stool and sat down. Quartilla brought him a bowl of fragrant stew; gobbets of boar meat sweetened by red fruits and wild onions. Esoros ate one spoonful with his eyes on Dinas, then put the spoon down. "I'm not hungry," he said.

Quartilla whisked the bowl away. "Then there's more for the rest of us."

To Dinas, who was sensitive to atmosphere, the room began to seem very small. Something had entered with Esoros; a tension like the heavy silence before thunder.

Cadogan felt it too. He tried to start a conversation with Quartilla but after a few words it dragged to a halt. She helped herself to more stew. Dinas cracked his knuckles yet again. Cadogan said the only thing he could think of that might get his cousin to talk. "You didn't tell me what happened to your stallion, Dinas."

"He's dead," said Dinas. He spoke with no emotion in his voice. There was stark agony in his eyes.

"Oh Christ, I'm sorry, I didn't—"

"I saw it happen," Dinas interrupted in a haunted whisper. "We all saw it, but we were too far away to get there in time. Meradoc and the stallion leaped up and out from a peak called Tintagel. The horse actually galloped through empty air. It looked as if they were flying." His eyes glittered wetly.

Never before had Cadogan seen his cousin cry.

"They were in the air forever, or so it seemed," Dinas continued. "Then they crashed to the rocks below." His voice died away; the last words almost inaudible. He was seeing it again. Seeing it as he would always see it, every day for the rest of his life.

A terrible silence filled the room.

When Dinas spoke again his voice was very low, but every word was audible. "When the fighting was over Otter and I buried them. Buried them both together at Tintagel. My saddle and saddlebags were still on . . . are still on . . ." He could not finish.

Cadogan felt almost an unbearable pity for his cousin. "Who was Otter?" he asked gently, trying to deflect the pain.

Dinas blinked. Dragged his thoughts back to the present. "Tostig. A friend of mine. He's gone to the high mountains too. The rest of my men were injured or killed outright that day, Cadogan. But in the end we won. If you can call it winning." Dinas sounded very bitter. "My mother once saw Tintagel in a vision, you know. She thought the vision was about me. *I* was supposed to be the one riding a horse in the sky."

"Your mother was a sorceress," a voice hissed.

Both men looked at Esoros. "What did you say?"

"She was a druid, a creature of the devil!" Esoros spat the words with fury. "She enchanted my lord master and ruined his life. He and my lady mistress were happy until Gwladys enslaved his soul. He had been a kind man but he became as cold and cruel as the sorceress. I'm glad I disposed of her."

Dinas leaped to his feet. *"You disposed of her?"*

Esoros stood to face him. "Vintrex taught me to be a Christian," he said proudly, "and God guided my hand."

"To cut her throat?"

"What else could I do? She was sending letters to my lord master and he was writing back to her. I was afraid she would ensnare him again so I went to stop her. And I did."

Dinas was ashen. "I thought my father killed her." He drew a deep, shaky breath. "When I found her murdered and the servants gone, I buried her myself and sent a message to the chief magistrate to inform him. I even identified Ocellus as the killer."

"You were wrong," Esoros told him.

Dinas ran a hand across his forehead. "But I could smell him on her!"

"They had been living together for a long time."

"You could probably smell Cadogan on me," Quartilla interjected.

Dinas tried to recall the exact sequence of events. Trying to make it clear again, to find his way through horror to truth. "I waited for some word from Vintrex but none came. Eventually I went to Viroconium myself to learn what he intended to do. When I reached the city he was not there, but the barbarians had been."

Cadogan said, "At least that explains why Father went to Londinium: to bring charges against Ocellus and arrange for his arrest. Ocellus was an important man and everything had to be done at the highest level. It must have been very painful for Father; they were brothers after all."

Quartilla could not bear being left out of the conversation. "You found me after you left Viroconium, Dinas. Now I know why you seemed so distracted. I'm not used to having men ignore me the way you did then."

He was not listening. "Are you sure my father was innocent, Esoros? He had a temper, I know because I've inherited it."

Esoros was unwilling to have his triumph over evil credited to someone else. "Mine was the hand that held the knife," he insisted. "Ocellus was no longer at their villa; he had abandoned her because she was communicating with Vintrex again."

"Father always said Ocellus was a shrewd man," said Cadogan. "Perhaps he decided to leave Britannia altogether, before the situation with the foreigners grew any worse. By now he might even be—"

"You can say 'dead,'" Dinas interrupted. "I've heard the word before."

"Enough talk of death and dying. There's *life* here, Dinas," Cadogan stressed. "Stay with us! You know most of the people in our settlement. We'll help you forget these terrible things."

"What if I don't want to forget them? If I forget Gwladys, and Meradoc, and the stallion . . . if I forget them I'll lose them, and I refuse to do that. I'll take them with me until I die."

Cadogan knew that resolute face; there would be no talking Dinas around. He still felt pity for his cousin, yet envy, too. Whatever came, Dinas would experience it to the full. He was not a man for the rolling hills and the snug little forts. His were the mountains and the abyss.

Esoros was watching the same face. Tardily he realized the full import of the confession he had made. He had killed this man's mother. Dinas did not look like the sort of man who would forgive.

Esoros began to back toward the door. Dinas raised one eyebrow.

The steward's nerve broke; he turned to run. Dinas caught him in one long stride and lifted him by the neck until his heels drummed the air. "Murderer," Dinas said in a deadly soft voice.

Quartilla made a little sound of protest.

"I could crush his throat and strangle him," Dinas remarked as if he were making casual conversation. "What do you think, Cadogan? Would I be justified? With Vintrex dead, is there a magistrate who would find against me?

"I've killed before, it isn't difficult. But you know that from experience, Esoros. Did my mother beg for her life? I suppose my father had taken the servants with him. Was there no one left to defend her when you came like a thief in the night?"

Esoros was making desperate squawking sounds.

Dinas lowered him—slowly, almost gently—until his feet touched the floor. But he kept his hands around the man's neck. "I'm not going to kill you, Esoros. When I knelt beside that grave on Tintagel . . ." He paused to compose himself. "Tintagel is a strange place and it can have a strange effect on a man. That's why I'm going to let you go. Run as far as you can, as fast as you can, but don't look back. Never look back. Because I might change my mind, and I can find you wherever you are." Dinas smiled. The smile of the wolf with its teeth at the throat of its prey.

He opened his hands and released the man's neck.

Esoros swayed on his feet, choking. Gazed wildly around the room. Turned and fled from the fort.

The three who remained looked at one another.

"That was a cruel thing to do," said Cadogan. "Almost worse than if you'd killed him. He'll be terrified for the rest of his life. Every time he hears someone behind him . . ."

"Yes," said Dinas.

He stayed with them for three more days. Esoros did not return; no one had seen him and Cadogan did not expect him. There were plenty of dangers waiting for a man alone and inexperienced at self-defense. Barbarians and wolves and accidents and ordinary people who were afraid of any stranger and might react with violence. Dinas did not need to take revenge. It would be done anyway, in its own time.

On the morning when Dinas was preparing to leave, Cadogan inquired, "Have you thought about going to the high mountains to be with your friends?"

His cousin responded with a negative shake of his head. "Other men's lives," he said dismissively.

"What about your own life?"

"I intend to live it. Hand me that lead rope, will you? I'll ride the bay today and lead the mare. The yearling colt will follow her."

"When will we see you again, Dinas?"

He gave a careless shrug. "I can't answer that, Quartilla. Maybe next month, maybe never. I'm looking for something, and I'll have to keep going until I find it."

"What is it?"

"I don't know that either," Dinas replied. Gazing past her to the meadow, the trees. The far distance.

Cadogan and Quartilla stood together outside their door and watched him ride away.

I left them there in their little fort, with their future planned and as predictable as a future can be. Hard work and a modicum of security; children perhaps. Cadogan would make a good father. As for Quartilla . . . who knows what depths are in that woman? She will continue to surprise and infuriate him to the end of their days.

Summer fading into autumn and the harvest. And then winter. For them, for me, for all of us.

I am happy for them, though I do not want what they have. It is my fate to seek an elusive prize without a name, perhaps even without substance. Yet I know it exists. The irresistible pull it exerts on my spirit is proof of that. I have sought it in the wrong way and learned a terrible lesson, but someday I will find it. I have faith.

Faith. "Fides" in the Latin language. What a slippery word that is! It translates as trust, confidence, belief. The belief of simple people who do not know the larger truth of existence; people who do not realize the great pattern underlying everything because they have not seen it in action.

I have seen it in action. Yet I too have faith.

While my search continues the dark yearling is growing up. His training goes well, he is becoming a fine stallion like his sire. If I am not happy at least I am content, which is perhaps the greater gift. My life is full. I ride across the land and sleep beneath the stars—or under my cloak if it's raining.

It rains so often in Albion.

AUTHOR'S NOTE

In the decades following the departure of the legions a new, indigenous form of architecture developed. Rectilinear thatched houses took the place of the round huts of Celtic Britain, as well as the later constructions patterned on the Roman style. Archaeologists recently discovered a massive timber hall, of unmistakably British design, built on the fire-ravaged site of Viroconium—now Wroxeter. Similar finds are being unearthed elsewhere. In time whole towns were built free of Roman influence. Intelligent minds were at work.

The so-called Dark Ages were primitive rather than dark. Literacy was not totally lost in Britain. Some descendants of the educated elite and a few monastic scholars retained the ability to read and write. But the pervasive influence of the Saxons, and to a lesser extent the other tribes who invaded the island during the fourth and fifth centuries, meant that Britain would no longer be Celtic.

Most modern historians accept the historical reality of Vortigern and the two Jutish mercenaries, Hengist and Horsa, though their actual dates vary widely depending on the sources consulted. There are no reliable eyewitness accounts from Britain during the years covered by this novel. The earliest information on the post-Roman period relies on the work of two monks: Gildas (*De Excidio et Conquestu Britanniae*), a Briton who died c. 570, and Bede (*Historia Ecclesiastica*), an Anglo-Saxon theologian who died in 735.

Both men were born long after the events related here, and wrote in the seclusion of monasteries. Their works bear testament to their religious convictions if not their historical acumen. They reputedly took their information from earlier letters and manuscripts that have since disappeared. The authors of those documents are unknown and their authenticity unproven. All we can know for certain is that the Romans invaded and conquered—then left.

In the long run, the fall of one civilization is very much like the fall of another.

Only the land remains.

GLOSSARY OF NAMES

Ancient and Modern

Albion—England
Caledonia—Scotland
Cymri—the Welsh
Cymru—Wales
Deva Victrix—Chester
Durovernum—Canterbury
Eire; Hibernia—Ireland
Erse—the Irish
Eryri—Snowdonia
Fretum Gallicum—The Strait of Dover
Glevum—Gloucester
Isca Dumnoniorum—Exeter
Londinium—London
Mamucium—Manchester
Oceanus Britannicus—The English Channel
Oceanus Germanicus—The North Sea
Oceanus Hibernicus—The Irish Sea
Ratae Coritanorum—Leicester
Vallum Aelium—Hadrian's Wall
Viroconium Cornoviarum—Wroxeter
Venta Belgarum—Winchester

SELECTED BIBLIOGRAPHY

Bowen, E. G. *Britain and the Western Seaways.* London: Thames & Hudson, 1972.

Campbell, James. *The Anglo-Saxons.* Ithaca, NY: Cornell University Press, 1982.

Cottrell, Leonard. *A Guide to Roman Britain.* New York: Dimension Books, 1966.

Cunliffe, Barry. *Rome and the Barbarians.* New York: Henry Walck, 1971.

Gildas. *On the Ruin of Britain (De Excidio Britanniae).* London: Dodo Press, n.d.

Johnson, Stephen. *Later Roman Britain.* New York: Scribner, 1980.

Laing, Lloyd. *Celtic Britain.* New York: Scribner, 1979.

Oliver, Neil. *A History of Ancient Britain.* London: Weidenfeld and Nicolson, 2011.

Owen, Gale R. *Rites and Religions of the Anglo-Saxons.* Totowa, NJ: Barnes & Noble, 1981.

Randers-Pehrson, Justine Davis. *Barbarians and Romans.* Norman: University of Oklahoma Press, 1983.

Scullard, H. H. *Roman Britain: Outpost of the Empire.* London: Thames & Hudson, 1971.

Stenton, Frank. *Anglo-Saxon England.* London: Oxford University Press, 1971.

Tacitus. *The Annals of Imperial Rome.* London: Penguin Classics, 1977.

———. *The Histories.* London: Penguin Classics, 1972.

Thwaite, Anthony. *Beyond the Inhabited World.* London: Andre Deutsch, 1976.